Hope Chest

by
Cherie Tucker

Disclaimer:

Delta Phi Tau is a fictional sorority, as are Iota Beta Pi and the Rho Gamma Epsilon fraternity. The initiation ceremony for Delta Phi Tau is completely made up from an English/Greek dictionary and the author's imagination. If any of those symbols or their explanations happen to be a part of any organization's ritual, it is simply a coincidence. This is a work of fiction. Except for the University of Washington's victory in the 1961 Rose Bowl, names, characters, places, and incidents are either a product of the author's imagination or are used fictitiously. Any resemblance to actual persons, living or dead, events, or locales is entirely coincidental.

Copyright © 2012 Cherie Tucker

All rights reserved.
No part of this book may be reproduced, stored in a retrieval system, or transmitted by any means, electrical, mechanical, photocopying, recording, or otherwise, without written permission from the author.

ISBN: 1479162825
ISBN 13: 9781479162826

To my father, who urged me to write

Chapter 1

April 1958

"What's this, Kathleen?" her mother asked, holding up a glossy brochure. On the cover, a handsome man and a shiny-haired co-ed walked hand in hand down a leaf-strewn path under a bower of autumn foliage.

"We had college conferences at school for the seniors today, Mother. That's from Western Washington State College in Bellingham. I hosted their representative." She moved to her mother's side. "The campus looks gorgeous."

"Kathleen, Western is a teacher's college."

"I know. You and Daddy have always told me that I should consider teaching."

"Of course we have told you that. Teaching—like good secretarial skills—you can always fall back on, especially when your children are grown. But you don't want to go to a teacher's college."

"I don't?"

"Heavens no! The men you'd meet there are also planning to go into teaching, and if you marry a teacher, you'll have to scrimp and save the rest of your life."

"Mother, I'm not going to college to get married."

"Kathleen, your college years will be the best, perhaps the only period in your life to meet eligible men from good families. That's why we've always said you'll go to the University of Washington right here in Seattle where you can join a sorority. I'm sure there are no sororities at Western."

"A sorority?" Her mother had never mentioned sororities before. Kathleen had talked about sororities with her friends at school, but she'd not given them much thought.

"They have lots of parties and dances, and you will meet lots of young men in fraternities who come from the right kinds of families."

"Daddy was never in a fraternity, and you managed to meet him."

"Times were different then. There was a war coming. People didn't have time for college, much less fraternities. You'll hardly be able to help out at a canteen and meet some nice officer in 1959. But in a sorority you'll meet all kinds of young men. Besides, going through Rush will be such fun."

September 1959

Kathleen Andrews counted forty-three rushees in her tour group—"A-C." She didn't know one of them.

"Welcome to Sorority Rush, ladies," the tour leader greeted them for their orientation in the Husky Union Building, called the HUB. "You're in for such a fun week. You'll meet new people and make great new friends. Just be sure to keep an open mind. Remember, there is a house for everyone."

"I don't know about that," a voice behind Kathleen muttered. "My girlfriend went through Rush last year, and she didn't get the house she wanted."

"What'd she do?" someone whispered.

"She dropped out of school."

"You're kidding," came the shocked response.

Hearing this snippet, Kathleen's excitement changed to uneasiness. How could anyone know which sorority she wanted at this point? They hadn't even been to one yet.

They followed the tour leader across the street that divided the University of Washington campus from Greek Row and stopped outside a graceful, white-brick house. Its tall columns and dark shutters glistened with last night's rain, which had mercifully stopped before Rush began, but the sharp smell of wet pavement hung in the air.

"What happens now?" asked a girl from the back of the group.

Kathleen was relieved that someone else didn't know. The orientation had told them about the mechanics of the day and about Panhellenic rules and that Panhellenic meant "all Greek" and was the sororities' governing organization, but Kathleen didn't know what to expect.

"We zip into ten sororities for thirty minutes each," was the *sotto voce* reply. "You meet everyone inside and try to smile the whole time while not saying anything stupid or tripping on the stairs."

Kathleen turned to the voice on her right as a smatter of nervous giggles erupted.

"Hi," said its owner. "I'm Mary Bergstrom—from Ballard High in Seattle."

"Hi. Kathleen Andrews. I'm from here too. Richmond High."

Mary had baby-fine hair in a fluffy bubble that framed her heart-shaped face. She was not quite beautiful, but she had an air about her, Kathleen decided, as if she knew the punch line.

"My sister's a Del Phi. We had to live through this when she went through Rush two years ago."

"Del Phi?" Kathleen asked.

"Delta Phi Tau," Mary told her, "but they go by Del Phi."

"You're lucky, then," Kathleen said shaking her head. "I'm the first girl in my family to go to college, let alone Rush. I'm just thankful it quit raining so my hair won't frizz!" She touched her dark curls nervously. "If it rains, I turn into a Brillo pad."

"Mine wouldn't curl if I slept with my finger in a socket," Mary said. "Some people have all the luck."

"I'll need more than luck. I can't even figure out these Greek names! They all sound alike."

Mary laughed. "Don't worry, by this time tomorrow you'll have them down pat— you just won't be able to remember your own!"

Kathleen didn't think she would have anything down pat, tomorrow or any other day. "How will you ever choose which house to join? I mean, there are so many."

"Well, my dear know-nothing-about-sororities, the first thing you need to know is they choose you, you don't choose them."

"What?"

"They'll look us all over and decide which of the lucky ones get asked back. You can drop houses you don't like, of course, but you can't call one back that's dropped you."

Dropped. Kathleen's stomach did just that. She and her mother had spent days studying the Rush Handbook and planning what she should wear. She'd thought arguing with her mother over a hat that didn't perch on her curls and make her look like one of the Marx Brothers was the most difficult thing she had to do.

In the summer, her high-school buddy Jake had given her a tour of Greek Row. He'd been rushed by several fraternities, so he knew his way around. She'd imagined herself a part of this scene, living in one of the beautiful old houses, walking to campus with sophisticated girls wearing flowers in their smooth pageboys, laughing and flirting with handsome fraternity men. It never occurred to her that she might not get in.

She stared dumbly at Mary, opening her mouth to ask another question, when a loud cheer came from inside the house. Kathleen jumped as the double doors burst open and the girls inside flew down the porch steps, clapping and singing something unintelligible. They had on tartan skirts and black sweaters, and each wore a strand of pearls. They smiled and clapped as each rushee was paired with the next girl in line and whisked into the house.

"Hi, I'm Wendy. Welcome to Lambda. What's your name?" A chubby girl with a ponytail grabbed Kathleen by the arm and ushered her up the brick stairs. She was a couple of inches shorter than Kathleen, who at 5-foot-3 rarely got to look down on anyone over age fourteen. Kathleen realized she had been picturing all sorority girls as tall and slim. Wendy was a shock.

"I'm Kathleen Andrews."

"Well, Kathy, we'll just put your coat in the powder room," Wendy said.

As Kathleen removed her coat, she had a sudden realization that if what Mary said about not being able to go back to a house that dropped you was true, this round might be the only time she would see some of these houses. The rushee just ahead of her had on a matching skirt and sweater in a pale pumpkin shade that showed off her auburn hair. Her belt seemed to be a circle of copper. Kathleen's white sweater and tweed skirt suddenly appeared painfully ordinary.

"Here's a name tag. You'll be thankful for these before the day is over!" Wendy pinned the glittery tag with "Kathy" on it onto Kathleen's sweater and maneuvered her deftly into the living room with a chubby arm placed firmly about Kathleen's waist.

"What's your major?" Wendy asked.

"I'm a pre-major so far," Kathleen admitted. She had no idea what she wanted to major in, probably education, but until that moment, it had not bothered her. Now her indecisiveness seemed to go with her unremarkable outfit.

"I was too my first year." Wendy winked, letting Kathleen know "pre-major" was OK.

It grew warm where Wendy's arm rested, and Kathleen's sweater was beginning to prickle. Wendy steered her to a group forming by a grand piano and introduced her. Someone asked what her major was, but Wendy answered for her. The other rushees declared in order that they were majoring in nursing and dental hygiene. One of the Lambdas squealed that she was in dental hygiene and that the rushee would just die during the chemistry section but not to worry, everyone did.

Suddenly a bell tinkled, and everyone quickly found a place to sit, which for most was the floor. All the smiling Lambdas turned to face the sorority sister who was still standing. She welcomed the rushees to Lambda and led the Lambdas in a song about sisterhood, during which Wendy kept pressing little squeezes onto Kathleen's arm.

Kathleen's face felt frozen in an unnatural smile, and her right leg was going to sleep. When the song finally ended, she rose as gracefully as she could, praying that her tingling leg wouldn't buckle.

Before she could think about it, however, Wendy was steering her to another group for introductions and what-is-your-majors. She met many of the girls in her tour group as well as the Lambdas, who all said they were s-o-o-o-o delighted to meet her and wherever did she get that beautiful sweater. Her self-confidence ebbed further.

The bell tinkled again, and the Rush Chairman announced it was time to leave.

"Have to take this," Wendy said, removing the nametag. "Panhellenic rules."

Now all the rushees were back out on the sidewalk as the smiling, clapping Lambdas sang and waved a last toothy farewell before disappearing into the house.

"Now you see why they call it Rush," their tour guide said and beckoned for them to follow her to the next sorority.

"How did you like the Lambdas?" Mary asked, catching up to Kathleen.

"I don't know what I expected, but this is wild. Do they always guide you around by the waist? It seemed kind of weird."

"Only the Lambdas. My sister says they're famous for it. Maybe they think if they let go of you, you'll escape. It gave me the creeps!"

They giggled, and Kathleen felt a surge of warmth for this new friend, but as they waited together in front of the next house for the now-expected shriek, she felt the butterflies start in her stomach again. Why hadn't she worn something more exciting? The Rush Handbook said "school clothes" for these first rounds, so she and her mother had concentrated on shopping for outfits for the dressy parties, including the dreaded hat. She should have paid more attention to these first parties. True, her white sweater looked good on her because her hair was so dark, but her outfit was definitely not memorable.

This time the girls who swooped down the stairs wore matching skirts and sweaters of varying colors. Their sorority pins—perched at precisely the same spot on each sweater—gleamed softly with pearls and gold and bobbed in time to the clapping and singing.

"I love you, say you love me,
For you-oo-oo we pine."

A tall girl named Libby smiled warmly at Kathleen and steered her by the elbow into the modern sandstone house. As she pinned a large round nametag onto Kathleen, Libby's shoulder-length pageboy fell softly forward and then settled back, as if it had never moved. Kathleen had to stop herself from smoothing her own curls.

After introducing her to the housemother, Libby led Kathleen into the living room and began the now-familiar routine. This time when the bell tinkled, she knew what to do, and even managed with Libby's help to snag a seat on a sofa instead of the floor.

Eight houses later, Mary and Kathleen walked back to the dorm and compared notes.

"I don't think I made a very good impression on anyone today," Kathleen confessed.

"Don't be silly. Besides, we don't really get to the good houses until tomorrow," Mary assured her.

"I wish I had brought something more spectacular to wear."

"You look terrific. I wish I had your hair. You could give me half and not even miss it."

Kathleen made a face. Her curls had driven her crazy for as long as she could remember. Her blonde mother, whose immaculate French roll always looked perfect, kept telling her she would appreciate them some day, but today wasn't it. Even though her new friend's comments reassured her a bit—after all, Mary had a sister in one of the *good* houses—Kathleen had not felt comfortable once today.

"What do housemothers do?" she asked Mary.

"They're like live-in chaperones. Fraternities don't have them, so you can never go into the guys' houses unless they're having a special function. Then they import some adults."

7

"Weird," Kathleen said. Then, trying to sound casual she asked, "How will we know if we are invited back?"

"We'll get bids back before the next round. I don't expect to get too many though, being a Del Phi legacy and all."

"Legacy?"

"Girls with a mother or a sister or a grandmother who was in the house. Unless you're some kind of monster, they sort of have to invite you back at least once. And if you have a sister who is currently in the house, the other sororities won't waste a bid on you. They figure you'll go with your sister."

"Will you?"

"Probably. We're good friends, and I've met a lot of the Del Phis. They're great."

"Boy, I didn't realize how ignorant I was about all this stuff. Thanks for filling me in. You're really lucky to be a legacy."

"Don't worry so much," Mary said. "What was your grade point?"

"A 3.9. Why?"

"How about activities? You on the cheer staff?"

"Is it obvious?"

"It's perfect. You're exactly what they're looking for: good grades, good activities, good looks. You even have visible eyebrows. Whoever said blondes have more fun didn't take into account all the time it takes to draw on a face!"

"Be serious. Some of the girls in our group seem so sophisticated. I mean, there's what's-her-name who spent last year in Germany as an exchange student, or Miss Seattle, thank you. Or how about the one on the Olympic swim team, for heaven's sake!"

"Oh, for heaven's sake yourself," Mary said. "Stop fretting. You'll do fine. I told you, they *love* cheerleaders."

Kathleen smiled wanly at her friend, fervently hoping Mary was right. She found some consolation in the fact she had a different outfit for tomorrow's day with the "good houses," but she had a hard time getting to sleep. She kept hearing Mary say, "You don't pick them. They pick you."

The next morning they stood outside the Delta Phi Tau house.

"Well," Mary said. "Now you will see what a real sorority looks like."

"They all looked pretty much alike to me yesterday," Kathleen returned honestly. She was having a hard time separating all the faces and matching outfits and songs. Now she was about to add ten more to the confusion.

The Delta Phi Tau house was another of the antebellum, white-columned structures that dominated Greek Row. A huge weeping willow in the front trailed its slender branches over the rockery of the high bank surrounding the house and nearly touched the sidewalk. The swaying of its curtain of leaves calmed Kathleen somewhat until the Del Phis swept down the stairs clapping and singing, wearing Ivy-League sweaters exactly like the red one Kathleen was wearing. The only difference was that theirs were monogrammed in white two inches below the center of the crew neck. So much for a better outfit.

A laughing blonde who had to be Mary's sister disengaged herself from the line and grabbed Mary. There was no denying their bone structure. Then a slim, lovely girl named Beth introduced herself to Kathleen, and they went into the house together. Beth pinned the delta-shaped nametag onto Kathleen's sweater, saying with a smile that it was lucky she hadn't had it monogrammed yet or everyone would mistake her for a Del Phi. She smiled, and Kathleen felt herself relax.

"Kathleen," came a voice over the noisy room. "Marcia Warden. Do you remember me from Richmond High? I'm so happy to see a familiar face come through this crowd."

Familiar face? Kathleen was surprised Marcia remembered ever seeing her before. She was two years older, and Kathleen had always admired her. She had been the Girls' Club president and had gone steady with the captain of the football team of their rival school.

"Ours was a small school," Marcia explained to Beth. "I couldn't believe all this crush when I went through."

Marcia had been nervous! Kathleen smiled at her gratefully and began to enjoy herself for the first time since the whole thing had begun the day before. The girls she was introduced to seemed more genuine in their responses. She thought they even sang better. Kathleen wondered if she would feel this way if she had not met Mary yesterday, but there was a friendliness about this group that she had not sensed before in the other houses. It seemed as if she had been there for only a few minutes when Beth said, "I really enjoyed meeting you, Kathleen, but it's time to go," and removed the nametag.

Outside again, Kathleen waited for Mary, who was one of the last ones to be clapped down the stairs.

"Well," she said to Kathleen, as they walked up the block. "What did you think?"

"You were right. It's the first time I haven't been totally nervous!"

"Good, because the next house is 'The Ice House,' and you can remember having fun with the Del Phis while you endure it."

"Ice House?"

"Iota Beta Pi. More money per cubic inch than any place else on earth."

The Iotas wore pastel cashmeres and pearls. Real pearls, Kathleen suspected. The door greeters wore gardenias in their hair, giving the entire house a sweet, expensive fragrance. Kathleen stuttered through the flawless introductions and the small talk. She felt dowdy and unsure of herself.

"They were nice enough," she told Mary when they were finally outside, "so why did I feel so stupid?"

"Because they're perfect! I think it's the way they look at you, sort of at a tilt. Makes you feel really short, or that your slip is showing, or that you stepped in something just before you came into the house."

Then Mary tipped her head back, flared her nostrils slightly, and looked down at Kathleen with half-closed eyes.

"You look just like them, Mary! What will your sister say when you pledge the Ice House instead of Delta Phi Tau?"

"It won't matter, of course. As an Iota, I wouldn't let her speak to me."

The rest of the day flew by in a blur of songs and nametags and meeting everyone in her tour group over and over again. There were no houses that Kathleen liked as well as she had Delta Phi Tau, although there were others she would like to see again.

"We'll see what becomes of us when we get our bid envelopes in the morning," Mary said. "So let's go get dinner while we still have a future."

"What a cheerful thought," Kathleen replied as they set off together.

The next morning the tour leader greeted them with a smile, but Kathleen felt there was going to be a stiff-upper-lip sort of speech.

"You've met a lot of people in the last two days, and I hope you're all keeping an open mind. Now you'll have time to look at the houses during a longer party. Mark the 'accept' bubble on ten cards. For those who might have fewer than ten cards, mark them all. You *must* return to all ten of the houses that invited you back. No skipping. Get to know the girls; let them get to know you. It's far too early to have your minds made up yet. Remember, there is a house for every girl in this room."

The tour leader called their names alphabetically and handed each girl a long, thin envelope. Biting the inside of her lip, Kathleen opened hers quickly and took out fifteen computer cards. She had been invited back by all the houses she liked, including the Del Phis, and to her absolute amazement, by the Ice House. She let out her breath, not even realizing she had been holding it. Mary was smiling at her.

"The word must not be out I'm a legacy! I got fourteen invites," Mary whispered "Ice House," Kathleen mouthed, waving a bid card.

"They knew they didn't have a chance with me." Mary looked down her nose.

The Tour leader frowned at them, and they returned to marking their cards. "Do you think the Ice House might realize their mistake and ask you back for the next party, Mary?" Kathleen asked when they left the room.

Mary patted Kathleen on the shoulder as if she were a small child. "No, dear, they won't. I told you before, after First Period Parties, the houses have to cut the number they invite back. They want a second look, not a first one. They'll just have to struggle along without me. Pity."

Despite Mary's joking, the surge of relief Kathleen had felt at finding all those invitations in her envelope was ebbing fast. She could be dropped by any of the houses next round. It was possible that she might not get into a sorority at all, let alone one that she actually wanted. She shuddered at the prospect of having to tell her mother that she had been dropped by all the houses and would never be able to meet a suitable prospect to marry. She shook her head and walked with Mary back to their dorm.

"I'm going to call my mother," Kathleen said and went to find a phone.

"How is it going, dear?" her mother asked before Kathleen could say a word. "I spoke with Mrs. Lavik a few minutes ago, and she said Trudy is having a wonderful time. Apparently she got invitations from every one of the houses she went to."

Kathleen smothered the wave of frustration she felt. She and Trudy Lavik had been at odds since both of them were elected to Richmond's Pep Staff. Whatever Kathleen suggested, whether it was a new step for a routine or an idea for uniforms, Trudy opposed it. She wanted to do dance routines that were smooth and pretty and didn't muss her perfect hair. Trudy would execute the motions with the grace of a Pavlova, always on the beat but strangely out of sync. It drove Kathleen crazy. They ran in different circles at school, but since they were the only two girls from Richmond High going through Rush, they had gone to the Panhellenic orientation together last spring, and Kathleen knew they were bound to run into each other during Rush.

"We go back to ten houses next, Mother, and I'm going back to all the houses I really liked."

"Why only ten, Kathleen? I'm sure Trudy's mother said there were twenty."

"There are twenty sororities, but we can only go back to ten, Mother. Even Trudy doesn't get extra." She wouldn't mention that five houses had dropped her, even though two of them were the Jewish sororities, who wouldn't pledge her anyway, and the other three she hadn't liked at all.

"Oh, then you got a full card, dear. That's just grand. And, Kathleen," her mother paused.

"Yes, Mother?"

"You will remember to watch your posture, won't you? They might not think well of you if you slouch."

"I'll stand up straight, Mother. Thanks. And give my love to Daddy. Bye." The phone felt heavy. She hung it up and walked down the hall to her room.

Warm sunshine did not make her feel better the next morning. Her first party was with the Iotas, and even though she and Mary had both been invited back to many of the same houses, they wouldn't be going to any together. Kathleen realized how much she had counted on Mary's presence.

"Well, Kathleen."

She turned at the sound of her name to see Trudy Lavik also joining the small group outside the Ice House.

"Imagine, the two of us at the same party." Trudy patted her hair and ran her tongue over her teeth, quickly switching to a smile when she noticed several fraternity guys dangling over their balcony to get a better view of their group.

"Hi, Trudy," Kathleen said, thinking how odd it was that she was happy to see a familiar face, even Trudy's. "How's Rush going for you?"

"I just love it, don't you? It's such fun! I don't know how I'll decide which house to join."

"Yes, it's fun, but don't you think you should get a little better look before you worry about that? I mean, Tours was a blur. How can you tell this soon?"

"Oh, Kathleen," Trudy said, tilting her head. "I can tell just by looking."

Trudy's confidence was galling, and Kathleen's feeling of relief at seeing her evaporated. She turned and looked hard at the double doors. Familiar shrieks greeted them, and Iotas dressed in jungle costumes streamed out in two lines, singing their door chant. Kathleen's hostess had her honey-blonde hair pulled smoothly into a pony tail on top of her head where it wrapped itself around a large plastic bone. She introduced herself as Sissy as they ran up the stairs and into the house.

The long entry hall was draped with vines and ivy, with spears and African-looking shields scattered here and there.

"You must have been up all night doing this," Kathleen exclaimed to Sissy.

"Oh, that's part of the fun," Sissy said in a breathy voice. "All the guys from the Beta house came over to help us. We could *never* have strung all these vines without their help."

The Betas were Big Men on Campus. Even Kathleen knew that. It was one of the houses Jake had considered pledging before he decided on Rho Gamma Epsilon, which he'd informed her they called the Rogue House. Kathleen imagined what fun it must be to have a whole fraternity drop in and help string ivy. She couldn't wait to be part of all this.

Sissy broke into her reverie by introducing her to a group of people who immediately asked her where she was from.

"I'm from Richmond," she replied.

"You're from Richmond!" a willowy brunette in leopard skin and black face asked in a soft drawl. "Ah'm from Newport News! This was mah daddy's school, so that's why Ah'm here. How 'bout you?"

It was the first spark of interest in her since she entered the Ice House, and it felt very good. Kathleen smiled at her and said, "No, Richmond High School. Here in Seattle."

The brunette's smile stayed bright, but Kathleen felt dismissed. "Mah," she said. "How nice." Then she turned to the others in the circle and announced she had to go get ready for the skit. She never glanced at Kathleen again. Kathleen wondered if Trudy would get that response to good old Richmond High, but somehow didn't think she would. She spotted Trudy surrounded by a cluster of Iotas who seemed to be hanging on her every word.

Another Iota was saying, "Donna here was homecoming queen at her high school, Sissy, just like you." Donna and Sissy gave each other Aha looks. "I was just telling her that five out of the last eight homecoming queens here at the U have been Iotas."

Kathleen started to comment that they didn't have homecoming queens in the Seattle high schools, but she thought it sounded sort of feeble, so she didn't.

Mercifully, it was time for the skit. They settled themselves on the floor as Miss Newport News and two other black-faced girls wearing woolly wigs and leopard skin outfits entered the room. Drums started pulsing, and the three "cannibals" did a clever and complicated dance while looking for someone to put into a large cooking pot.

"The girl in the middle is a Husky cheerleader," Sissy whispered.

As Kathleen turned to comment on how creative she thought the dance was, she realized that Sissy was talking to Donna again and not to her. No sense mentioning that she had been a cheerleader, she decided. The space to tell it in was too large and the audience too small.

A petite blonde wandered around, lost in the jungle. Just as it seemed she would fall prey to the cannibals, three Iota "missionaries" gave chase in hilarious slow motion that had the whole room in hysterics. Then the tiny blonde, safe at last, was offered the haven of Iota love. The missionaries pinned the diamond-shaped pin onto her dress, and everyone burst into song.

The group mingled again, commenting on how clever the skit had been, and then it was time to go. Sissy bade Kathleen a vague good-bye as she sped her to the door. There she seemed to forget Kathleen altogether as she waved homecoming-queen waves at Donna, who waved back from the group forming on the sidewalk. Several voices called out "Good-bye, Trudy," and Kathleen saw Trudy smile her gleaming smile back at them. No one was waving at Kathleen, and it felt very odd. Being a cheerleader at Richmond had been an enviable thing. People looked up to the cheerleaders, and they were part of the "in crowd." Kathleen had never experienced this sort of invisibility before. She hoped it was just because this was the Ice House.

Trudy appeared beside her. "I just loved the Iotas, didn't you? Maybe we'll meet at another party. See you then."

"See you." Thank God they were going in opposite directions, Kathleen thought. Perhaps things were looking up. And maybe she would have fun with the Lambdas. As their Tour leader had said, it was still too early to make up her mind.

"Hi, Kathleen. Mind if I walk with you?"

A girl named Alice from her tour group hurried to join her. "I'm going to the Lambda House," Alice said. "I can't wait. I just loved them during Tours. They were so warm!"

"Yes, they were," Kathleen agreed, remembering Wendy's arm around her waist. "I'm going there too."

"I wonder what their theme will be."

They didn't have to wonder long. After the usual shriek, two Lambdas came down their stairs unrolling a length of yellow cloth with a brick design painted on it.

"Follow the yellow brick road!" they shouted cheerfully, and Munchkin-clad Lambdas headed two-by-two for the group of rushees. The first one grabbed Alice in a joyous reunion and rushed her up the stairs. Kathleen found herself staring at Wendy.

"Kathy!" she said and grabbed Kathleen by the waist. "I'm so glad you're back."

"It's Kathleen," Kathleen shouted over the singing.

"Oh, that's right," Wendy said and then waved her chubby hand as if names were minor details. "I don't know, you look like a Kathy to me."

They dashed about meeting more people, and then sat for the skit. Poor Dorothy—sans Toto—wandered forlornly looking for a place where she could belong. The Good Witch appeared and pointed to the Emerald City of Lambda ("The emerald is our jewel," Wendy whispered) where the Wizard would be able to help her. After Dorothy and friends discovered that there was no place like Lambda, the assembled cast sang a song to the tune of "Over the Rainbow" about Lambda sisterhood.

They ate little green cookies, drank cloyingly sweet "Emerald Punch," and then follow, follow, followed the yellow brick road back outside. Kathleen felt as if her face had frozen into the world's phoniest smile as Wendy waved and waved, and several people called good-bye. Alice stood next to her, beaming.

"Oh, Kathleen, I *love* this house," Alice said reverently as the Lambdas went back inside.

"God, that was *awful!*"

Kathleen turned to see a tall girl behind her rolling her eyes.

"I thought it was wonderful," Alice said, looking wounded and surprised at the same time.

"Gawd!" the tall girl said again, louder. Then she tossed her long hair and walked off.

"We've been erased," Kathleen said to Alice, trying to cheer her up. "Maybe it proves that what our tour leader said was true. There's a house for everyone. Obviously this one's not for her." Alice seemed a bit cheered, but Kathleen wasn't. What if everyone but the Lambdas dropped her? Would she pledge them just to be in a sorority? What would it be like being in the same house with Wendy? She shuddered.

"Where do you go now?" Alice was asking her.

"Delta Phi Tau."

"They didn't ask me back," Alice said. "I heard they're kind of snobby."

"Did you? I really liked them during Tours. I can't wait to see what this party is like."

"Well, good luck. Maybe I'll see you at the next round."

They parted, and Kathleen headed up the street. As she turned the corner, she could see the beautiful willow tree branches swaying in a graceful, beckoning motion. Her heart beat a little faster as she joined the crowd standing in front of Delta Phi Tau. She recognized a few girls and vowed to pay more attention to names this time.

Soon the doors opened, and the Del Phis poured out in colorful ski outfits. Mary's sister skipped past the two greeters and came right for Kathleen.

"Kathleen, welcome back. I hoped we'd see you again."

She did? Then as they went through the double line of girls toward the front door, two or three girls called out, "Hi, Kathleen." Wonder replaced her nervousness.

Inside, the house had been transformed into a ski lodge. Skis lined the halls. Fragrant cedar and pine boughs festooned the living room, where despite being in the 70s outside, a huge fire roared in the fireplace. An enormous bearskin rug stretched in front of it.

"Can you believe how warm it is today?" Julie asked her as she pinned a nametag on Kathleen. "The weather gods wait all year to get their little revenge on us by turning on the heat for our ski party."

"But it looks wonderful in here," Kathleen heard herself say and then immediately felt stupid again.

Julie seemed not to notice. Still smiling she said, "Come on in. I want everyone to meet you, especially our two Husky cheerleaders. Do you think you'll try out in the spring?"

"I hadn't even thought about it, to tell you the truth," Kathleen said, amazed that Julie remembered she had been on the rally squad.

"Billie, come meet Kathleen Andrews. We were just talking about you cheerleader types."

"Good stuff, I hope." Billie was a short redhead with a million freckles and a slight overbite. Her smile lit up her face and caused her eyes to wrinkle shut. She wore a rust and gold ski sweater and gold stretch pants. Kathleen liked her immediately.

"All good," Julie assured her. "Kathleen was a cheerleader at Richmond High here in Seattle. I was just telling her about you and Patty."

"Thinking about trying out?" Billie asked.

"As I told Julie, it hadn't even entered my mind. I'm still reeling from all these parties." Mercifully they both laughed as if she had said something truly witty.

"Well, think about it. The Husky band is the best, and the team's on a roll. We could even go to the Rose Bowl this year!"

"Hey, Patty," Julie said to a tall, slim girl with a short pixie hairdo. "We're having a cheerleading convention over here."

"I'm trying to convince Kathleen here to think about trying out in the spring. She was a cheerleader at Richmond," Billie told her.

"I went to your game against my old alma mater to watch my little brother play last year," Patty said. "Your squad was terrific. I even stole a step from you."

"You did? Which one?" Could she sound any more insipid? Kathleen felt her face grow hot.

"I'll show you. I think it was the beginning of your fight song. You were in a circle and did a peel-off with your pom-poms like this." She demonstrated Trudy Lavik's least favorite step—the one that mussed her hair. Kathleen relaxed again and beamed at Patty. It was a Sign.

"I *knew* you weren't clever enough to make that up yourself, Patty!" Billie said.

"On the contrary. It takes a very clever person to steal a step that goes by that fast and get it right. And if you come to the game Saturday, Kathleen, you'll see it."

"I'm leaving you fanatics to yourselves," Julie said, shaking her head. "I'm in the skit, Kathleen, but I'm sure none of you will miss me while I'm gone. Just please don't practice any kicks—it's too crowded!"

"People who haven't been cheerleaders just don't understand," Patty said.

"I had a boyfriend once who asked me why I wanted to be a cheerleader," Billie said. "I explained how much fun the choreography was—the making up of routines that finally clicked and how you could tell when the crowd was with you and all. I got very rhapsodic, but it was wasted on him. He said I only did it to show off my legs and why didn't I face it."

"You're kidding!" Patty exclaimed. "How long did you go with him?"

"About five more minutes." They all laughed, and Kathleen felt a sense of belonging that warmed her. When the bell tinkled, they settled themselves on the bearskin rug. Kathleen was tempted to rest her elbow on the shaggy head, but it seemed rude somehow.

Marcia, the Del Phi from Kathleen's high school, tap-danced into the living room holding a foil-wrapped toilet plunger that was supposed to be a microphone. She wore a huge fuzzy coat and sported a large yellow mum with a purple W on it.

"Welcome to the Del Phi Lodge here on Mt. Rush Rush," she said. "We will be interviewing some of the skiers here today to see how they are enjoying themselves. Oh, here comes one now."

Julie stumbled in, her nose in a copy of *War and Peace*.

"She's perfectly cast," Billie whispered to me. "She has the highest grades in the house, and she hates skiing."

"A little light reading?" Beth asked her.

"Something to do on the chair lift. The rides are so long, it seems a shame to waste all that time."

Then a petite redhead in a one-piece stretch suit slithered in. She had a perfect figure and flawless skin, but she wore huge, silly, rabbit-fur earmuffs.

"Are you enjoying the slopes?" Marcia asked her.

She said nothing.

"I said, are you enjoying the slopes?"

The bunny smiled vacantly.

Finally, Marcia lifted one of the earmuffs and spoke into her ear. "Are you enjoying the slopes?"

"Oh, yes!" she trilled. "I'm just a beginner . . ."

"No!" Marcia interrupted and then mugged at the audience.

"Yes! But my instructor says I already make the best sitz marks on the hill!"

Marcia interviewed a few more hilarious types—some tall, some pretty, some athletic looking. It occurred to Kathleen that aside from the fact that the Del Phis made her feel important and welcome, she liked them because they were all different from one another. The Del Phis didn't seem to have a "look." The Iotas were all so sleek, and the Lambdas were all sort of frumpy. But maybe it was that everyone dressed alike during Tours. She would have to look more closely at the houses.

"Have you actually read *War and Peace?*" Billie asked Julie as she rejoined them.

"Of course she has, silly," Patty replied. "She had phone duty for a whole hour once. I think she read it then."

Julie laughed and pulled Kathleen away, saying she wanted her to see a more representative group than just cheerleaders who never read. Marcia came up and told Kathleen she was happy she was back. By the time everyone was clapped out, Kathleen knew this was a house she could love. People were waving and saying good-bye to her by name. She felt so much better than she had outside the Ice House.

Mary stood at the corner waiting for her. "Come on, it's time for some dinner and comparing notes."

"I'm having trouble with this open-mind business, Mary," Kathleen confessed over meatloaf and mashed potatoes. "Some of these houses are just not for me. I know that going back to them is a complete waste of time."

"Yeah," Mary agreed. "I went to Oz today too." She made a Munchkin face that caused Kathleen to swallow wrong.

"At least I wasn't nervous there," Kathleen said when she stopped coughing, "because I didn't care. Then at Del Phi your sister grabbed me from the beginning, and everyone was great. Their skit is hilarious, by the way. Wait till you see your sister."

"I told you you'd like them." Mary looked smug.

"But the Ice House! You should have seen Miss Newport News's face when she found out I wasn't from *her* Richmond. It was as if she might catch something horrible by just being near me."

"Well, don't feel alone. I could've fallen on my face today at one house, and no one would have even noticed. Miss Seattle came in behind me, and people practically walked over me to get to her. I nearly drowned in the ooze. The worst part is, she's really nice, so I couldn't hate her."

"Pity."

"Oh, well, eat up so we can go rest our smiles. You know, I heard that beauty queens put Vaseline on their teeth so their lips can slide up easily. I should have asked Miss Seattle." She started curling her lips up like a chimpanzee.

"That'll get you into the house of your choice. Hold that look while I go give my mother a call. She's probably sitting by the phone."

Her mother answered on the first ring.

"Hi. I just have a second, but I thought I'd check in."

"How are you doing, dear?"

"Well, the parties have been interesting. Some are more fun than others. I really liked the Delta Phi Tau house today. They had this neat ski party . . ."

"Is that the one you were at with Trudy? Her mother says you were at the good one together."

"No, that was at a different house, one I didn't think was so good." Kathleen tried to keep her voice from rising. "The one I really liked was—"

"Mr. Lavik's partner has a daughter in that house. She was a debutante last year. Mrs. Lavik says it's really the best one."

"Trudy doesn't know any more about the houses than any of us do, so don't listen to Mrs. Lavik."

"Well, it's a positive sign that you two were at the same party."

Kathleen knew that it would be fruitless to try to explain anything further. She said good-bye and walked slowly back to where Mary waited.

"Who stepped on your face?" Mary asked.

"It's so hard to talk to my mother sometimes. She gets a little piece and thinks she understands it all. And no amount of explanation can dislodge her." Kathleen shook her head and then smiled. "Well, maybe I'm not the best one to explain Rush to her anyway. I don't seem to get it fully myself."

"You're getting better," Mary reassured her. "Let's head back and see what new treats are in store for us."

Kathleen smiled her way through cowboy parties, Roaring Twenties parties, underwater parties, and an outer space party. Each house she went to was more elaborately decorated than the last. There were pictures of every queen or cheerleader who had ever worn the pin.

"Did you count the number of houses the Betas personally decorated?" Mary asked her when they were finally back at the dorms after the last party.

"Only about all of them! I just wish I had some sense of where things stand. I'd give anything to know if the houses I like really like *me*. It's impossible to tell."

"Well, they can't say anything, you know. If they even hint that they want you and Panhellenic gets wind of it, they're in big trouble for 'dirty Rush.'"

"What the heck is that?"

"My sister told me that last year one house really wanted this girl, so one of the girls whispered to her that they were going to ask her to pledge. You know, so she'd pick them and not some other house. Well, she was so excited that she told someone who told someone, and it got back to Panhellenic. The house was on social pro for two quarters."

"Social pro? It's like a different language!"

"Social probation. They couldn't participate in exchanges with fraternities or have any social functions until spring quarter. You know, no formals or stuff."

"Panhellenic can *do* that?" Kathleen was dumbfounded.

"You bet. They could have put just the girl on social pro, but they slammed it to the whole house. So everyone is being really careful this year. My sister and I can't even call each other."

"Wow, that's pretty amazing. But I can tell you honestly that no one's been whispering anything to me. I can't wait to see who asks us back."

"We'll know in the morning."

After breakfast, they gathered back at the HUB where their Tour leader stood behind the now-familiar stack of envelopes.

"You must choose six houses from these bids," she informed them with a huge smile.

"What if we don't want to go back to six of them?" a voice in the back asked.

The smile faded ever so slightly. "If you have six or more cards in the envelope, you must choose six. Otherwise the computer will automatically assign you to whatever houses asked you back until you have six cards. It's still way too early to make up your minds." She passed out the envelopes.

Kathleen was almost afraid to open hers. She pulled the whole stack out at once and fanned it slightly. There was Delta Phi Tau. She discovered she had been holding her breath again and now let it out. The card from the Lambdas was next, followed by a house she had sort of liked. The rest didn't really matter, but she was startled to see a card from the Iotas. Well, things were certainly getting interesting. She glanced at Mary, who was doing her chimp face back at Kathleen. Kathleen figured Mary was pleased too.

She marked her cards easily except for the Lambdas'. As much as she dreaded going back there again, if she dropped them, she would have to choose between two houses she liked even less. Please don't let me end up with Wendy again, she prayed as she blackened the circle on the card and put them all back into the envelope.

"Well?" Mary asked when they got outside.

"Well, yourself. Delta Phi Tau asked me back, and . . ." Kathleen tried to look mysterious.

"Do I detect a drum roll here?"

"A big one. So did the Iotas!"

"No! Their numbers must be way down. They sound desperate! Perhaps you didn't make it clear to them that you shouldn't be having a good Rush."

"Oh, stop it," Kathleen said and laughed. "Maybe they have a thing about cheerleaders as well as homecoming queens. Either way, I'm shocked."

Before any of the parties resumed, however, everything came to a halt for the opening Husky football game. It was perfect football weather, sunny and bright and not a cloud anywhere. Kathleen and Mary followed the crowd down a beautiful wooded path that wound behind the dorms to the stadium. It was cool and shady and smelled of wet leaves. The girls came out of the woods at a concrete footbridge into the dazzling sunlight and melded with hundreds of fans. Tall, lean rowers from the Husky crew hawked programs next to pot-bellied men from Kiwanis selling bright red apples.

"Want an apple, Mary? My treat," Kathleen said.

"Sure, but don't you think what we *really* need is several programs?" Mary was staring at the handsome guys from the crew.

Kathleen pushed her along toward the gate to the student section. Once they walked through the entrance tunnel, they found themselves high above the field at the top of a steep flight of concrete stairs. Blocks of seats had already been staked out by shirtless fraternity boys showing off their summer tans. Interspersed with them in colorful clusters sat well-dressed sorority girls in soft sweaters and skirts, their pins twinkling in the bright sun. A thrill ran through Kathleen as she realized that by the next game she might be sitting with such a group and maybe even *know* some of these guys.

"Have you ever seen so much gorgeous manhood in one place, Kathleen?" Mary poked her in the ribs. "And they're all just waiting to meet us."

They made their way to an area far down in front where no seats had been saved. A large sort of moat separated the stands from the track and the football field. They were close enough to the cheer squad that they could hear their shoes crunch against the cinders on the track.

"God, what a view," Mary said. "Look at all those boats."

On the Lake Washington side of the stadium, streams of boats pointed their way to the game and tied up to one another. Beyond them and the sparkling blue lake, the Cascade Range stood sharp and green against the sky.

Suddenly music erupted as the team came running out onto the field, and the announcer's voice boomed over the cheering crowd to welcome everyone to Husky Stadium.

"Hey, look!" Mary said and pointed to the stands behind them.

Kathleen turned to see a body being passed hand-over-hand up through the fraternity section. The shirtless boy was laughing as he was pushed and dropped and tugged to the top of the stands.

"What a hoot!" Mary exclaimed.

"I'd hate to have that happen to me," Kathleen replied.

"Yeah, but I don't imagine even these crazies would grab a girl in a skirt and nylons. It's hard enough to keep your knees together just sitting in a chair. Imagine how tough it would be doing that."

Then it was kick-off time, so the attention of the crowd turned to the field. A non-conference game, it wouldn't count in the standings, but the Huskies scored in the first two minutes and never trailed.

"The only problem with so many touchdowns is that the cheerleaders have to keep doing the fight song over and over. It doesn't give them a chance to do any other routines," Kathleen explained. Mary looked at her friend.

"I'll bet no one has ever pointed that out to the coach. I'll send him a note and tell him to have his team knock it off." Mary rolled her eyes. "I didn't realize cheerleading was a sickness."

"Sorry."

Kathleen was disappointed at the halftime, because the Husky Marching Band she had heard so much about wasn't performing. Instead there were several local high school bands.

"Maybe everyone isn't back at school yet, do you think?" she asked Mary.

"I'm sure that's why they aren't here, dear. But if they had known how important it was to you, they'd have made the effort. But tell me, is that all you like about football?"

"Pretty much. You can't see the games much from the sidelines anyway because your back is usually to the field."

"This is truly fascinating," Mary said. "I had no idea."

The score was hugely in favor of Washington when the game finally ended. The girls headed back to the dorms to change into heels and "nice dresses" for the next round of parties.

"I hope my feet hold out," Mary wailed as they went to pick up their schedules at the HUB a short time later.

"You and me both," Kathleen agreed. "It was hard to get heels on after walking so much in flats today."

"Where do you go now?" Mary pulled Kathleen's schedule from her hand as they walked off campus toward Greek Row. "Nope, we don't go to anything together until tomorrow morning at Del Phi. I'll see you back at the dorms after the last party."

"Wow them all, Mar." Kathleen waved good-bye and started to walk the short block to her first party when she heard someone call her name.

"Wait up, Kathleen!"

It was Jake, sprinting down the stairs of the Rogue house to join her. "How's Rush going for you? I haven't seen you since it started."

"It's pretty confusing, if you want to know the truth." Kathleen was delighted to see him. For a few moments at least she could be totally herself with someone besides Mary. "When you showed me around this summer, you didn't tell me how scary it would be!"

"Scary, why? Although I will admit some of those songs are pretty frightening."

Kathleen laughed and felt an affectionate rush of warmth for him. "I just didn't know it would be so—I don't know— so serious. It's like applying for a job, only worse."

"Oh, come on, Kathleen. All these lovelies I've been watching look like they're having a wonderful time. What's your favorite house so far?"

"Well, I really like Delta Phi Tau best, but I hate to even say it out loud. I don't want to jinx anything. I'm going back there tomorrow."

"Delta Phi Tau. That's great. They're supposed to be really good. One of my Rogue roommates is pinned to a Del Phi. Her pictures are all over the room."

"Keep your fingers crossed for me, Jake. The other houses just don't feel the same. But I'd better go now, or I'll be late to my party. Are you moved into the fraternity yet?"

"That's how I got a roommate, Kathleen. Not nervous are we?"

Kathleen swatted his arm. "Don't pick on me, I'm wearing heels!"

Jake laughed and offered his arm. "Want me to help you hobble? It would be very impressive to show up on the arm of a Rogue, you know."

"Thanks, but I don't want the other rushees to get jealous."

"You always were considerate. OK, I'll be watching the newspapers to see what you pledge. Good luck and stop worrying."

She left Jake, feeling much better than she had a few minutes earlier, and walked as quickly as she could in the unfamiliar heels to the sorority house for the next party. There were only a dozen or so girls waiting outside, she noted, less than half of what she was used to. She didn't have time to think about it much, though, because the familiar door chant started almost immediately.

Her hostess introduced herself as Heidi and led her to a beautiful table set with silver and china in the dining room.

"Have a cup of tea, Kathleen, and some of this delicious cake." She handed Kathleen a delicate cup and saucer and a plate with a square of lemon cake on it. Kathleen took one item in each hand and followed Heidi into the living room. She sat as directed in a high-backed wing chair, balancing the teacup and cake plate on her knees. There was no way she could drink or eat from either.

Several sorority sisters gathered in a little group on the floor in front of her and after introductions, sat looking up at Kathleen and smiling.

"This is the good part of the computer foul-up," Heidi said. "We get to spend some time with you for a change."

"Next party we have fifty-four or something like that!" a girl named Susan said. "Honestly, every year those computers go nuts at least once. It's so annoying."

"I thought it was a little strange to see so few of us outside," Kathleen ventured.

"You thought maybe no one chose to come back to our house?" Susan said.

Kathleen's face burned and then froze. How stupid could she sound? "I . . . No, of course not. It's just that . . ." She wanted to evaporate.

Susan started to laugh, and the other girls joined her. "Don't mind Susan," Heidi said. "She has a warped sense of humor. Did you go to the game?"

Kathleen was weak with relief that the focus of the conversation had turned from her gaffe. "I did. It was so exciting. Do they always pass bodies around?"

One of the other girls at her feet said, "It's the fraternity jocks. They think it's so cool. I was nearly squashed last year when some big lunk fell on me."

Kathleen closed her eyes as she laughed with the rest of them at this remark and didn't see a small, white poodle fly out of nowhere and land on her lap. She nearly dropped both plates, but she had them so tightly in her grasp that they seemed to be a part of her arms by now.

"Get down, you naughty dog," Heidi scolded. "She belongs to our housemother and thinks she owns the place."

"She likes you," Susan said. "And besides, it's her chair."

"No, it's all right. I like dogs." Kathleen felt like one of those moths pinned to a board. She couldn't move. The dog had begun to curl up in her lap when a large bang sent it leaping to the floor, knocking the cake off its plate and onto the rug. Kathleen started to lunge for it, but stopped just in time to avoid spilling her tea on the girl just next to her knee.

"I'm so sorry," she said, mortified.

"I'll just go get some napkins," Heidi said. "Don't worry about it."

The girls seated at her feet smiled and gathered up crumbs from her disaster while Kathleen wished some magic would transport her to another planet. Mercifully the pirate skit had begun. The noise had come from a large black gun fired by one of the pirates. There was the sharp remembered smell of cap guns and a lot of smoke, but not enough to hide in. Kathleen couldn't wait for the whole thing to be over.

When she was finally out on the sidewalk again, she drew a shaky breath. The perfume of autumn that had lifted her spirits before the game today did nothing for her now. So much for that house, she thought. She'd rather liked it before and considered it a possibility if Delta Phi Tau dropped her. Now that option was out. And with gathering dread she realized her next house was the Lambdas.

Stationing herself near the back of the rushees behind a tall brunette, she saw Wendy come flying down the stairs in the other direction and squeal at someone else. Amazingly, the girl looked happy to see Wendy. Much relieved, Kathleen went into the house with another Lambda. Several of the girls came over and squeezed her arm and told her how happy they were to see her back. They do a lot of touching in this house, Kathleen thought, but her hostess did not steer her around by the waist as Wendy had.

She was glad when the party ended, but after the disaster at the previous house, Kathleen had to admit that it felt good to be fussed over a bit. Still, she knew she could not be happy there.

She spotted Mary waiting at the crosswalk, and they headed to the dorms together.

"Do you think you could carry me, Kath, old pal," Mary said, limping dramatically. "My feet died about two hours ago."

"Mine too," Kathleen agreed. "I don't know how we're going to make it through the next few parties in heels! Whose idea was this, anyway?"

"So, other than your feet, how'd it go?"

"Oh, Mary, you will *not* believe what happened to me at the first party." Kathleen told her the story of the poodle and the cake. The pain of reliving it made her face burn, but by the time she got to the big bang that startled the dog, Mary was hysterical.

"How can you laugh?" Kathleen shouted at her. "I wanted to die!"

"Well, at least you didn't throw up. A girl at my last party was so nervous she lost her lunch."

"You're making this up to make me feel better."

"Scout's honor," Mary said holding up three fingers. "She headed for the powder room just as the skit started, but she didn't make it. I heard she's moving to Argentina."

"Oh, poor thing. I guess it could have been worse."

"Not for her!"

"No, I meant for me. Right now I just want to get something to eat and go to bed. I feel like I could sleep for a month."

"I just want out of these high heels," Mary said. "I may never be able to put my feet flat on the floor again. Think of it. For the rest of our lives on the beach we'll have to walk with our toes sticking straight up in the air."

The next morning they were both going to Delta Phi Tau first. Kathleen crammed her aching feet into her black pumps and fastened a gold circle pin onto her red wool dress. She studied her hair critically in the mirror. She would have to wash it tonight for sure. If she stayed this tired, she wouldn't even mind sleeping on rollers. At least she remembered to pack the little sponge pads so the brushes in the rollers wouldn't perforate her scalp.

She tapped on Mary's door, and they went to breakfast together.

"I wonder if this is how it felt to have your feet bound," Mary said. "These shoes were the right size when I bought them."

"I know. Mine shrank too. Must be the climate."

They walked as quickly as their high-heeled feet permitted to Delta Phi Tau, where they waited with the other girls near the willow tree. Kathleen watched the gentle branches and took deep breaths.

"Relax," Mary whispered. "These are the nice ones."

"I just hope I don't do anything stupid in here," Kathleen whispered back.

The Del Phis whooshed out dressed in sarongs. Patty, the tall Husky cheerleader, broke from the line and grabbed Kathleen, putting a blue plastic lei around her neck.

"I'm so glad you're here, Kathleen," she said, and sounded to Kathleen as if she really meant it. "Did you get to the game?"

"Oh, yes," Kathleen said. "But I can't wait to hear the real band."

"Neither can we. High school band day is such an ordeal. We can't do much when the high school kids decide to play two or three different songs simultaneously like Saturday!"

"I noticed that."

"I'm sure everyone did. But did you notice your step in 'Bow Down'?"

"I did! It looked great." Kathleen couldn't believe Patty remembered their earlier conversation.

Patty led Kathleen into the dining room. A fountain in the center of a grass-like carpet splashed noisily, ringed by mounds of spiky pineapples, green-tipped fingers of bananas, oranges, apples, and thick clusters of purple and green grapes. Fishnets lined the walls and ceiling, studded with antherium and delicious-smelling flowers. Kathleen felt herself relaxing in the cool, perfumed room.

One Del Phi after another came up and called Kathleen by her name without even looking at her name tag. She was amazed to be remembered; it felt good. She and Patty sat next to Mary during the skit, which consisted of several intricate Hawaiian dances and a comic hula. None of the cheerleaders performed, and Kathleen was struck by how much talent there must be in this group to find so many other girls who could dance. What fun it must be to choreograph all this.

Unlike the interminable party at what Mary now called the Cake and Dog House, this party flew by. Before she knew it, Kathleen was returning her lei to Patty and leaving the house. She and Mary stood beside the willow tree and waved. Many voices called goodbyes to them by name.

They separated once again and went to one more party before lunch and two before dinner. Kathleen felt that none of the houses could hold a candle to Delta Phi Tau. What could she possibly choose if they didn't ask her back? She knew the Iotas probably wouldn't, but that was fine with her. Their skit was hilarious, but the girls didn't seem to remember that she'd been there before. It didn't feel good to be there. Streams of rushees passed her as she waited anxiously for Mary, and she was surprised to realize how many of the faces were becoming familiar to her. Finally Mary's blonde head appeared in the crowd.

"Let's go to the Ave for dinner. I can't face dorm food tonight." Mary said.

"You mean walk? Uh uh, you'd have to carry me."

"I mean in real shoes, not heels. Let's go get a pizza."

They walked slowly and painfully back to the dorms and changed into skirts and sweaters and saddle shoes. "Much easier to walk in these," Mary said. "Let's hit the Ave." It was still pleasantly warm, but the evenings were beginning to cool down, so Kathleen grabbed her coat.

"You know, when I first heard people call it 'the Ave,' I thought they were showing off," Kathleen admitted.

"Call it 'University Way' and everyone will know you just got here."

They went into Pizza Haven and slid gratefully into an empty booth. "Even in my old saddles, my feet just don't recognize themselves," Mary said with a groan.

"Looks like everyone going through Rush decided on pizza tonight," Kathleen said, noticing rushees at the other tables. There were a few waves and tentative smiles.

"If I ring a bell, do you think they'll all wait for us to do a skit? Let's try it, Kath."

"Will you stop that! What kind of pizza do you want?"

They gave their menus and their order to the waitress, who wrote it down without smiling or making eye contact with either of them.

"Are you ready to narrow it down to three tomorrow?" Mary asked.

"I wish I knew what was going on, Mary. Did your sister say anything to you at the party today?"

"Are you nuts? I told you before, she can't even tell my mother what's going on. They'd be in so much trouble."

"Oh, my God, I forgot to call my mother!"

"Kathleen, you talked to her yesterday, or the day before."

"I know, but she's probably sitting by the phone right now fuming. I'll be back in a second." She rummaged through her purse. "Darn it, Mary. Can I borrow a dime?"

"Two nickels, and I want a receipt." Kathleen swatted at her with her napkin and slid out of the booth to find the phone. The yeasty smell of the pizza dough coupled with the other pizza fragrances made her mouth water as she dialed. Her mother answered on the first ring.

"Well, we finally hear from you," her mother said. "I wouldn't let your father use the phone at all last night in case you decided to call, but I guess you were busy."

"Actually, we had two parties after the football game, so we didn't get back to the dorms until late. My feet were killing me from walking in heels, and I couldn't wait to get my shoes off and get into bed."

"I hope you didn't take off your shoes at any of the sorority houses."

"Of course I didn't, Mother. Even if I'd wanted to, my feet were so swollen, I knew my shoes wouldn't go back on." She tried to make a joke, but she could feel her mother not laughing.

"Well, what do you do next, dear?"

"Tomorrow morning we get our bids for first-, second-, and third-preference parties. We have to choose the houses in the order we like them and then go to the parties. It's also hat day, so I hope I don't look like a fool."

"Let's not have this conversation again, Kathleen. That hat is positively the smartest thing you tried on. You look very sophisticated in it. Wear it proudly and hold your head high."

"OK. Have to go now. Mary—my new friend I told you about—and I decided to come to the Ave for a pizza, and I think it's ready."

"'The Ave'? What is that, a restaurant?"

"No, it's University Way. Mary and I were just talking about how everyone calls it that."

"I hope you are not adopting affectations, Kathleen. They are so unbecoming."

"I really have to go. Please tell Daddy I said hi." She hung up and walked back to the booth. Mary was pulling a steaming triangle onto her plate while strands of white cheese clung to the main pizza.

"Something wrong?"

"No, it's just my mother. Even though she knows less about Rush than I do, she's always giving me advice."

"How could anyone know less than you do?" Mary said between bites.

"Hard to believe, I know," Kathleen responded, reaching for a slice of pizza. "But she's so afraid that if I don't get into the 'right' house, I won't meet Prince Charming or something. I don't know."

"I don't either, but I will say I've seen plenty of the princely types hanging around the fraternities as we walk past. Tell her the pickings look good."

Kathleen chewed thoughtfully for a moment. "Yeah, they do, come to think of it."

"That's the attitude. And stop fretting. You'll be in a good house—both of us will, and then our biggest problem will be that there are only two date nights on a weekend. Poor princes. They'll have to get in line."

The next morning they walked to the HUB together for the 8 o'clock meeting. The tension in the room was palpable as the chairs gradually filled. As she prepared to pass out the envelopes with the bid cards, the tour leader gave another little pep talk about its being still too early to have your mind made up.

Kathleen didn't believe her for a minute, and she could see from their expressions that most of the other rushees didn't either. She opened her envelope quickly, the way they tell you to remove bandages, she thought. The card for the Lambdas was there on top. Then amazingly, there was a card from Cake and Dog! Then Delta Phi Tau. Kathleen was so relieved she let her breath out in an audible puff, then looked around quickly to see if anyone had noticed. No one was doing any looking around; all eyes were on the fateful bid cards. It was only then that she realized that there were still more cards in her packet. None from the Iotas—no surprise there—but the other houses she had gone to had invited her back. She filled in the bubbles for Delta Phi Tau and Cake and Dog and wished she didn't have to choose three. The tour leader told them that if they didn't, the computer would do it for them, so reluctantly she filled in Lambda. She was completely sold on Delta Phi Tau by now, although if Cake and Dog could invite her back after what happened, perhaps that could be an all-right second choice, but the rest of the houses held no appeal to her. She took her envelope to the tour leader and went outside to wait for Mary.

"Well?" she said to Mary as she bounced down the stairs.

"Delta Phi Tau?"

"Yep. You?"

"We'll be at the same party in our beautiful hats, Kath, old girl." They giggled like children and raced each other back to the dorm to get ready.

Kathleen was almost glad of the hat, since her hair after a night in rollers made her look sort of like Shirley Temple. She put on her navy suit and smashed the hat her mother had insisted on over most of the curls, allowing a few to poke out to prove she wasn't bald. She quickly put her lipstick and a clean hanky into her navy purse and smoothed on her leather gloves. Mary was waiting in the hall.

"Wow, do we look sophisticated," Mary said. She had on a camel and white tweedy suit with a large grosgrain ribbon bow at the neck. Her hat was a camel sailor that framed her face and made her look much older.

"*You* do, anyway," Kathleen said. "That suit is fabulous on you. You look positively wealthy!"

"Well, I was about to say the same for you. C'mon, let's go knock 'em dead."

They had to go to their third-preference house first, and Kathleen was completely unprepared for what met her at the Lambda house. There wasn't the usual shout as the door opened, and the Lambdas came out of the house singing, but the mood was somber. Kathleen thought at first that it was because the rushees were so dressed up and were behaving more formally, but she suddenly realized that all the Lambdas knew that everyone there had chosen their house last. It was like being at a funeral. Wendy hugged Kathleen and then started to cry.

"Oh, Kathy, I'm so sad to see you at *this* party," she sniffed. Others came up to her and did the same. Then they sang a song to the tune of "Sayonara" with dreadfully sappy words that caused the Lambdas to cry harder. When the rushees were finally led out at the end of what seemed like much longer than an hour to Kathleen, the Lambdas stood in their doorway, arms linked around one another's waists, swaying and sobbing and waving as if the girls on the sidewalk were being taken off to slaughter.

She walked to the next party with two girls who were also headed for Cake and Dog. Kathleen tried to concentrate on what they were saying, but she was steeling herself for the kind of reception she imagined must await her where she had made such a fool of herself.

To her enormous surprise, the girls there seemed to go out of their way to make her feel welcome. One girl even whispered that they had specifically locked up the housemother's dog. There were some tears during the songs, but the mood was not nearly as sappy as it had been at the Lambdas'. Kathleen decided that maybe she could be part of this house if the Del Phis dropped her, but the decision didn't make her feel good. It was getting too awful to think about. How simple it had seemed this summer when Jake had driven her around to show her the houses. She had thought she would just pick the one she liked and move in.

She left Cake and Dog more anxious than ever to head toward Delta Phi Tau. The sight of Mary's sailor hat coming toward her at the willow tree cheered her, but they barely had time to say hi when the singing started. As one of the Deltas started to lead Kathleen into the house, Marcia Warden from her high school stepped smoothly between them and said, "I'll take Kathleen."

It was as if they were old best friends, Kathleen thought, pleased. "Thanks for taking me," she told Marcia.

"I am so happy to see you at *this* party." Kathleen knew it was as close as Marcia could come to saying they wanted her to pledge, and her nervousness changed to excitement in a blink. She even forgot she was wearing a hat.

Kathleen had met many of the rushees at other parties. There was the tall girl from Olympia who'd disliked the Lambdas' Oz party so much, and there was Miss Seattle, who looked better in a hat than anyone had a right to. But there were a number she had not seen before. She tried to imagine herself really, truly belonging here with these attractive girls. It felt so good. She caught Mary's eye, and they both smiled.

As they stood outside afterwards, she heard many voices call out, "Good-bye, Kathleen," and "Good-bye, Mary."

"It's a Sign," Mary said, as they walked back to the dorms. "I'm sure we're in."

The next morning, to her extreme relief, there were three cards in her envelope for the final round, and she had to choose only two. Maybe Mary had been right, she thought as she marked the Delta Phi Tau card with "first preference" and Cake and Dog second. The Lambdas had invited her back too, and she was glad she didn't have to go back there again. She almost skipped to the tour leader's desk to turn in her cards.

"Del Phi, here we come," Mary said once they were both outside.

"I will be so glad when this is over."

"So will I," Mary agreed. "I'll never smile again, and I will never, ever tell anyone else what my major is."

Back at the dorms, Kathleen stood in line at the phones to call her mother, who answered as usual on the first ring.

"Well, only one more day. Delta PhiTau asked me back, and Mary thinks it's pretty sure that we'll be asked to pledge."

"Trudy's mother says Trudy will probably be pledging that Iota-something house. She claims it's the best one. Aren't you going back to that one?"

"No. They weren't really my type, but I can see why they liked Trudy."

"But if it's the best one, how could they not be 'your type'? That's nonsense."

"Mother, they're called the Ice House by people here. They're snobby. I didn't like them at all. Besides, Jake says Delta Phi Tau is one of the top houses, and he's in a great fraternity, so he should know."

"Jake wouldn't know quality if it bit him, Kathleen. I hope you aren't letting him influence such an important decision."

"I'm making up my own mind. Mother. I love the Del Phis. Everyone there is so nice, and they even have some Husky cheerleaders in the house. I have a lot in common with them."

"Well I hope you know what you're doing, dear. This is one of the most important decisions you will ever make. Please think about your future. Life is more than cheerleading."

"I'll be careful, Mother. Keep your fingers crossed for me." She hung up thinking how glad she was that she never mentioned to her mother that the Iotas had dropped her. Let her believe Kathleen dropped them if she had to. Trudy's mother would have a field day with that one.

Final Preference day was cloudy. Kathleen looked out the window at the dark sky. If it rained, her dyed-to-match satin pumps would be ruined, but worse, her hair would turn to frizz. Please don't let it rain, she prayed, just until the parties are over. She centered the satin rose on her wide belt and tried to see her hem in the not-quite full-length mirror. She wore pearl-drop earrings and a pearl bracelet.

Mary flounced into the room and struck a model's pose. "Well? It's as close as I can come to hot pink. But look at you! That shade of purple is death to blondes. You are *so* lucky. We are not so exotic in the Nordic countries as you dark-eyed beauties from the south. Our brightest color is navy."

"My dad's family and the dark hair are from Scotland, Mary. That's hardly the Southern Hemisphere. And you look stunning, Miss Blondes-Have-More-Fun."

The white skin of Mary's shoulders peeked out of little triangles cut into each rose satin sleeve. Triangles of pearls and rhinestones dangled from her ears.

"Let's head over to Second Preference before our feet get too numb to walk," Mary said, pulling on her coat. Kathleen shrugged into hers and they headed across campus.

"The Cake and Dogs will be destroyed when they discover you have not chosen them first, Kath."

"I think they'll survive, Mary. Besides, it's a pretty neat house. I probably would have chosen them if it weren't for the Del Phis, but I feel so much more myself with them, don't you?"

"Absolutely. I'll see you at the willow tree in a very long hour."

Kathleen didn't realize how prophetic Mary's words would be until she went into the house. The girls were all dressed in black, and the lights were dimmed. They handed each of the rushees an unlit white candle with a small lace doily around its base. There was a ceremony wherein each sorority sister recited a short poem about the rushee she was with. Then she lighted her candle and together they walked to a long table and placed the candle into a holder.

It was dreadfully serious. Most of the girls, both rushees and sorority members, were crying. Kathleen felt a lump in her own throat. Many of the girls in the house seemed to go out of their way to speak to her, and they were all being so kind. It was a wonderful house, and there were some terrific girls in it. But it was a relief finally to see the door close to end the party. She took as deep a breath as her merry widow corset would allow and walked quickly to Delta PhiTau.

"Mine was similar," Mary said as Kathleen told her about the party. "They did everything but human sacrifice! They want you to change your mind and join the fold while there is still time. It probably works on the girls who cry in movies."

"I cry in movies."

"Another theory shot."

There were no tears inside Del Phi. All the lights were on, and there wasn't a candle in sight. The Del Phis in white formals carried long-stemmed yellow roses, which they handed to each of the rushees as they went up the stairs. Billie, the red-headed cheerleader, took Kathleen inside. Everyone smiled. Everyone looked gorgeous too, Kathleen thought, with the many colors of the rushees' dresses standing in sharp contrast to the white formals.

Three senior girls told what belonging to Delta Phi Tau had meant to them. A few of their sorority sisters had tears in their eyes, Kathleen noticed, but not for the same reason as the tears she'd seen at the other parties. And one of the girls made them all laugh when she said that her closest friends were her Del Phi sisters, who would be her bridesmaids—if and when she ever found a groom. Kathleen reveled in how good it felt to laugh after the last party. She had no doubts; this was where she belonged.

"Make a wish as you place the rose in the crystal vase," Billie told her at the end of the party. Of course she wished for a Delta Phi Tau bid in the morning. Kathleen knew it was just a game, but she couldn't remember ever wishing for anything so much, except for maybe her bride doll when she was little.

"Well, this will be our last night in the dorms," Mary said as they walked back from the HUB after marking their final preference cards.

"Can they still drop us now, Mar?"

"It's possible, but I doubt it. Anyway, we'll know soon enough. Do you think we would look weird if we held hands to go up and get our envelopes tomorrow? I mean, in case one of us faints or tries to commit suicide or something."

"You are a crazy person! I can't even get properly nervous around you."

Mary laughed and waved as they went to their separate rooms. Kathleen hung up her dress and gratefully unhooked the merry widow. The stays had left long indentations over her rib cage and around her waist. She slipped into her nightgown and washed out her nylons before going to bed. She was exhausted but wide-awake. The shock of the cold sheets against her bare legs awakened her further.

Surely they wouldn't drop people at this late date. Billie was so friendly and had made her feel so welcome. Would she have acted that way if they were not planning to pledge her? Kathleen had no answers. She finally fell into fitful sleep, waking nearly every hour to look at her clock, sure she had overslept and missed getting her bid.

The next morning in the HUB, the envelopes their tour leader had in front of her were different. They looked like formal wedding invitations. Kathleen looked at Mary, who just shrugged. Apparently she didn't know about this part of Rush. The tour leader called each name, and the rushees walked to the front to get their bids. Kathleen was shaking as she reached to take the envelope. She waited to get back to her seat before she opened it.

Inside was the Delta Phi Tau crest in gold on a thick white card.

> The members of Δελτα Φι Ταυ Fraternity
> invite
> Kathleen Andrews
> to become a pledge on
> this
> Nineteenth day of September
> Nineteen Hundred and Fifty-nine

Mary waved an identical invitation and spun Kathleen around and around. Other girls were twirling and dancing.

"Girls, please!" Anne was trying to be heard. "Just wait here, and representatives from the sororities—*your* sororities—will be here to fetch you."

"This is it, Kath. Now we go from the dreaded dorms to lives of excitement, romance, and endless dates!"

"I hope so. In the meantime, I'd better call my mother."

Chapter 2

September 1959

Lugging her aqua Samsonite suitcases and laundry bags full of bedding, Kathleen followed Mary and their Big Sisters—Marcia Warden and Mary's sister, Julie—and left the dorms behind. At the Delta Phi Tau house, Kathleen looked with proprietary satisfaction at the willow tree as the four of them went up to the front door.

"We'll all be rooming together this quarter," Marcia said as she led the way up the stairs to the third floor. On every door there were huge signs welcoming the new pledges. Marcia stopped before one that said "Welcome Kathleen and Mary" in shiny gold letters. There were gold hearts scattered from top to bottom. One said, "We Love You." Another declared, "Our Little Sisters Are Tops."

"Welcome to your new home," Marcia said.

The large, square room held two desks, two dressers, a day bed, and three closets. What struck Kathleen most was the view of Mt. Rainier from the large window opposite the door.

The mountain stood in clear relief, its ridges and shadows and ancient snow majestic in the bright sunlight.

"It looks like a painting," Kathleen breathed.

"This is the best room in the whole house," Marcia said.

"Besides sharing our fabulous view," Julie announced, "Pledges share a closet. The middle one. And the dresser near the window is yours as well."

Kathleen looked at the dresser Julie indicated. It was no larger than the one Kathleen had had as a child, but she was thrilled with it.

"Well, Kath," Mary said, "you want the top two drawers or the bottom two?"

Marcia started to laugh. "There are four more drawers in the closet, and your formals and suitcases go in the ironing room. You won't have to cram everything in here."

"You might want to keep your semiformals handy for the pledging festivities, though," Julie added. "But first you have to see where we all sleep. Bring your bedding."

She led them to a heavy door at the end of the hall.

"This is the sleeping porch," Marcia said. "It is a sacred place. There is no turning on of lights, no closing of windows, and no talking in here. Ever."

"Amen," Julie added as the door closed softly behind them. "For now, put your stuff on whichever bunk you want. You can make your beds later."

Kathleen and Mary looked at the large uncarpeted room. There were rows of metal bunk beds from wall to wall. Windows made up the entire east wall, and they were all open.

"God, we'll freeze," Mary exclaimed, echoing Kathleen's thoughts exactly. Kathleen had never slept with an open window in her life, except in the hottest part of summer. And even then she would wake with a scratchy throat.

"Better to be cold than to suffocate," Julie said logically. They agreed, but Kathleen was already planning to ask Gram for the heavy old quilt from her back bedroom. It was filled with what seemed like a ton of cotton batting, and she was sure it would keep her warmer than the two blankets she had brought with her.

"Okay, girls, let's go get you unpacked. You have a pledge meeting in a few minutes."

They went back to the tidy room, and in a minute it was a blur. Kathleen took the closet drawers first, while Mary filled the dresser. Kathleen transferred her underwear from her suitcase to the top drawer, stacking it in neat piles in the shallow space. In the second drawer she put her bobby socks and her nylons and garter belt. There were two hooks inside each of the doors, so she hung her nightgown and her robe on one. Then she hung her skirt hanger with six skirts on it and her good wool dresses and her emblem jacket. Her blouses would have to be ironed, she thought as she stuffed them into what she estimated remained of her half of the closet.

"Ready to switch, Kath?"

"It's all yours, Mar. I left you plenty of space."

Kathleen was happy to note that the dresser drawers were deeper and wider than those in the closet, and all of her sweaters fit with just a bit of squishing.

"Let's get one of those shoe racks for the bottom of the closet, Kath. Otherwise we'll never be able to sort anything out in this tiny square. Unless you wear a 7 AA"

"Seven and a half, Mar. Sorry."

"You can stack shoeboxes in the space above," Marcia said. "That's what I do. It's kind of high up, but if you label the boxes, you can tell what's in them. We can do that later. Right now, let's get you down to your meeting."

As Mary and Kathleen followed their Big Sisters out of the room, their eyes met, and they smiled outrageously. Kathleen was so excited she wanted to shout, but she walked calmly down the stairs to the dining room.

Miss Seattle was there, and the long-haired girl from Olympia. There were several others Kathleen recognized from various parties, but many faces were new to her.

The pledge trainer turned out to be Marcia. She welcomed them to Delta Phi Tau and outlined what would be happening for the next few days.

"Tonight there will be the pledging ceremony in the living room where you will get your pledge pins. These are to be worn only with dresses or skirts, *never* with pants or jeans. They go over your heart, like so." Here she put her right thumb in the hollow of her collar bone, extending her fingers until the tip of her little finger rested just above her left breast. Kathleen and the other pledges followed suit. Mary stretched her fingers so the tip of her little finger landed on her rib cage. Kathleen choked back a laugh and refused to look at Mary for the rest of the meeting.

"You will wear semiformals for this ceremony, and immediately after will be the parents' reception. Those of you whose parents are not in Seattle will attend as well. We'll all share. Alumnae will be here also to see what this year's pledge class looks like.

"We're very proud of you, by the way. You are the largest pledge class of any house—we got an exception from Panhellenic and were able to take 42. That's two over quota.

"Your cumulative grade point average is a 3.1. That's the highest of any class in years. And besides being darling . . ." She paused while a ripple of self-conscious laughter went around the room. "Besides that, we have ten cheerleaders, four beauty queens, one National Merit Scholar, several other scholarship winners, and a debating champion. Not to mention several musical types. You are a terrific class, and we are so excited that you chose to pledge Delta Phi Tau."

Kathleen's heart swelled to be a part of all of this. She hadn't even imagined that it would feel so good.

"Now, let's get to know one another, shall we?" Marcia continued. They went around the room sharing names, where they were from, and, of course, their majors. Many girls were from out of state, but most were from the Seattle area. The local pledges who chose to live at home rather than in the house were called townies. There was a special "town girl" room where they could stay overnight if they needed to. Until school started, the townies would all be jammed into it for the pledging period. Kathleen was glad she was living in the house. She already loved her room, shared closet and all.

Hope Chest

After the meeting, the pledges charged up to the phones, lining up for a chance at one of the three lines out. Kathleen finally got her turn to call.

"It's so wonderful. My room has the most incredible view of Mt. Rainier. And Mary and I are roommates. I can't wait until you and Daddy see it. There is a parent reception tonight at 7:30, and I'll show you everything. I hope you will come."

"Of course we'll come. Don't be silly, we wouldn't miss it. I'm eager to see this place and to see the other girls. What are they like, Kathleen?"

"I just met them all at our pledge meeting. They're all so neat. There are cheerleaders and scholars and beauty queens. Everyone is really different."

"Trudy pledged that good house, Iota something. Her mother called first thing this morning." There was a note of irritation in her mother's voice.

"I couldn't call before, Mother. There are only three lines here, and we were so busy unpacking and going to the meeting, we couldn't use the phones until now. I'm happy for Trudy. She'll be a perfect Iota."

"Is this house of yours a good one, Kathleen? Trudy's mother said she didn't know too much about it."

"Trudy's mother doesn't know too much about *anything*. I keep telling you that. I don't know why you keep listening to her. Delta Phi Tau is fabulous. You'll see. The girls are smart and darling." Then she added, "Miss Seattle is in my pledge class."

"Oh, well!" Her mother's tone changed, and Kathleen hated herself for resorting to such tactics, but she knew she had given her mother something to throw back at Mrs. Lavik. "You'll have to introduce me tonight. Your father and I will be there at 7:30."

"OK. I'll see you then. Someone is waiting for this phone, so I have to go now." She hung up and went back to her room. She sat on the day bed and studied the mountain.

"OK, Pledge!" came Mary's voice. "Into your whalebone corset. It's time for ceremonies."

47

Hope Chest

Kathleen jumped up and hugged her new roommate. All the excitement came flooding back. She lived *here* now. It would be a whole new adventure.

❧

Kathleen followed the other pledges in a circle around the living room, stopping where they were told to receive the small pledge pin. Marcia pinned it onto Kathleen's dress and gave her a quick hug. Kathleen couldn't keep her eyes from looking down at it every few seconds, a golden delta divided by a blue bar.

They went to the dining room for dinner, sitting next to their Big Sisters. Houseboys in starched white jackets served roast beef and mashed potatoes on thick china plates.

"Wait for the housemother to lift her fork before you eat anything," Marcia whispered to Kathleen. "It is the responsibility of the person at her left to remind Mrs. D, because she gets to chatting and *never* starts to eat. Remember that if you ever sit there."

Immediately after dinner they filed into the living room and formed a line, by height, to receive their guests. Each pledge held a small bunch of violets, a gift from the men of Sigma Alpha Epsilon fraternity, as parents and alums came through, smiling and shaking hands and exclaiming over how beautiful everyone was.

Bouquets that had arrived all day long filled the living room: mums and roses and glads in every color banked the fireplace and covered the coffee tables. Kathleen had been stunned to receive an arrangement of tiny yellow rosebuds from her parents.

The fragrance of the flowers mingled with the girls' perfume, filling the warm room with a heavy sweetness.

"My feet are killing me," Mary whispered without breaking her smile.

"Mine, too. Have you seen your folks yet?"

"No, but they're always late. They'll be here. Are yours coming?"

"I just saw them walk in."

Kathleen's parents came around the corner, her father's huge smile lighting up the room for her. Her mother wore her best grey suit with the Persian lamb collar. Her perfect blonde hair, so different from Kathleen's, was swept into a smooth French twist. As she came through the entry arch, her eyes swept the room. She started toward the head of the receiving line, but Mr. Andrews took her arm and propelled her over to Kathleen.

"You look gorgeous, Kitten. This is some impressive piece of architecture you picked." Sweeping her into a hug, he whispered. "Too bad there's no parking!"

"Hello, dear," her mother said, giving her a kiss on the cheek. "This is quite a nice house." She sounded surprised.

"Mother, Daddy, this is my friend Mary." Kathleen tried to remember to look at her parents so they could hear Mary's name, as Marcia had taught them at the meeting.

"How do you do, Mary," Mrs. Andrews said formally.

At that moment Marcia appeared. "You must be Kathleen's parents. She has your lovely cheekbones, Mrs. Andrews."

Mrs. Andrews turned her most dazzling smile at Marcia, whom Kathleen could have kissed.

"This is my Big Sister, Marcia Warden, Mother. Do you remember her from Richmond?"

"Why don't you take your parents on a tour of the house, Kathleen. Show them your room. It's all right to leave the line now."

"Let's go see," Mr. Andrews said and offered his arm to his daughter. Kathleen took it and then took her mother's and led them first to her bouquet.

"Yellow roses are Del Phi's flower. How did you know?"

"I asked the florist. I called one in the University District and presumed they would know such things. I had to tell Trudy's mother about it. She wasn't aware that she should send flowers." She raised her eyebrows slightly, and Kathleen had to smile.

"Where's your room, honey?" Mr. Andrews said.

"Third floor." She held the door for her mother and then led them up to her room. Kathleen stood expectantly as her parents entered and looked around. She was filled with pride at how everything looked. Julie had brought a basket chair from home with a large red pillow. Marcia had angled a silver-framed picture of her boyfriend on the dresser. Little touches already made it look lived in.

"There's only one bed, dear. Where do you sleep?" Her mother kept looking around the room as if there were more beds somewhere that she just couldn't see.

"On the sleeping porch. We'll go there next. What do you think of the room? I wish it were daytime so you could see the view of Mt. Rainier."

"The room's quite small, don't you think? How many of you are there in it?"

"This is a four-girl room, Mother. It's one of the biggest."

"But there are only three closets. How is that?"

"Mary and I share the middle one. It's really quite fine." Kathleen opened the closet to show her mother the fit.

"Looks pretty super to me," her father said. "I think you're going to have a ball here, honey. And Mary seems pretty OK too. You did yourself proud."

"Thanks, Daddy," Kathleen said, hugging him. "I'm so happy."

"Let's see this porch thing, Kathleen," her mother said, exiting the room and turning the wrong way down the hall.

"This way, Mother."

"Now this takes me back to my old days in the service!" Mr. Andrews said as he eyed the metal bunks. "Except we didn't have any ruffled quilts."

"It's freezing out here. You'll catch your death. Can't you sleep in the room?"

"No one sleeps in the rooms, Mother. That way if you need to stay up late studying, you don't disturb anyone. I'm going to ask Gran for that old quilt. I'm sure I'll be fine."

They went back down to the dining room for coffee and cookies, and the feeling of pride and excitement swelled as she saw all the Del Phis smiling and showing off the house—*her* house—to their families.

Finally, all the guests were gone. Mary and Kathleen trudged up to their room and kicked off their high heels.

"Whew! That was something. Your parents are nice, Kath. Your dad's a sweetie."

"I can't get over how much you and Julie look like your mom. It's scary." Kathleen stepped out of her dress and put it on its hanger. "I thought I'd be too excited to sleep tonight, but I think I can sleep for a week!"

"I know what you mean," Mary agreed, pulling on her nightgown. "At least my feet do. Standing in heels is not their favorite thing to do."

They grabbed their towels and padded gingerly down the hall in their slippers to the large bathroom. On the far wall, Kathleen opened the cubbyhole assigned to her—two over from the left, third row down—and draped her towel over the small door. She loved the way everything fit so snugly into this tiny space that was now hers alone. There was room for her soap dish, toothbrush and toothpaste, deodorant, and shampoo, if she used the kind in a tube. Everything else she kept in her room.

"Pledges, two minutes! Everyone into bed," squawked a voice over the intercom.

Kathleen scrubbed her face and brushed her teeth quickly and dashed to the sleeping porch. It was cool there as she found her way in the dark to her upper bunk. The sheets were cold against her skin. Gran's quilt would be welcome, she thought, as she went over the amazing events of the day. Her eyes were just closing when the door burst open and all the lights went on.

Kathleen sat up with a start. There must be some kind of emergency for someone to have turned on the forbidden lights. Then all the actives poured onto the sleeping porch, clapping and singing the clap song from Rush. They pulled the pledges from their various bunks and herded them, giggling, down to the living room.

There each pledge was presented with a flannel nightgown with little blue triangles all over it and the Delta Phi Tau letters on the pocket. Pizzas appeared from the kitchen, and the pledges sat happily on the living room floor, watching the actives put on another skit parodying Rush. As everyone dissolved into tears of laughter, Kathleen was sure she had never been happier. And tomorrow night, Mary had told her, was the reception for all the fraternities. Finally they would actually be meeting the fellows who'd been hanging over fences and off balconies all week long. She couldn't wait.

Things were a bit more serious at the next day's pledge training. Marcia told them they would all be going out on dates after the pledge reception. Every Big Sister had fixed her Little Sister up with someone from one of the fraternities.

"My sister has abominable taste in men," Mary groaned as Kathleen shushed her. Linda, the Social Chairman, a beautiful blonde senior who had been a runner-up for Seattle's Seafair Queen the previous summer, took over the meeting. She reminded Kathleen of Grace Kelly.

"You must remember that you now represent Delta Phi Tau," Linda began, dazzling them with her smile. "Everything you do reflects on all of us, so you must always be gracious. If your date turns out to be the biggest glunch in the world, you must treat him as though he weren't. You don't ever have to go out with him again," she said over the murmurs from the pledges, "but *he* should want to go out with *you*."

She looked around at the wide-eyed pledges as if to confirm that they understood before she continued. "For example, what do you do if your date gets out of the car and doesn't appear to be coming around to open your door for you?"

"Open it yourself," someone in the back responded matter-of-factly.

"Eventually," the Social Chairman said with a nod. "But first you must give him time to realize that you are waiting for him. Busy yourself with your purse or your gloves so that if he looks to see why you aren't out of the car yet, he will see that you aren't just tapping your foot over his lapse. It will give him time to recover and get to your door if he is going to, or you can then let yourself out gracefully—we'll practice that next. That way he'll never know you were waiting to be helped out, and you won't embarrass him by calling attention to his shortcomings. Remember, ladies, men bruise easily."

Kathleen listened eagerly to everything, even to the instructions on how to light and hold a cigarette, though she didn't smoke.

"A lady never has a cigarette in her mouth without holding it between her fingers." Linda demonstrated with an unlit cigarette. "I don't smoke, but I'll show you how to light your cigarette the proper way." She took a match from a matchbook while holding it and the cigarette in her left hand. After closing the matchbook, she pantomimed striking the match with her other hand and lighting the cigarette. "Now you can light it easily. Or if your date offers to light it for you, take his hand and guide the match to the cigarette, but always look at him while you do. If you watch the match, your eyes will cross." Everyone laughed while she demonstrated crossing her eyes. "As you all must know by now, smoking is allowed only in the smoking room on the second floor, and downstairs in the library or the rec room."

Linda was everything Kathleen thought a sorority girl would be, and she hoped to be as poised as she was.

"A lady also never walks with a cigarette in her hand. If you must move about, put your cigarette in your ashtray and carry the ashtray across the room. And never, *ever* smoke while walking on the street."

They were also told that they were never to drink out of bottles except on picnics, always use a glass, and they could never date two men from the same fraternity at the same time. "Men talk, you know," Linda said. "Wait at least six weeks. Tomorrow we'll cover table manners. You won't be eating out tonight."

Finally they were dismissed to go shopping for girdles, which they would be expected to wear under skirts and dresses and nice pants. It would not do to jiggle.

After a flurry of shopping and eating and showering and dressing, all the pledges were once again standing in a line in the living room. This time they were in cocktail dresses, and the nosegays were from the Phi Delts.

"Why do they call it Stock Show?" Kathleen whispered to Mary as Linda walked down the line adjusting pledge pins or pointing out lipstick on the teeth.

"Beats me," Mary said.

The doorbell rang, and fraternity men—mostly pledges fresh from high school themselves, but some "older" actives—began to stream through. They came in groups of five or more, most wearing navy blazers and grey slacks, and most holding the newspaper list of Rush results. Very few went through the line, however.

Some did and tried to make small talk, but most stood back, looking the pledges up and down and making mysterious notes on their papers.

"What are they doing over there?" Kathleen asked Mary.

"I have no idea, but I feel like I'm on display."

"Now I get it—Stock Show. Clever."

Just then Jake's familiar face loomed above the shorter boys in the room. He spotted Kathleen and came over to her.

"Jake! I am so happy to see a familiar face. This is *awful.*"

"Not for us. We've been to ten houses already. There are some gorgeous girls in this year's crop. Especially here."

"Thank you," Mary said.

Jake looked at Mary, who was batting her eyelashes outrageously at him.

"Mary, this is my best friend Jake, also from Richmond High. He's a Rogue. Jake, this is my new best friend, Mary, from Ballard."

"Hi, Mary."

"Hello, Jake."

"Hey, Jake, what are those guys writing over there?" Kathleen asked him. "Practically everyone's toting a pen."

"Oh, they're making notes on the pledge lists. Future reference. That sort of thing."

"You've got to be kidding," Mary said. "You mean research? Like we're a term paper?"

Jake laughed. "It's not quite as serious as that. It just opens up the options. Winter formals are coming up sooner than you'd think."

"We're 'options,' Kathleen. It's a good thing we had all these days to practice our winning smiles."

Kathleen saw a group that had been looking in their direction suddenly move toward the other end of the line. She turned to look at Mary and bit her lip to keep from snorting. Mary had her eyes crossed and was smiling frozenly at them. Jake laughed even louder.

"I don't know which of you is worse," Kathleen said.

"Well, I'm off. Got to hit the rest of the sororities before the lines break up. Nice to meet you, Mary."

Jake moved down the line and then waved as he left.

"He's kinda cute, Kath. Does he have a girlfriend?"

"Not unless he found an 'option' tonight. Do you think he's cute? I never looked at him that way. He's a buddy."

"Forest for the trees, my dear. He's a doll."

After Jake's departure, the evening did not improve. Marcia had lined Kathleen up with a pledge in her boyfriend's house. The two showed up together, and the four of them walked around the corner to their fraternity. Once again, Kathleen's feet were killing her, and she longed to kick off her heels when they got inside the Tudor structure, but she knew not only from her mother's admonitions but from Linda's pledge training that kicking off one's shoes was forbidden. And she could hardly break one of the major pledge rules with Marcia right there.

Kathleen's date was tall and thin with a large Adam's apple that moved nearly two inches when he swallowed, which he did often and nervously. He was from Idaho and wasn't sure he should have come to the UW. He really wanted to be a veterinarian, and probably should have gone to Washington State. His mom wanted him to be a real doctor, so he thought he'd try pre-med to make his mom happy.

"And that was the sum total of our conversation," Kathleen told Mary later. "I had to pull even that out of him. He was so busy swallowing that I think he thought he was talking! Pity. He wasn't bad-looking, but he never said two words on his own."

"Well, you wouldn't have had to worry with Mr. Baseball Scholarship from Spokane," Mary said rolling her eyes to the ceiling. "He never shut up. I know every game he ever played, what his best pitch is, which schools tried to snatch him away from the UW. You name it, I can recite it."

"Oh well, Mar, Marcia really doesn't know me very well, and her boyfriend couldn't know my date too well, so they did the best they could. I'm sure there are zillions of dreamy guys out there just hoping to meet us."

"At least a zillion," Mary intoned, unconvinced. "This was not what I'd call an auspicious start considering how great a sacrifice my poor thighs have made spending all this time in this hideous girdle. It's giving me a headache!"

Kathleen called her mother the next morning.

"Thanks again for the roses, Mother. What did you think of the house?"

"Well, I thought it was lovely, Kathleen. And so were most of the girls. But I really can't believe you have to sleep on that dreadful porch thing, or whatever you called it. But Mrs. Lavik said even Trudy's house has the same arrangement."

"Every house does. But it's not that bad, and besides, we've been having a ball. Last night was kind of a bust though. We all got fixed up with blind dates, and Mary and I were not terribly lucky."

"Why ever not, dear?"

"Well, no one really knows what the pledges are like, so it wasn't exactly matching up known quantities. My date was so shy he couldn't even talk."

"What is he studying, Kathleen?"

"He's in pre-med."

"My, my, a doctor! Well shyness isn't the worst thing in a person. A clever woman can make a shy man feel very important. Did you ask him about himself?"

"Mother, I asked him about everything I could think of. I'm sure I'll never see him again, so don't get your hopes up."

"But, Kathleen, a doctor. If he calls back, I hope you'll give him another look. Still waters run deep, they say."

Neither of their dates called back, and both girls were relieved. Kathleen had a nagging feeling, though, that if she had been more interesting, hers would have. With an effort she dismissed the memory of the Social Chairman's admonition that all dates should want to ask *you* out again.

꩜

After classes started the following Monday, Kathleen was too busy to give her disastrous dating debut another thought. She had never had so much homework in her life. For her Western Civ class alone, there was a mountain of reading. Every night she dragged piles of books to study table in the dining room where the pledges studied from seven until ten every school night. No phone calls.

After overcoming the shock of seeing people underlining in their books as they studied, Kathleen brought a ruler to study table and underlined passages in practically every paragraph, hoping it would help with retention.

She labored over her paper for English 101 and got the first C of her life. She could scarcely breathe. A C! "This is a peculiar combination of keen observation and odd oversights," the professor had written. She had no idea what that meant.

She called home that night and was relieved when her father answered.

"Hey, how's my girl? You studying hard?"

"Oh, Daddy, it's really tough. I worked like a dog on my English paper and only got a C! I don't know what they want."

"Don't worry too much about it, Honey. When I went to school, I thought a C was as high as it went. I'm sure you'll do fine next time." He laughed heartily at his little joke, and Kathleen felt her spirits lift a bit. Then she heard her mother's voice in the background.

"A *C!* Give me that phone."

"Here's your mother, Kitten."

"What's wrong, Kathleen?"

"Nothing's wrong. I just got a C on my English paper, and I don't know why. I thought it was pretty good."

"Well, obviously pretty good isn't good enough. Did you spend enough time on it?"

"Hours, Mother. I have an appointment with the professor to see what I should be doing differently. Maybe I misunderstood what we were supposed to write."

"Tell him you are on the dean's list of entering freshmen. You've never had a C in your life. I don't understand."

"No, neither do I." Kathleen was sorry she'd called. "I'll let you know what he says. I'd better go study now. I don't want to get any more grades like that, and I have a psychology quiz tomorrow."

"Has the doctor called you back?"

"The doctor?"

"You know, that boy you went out with."

"Oh, him. No, he hasn't, and I don't expect him to. We have our first exchange this Saturday. Maybe I'll meet someone there."

"An exchange. What's an exchange?"

"We all go to some fraternity for a couple of hours and meet everyone there, I guess. I'm not quite sure, but I'll call you when I get back and give you all the gory details."

"Oh, Kathleen, try to be serious. This could be a wonderful opportunity for you."

"I will, Mother. I'll talk to you Saturday. Bye." She hung up just as the intercom blared that there were only five minutes until study table. She went to her room and got her books and the Delta Phi Tau coffee mug Marcia had given her and headed down the stairs to the dining room. She had never drunk much coffee before, but here it seemed like part of studying. The cook wheeled out a huge coffee maker just before study table and everyone filled up. Kathleen was getting used to the bitter taste.

On Wednesday a list was posted on the bulletin board on the second floor landing. Each pledge's name was paired with the name of a pledge from the fraternity next door. Kathleen's exchange date was a Barry Brown. Pledges were running around asking anyone who might know anything about their exchange dates. Girls who had gone to high school with some of the pledges next door were able to shed some light on a few names, but most were mysteries. The consensus was, however, that there were some really neat guys in that fraternity. Kathleen felt a thrill of hope that finally she would meet one of the handsome types she had seen when Jake took her on their tour last summer.

"Do you know how they paired us up with our exchange dates?" Mary said in a strangled voice after they stood to sing grace before dinner that night. She yanked her chair out with a vicious tug and flopped down next to Kathleen. "By height!"

"So?" Kathleen said, putting her napkin on her lap. "Height, alphabetical order, what's the difference?"

"In case you never noticed, I'm only 5-foot-2." Mary wailed.

"Oh, well," said the girl next to Mary, "at least it's only an hour and a half. How bad could it be?"

The morning of the exchange, Kathleen struggled into her panty girdle and fastened her nylons into their hooks, smoothing the girdle legs down over the garters. Her blouse needed ironing after being crushed in the crowded closet, so she put on her slip and ran down to the ironing room. The smell of the steam iron and the damp ironing board announced that she had to wait.

"I'll just be a second," said a jolly active named Penny. "I just hemmed this skirt and wanted to press it. Getting ready for the exchange?"

"Yes, but my blouse looks like an accordion," Kathleen said, holding up the crumpled garment.

"OK, it's all yours," Penny said, sliding her skirt off the ironing board. "It's set on 'wool,' so you may want to change it. Have fun at the brunch."

Alone in the small room, Kathleen waited for the iron to get to "cotton" and glanced around at the rainbow of formal gowns and "good coats" hanging from clothes racks. Scarlet satin and pale blue tulle hung between gold brocades and velvet-topped Black Watch taffeta. Behind the racks, trunks and suitcases were stacked to the ceiling. Thank goodness she didn't have to cram her formals into her closet, or they would all look like her blouse. She pressed it, turned off the iron, and slipped her arms into the still-warm sleeves, hoping that Barry Brown would be worth all this effort.

The pledges dutifully walked past Linda before entering the living room to wait for their exchange dates to arrive. Linda gave each of them a pinch to make sure all were wearing girdles. Satisfied, she joined them in the living room to give last-minute instructions.

"OK, everyone, this is your first exchange. You may or may not like your date, but it's up to you to be sure he likes *you* and Del Phi in the process. Do not say anything negative about any other fraternity or sorority, compliment him on his house or his shirt or whatever, and mind your table manners during brunch. Some of you are still buttering the whole roll. Break off a piece that will fit into your mouth in one or two bites and butter only that small part, not the whole roll. And don't cut the roll; break it gently with your fingers. Any questions?"

"What if we get asked out for tonight?"

"Good question, Sally," Linda said to the girl from Olympia as Mary rolled her eyes at Kathleen. "Generally exchanges are at night, and you should not go out that same night with your exchange date. You don't want him to think you had no other plans for a Friday night, now do you?"

Nervous laughter peppered the room.

"However, if your date wants to take you to the game today, that would be all right, but only to the game. It is Saturday, after all, so he will probably assume you already have plans for the evening."

As they were digesting this latest bit of strategy, the doorbell rang, and a long line of the fraternity pledges filed in. Some were indeed quite good looking, and Kathleen felt a shiver of excitement in the pit of her stomach.

Linda and the social chairman from the fraternity stood in the middle of the living room and began calling out names from the lists they both held.

Kathleen didn't have to wait long, as the names were in alphabetical order. She looked hopefully into the crush, but as Barry Brown stepped forward, Kathleen's heart sank.

He was taller than she could have hoped for, but the rest of the news was bad. He had dark, indeterminately colored hair that would be curly if it were not cropped so close to his head. His drip-dry shirt must have been white once, Kathleen thought, but it now lacked a genuine hue. With scarcely any eyebrows at all to give his face definition, the only color visible on Barry Brown was the painful red of his serious acne.

He looked at the carpet as introductions were made, and Kathleen walked silently beside him as they covered the short distance to his fraternity. He opened the door, but not for her, and she followed him into the stucco house. They joined others in the Spanish-looking living room, but Barry did not introduce her to anyone.

"So, Barry, where are you from?" Kathleen asked, trying to make conversation.

"Spokane," he replied.

"Hey, there's a girl in my pledge class from Spokane, Ellie Miller. Do you know her?"

"No."

"What are you majoring in?" Kathleen tried again, feeling as if she were still going through Rush, but on the other side.

"Accounting," he replied.

"That's nice," Kathleen murmured.

Mercifully a bell rang and they went into the dining room for brunch. Kathleen waited a second for Barry to pull out her chair, but he sat down quickly without looking at her. She seated herself and smiled as Mary and her date sat down across from her. Mary's date was fairly nice looking and wore a crisp oxford cloth shirt under a blue sweater. He was from Ohio and said he had fallen in love with the Northwest, and getting to speak to two natives about his discovery was the best thing that had ever happened to him, so he kept the conversation going during the meal. Barry spoke once to ask the active serving them if he could have apple juice instead of orange juice.

"No, Barry, this is it," the active hissed. Barry then picked at his meal, pushing globs of scrambled eggs around the plate with his fork.

"This is delicious," Kathleen said, trying to draw him into the conversation again. "You must have a good cook here."

"I hate scrambled eggs," he replied, dropping his fork loudly onto his plate. He then stared off into space and began squeezing the large pimples on his face with his thumb and forefinger until tiny dots of blood pooled on his thin cheeks. Kathleen knew she could not look at Mary if the honor of Delta Phi Tau were to be upheld, so she concentrated on placing her silverware across the plate to indicate she was finished, as Linda had taught them. It was the longest hour and a half she had ever endured.

"God, Kathleen, you must have been bad in your last life," Mary howled between fits of laughter when they finally were able to return to their own house. "I thought he was going to bleed to death right there in front of us!"

"I couldn't even look at you. I knew we would probably spray scrambled eggs all over the table and Linda would have our heads."

"You have one of these every weekend until summer, girls, so you may as well get used to them," Julie stated calmly as she came into the room. "Was it really that bad?"

"Not for Mary it wasn't," Kathleen replied. "Her guy was darling. Mine was very strange."

"Well, cheer up," Julie said. "Sometimes you meet someone quite nice on exchanges. I did. Once."

"Actually, my guy said he would give me a call next week," Mary admitted. "Don't you just pray Barry will ask you out? Maybe we could double," Mary said sweetly and then burst into laughter again.

"Thanks a bunch, Mar. I don't know. First my Stock Show thriller, now Vampire's Delight. Where are all the gorgeous men I thought we'd be wading through?"

"There's another exchange Friday. Maybe we'll have better luck then."

But the social picture didn't improve through the fall. To make things worse, it seemed to rain every day—hard, pouring rain. Kathleen's plastic rain bonnet did nothing to prevent her curls from coiling tightly to her head, and the sharp little edges of the strips that tied under her chin acted like conduits for the run-off. She was damp and miserable and had one cold after another. She couldn't decide if they resulted from the freezing air of the sleeping porch or from sitting in class with her wet bobby socks chilling her ankles. Or from her unfortunate decision to take swimming.

Everyone who wanted to graduate from the University of Washington had to pass a swimming test or take the basic swimming class. Since all freshmen had three required quarters of P.E. anyway, Kathleen decided just to take the class.

She had registered for the 4 p.m. class on Mondays long before she knew that Monday night was chapter night on Greek Row.

Every house had its weekly chapter meeting that night, preceded by a formal dinner.

Kathleen's hair would be soaked after her hour in the pool, even though she wore a bathing cap. There was a sort of hair dryer attached to the wall of the dressing room in the pool, but the one time she tried it, it turned her hair to frizz. So she would towel it as dry as she could and hurry back to the house. In the rain, the ten-minute dash wearing the plastic rain bonnet steamed her hair to an unmanageable tangle. By the time she got into her nylons and heels for chapter dinner, there was no time for rollers or hair dryers, so she just ran a comb through it and ate dinner with damp hair.

The third week of swimming she got back to the house even later than usual and barely made it to dinner on time. During dessert, one of the seniors came into the dining room carrying a nosegay of rust and gold chrysanthemums surrounding a lighted taper. Slender streamers of satin ribbon in pale yellow wrapped the base of the candle and trailed below it. The senior handed it to the girl at the end of the first table.

"What's happening?" Kathleen asked Marcia, who was sitting next to her.

"Someone's engaged! The ring's attached to the flowers so we'll get to see it. Whoever owns it will blow out the candle."

The bouquet passed from hand to hand as little Oohs and Aahs accompanied it. Tied to the candle with the same yellow ribbon was an old-fashioned looking engagement ring. The tiny solitaire diamond was set in the center of an ornate white-gold setting that seemed designed to make the diamond appear larger. After the candle had made the rounds of all the long dining tables, it was passed back along the route it had traveled. Whispered guesses and "Whose is it?" followed the candle. Then with a giggle, a senior named Barb blew out the flame. Everyone shrieked and rushed to the now-engaged sister and watched as she removed the ring and slid it proudly onto her finger. Then she stood and held the bouquet in front of her as if she were already a bride.

"Jim and I will be getting married this time next year, so these will be my colors."

She indicated her flowers.

Everyone clapped, and those near her crowded to see the ring again and to hug the bride-to-be. Then Dena, the songleader, tapped her glass for quiet. "The Sigma Nus will be here for the serenade right after dinner. We'll have coffee in the living room, so go upstairs and comb your hair and put on some lipstick and be back down in two minutes."

The housemother stood so all the girls could leave without waiting further. Kathleen cast a questioning look at Marcia.

"Her fiancé is a Sigma Nu, so they'll all come down for the engagement."

"Oh, great. My hair looks like Brillo!"

"You look darling. Don't worry about it."

But Kathleen was miserable. They had an exchange scheduled with the Sigma Nus in November, and everyone was looking forward to it because they supposedly had a terrific pledge class. Now she would look her absolute worst when they came over. It wasn't fair. She dragged the comb through her tangles and went back downstairs with Mary.

Mrs. D was seated on one of the sofas with the silver coffee service on the table in front of her, as well as a large tray of tiny demitasse cups. The girls arranged themselves on the rest of the sofas and on the floor facing the grand piano, but Kathleen squeezed behind one of the sofas and perched on the wide window ledge. Mary soon joined her.

"Why are we way back here?" she asked.

"So no one can see me."

The Sigma Nus trooped in and formed a semicircle at the piano. They were impressive in the usual navy blue blazers and grey slacks. Kathleen shrank into the draperies.

Then the engaged couple stood in front of them, their arms wrapped around each other's waists. A tall, handsome senior stepped forward and made a great show of clearing his throat. "As much as we hate to see one of our esteemed brothers bite the dust in this way, we have to agree that he couldn't have chosen a better girl than Barb."

Barb blushed as Jim's fraternity brothers clapped and whistled.

"Now, Jim, for you and your sweetheart, many good wishes and . . ."

A clear note sounded, and the men broke into a slow song about love that lasts forever. Barb and Jim stared into each other's eyes. Then the Del Phis sang back about Delta Phi Tau love so true. When they finished, the Sigma Nus clapped and whistled some more, and everyone rushed up to the couple to offer congratulations and best wishes and to see the ring.

Mrs. D began to pour the coffee, and girls served the men, who took the tiny cups in their huge hands. Kathleen watched one enormous fellow try to put his finger into the cup handle. He failed, and then didn't know how to pick up the cup, so he just set cup and saucer down on the piano and stuffed his hands into his pockets.

Finally the fraternity left, and the pledges went to their rooms to get ready for study table, while the actives went downstairs for their chapter meeting.

"Well, the exchange with them might be *all right*," Mary said, hanging up her dress and shrugging into her muu muu.

"I don't know. They might have a Barry Brown hidden away that they don't bring to engagements. With my luck, I'll get him. In the meantime I have a huge paper to write for English 101 on John Stuart Mill's 'On Liberty,' and I haven't even read it yet. Plus I have a ton of pages to read for Psych. I've never been so swamped."

They carried their books and notebooks down the stairs, stopped to fill their coffee mugs, and then headed for the dining room. Going to study table was the only time they could pass by the living room area wearing anything besides skirts or dresses. Kathleen had on her cut-off jeans, a sweatshirt, and her turquoise fuzzy slippers. As they rounded the corner to the dining room, there stood three Sigma Nus still talking to Barb and Jim. They glanced at Mary and Kathleen and then resumed their conversations.

"Did you see the great reaction we got? I didn't need to hide in the curtains. My lovely hair makes me invisible!"

"I guess that's why we have to dress up to be on this floor. Although, I think my muu muu is quite fetching." Mary struck a pose.

"The way I look, I don't think anything would help. You don't know how lucky you are to have straight hair!"

There was no active supervising study table because they were still in the Monday night chapter meeting, which had been delayed because of the engagement. Nevertheless, all the pledges fell silent as they attacked their books. Kathleen concentrated on Mill's essay but found that after a half page, she had no idea what she had read. Nothing at Richmond High had prepared her for this kind of homework. Nor had her meeting with her professor helped that much. At Richmond every assignment had been structured: Do a 20-page notebook on one of the following topics: the rise of Communism or the history of Greek drama. No one ever asked her to discuss an author's point of view as it related to something. As long as she chronicled the event and got the dates right, she got an A. All this interpretation was hopeless.

Over the next weeks, she spent hours in the library, even trudging onto campus at night after dinner, thinking that the atmosphere of the beautiful Suzzallo Library might inspire her. She agonized over each paper, writing and rewriting, cutting out paragraphs and taping them onto other pages, drawing symbols and arrows to insert new thoughts, and finally typing it on her portable Smith Corona, often typing well into the early morning hours. She prepared for every exam as if it were a final. Never had she studied so much or so hard.

It seemed the only breaks she took were the weekly exchanges, none of which were great improvements over the first, and the football games. The games at least were exciting. Time and again the Huskies won in the last few seconds. Kathleen and the other Del Phis screamed themselves hoarse as, game after game, the Purple and Gold squeaked out victories. Rose Bowl fever struck at midseason, and now it was a reality: the UW was going to Pasadena.

Kathleen spent most of game time watching the cheerleaders going through their routines. At lunch, she usually sat with Patty or Billie and talked about cheering. All three agreed that the Husky band was the best, and Kathleen wondered what it might feel like to do routines to that big sound in that even bigger stadium. But she didn't have much time to contemplate cheerleading with a mountain of reading to do every week.

"At least all our dates aren't affecting our studies," Mary quipped one Friday night as they walked to the Ave for ice cream after an exchange.

"Where are they all?" Kathleen said.

"Probably just working up the courage to approach us, I would imagine."

"Probably."

She really didn't know how she would manage a boyfriend right now when she barely had time for herself. But she was disappointed that the promise of a glorious social whirl had not yet come true. If it weren't for Jake, whom she had invited to the pledge dance but who had not invited her to his, she didn't date at all. When she wasn't studying, weekends were spent going to a movie or for Chinese food on the Ave with Mary and some of the other pledges or going home to do laundry and spending the weekend with her parents. Her father was always so delighted to see her that for a few moments she was glad to be home. But her mother's constant references to Trudy Lavik's social success, as told by Trudy's mother, and her hints that Kathleen could do more about her lack of dates if she really tried ("Are you sure you give yourself enough time to put on makeup before you go to class every day, dear? You never know when you might run into Mr. Right, and you want to look your best") caused her to spend most of her weekends at the sorority.

Finally the quarter ended. Back at the house after her last final, Kathleen threw her books down in relief.

"If I never see another white rat again, it'll be too soon! I will *never* take another psychology course."

"What are you talking about, Kathleen?" Mary was packing to go home for Christmas break. They would have new rooms and new roommates next quarter, so they had to remove all their belongings.

"Psych 101. Our lab instructor always brought this huge, hideous white rat to the labs. We all sat around a long table, and she'd let the rat roam all over it. I could hardly concentrate on what she was saying for fear the nasty thing would twitch its way to me. Ugh."

"Well, it's all over now, and we can get on with our lives. Think you made the dean's list?"

"I just hope I made my grades to be initiated," Kathleen said.

"Oh, come on, Kath. You only need a 2.3, and you were the great scholar from Richmond. You'll do better than you think."

But despite the hours of diligent study, she barely squeaked past the required 2.3 for initiation. She could not believe her eyes when the grade envelope arrived just after Christmas. She managed a surprise B in Psychology, despite the white rat, and a B in swimming that she was already aware of. But the dreaded C she had on her first English paper had spawned more, and she also got a C in Western Civ. Knowing every date of every event that ever happened in the early world didn't help her answer the questions on the blue book exam that, like her papers in English, dealt with concepts, not facts. The information she had been so confident about going in was not even relevant to the questions on the final.

She called Mary right away, thinking that one good thing about being at home was that she didn't have to wait for a phone to be available.

"I can't believe it, Mar. I've never had a C before, and now here are two big ones! I couldn't have studied any harder. How did you do?"

"I got a couple of Cs myself. High school chemistry wasn't that hard, but here it nearly killed me. I think I'm out of dental hygiene."

"My mom is always after me to take shorthand and more typing. She claims I can always fall back on secretarial skills, but my typing is the worst. I would die if I had to do that all day long. She'll really push me when she sees these grades."

"Well, I couldn't be a secretary either. And nursing is out. Besides the science classes, I couldn't give anyone a shot. When Lindy was practicing her demonstration speech on hypodermic needles that night at study table, I nearly passed out watching her. And she was only stabbing an orange!"

"How long can you be a pre-major, I wonder?"

"I hope indefinitely, Kath, for both our sakes. But don't worry about the grades. At least we get to be initiated."

Kathleen hung up, not feeling much better, and went in to set the table for dinner. She decided to wait until her father was there to discuss her grades. Surprisingly, however, her mother was not upset.

"The important thing is that you'll be initiated, dear. It would never do to have paid all that money and then have to tell people you didn't make it in the sorority." A shudder passed over her mother's slender shoulders and she shook her head.

"College is a big adjustment, Kitten," her father said, patting her hand. "I'm sure next quarter will be lots easier."

"Thanks, Daddy," Kathleen said. "I hope you're right."

Chapter 3

January 1960

Back in the house for the next quarter, they had barely settled into their new rooms when it was time for the initiation ceremony. Kathleen missed rooming with Mary, but one of her new roommates turned out to be Billie, the Husky cheerleader. The other pledge was Chris Travis, a nursing major. They shared a three-girl room that looked out over the tree-lined street instead of at the mountains. It was much smaller than last quarter's room, but it had a cozy feel, and Kathleen liked watching all the activity going on in front of the house.

After a light lunch of cold cuts and salad, Marcia hustled the pledges upstairs to get into their white formals for initiation. Three of their pledge sisters had not made their grades and would come back tomorrow. Tonight only members could be in the house. Even the housemother and the houseboys were gone, which, Billie explained, was the reason for the "pick-up" lunch and the paper plates. They would have a formal dinner later.

Hope Chest

When they were dressed, Marcia assembled them in the library. "Last moments as pledges, ladies. Here we go." Marcia, holding a lighted taper, led the initiates to the chapter room, single-file.

Inside, small tables draped in white had been placed at various spots around the perimeter of the darkened room, each holding an unlighted candle and a small bouquet of yellow roses. A white-robed active stood behind each table, and the rest of the actives sat at one end of the room. The initiates circled the room once behind Marcia, and then she led them to the first table where Mary's sister told them the significance of the Delta.

"The Delta is the first letter of the Greek word *didonai*, which means 'to give.' It has a twofold charge for us. The first aspect of *didonai* applies to our sisterhood. We give to one another because of the bond we have in Delta Phi Tau, and Delta Phi Tau gives back to us with life-long friendships. Beyond our fraternal bonds, however, *didonai* speaks of selflessness, a quality of character that is noble and gracious. One who gives does not put herself first, but instead, she values others by giving of herself and her talents. We give to our sisters, our families, our community, and our country. This is *didonai*."

Marcia lit the candle on the table with hers and led the girls to the next station. There, Barb, her engagement ring twinkling in the candlelight, revealed the mystery of Phi.

"Phi is the first letter of the Greek word *philosophos*, lover of wisdom. One who gives, but has not love of wisdom, gives insignificantly. But one who loves wisdom studies truth. This student seeks to know all peoples and all ideas, and therefore becomes one whom others wish to know and emulate. A wise and giving woman is a worthy friend, a valued partner, a good citizen, and a joy to all who know her. This is *philosophos*."

Again Marcia lit the candle on the table and motioned for the girls to follow her. At the next table, Linda, the social chairman, told them of the meaning of the final letter, Tau.

"Tau is the first letter of *time*, the Greek word for honor. It was used to describe acts of excellence that merited honor, and it is these kinds of acts that we must strive for in our lives. A wise and giving woman, as you have learned from Delta and Phi, is one who merits honor. *Time* is the highest of goals, to live so that your actions with your sisters, your family, your country, and all who know you bring honor to you and also to Delta Phi Tau. This is *time*.

At the next table was a small brass chest with pearls spilling out of it.

"The pearl is our jewel," they were told. "Pearls do not have to be faceted or worked in any way for their beauty to shine through. They have an inner light, a luminosity that shines from them just as they come from the sea. Even pearls with imperfections have a beauty. No two are alike. They symbolize the inner and unique loveliness of each of our sisters. Every new member of Delta Phi Tau joins an unbroken strand of jewels from the first initiates, encircling all of us in the sisterly love of Delta Phi Tau."

Marcia lit the candle and led them to the next station. Here Patty held up the pin.

"On the back of your pin are the letters *alpha pi*. They stand for Delta Phi Tau's most sacred motto: *Aionios pistos*, eternally faithful. This motto is the core of our sisterhood. Delta Phi Taus pledge our loyalty to our sisters through this motto; it is a bond amongst us for life—and for after. It means that we will always uphold the traditions of Delta Phi Tau, that we will be true to all she stands for, that we will never divulge her secrets, and that we will be steadfast to our fraternity and our sisters known and unknown. If on life's road we encounter another Delta Phi Tau, the love and friendship we feel here will extend to that sister. Wherever life takes us, we have a place to belong within the circle of Delta Phi Tau."

Kathleen felt a sting of tears start behind her eyes. She was filled again with so much love for these sisters and with so much pride to be a part of such a group. They moved on to the next stop, where they were shown the secret grip that would allow them to enter a chapter meeting at any Delta Phi Tau house in the country and pledged never to reveal any of the mysteries of Delta Phi Tau.

Finally they stopped in front of the president. At this point, Marcia fanned them into a semicircle, and the Big Sisters came from where they were seated to stand behind them. Marcia placed her candle into the holder and slipped behind Kathleen.

"Now you will receive the badge of membership in Delta Phi Tau. It is to be worn with pride and respect. It is always to be worn next to your heart. It is a symbol of sisterhood, a symbol that those who wear it share the secrets and the pride of Delta Phi Tau. We welcome our new sisters."

The initiates all turned to face their Big Sisters, who were holding the gold and pearl pins. Kathleen held her breath as Marcia fastened hers to her bodice.

"Welcome to Delta Phi Tau, Kathleen," Marcia said and folded her into a warm hug. Now the tears came for real. The actives sang a chorus of "Delta Phi Tau Pearls," and Kathleen dabbed at her eyes. She heard sniffling around her and looked for Mary down the line. Mary smiled at her and pulled back her shoulders to show off her pin. Kathleen stifled a giggle, despite the lump in her throat. Even if she didn't quite have the grades she was used to getting, she had made it to initiation. She belonged.

⁂

"So, how are your classes going to be this quarter? Any better?" Mary asked her at lunch the following Monday. Both girls proudly wore their new Delta Phi Tau pins on their sweaters.

"It's hard to tell," Kathleen said. "I still have that huge Western Civ class—102—but this time I know that 'supplementary readings' aren't for extra credit, they're required. Tomorrow I go to Creative Dramatics for Children. That ought to be interesting."

"Why that one? Are you thinking of going into teaching?"

"Possibly. My mother always says it's a good profession to fall back on. And I like kids. Besides, I needed a three-hour class, and that was the only one that sounded interesting. Please pass the blue milk."

"I don't know how you can drink that stuff." Ellie Miller, the girl from Spokane, made a face as she passed the pitcher of skim milk to Kathleen, handle first.

"Oh, I see. Nutrition has nothing to do with home ec?"

"I'm in the fabric side, dear, not the kitchen."

"Any super guys in your classes this morning, Chris?" Kathleen said to her roommate, who sat across from them.

"In nursing? I don't think so. How about you, Ellie?"

"Tons. They were swarming all over the sewing machines."

"You know," Kathleen said, "There must be three hundred people in that Western Civ class, and I haven't seen one interesting guy. It's amazing. Where are they all?"

"They're sure not in home ec, I can tell you," Ellie said.

"And probably not in creative dramatics for children either. I don't get it. Last summer when I drove around here with Jake, they were everywhere. Washing their cars, playing basketball, sitting on lounge chairs. Now, poof!"

"It could be seasonal. I think maybe they only come out when there's no school."

"Oh, Chris, how depressing."

"Well, they sure don't come to exchanges," Mary said.

"And we have that on empirical evidence, which I learned about in my Psych 101 class," Kathleen added. "First-hand observation. Can't beat it for proof."

"What time is your next class, Roommate?" Chris asked Kathleen.

"One o'clock."

"Mine too. We'd better get the room clean pronto. I have to go all the way to Health Sciences. I'll never make it if we don't hurry."

"I'll do it, Chris," Kathleen told her roommate. "You and Billie are such neatniks, there's nothing to do. We'll never have a demerit, even if we don't do anything."

"I thought that when we got initiated we wouldn't have to do this pledges-clean-the-room stuff," Mary said. "I guess we're pledges all year."

Up in the room, Kathleen hung up a stray belt and fluffed the pillows on the day bed and then turned to close the closet door. She caught a glimpse of herself in the mirror and smiled when she saw her gold Del Phi pin gleaming on her sweater. She closed the door and headed downstairs to leave for class.

She had gone to the bookstore, but there was no text listed for this class. She didn't quite know what to expect, so all she took with her was a small spiral-bound notebook.

There were about a dozen people in the classroom when she arrived, and a few more trickled in after her, but no familiar faces. She took a seat in the circular row and waited.

Suddenly, the door flew open and a short, redheaded dynamo swept into the room.

"Good afternoon, everyone, and welcome to Creative Dramatics for Children. My name is Professor Hawkins, and I want to know yours."

She looked right at Kathleen when she said it, so she answered, "Kathleen Andrews, Professor."

"Welcome, Kathleen Andrews. Tell me now, why are you in this class? Do you know what you are going to do with the rest of your life?"

Kathleen felt her face grow warm. "I'm afraid not, Professor. I don't even have a major yet."

There were nervous titters from the students around her, and Kathleen stared straight ahead. "Wonderful!" Professor Hawkins said, clapping her hands. "I never knew either. Still don't. But I've discovered that while I was trying to figure it out, I kept discarding the things I didn't like and sort of hanging on to the ones I did, and what do you know?"

The whole class seemed to be leaning forward.

"Here I am, doing what I love. And you will too, Kathleen Andrews. You will too. All of you will, but you have to keep a sharp eye out. And that's what I'm here to help you do. Let's meet the rest of you first, shall we?"

They went around the room saying their names and giving their majors—those who had them—and all smiling self-consciously as the professor darted from desk to desk.

"What a wonderful class this is going to be. I can tell. The first thing I want you all to do is get yourselves a little notebook that you can carry with you everywhere. In it, you will record your daily observations. Little things, like the various personalities of lawn sprinklers."

"Lawn sprinklers?" came an incredulous voice.

"Of course," Professor Hawkins replied. "Why some are so graceful, for example. Almost like ballerinas as they arch gently across the lawn. Others," she continued, hunkering down and looking up at the class from under drawn brows, "others spit and fitz as if they were furious at you for watching them. And still others barely have the energy to get the job done."

A shiver of wonder passed through Kathleen. She had never heard anyone, not even her beloved Senior English teacher at Richmond, so clearly state things that she had always felt but had never given voice to. The rest of the hour passed by in no time, and she was disappointed when it was over. The campus she hurried across to get from one class to another suddenly seemed brand new, and she walked back from class clutching her notebook and searching for things to notice. The stately brick buildings of the Quad glowed in the pale winter sunshine. The carillon in Denny Hall began to chime the hour. She stopped to listen. Had she heard these bells every day, or just now for the first time? She knew that someone played songs on them every morning, but she could not remember hearing a single melody before. How could she not have heard something so beautiful? She continued up the path and sat on the steps of Denny Hall and just watched and listened.

Students in warm coats streamed by her. The coats were mostly dark—navy, brown, forest green—brightened here and there by a silk bandanna or a red ski cap. It was like looking through a kaleidoscope. How could one lecture, one professor so open her eyes?

She looked at everything with new eyes and couldn't wait for class each day. Even Western Civ became interesting. She now watched the professor who had seemed so boring last quarter in order to describe him, monotone and all, in her notebook. Describe wasn't even the word she wanted. Capture, that was it. She studied his shapeless jacket until its very shapelessness took form.

The only thing she didn't have to observe was any progress in her social life, but at least her classes were improving.

"Can I borrow anyone's hair spray?" said Lynne Lewis, a senior from Mercer Island, across the floating bridge from Seattle. "Mine just died."

"Here, use mine," Mary said, tossing Lynne a can of Aqua Net. "Although your hair never looks like it moves around too much."

Lynne laughed a silvery laugh. "How do you think I get it that way? It's pretty straight unless I spray it to death."

"A woman after my own heart," Mary said.

Lynne moved into the doorway and began spraying her blonde bubble in large arcs. "I heard you two complaining about meeting guys, and I'll tell you where I've met some really nice ones—and girls too for that matter," she said.

"You jest," Mary said.

"No, really. Here's your hair spray, thanks. It's called Fishers. It's a non-denominational Christian group that meets on Wednesday nights."

"I'm not very religious," Kathleen said.

"Oh, it's not *religious* religious," Lynne said. "It's just fun. We sing and talk and have coffee and get to know people. You'd like it."

"Fishers?" Mary said.

"From 'fishers of men,'" Lynne said.

"Hey, I remember that song from Sunday school," Kathleen said, and began to sing, "'I will make you fishers of men, fishers of men, fishers of men.'" She pantomimed casting out a fishing line and reeling it in as she sang. Lynne started to laugh and joined in.

"'If you faa-low me, if you faaa-low me. I will make you fishers of men, if you faaa-loow me.'"

"I don't think I can bear this," Mary groaned. "Promise me you won't wear your pins or make eye contact with me if I go with you."

"I didn't think the Lutherans did much singing, Kathleen," Lynne said between giggles.

"Hey, not true," Mary quipped and burst into a slightly off-key chorus of "A Mighty Fortress Is Our God." "Martin Luther wrote lots of hymns."

"Besides the singing, Mary," Lynne continued, "there are some really neat guys there. Why don't you both come with me next week and see."

"Do we get a refund if there are no guys?' Mary asked.
"Double your money back. You can't lose."

The three of them walked briskly in the cold night to the meeting the following Wednesday, still talking about the big event of the last weekend. One senior had gotten back to the house after the 2 o'clock curfew on Saturday night. Mrs. D had already locked the deadbolt, to which she and the standards chairman had the only keys. The standards chairman always waited by the door for the ten minutes allowed for grace period after 2 a.m., but after that there was no way to get into the house except by ringing the bell and getting Mrs. D to unlock the door.

"I still don't see why she got campused when it wasn't even her fault. Ginny said she begged him to bring her back, but he just wouldn't!" Kathleen said.

"I heard he was pretty drunk," Mary said. "What a creep."

"But she did get some beautiful roses," Kathleen said. "He can't be all bad to try to make up like that."

"Roses are the penalty when a guy causes you to get campused," Lynne said. "It's standard. And the flowers are usually quite dead by the next weekend when you get to stay in, so you can't even spend all that long time contemplating them."

"I would hate being stuck in the house all weekend. Especially Friday night dinners. They are the worst!" Mary said. "Fish sticks every week. And all the Catholics sign out. You would think their consciences would make them stay and do penance with the rest of us for inflicting fish sticks on others. No wonder Martin Luther started his own church, bless him."

"You are too funny," said Lynne, leading them up the stairs of a large modern building off Greek Row that housed a number of organizations. They followed the signs to Fishers in the main hall. The room was full, and the girls found a place to sit on the floor in front of one of the couches. A pretty Tri-Delt Kathleen remembered from Rush passed out songbooks.

The leader was a handsome charismatic type from Tennessee named Guy, with a charming Southern accent and a droll sense of humor.

"Happy to see so many new faces tonight!" he boomed at them. "Welcome to Fishers. We all come together here every week because we love the Lord and want to share what He has done in our lives with all of you so that you, too, might come to know Jesus Christ as your Lord and Savior. Let's begin with a song."

They sang a number of tunes, some familiar to Kathleen, but most were new. There was an easy atmosphere, and as Kathleen glanced around the room, everyone who met her glance smiled back at her. She saw several sorority pins on the girls and recognized a few faces. And there seemed to be an equal a number of guys. Perhaps this would be a good place to come.

Guy opened his Bible and in his soft accent began to read from the New Testament about Christ's first miracle at the wedding at Cana where he changed water into wine.

"And y'all know what was so amazing about this miracle? Not just the water becoming wine, no sir. It was the water that was in big old jugs by the door that people used to wash their dusty feet in. And the Bible says it was the *best* wine. He took the scummiest old water around and revealed Himself to the whole world at that moment to help the host from being embarrassed by running out of wine before the wedding guests were ready to leave.

"And that's what God can do for you through His Son, make even the crummiest of us into the very *best*. Think of that—the *very best!* And that's what we want to do here at Fishers, be instruments—myself, Gail (he pointed to the Tri-Delt), all of us—be instruments to help you know, really know, our Lord and Savior."

Kathleen looked over at Gail who was smiling and nodding.

"Now I know a lot of you go to church," Guy went on, "But back in Tennessee we have a saying that going into a church don't make you a Christian any more than going into a garage makes you a car." He paused to let the light laughter die down.

"Some of you—heck, all of you—might even be baptized, and that's a fine thing. But," he paused again. "But you can have a real, stand-beside-you, talk-to-me friend in the Lord if you just open your heart and let Him in. Just say, 'Lord Jesus, I give my life into Your hands. Come into my heart and make me Yours.' It's just that simple, and you can start right now, tonight, being the best you can be. Think about it."

He looked around the room and seemed to smile right at Kathleen. She held her breath, but his eyes moved to take in the rest of the crowd.

"Let's bow our heads in prayer," he said finally. There was a soft rustling as people shifted their weight and bowed their heads.

"Lord, we know that You are there with Your hand extended just waitin' for each and every one of us to reach up to You. Help us to open our hearts and receive Your excellent love and guidance in our lives. Help everyone in this room to come to know You in a personal way, to know the peace and the joy that comes from walking every day with You. Thank You, Lord, for the most excellent gift of Your Son, Jesus, in Whose Blessed Name we pray, amen."

A chorus of barely audible amens followed, and eyes opened. Guy was still smiling his handsome smile at them. Kathleen was transfixed. She looked around the room at the healthy, glowing faces. There was a feeling of harmony in the room that drew her. They had begun to sing again, and she was pulled out of her reverie to flip through her songbook to find the right page. After the final song, people moved over to a long table by the wall for cookies and coffee. Gail came up to the girls as they got their refreshments.

"How nice to see you here," she said to Kathleen and Mary after Lynne had introduced them. "Did you enjoy it?"

"It was wonderful," Kathleen heard herself say. She saw Mary glance quickly at her with a smile on her face that evaporated as soon as she saw that Kathleen wasn't just being polite.

"Well, I hope you will all come regularly. We have a Bible study group as well on Tuesday afternoons at four, right here. Everyone's welcome."

She moved on gracefully to greet other newcomers, and Guy came up to them. Lynne performed introductions again, and he took their hands in turn, enveloping them in his huge paw.

"I'm truly delighted to meet you both. We have a super time here every week, and I hope we'll be seeing a lot more of both of you."

As they left, he was at the door saying good-bye (which to Kathleen sounded delightfully like "Bah") to everyone again.

"Whadja think?" Lynne said.

"I think I'll stick to the good old Ballard Lutherans and the lutefisk-eating contests. This is too much Bible-thumping for me," Mary confessed. "I felt like we should have been in a tent."

"I don't know, Mar," Kathleen said thoughtfully, "I thought it made a lot of sense. I mean, I pray occasionally—finals week, for example—but other than that, I don't think too much about God, except at Easter. Maybe that's because that's the only time my family goes to church. My dad says we're 'holiday Christians.'"

"There is such a feeling of community among the Christians at Fishers," Lynne said.

"That's true," Kathleen said. "I felt it too. Plus, you were right, Lynne. There were some cute guys there."

"You make it sound like a fraternity," Mary said.

"Well, it is sort of like that, I guess," Lynne answered.

"Not to me. You two will have to commune without me from now on, I'm afraid. But I will grant you one thing, that Guy person is a doll."

April 1960

"Who are you taking to the Spring Formal, Kath? Jake again?"

"I hope not, Mary. I know he'd go if I asked him, but I think he's dating someone, so that wouldn't be too cool. Actually, I was kind of thinking of asking Guy." She looked at Mary and then looked out the window quickly. Her heart was pounding.

"Guy? As in Fishers Guy?"

"Well, why not?"

"Why not what?" Lynne said, bouncing into the room and flopping down next to Mary on the daybed.

"I told Mary I might invite Guy to the formal." She sounded defensive even to herself.

Lynne looked at Mary, who shrugged, and then back at Kathleen. "I don't think he dates anyone who goes to Fishers, Kathleen."

"How do you know?"

"Well, I think it's policy or something. Kind of like not dating people you work with."

Kathleen felt her heart sink. Guy Mathers was by far the most interesting man she had met since coming to the U. Besides being inordinately handsome, there was something attractive about him that she couldn't describe. Maybe it was that he was older and seemed more sophisticated than the fraternity boys she had met. Maybe it was that he was the leader of the group and always seemed so in charge. Since that first meeting with Mary and Lynne, Kathleen had not missed a Fishers meeting. She found herself volunteering to do little things that put her into contact with Guy, things like passing out songbooks and staying to clean up. It meant she had to walk back to the house alone if Lynne hadn't come or couldn't stay, but she didn't mind. It was only a couple of blocks.

Despite all her volunteering, however, Guy had done nothing to indicate any special interest in her. He bestowed his incredible, perfect-toothed smile on everyone equally. Once he had put his arm lightly around her shoulders, causing her heart nearly to stop and the color to rise in her face. She relived the moment for a whole week until she saw he did the same thing to several others—girls and guys—equally at the next meeting.

The fact that he had a warm word or look or touch for everyone in his circle didn't stop her from dreaming, however. She could invite Jake again to the formal, but she imagined herself on Guy's arm. She had almost asked him last week, but chickened out at the last minute. Now she thought about what Lynne had just said and was flooded with relief that she had not spoken to him and humiliated herself.

Of course he couldn't go out with someone in the club. How could she have been so stupid? Didn't Delta Phi Tau have much the same rule that you couldn't date two men in the same fraternity unless you had waited a full six weeks between them? It would be even more awkward for him at Fishers to have to smile at some freshman with a crush. And what if he had gone with her, and the date turned out to be a disaster! She could never face him again. Her cheeks were burning.

Thank God she had not mentioned him to her mother. In fact, she had not even told her about Fishers. Somehow Kathleen felt her mother would not understand the group. She was not what Kathleen would describe as religious in the sense Kathleen was now coming to understand at Fishers. She was sure her mother did not have a "personal relationship with Jesus." The elaborate ritual of the Episcopal church they attended on holidays, where people dressed well and exchanged gloved handshakes in the fellowship hall afterwards over coffee (poured into china cups from silver servers) was what Mrs. Andrews expected from her church. She even cast an occasional disparaging remark about Gran's devotion to her Presbyterian roots.

"Grape juice and Wonder Bread cubes," she sniffed. "What kind of Communion service is that?"

Kathleen turned to Lynne with as much nonchalance as she could muster. "I suppose you're right. It's just that there is no one I really care to go with."

"It's going to be so neat. Have you ever been to the Chinese Room at the top of the Smith Tower?" Lynne asked. "It's all decorated in old carved dragony stuff, and you can walk all around the outside on the balcony. You can see everything from there, the lights of the city, the ferries on the Sound. It's a shame to waste such a romantic place on just anybody."

"You taking someone special, Lynne?"

"I hope so, Mar. I asked that cute Delt I had a coffee date with last week. I figured, what the heck. All he could say was no, but he said yes. How about you?"

"I'm not sure. Maybe I'll ask this Alpha Delt from my psych lab last quarter. We really had fun in class, but I don't know."

"All I had in psych were rats," Kathleen said. "Definitely no Alpha Delts."

The gong chimed for dinner, and they all went down to eat. The gnawing fear that had haunted her ever since she first thought of asking Guy to the formal was gone, and Kathleen found that she was ravenous. She dived into the thin slices of roast beef with gusto. Their cooks were wonderful, but tonight's dinner tasted especially good. There was even her favorite dessert: angel food cake with chocolate whipped cream and slivered almonds. She had been saved from certain embarrassment, and she thanked her lucky stars for her sorority sisters and their timely interference. So many times these new friends had come through for her. But now she was at a loss. She could ask Jake if all else failed, unless of course he was serious about his new girlfriend and she objected. But the Smith Tower sounded too romantic for good old Jake. Oh well, maybe something would turn up. She had a few weeks to decide.

In the meantime she was working with Billie on a routine for Husky cheerleader tryouts. They were scheduled for the middle of April. There had been an orientation meeting already, and more than a hundred girls had signed up, including Trudy Lavik.

Kathleen had not seen much of Trudy since Rush, but her mother related Trudy's progress to her at each phone call. Trudy had the most interesting classes and was dating just about everyone who was anyone in simply the best fraternities. Kathleen could hear the frustration in her mother's voice that she was not able to parry each of Mrs. Lavik's thrusts with a superior accomplishment from her own daughter. At least Kathleen's grades for winter quarter had been a more respectable 3.0 to Trudy's 2.5, but Trudy's scholarship had never been her strongest suit.

Kathleen found herself doing her tryout routine in her head as she walked to class or took phone duty or waited to be served at dinner until it became second nature to her. It had to, so if she got a case of the nerves during tryouts, her body would keep going even if her mind froze. The night before tryouts she fidgeted and changed positions so much in her upper bunk that the girl below her gave Kathleen's mattress a kick. Finally she dragged Gran's quilt off the sleeping porch and went to her room. She flopped down on the day bed and realized she had no pillow, but she didn't have the energy to go back to the sleeping porch. She laid her head on her arm and finally fell asleep.

She made it through her classes the next morning, though the hours seemed to drag, and finally it was time for her and Billie to head to the HUB for tryouts. The sight of Mary waving a hanky dramatically from the upstairs window finally lightened the tension a bit, making both girls laugh.

"She's so crazy," Kathleen said. "Look at her, waving like a *Life* magazine photo of mothers sending their sons off to war. Will it be that bad?"

"You'll do fine, Kathleen," Billie assured her. "I just hope I don't make a mess of things."

"Oh, Billie, you'll make it again for sure. Patty won't ding another Del Phi Tau."

Patty had been elected captain by last year's squad and would be running the tryouts. Even so, Kathleen knew Patty would be fair and that being a Del Phi wouldn't help Kathleen if she didn't do a good job in these tryouts. The girls took their places with the crowd of bouncing, high-kicking hopefuls who were practicing all around the room. Trudy was already there, Kathleen noted.

They were all given large white squares with numbers on them to wear. Kathleen was number 35; Billie 36. Dozens of girls had lined up behind them to register. Kathleen and Billie went to the center of the ballroom to do some warm-up stretches.

The judges' table was on the stage at the far end, and all the judges were standing around Patty, who seemed to be explaining the procedure to them. Heads nodded as she gestured to a clipboard she was holding. The yell king was there and the band director and the graduating girls from the current squad who wouldn't be trying out again, but Kathleen didn't recognize any of the other judges. She assumed they were from the Rally Girls and the Sundodgers, the women's and men's spirit groups, and maybe the card stunt committee. They seated themselves around a long table.

Patty finally came down from the stage and clapped her hands for quiet.

"Welcome, everyone," she said into the microphone. "I'm thrilled to see so many of you here. The procedure will be simple. First, we'll teach you a routine that you will perform in groups of four for the judges. They will then select the semifinalists. Then we'll have that group do their individual routines one at a time. The judges will select the finalists from that round. At that point, we will play a piece of music for the finalists to make up a routine on the spot. OK?" Heads nodded. "Right now we'll show you the tryout routine. Sunny, hit the tape recorder, please."

Patty and the others lined up and launched into a routine to "Singin' in the Rain." To Kathleen's tremendous relief, the routine looked very easy. It was also to a song their band at Richmond had never played, so she didn't have an old routine in her head to confuse with the new one. She felt a tiny bit less nervous.

They were divided into different groups to learn the dance. When Kathleen looked around, there was Trudy right behind her, every perfect hair in place.

"Hi, Trudy. Nervous?"

"Not really. I've had my routine ready for ages. How about you?"

"I'm not worried about my routine, but there are so many trying out. We'll soon see how much talent is here."

Trudy made a face as if to say Kathleen was being foolish and turned to Sunny, the leader of their group. The short brunette began teaching them the routine. It was easy, Kathleen thought, because it was predictable. If there were two steps to the right, there would be two to the left. If they kicked with the right foot, the next step would be a kick with the left. Two turns to the right, two to the left. Kathleen had it the first time through, but there were a couple of girls in the group who had some trouble getting the steps. Sunny divided the group again and went to work with the strugglers.

"The rest of you practice it in your lines. Work on keeping them straight, and watch your spacing. I'll be right back with you."

Kathleen stood next to Trudy and watched her out of the corner of her eye. Predictably, she turned "Singin' in the Rain" into a ballet, gliding smoothly through the steps as if she were on ice. The girl on Kathleen's other side bounced and jiggled as if she had drawn in the energy Trudy wasn't using. Kathleen tried to blend with them so she wouldn't look out of step.

Finally they all tried it to the music. Kathleen concentrated on the steps and the line, but found herself overwhelmed by the entire room full of girls in the required white blouses and dark shorts, all of them swinging and kicking in unison. Suddenly she felt a different kind of nervousness. In worrying about her routine, she had not given much thought to the competition. Well, here it was all around her. Attractive girls with wide smiles and lots of pep, straight backs, and straighter kicks. The room was getting warmer, and the mingled smells of dust and sweat and hair spray and perfume were getting stronger. She felt hot and worried. She took a deep breath and forced herself to concentrate.

After about ten minutes, Patty took the microphone again. "Take a seat along the sidelines, girls. You all look really good. We'll call you up by number in groups of four, and you'll do the routine twice through so the judges don't have to look at you in Cinemascope. Sometimes they need a second go-through to see you all."

There was a shuffling as people seated themselves around the edges of the ballroom floor, some in the few chairs, most on the floor. Kathleen sat next to Billie on a window ledge where someone had mercifully opened the window. They reveled in the cool breeze. Trudy sat across the room from them with several Iotas who were trying out.

"None of the Iotas over there are even perspiring," Kathleen whispered to Billie. She was feeling sticky and rumpled despite the breeze.

"They're not allowed to. It's part of the pledge training."

The groups of four did the routine for the judges, who smiled equally at everyone and then scribbled furiously on yellow sheets in front of them.

Trudy went up in the third group, and Kathleen had to admit that even with her overly smooth style, she looked better than most of the girls performing with her. She dazzled her perfect smile at the judges throughout both routines. Her blouse remained firmly tucked into her dark shorts, and her kicks were the highest in the line.

Kathleen and Billie went up together, which was comforting to Kathleen, even though they were competing against one another. They sailed through the song, and it felt good both times.

After all the groups were finished, the judges conferred for several minutes.

"Break time, girls," Patty said. "Go get a drink of water."

Everyone made a break for the drinking fountains and the bathrooms. There were lines of girls everywhere fanning their flushed faces. It was much cooler in the hall. Kathleen untucked her blouse and ruffled it to speed the cool air to her skin. Her stomach was aflutter. This would be the first cut. She prayed that she would make it.

In the bathroom, Kathleen tucked her blouse back into her damp waistband and made her way to the mirror. Her hair was curling wildly around her face. She smoothed it with her hands and watched in frustration as it sprang back into its own style. She splashed cold water on her face and let it dry in the air as she headed back. The ballroom was quiet as the girls returned. Everyone sat around the sides waiting.

Finally Patty stood on the stage holding the yellow sheets. "I want to thank all of you for your interest and for all the work you have put into this. I will read the numbers of the people who have made the first round. When I do, will you please come to the center of the room? The rest of you are welcome to stay if you wish."

Then she started reading the numbers, "One, four, nine . . ."

Trudy jumped up when her number was called and ran with tiny steps to the growing circle of girls in the center.

"Twenty-five, twenty-seven, thirty, thirty-five, thirty-six . . ."

Kathleen and Billie hugged each other and ran out to the middle. The bouncy girl who had been next to Kathleen was not called. Kathleen didn't look around for fear of catching her eye.

Patty finished the numbers and smiled at the lucky ones. There were a few tears on the sidelines, Kathleen noticed, but no one left.

"Now," Patty said to the group in the middle of the ballroom, "it's your turn to show us your originals. To be fair, this time we'll start with the larger numbers and work backwards. So 99, you're on. The rest of you just sit toward the back."

While the other semi-finalists went back to the sidelines, Number 99 stayed where she was in the center of the room. She licked her lips and flashed a smile at the judges. Her routine was excellent, and she did it flawlessly, as did most of the girls who performed before it was Kathleen's turn. Billie's routine went perfectly. Kathleen knew it by heart. Billie's red ponytail flipped and bounced in rhythm, making her look even peppier. Her style was sharp and precise, with all the polish but none of the studied smoothness that Trudy had. Kathleen was sure Billie would be back.

Finally, Kathleen was in the middle of the floor and smiling at the judges herself, concentrating on Patty, who gave her an encouraging wink. Then the familiar tune started, and Kathleen went through her routine. In a flash it was over. The judges were writing, and they were smiling.

"You looked fabulous!" Billie said as Kathleen went back to her seat. "Not a glitch."

Kathleen was breathing hard, but she felt good.

When the music and the light applause finished after the final contestant, the only sound in the room was the scratching of the judges' pens or the rustling of their papers. There was a collective holding of breath as the girls on the sidelines trained their eyes on the stage. Finally Patty took the microphone again and read the numbers.

"Here are the finalists. Thanks to all of the rest of you for coming today. Again, you may stay if you wish."

Kathleen heard nothing until Patty said "thirty-five" and she realized it was her number. She nearly wept with relief. Then Billie's number was called, and she joined Kathleen in the center. Trudy, another Iota, and "99" also joined them. Kathleen did a quick count: there were 30 girls in the finals—for seven spaces.

"Here's the music. Make up anything you'd like us to see. And relax, it's only sixteen bars." Patty played a sprightly version of "Alouette" for them. "That's it, girls. See what you can do. We'll play it a few more times, and then you have five minutes."

"Alouette"? Kathleen's mind went blank. She had expected what? John Philip Sousa? Not "Alouette." She gulped in a few breaths to calm herself and closed her eyes. Do kicks, she decided. And something with her back to the judges. And nothing predictable.

She began to bounce slightly to the rhythm. As her feet began to move, her heart began to beat again. She started with a simple step and stopped, moving only her shoulders to the afterbeat. It worked, so she repeated it in the same pause after the next measure, only she reversed the direction of the motion. The rest of the steps seemed to form themselves, and she ended with a high kick and a Charleston pose with her hands over her head. She noticed that everyone else was ending with a jump.

"OK, that's all the time you get." Patty's voice stopped all the movement. "Form circle in the order of your numbers. What we'll do is play the music, watch your routine, and then move you to your left one spot so you can do it again. We'll keep doing it until everyone has performed in front of the judges. You'll be perfect when this one is over!" There was nervous laughter. Kathleen moved to the circle and found herself in the back, almost opposite the judges. She would have time to polish as she moved along.

The music started and so did the routines. Over and over. Kathleen vowed she would never listen to, whistle, or sing "Alouette" again. At last she was in the front. She smiled at the judges, lifted her head, and took a deep breath. As before, it was over in a flash, and she moved to her left. Finally she was back where she'd started, and that portion was mercifully finished.

Patty motioned for them to return to the sidelines and sit. "The judges want to take a couple of last looks, girls, so please come up in groups as I call your numbers and do the routine we taught you today."

She called Kathleen and Billie and Trudy and four other girls, including 99, as Kathleen had begun to think of her. They lined up and did the routine. Then Patty called three new numbers to replace three girls in the line. There was one more shuffle and once more through the routine. Kathleen and Billie exchanged worried looks.

"Last time, girls. I promise," Patty assured them.

The music started again, and when they were finished, the judges stood and clapped. Patty said, "Congratulations to the new 1960-61 Husky Rally Squad."

Kathleen looked at Billie and then at Trudy. Everyone looked puzzled. Then it dawned on them. They had won! This was the new squad. Pandemonium broke out as they hugged each other and the judges, who had come down from the stage to congratulate the winners. Even girls who had been eliminated were hugging everyone.

"We made it," Billie shouted over the din.

"I can't believe it," Kathleen shouted back.

"Well, it looks like we'll be cheering together again, Kathleen," Trudy simpered. "Just like old times."

The three Del Phis walked back to the house together. Mary saw them coming from the window and met them at the door. "I told everyone to meet in the smoking room. How'd you do?"

Kathleen kept her eyes down. Patty shooed Mary up the stairs ahead of her, and the three followed her to the Smoker. Mary cast a worried glance at Kathleen over her shoulder, but Kathleen didn't respond.

"Well?" said several voices as the girls came into the room. It seemed to Kathleen that the whole house was there.

"Well, Billie made it again, as we all expected," Patty said, and a cheer went up. It fizzled as everyone suddenly looked at Kathleen. They dropped their eyes when she didn't smile back at them.

"And Kathleen made it too, of course," Patty said finally. The room erupted in noise.

"You rat!" Mary said, hugging Kathleen, who was now laughing and crying at the same time. "Pretending to be a failure to me, your oldest friend."

The Del Phis crowded around her and Billie, hugging and clapping and cheering.

"*Three* cheerleaders in the house."

"Too much!"

"This will be so great for Rush next year!"

"And you'll probably get to go to the Rose Bowl!"

There was a sudden silence. "Rose Bowl!" Kathleen shrieked, and she and Patty and Billie held hands and jumped up and down.

"Pass me my smelling salts," Mary said. "This is too much excitement for me."

"Well, you go lie down, old thing. I have to go call my folks." Kathleen went excitedly to the nearest phone.

⁓

Now campus life had new meaning for Kathleen. The twice-weekly practices became her focus. Here was something she could understand and control. There were no trick questions in music, only rhythmic problems to be translated into movement in a way no one had thought of before.

With the possible exception of Trudy, the pep squad was a diverse and delightful group. There was a short, attractive blonde named Penny from Santa Rosa, whose style was different from anything Kathleen had ever seen before. There was also a stunningly beautiful Iota named Elspeth Holm, a dancer who had long, white-blonde hair, perfect skin, and as Mary said when she saw her, "miles of legs." And "99" was Gabby Anderson, an Alpha Gamma Delta from Mary's high school, who ended up standing next to Kathleen in the lineup. She had a long brown ponytail, a tiny nose, and enormous blue eyes. Finally there was Cindy Trapp, a Tri-Delt from Bellevue, who had been a cheerleader, not a songleader, as the Husky squad was actually called because they performed to music, not cheers.

"Our moves were really different, you guys, because we did cheers. Unlike you in the big city, we didn't have any boys on cheer staff, just girls. The songleader squad danced to the band, but we didn't. In fact, these tryouts were the first time I ever did anything to music!" She sounded apologetic.

"Whatever you did, it looked terrific," Patty said. "Let's see it."

They spent the first few practices like that, sharing routines and comparing styles and listening to Trudy object to anything that seemed "not very graceful." Kathleen was pleased that Trudy's objections were almost always overridden by the other girls, including the beautiful Elspeth, so there was no need for Kathleen to say anything. Her fears that the tension between her and Trudy in high school might follow her here vanished. Soon the squad had made up several routines and looked as if they had been together for much longer than a few weeks. Kathleen was thrilled and could hardly wait until football season, which seemed a very long way off.

In the meantime, her continuing work with Professor Hawk's creative dramatics classes, coupled with the excitement of cheer practice, gave college a whole new dimension. Kathleen waded willingly through the dusty textbook for Sociology 101 with the goal of getting it behind her so she could think about new routines. In contrast, the readings for her class on children's literature were magical. She read the Caldecott and Newbery Medal winners and marveled over them all. The illustrations were breathtaking, and many of the stories caused her to laugh out loud—or to cry. She had never read any of the Winnie the Pooh stories as a child, a fact her classmates had a hard time believing. She adored Eeyore, the gloomy old grey donkey, and drove Mary crazy by always responding to her "How are you?" with Eeyore's "Not very how, thank you."

The campus also changed. Rhododendrons burst into pink and red beneath the evergreens. Tulips and daffodils blazed around the sundial and Frosh Pond, and everywhere there was color. The Del Phi willow was once again green and full. The grey days were gone.

"Hey, Kath," Mary said, catching up to her near the HUB. "Guess what! I have a coffee date right now in the HUB with a super-cool guy. Maybe our luck is changing."

"Who is he? Where did you meet him?"

"He's in my econ class. I never thought anything good would come from it, but here we are. He's a Beta, and he's really cute."

"In the HUB? Good. Instead of going to practice, I'll hide behind a potted palm and spy on you. Rub your nose if you need to be rescued."

"Don't you dare! If this turns into anything, I'll at least have a date for the formal. Keep your fingers crossed."

Mary dashed off, and Kathleen realized she had not thought about the formal since tryouts. It didn't seem so daunting now. Maybe she would just ask Jake and call it a day. They always had fun. That decided, she went up the stairs to practice.

At dinner that night, Mary was bubbling. "Not only is he cute, but I think he has a brain. He's a business major from Bellevue. And . . ."

Her sister Julie and Kathleen stopped chewing and looked at her. "And?" they said together.

"And we're going out Saturday. I can't even believe it. Somebody pinch me."

"Oh, Mary," Julie said. "You are such a nut. Where's he taking you?"

"To a movie, I guess. Who cares?"

"Wow, a real date. After only two quarters. Maybe there's hope for me yet," Kathleen said.

"Well, somebody preferenced you for the exchange Friday," Lynne said.

"What?" Kathleen was surprised. She knew that fraternity men could "preference" someone from the house, even someone who wasn't a freshman, but it had never happened to her. Like all the other pledges, she just got lined up with someone her height every time. No one had ever "preffed" her for an exchange, but some of the older girls, who didn't have to go to exchanges, had found themselves on the list. Usually they didn't want to go, but they had no choice if they'd been preffed. The only exceptions were girls who were pinned or engaged.

"I saw the list as I came down to dinner. You were right on the top under 'Preference,' big as life."

"Who is he?" she asked Lynne.

"I didn't look at the name. I just noticed yours."

"Well, for heaven's sake. I don't even know anyone in that house."

Mary gave her a little push. "Go look. We want to know who he is."

"I can't leave until after dessert. Mrs. D won't excuse me just to go look at a list."

"Tell her you got your period, silly. She'll excuse you for that. We *have* to know."

"Are you serious?"

"Absolutely, Kath. This is big. Go. Go!"

Kathleen placed her napkin on her chair and approached Mrs. D's table. "May I please be excused, Mrs. D? I'll be right back."

"Of course, dear," the housemother said, barely glancing up.

Kathleen returned a few minutes later.

"Well?" They all said it at once.

"Ben Davis. Anyone know him?"

No one did. It was a mystery. Then Mary said, "Aha!"

"Aha? What does that mean?"

"He preferenced you because you're a varsity Husky songleader now. What price fame."

"You know, she's probably right, Kathleen," Billie said. "It happened to me last year right after tryouts."

"But how would he even know who I am?" Kathleen said.

"The article with your picture was in the *Daily*, Miss Important Somebody," Lynne said.

"Well," Kathleen said, laughing, "is Mr. Ben Davis ever in for a big disappointment!"

"On the contrary," Mary said. "He's probably a big glunch who will never have another chance to date such a hot number. Do be kind to the nobodies, dear. Their lives are so miserable."

Kathleen swatted her with a napkin, and they all dissolved into laughter, causing Mrs. D to look their way and frown. "We all know there are no big glunches in that fraternity, Kathleen," Billie added. "This should be interesting."

Ben Davis was anything but a glunch. Kathleen felt her heart jump a bit when they called her name and she realized he was her date. He was tall, blond, and muscular and with light blue eyes.

"Hi, Kathy," he said.

"It's Kathleen," she said and then felt her face burn. Had she sounded too sharp? Here was the first interesting possibility she'd come across since Guy at Fishers, and the first thing she did was to correct him. She looked at him, concerned, but he was still smiling at her.

"OK, Kath*leen*."

"Sorry, I'm just so used to having to correct people."

"I don't have much trouble with Ben."

"No. I wouldn't think so." She laughed, but it sounded forced. He held the door for her, and they left for the fraternity. They walked nearly half a block in silence. Kathleen's mind raced to think of something else to say. She felt absolutely stupid.

"I was surprised you preferenced me," she said, and then wished she hadn't.

"Well, I saw your picture in the *Daily* and knew we had this exchange coming up, so I figured it would be a good way to meet a Husky songleader."

So, Billie was right. And he hadn't really even wanted to meet *her*, just someone on the squad. Suddenly she didn't feel stupid anymore. She looked at Ben, who was still making no effort at conversation, and laughed with relief.

The exchange turned out to be fun. They went on a scavenger hunt in groups of six. They knocked on the doors of the few private homes and boarding houses that dotted the edges of Greek Row to find outrageous things like a pair of size 13 sneakers—which no one found—or anything from Montana—someone came up with a map—and a tuna sandwich on white bread—an elderly woman made one for Kathleen's group. She didn't even seem surprised to have six college students knock on her door and ask for a sandwich.

To Kathleen's amazement, many of the fraternity brothers congratulated her on being chosen for the rally squad. They were friendly and cute, and it was the best exchange she had yet been to. Ben, however, did not talk much more during the exchange than he had when they walked to the house. The others in their group had done most of the talking and ringing of doorbells. Ben hadn't seemed too interested in her or the scavenger hunt. She had asked him a few questions about himself and found out he was a sophomore majoring in physical education and wanted to be a tennis coach. He didn't ask her anything about herself, however.

Well, she thought as they walked back to her sorority, now he's been out with a Husky songleader. It doesn't seem to have thrilled him.

"Thanks for preferencing me for the exchange," she said at the door. "It was really the most fun one I've been on."

"So are you doing anything tonight? I mean, you want to go to a movie or something?"

She couldn't believe her ears. He had seemed totally unimpressed with her all evening. "Sorry, Ben, but I'm busy tonight. Maybe some other time?" She wasn't busy, but Linda's admonition against accepting a date on the same night as an exchange rang in her ears. Besides, if her picture hadn't been in the paper, she wouldn't have piqued his interest at all. His fraternity brothers had been more attentive—and more fun. Still he was attractive and the first man who had asked her out since she came to the university. She might say yes if he asked her out again, but not tonight. She smiled what she hoped was a sincere smile at Ben.

"Yeah, OK. I'll give you a call." He didn't sound as if he meant it.

"Please do." Neither did she.

She went to the formal with Jake after all. They doubled with Mary and her Beta friend, Mark, whom Mary had been seeing since their first coffee date, and the four of them had a wonderful time.

"How come you can't get excited about Jake?" Mary asked after the dance. "He's cute and funny, and he can dance—sort of."

"He's just a friend, Mar. I don't think of him in any other way. And he doesn't have any romantic feelings for me either. Besides, my mother would die if I ended up with Jake. She thinks he'll never amount to anything. She keeps telling me it's just as easy to fall in love with a rich man as a poor one."

"Yeah, it's just harder to find them, that's all."

Spring elections came for sorority officers, and Kathleen was elected social chairman. She was so surprised and so proud that she burst into tears.

"You'll cry different tears when you see how much work it is next year," Linda whispered and then hugged her. "You have to train all those ignorant freshmen how to appear to have been well-bred. And you have to follow in my footsteps. That could be the hardest part."

"I had such a good example, Linda, how could I fail?" She couldn't wait to call her parents.

"Why, Kathleen, that's wonderful," her mother said. "What do you have to do?"

"Well, besides training the pledges in social graces, I'll be responsible for setting up all the exchanges next year with the social chairmen of the fraternities. I'll be the only active going to all the exchanges, but most of the social chairmen are really neat, so that might be a lot of fun."

"I would think so!" Her mother's voice sounded full of pride. Kathleen smiled and shook her head. "Wait until I tell Mrs. Lavik about this. Now I know you will meet someone special, Kathleen. This is just the opportunity we've been waiting for. I don't think Trudy has been elected to anything at her house."

"I haven't talked to her about it, Mother, so I wouldn't know." Kathleen hung up shortly, still shaking her head, and went back to her room to study for finals.

෨

Spring quarter ended, and Kathleen moved back home for the summer. She got a job working at her father's construction office posting invoices and helping with payroll. She hated all the numbers, and it took her days to master the ten-key adding machine, but she was making a $1.50 an hour, more than she could have made clerking in a department store, so she wasn't complaining.

The office was in an industrial part of town with huge trucks rumbling by all day. Her little cubbyhole was really a partitioned section of the accounting department. There was a tiny desk with the adding machine, some black, metal in- and out-boxes, a telephone, and no window. She brought in a picture of some white daisies in a blue bowl and a green plant in small terra cotta pot, both of which helped to brighten up the drab surroundings for awhile, but the lack of sunlight soon made the plant droop sadly, and Kathleen finally took it home.

Despite the tiny space that was hers, she liked being at her father's company. Sometimes when he was in the office, he would pop in and smile at her, and then they'd go to lunch at the nearby truck stop, aptly named The Other Side of the Tracks for the old train tracks that ran in front of their parking lot. They made the best club house sandwiches Kathleen had had since Gran used to take her to The Bon Marché after ballet lessons when she was small.

"Too bad you'll be getting married someday, Kitten," he told her one day. "You catch on pretty quick to this business. But I can't see you building houses; more like decorating them for your kids."

"I can't see me building houses either, Daddy," she agreed. "But I can't imagine getting married either. I didn't meet a single neat guy this whole year."

"Give it time. You only just started. And now that you're a varsity songleader," he rolled his eyes, "that phone'll be ringing off the hook sooner than you know it."

She laughed and told him about the exchange with Ben Davis.

She and Trudy carpooled to summer practice every Tuesday and Thursday night, since they lived only a few blocks apart.

"How's being on the College Fashion Board, Trudy? Is it fun?" Kathleen asked her the first night.

"It's so hard!" Trudy said. "We have to be on the floor and wait on people just like the regular employees."

"Well, what did you think you'd be doing at a department store?"

"I thought we'd just sort of float around and give tips to the girls who were shopping for college. Especially the ones who are looking for Rush things. But, no. We have to wait on everyone—fat old ladies and all." She gave a delicate Trudy-shudder. "At least we get to wear these *darling* outfits. And we get to keep them. The regular clerks have to wear black or brown or navy blue. I'd die!"

"I guess I'm lucky," Kathleen said. "I just wear regular summer dresses to my job. No one really sees me but the other people in the office."

Trudy didn't respond, and Kathleen could tell her mind was already elsewhere.

Except for the long rides with Trudy, the summer was a good one for Kathleen. The weather was perfect, and most of the time the practices were held outside on the lawn of the HUB in the cool shade of the chestnut trees. The other girls on the squad were friendly and talented, even Elspeth, whose beauty made her appear aloof, but who was turning out to be quite fun. They were all having a ball combining their various styles and ideas into clever new routines.

Kathleen also had lots of meetings to get ready for Rush. She had no inkling when she went through last year that the sophisticated girls she so admired worked so hard inside their grand sorority houses. There were costumes to make, skits to develop, and props to buy. Much of the summer work fell to the Seattle girls, who were in town, and Kathleen loved the bustle of it all. She could hardly wait to experience Rush from this side.

Jake called her in August and invited her to a Rogue rush party on Vashon Island.

"I still can't get over the way you guys do Rush," Kathleen told him. "It's so disorganized."

"You mean because we don't decorate our houses and come skipping out to meet all the fellows in our costumes?"

"You know what I mean. Yours just goes on and on. What's happening at this party?"

"The usual. Bunch of guys in the house and a few outstanding athletes from select high schools who would sell their souls to be Rogues. Same old stuff. Especially when they see the outstanding caliber of women we date."

Kathleen stopped breathing for a second. Not Jake. Surely he was only asking her to the party because he needed a date and they were such old friends. Jake would never parade her around because she was a Husky songleader.

"Beach clothes, then? Shall I bring anything?"

"How about one of your fabulous chocolate cakes, Kath. That'll convince any reluctant rushees to sign. We'll give them a small taste and not let them have any more until they pledge."

Kathleen laughed from pure relief. Not Jake. No, not Jake. "One chocolate cake, coming up. What time will you be here?"

"We have to catch the 11 o'clock ferry, so I'll be by about 10. And throw in your bathing suit. We might go water skiing if one of the guys can get his boat over there."

Kathleen got up early that morning so her cake would be fresh and made it in the sheet pan with a snap-on lid that they used for picnics. After it had cooled, she frosted it with Jake's favorite fudgy frosting and taped an old knife to the bottom, just in case.

It was comfortable to go places with Jake because it didn't matter what she wore or how she looked. There was no pressure, although her mother always admonished her that you never knew whom you might meet, so you should always look your best. She thought a second before she grabbed a new pair of white shorts and a plum-colored top instead of her more comfortable cut-offs. The color was good with her hair, and the white shorts made her passable tan look even darker.

Jake was there at 10 on the dot. He sniffed the cake tin appreciatively and held the door for her as her father told them to have fun and her mother said good-bye without looking at Jake.

As they approached the car, Kathleen noticed another couple in the back seat. "Are we doubling?" she asked him.

"Oh, yeah. I guess I forgot to tell you," Jake answered as he helped her into the car. "Kathleen, this is my friend, Paul Gordon."

Kathleen turned to acknowledge the introduction and nearly stopped breathing. There in the back seat was the most gorgeous man she had ever seen.

"Hi," he said and smiled at her. He was incredibly tan, and the contrast between the brown of his skin and the brilliant blue of his eyes was startling. The sun had streaked his straight blond hair like a lifeguard's and had bleached white the hairs on his well-muscled arms. She didn't hear his date's name at all.

"Paul's family and mine have been friends forever," Jake was explaining to Kathleen. "Our mothers went to school together.

And even though he went to some strange school back East, he at least had the good sense to pledge a decent fraternity back there and has graciously agreed to come help us with the Rush parties."

"I never turn down a party, Jake, Rush or otherwise. Might miss something." He looked at Kathleen until she turned around to face the front.

Jake and Paul then resumed a conversation they had obviously started before Jake went in to get her, about which was the best way to the Vashon ferry. Kathleen was thankful she didn't have to speak. On the ferry, they left the car and went up on deck. All four of them stood in the strong wind of the bow on the short ride to the island. Paul spoke of his recent Mexican trip, which Kathleen realized must explain the tan, while his too-blonde date smiled up at him as if he were declaring the world free from disease. She had his left arm securely wrapped in both of hers.

Kathleen couldn't look at him. She concentrated on the curling waves of the ferry foaming away from the bow and searched the dark water beyond the white trail for jellyfish, as if spotting one counted for something. She could imagine what the wind was doing to her hair.

The house where the party was held was a sprawling V-shaped affair that seemed to have views from every possible room. Kathleen took her cake into the kitchen, which was crowded with people drinking beer or Pepsi, but there was no food there.

"On the deck," someone said to her, noticing her dilemma.

"Thanks," she said and went in the indicated direction through sliding glass doors off the kitchen. From the deck that swept around the entire front of the house, the lawn sloped down to the Sound where barnacled rocks studded the shore. The tide was way out, exposing a smooth sweep of sand, and a dozen or so partygoers were digging clams. The pungent smell of kelp drying on the beach mixed with the scent of newly mown grass. She knew that this was only a "summer home" to Jake's frat brother and wondered briefly what his father did to afford all this luxury. She knew that many of the boys in this fraternity were from wealthy families and imagined her mother's disbelief to see Jake in such an environment. The thought made her smile.

She looked for a space to put her cake down. Several long tables were already filled with food, mostly chips and cans of nuts, but Kathleen was happy to discover that there were few desserts, and nothing that looked remotely as delicious as hers.

"Can you find room for that?" she heard a deep voice say behind her. She turned and found herself inches from Paul Gordon. He had two beers by their necks in one hand, and with the other moved a plate of store-bought cookies out of the way. "There," he said and smiled at her.

"Thank you," she managed and placed the cake on the table, removing the lid.

"Looks good. I may try a piece later. You make it yourself?"

"Yes," she said. "Jake asked me to. It's his favorite." Why had she said that, of all things. Now he would think that she and Jake were an item. But since he knew Jake, then he must know that Jake wasn't going with anyone. She tried to think of something to say to undo this wrong impression, but as she struggled with herself, Paul Gordon took his smile off to his date, and she was left standing by the table alone.

Suddenly, to her great and unexpected relief, she saw Billie heading toward her. They had become good friends over this summer's many practices, and her timing just now couldn't have been better.

"Kathleen, I'm so glad to see you here. What a neat surprise. And, by the way, *who* was that?"

"Jake's friend. He's a Rogue from Dartmouth." Kathleen was relieved to hear her voice sound so normal. "We doubled."

"What a doll!"

"I didn't know you were dating a Rogue," Kathleen said, changing the subject and lowering her voice a bit in case Billie's date was nearby. "You never said a word at practice."

"Just started. He's so cute. Wayne Johnson. That's him over there in the blue shirt by the volleyball net."

"Not bad," Kathleen said, signaling her approval with her eyebrows, grateful for some unknown reason that they weren't talking about Paul anymore.

"Hey, Billie," Jake said, emerging from the kitchen with a beer and a Pepsi. Billie took the Pepsi from him, even though it was obvious he had brought it for Kathleen.

Billie gave Jake a hug. "I promise I'll behave. How did you know I was out of pop?" She lifted the Pepsi in a toast to him.

"You Del Phis," he said. "Such lushes. Back in a sec, Kath."

He disappeared into the kitchen. Billie looked at Kathleen.

"He's so nice. Are you sure you aren't just a little bit interested in him?"

"Like a brother, Billie. We know each other too well."

"I hope you two don't get drunk on these Pepsis and start cheerleading all over the place," Jake said as he returned with another pop for Kathleen.

Billie laughed and touched her drink to Kathleen's. "Let's go see what's happening down there. And I want you to meet Wayne. Thanks, Jake."

The girls went down the stairs to join Wayne and also to meet some of the rushees. Kathleen couldn't help noticing that all the girls at the party were affected by Paul's presence. They swarmed around him, Kathleen thought in disgust. She made it a point to avoid him, which proved to be unnecessary since he never looked at her the rest of the day. He never looked at his date much either, Kathleen noticed, shaking her head at the blatant fawnings of the other girls. He was obviously used to the impact his good looks had on women and handled all of them with practiced smoothness.

Everyone ate, played volleyball or croquet, and some brave souls went water skiing.

"That water's too cold for me," Kathleen told Jake when he dared her to go. Besides, she thought, if my hair looks bad from the ferry, what would salt water do to it?

When Jake dropped Kathleen off at home that night, Paul flashed her his brilliant smile over the head of his sleeping date, who had draped herself over him like a mantle. She thanked Jake for the party and went inside feeling unsettled. Paul was exactly the type she'd expected to find in abundance at the U, but until now hadn't even glimpsed. Even Guy at Fishers with his slow, Southern charm was not in Paul's league. She was desperately glad she had worn a better outfit than she had planned to originally, but even at her best she had made zero impression on him. It would take more than a great pair of shorts to impress Paul Gordon, but Kathleen wasn't sure what that might be. He probably went for the beauties, but his date was nothing to write home about. Mary would have called her a fuzz head, as much for what was outside as for what obviously wasn't inside her head.

Oh, well, she thought as she climbed into bed later, he was probably so conceited, there was no getting through to him. And she probably would never see him again anyway. Still, it took her a while to fall asleep.

Chapter 4

September 1960

At the end of the summer, Kathleen moved back to the sorority house for Work Week. There was much hugging and lots of noise as summer stories were told and retold. Kathleen's pledge class was minus about ten girls. Five of their classmates had passed the coveted candle at chapter dinner last year, including Miss Seattle and Sally from Olympia. Three had gotten married, and the other two had quit school to go to work and "save up for the wedding."

"Looks like we'll be here right up to our senior years, Rushing our little hearts out," Mary said.

Kathleen realized how much she had missed her zany friend during the summer. They had seen each other at the Rush meetings and had gone out to movies a couple of times, but since they lived so far apart and Mary had an evening job at a local burger place while Kathleen worked days, their meetings and even phone calls had been infrequent.

They moved their things into their new rooms, which were assigned by seniority, seniors and juniors getting first pick of location and roommates, sophomores filling in the rest. Kathleen was thrilled to wind up in a corner room with Billie on the second floor right behind the willow tree. There was a window on each outside wall, one with a window seat, and the room was filled with light.

Mary was in the identical room on the third floor just above them. "I'll just stomp on the floor if I need to talk to you. Or maybe we could do that waxed string thing with orange juice cans and have our own phone line through the windows. It would sure beat running up and down the stairs."

"If we get a break, let's hit the waterfront import shops for some pillows," Billie suggested to both of them. "That would make those window seats look so darling."

"And so cozy while we chatted on our juice cans," Mary added.

"And we could pile some more pillows on the day bed," Kathleen said. "I love this room."

But Work Week was aptly named, and it was several days before they could escape anywhere. They practiced songs, especially their clap song, to be sure the sophomores understood how their lines moved up so they could grab the next rushee. They divided into groups and worked on skits. A Del Phi alum in her forties came and reminded them with introductions that the rushees already knew their own names and to be sure to face the Del Phi, not the rushee, when speaking it. They drilled on how to get down to and up from the floor gracefully.

"Drop gently to both knees, ladies, and then sit on one hip or the other. Then, with your feet together, push yourself onto your feet and rise. Never get back to your knees and put one foot and then the other up in front of you. Everyone for miles can see right up your skirt that way!"

They put photos of girls in the house who were queens or officers into attractive silver frames and arranged them on various tables throughout the living room, including a shot of the three songleaders in their uniforms waving their pom-poms. During the first round of parties, the three of them in uniform would perform

"Bow Down to Washington," so during skit practice they worked on perfecting the routine. Also, in the middle of everything, the three would dash to the HUB for their regular practice, because the first game would be Saturday, during Rush.

"If nothing else," Patty said, "we should come out of Rush in terrific shape."

"Or dead from exhaustion!" Kathleen said, wiping the perspiration from her forehead with the sleeve of her shirt. "These pom-poms are getting heavier by the minute."

In high school they had made their pom-poms by cutting crepe paper into strips and gathering them in the middle with adhesive tape. They were virtually weightless. The Husky pom-poms came from a supplier and were made of thin, machine-cut strips of crepe paper wrapped around and around a wooden block, over which a plastic handle was fastened. There was a loop across the block for the hand to slip through. The first time Kathleen saw them, she was impressed. They looked so much sharper than the homemade ones, and they didn't "grow" in the damp weather. They stayed crisp and beautiful and made a wonderful swishing sound as she shook them. But as the practice grew longer, the wooden blocks seemed to weigh a ton. The morning after the first full practice where she had used them, her arms felt as they had the first time she tried water skiing. She could barely pull up the sheets to make her bed. She couldn't believe that something as innocuous as a pom-pom could wreak such havoc.

"I must be really out of shape," she complained to Billie.

"No, it's like the old Indian clubs they made us use in gym. It builds up the upper body. Maybe even the boobs, who knows?"

Finally, it was the first day of tours. Everyone filed in front of Molly Chambliss, the Rush chairman, to be checked for girdles and makeup. The Del Phis wore the same monogrammed sweaters over white blouses that Kathleen remembered from last year, and she thought they looked wonderful. But this was the first time she was wearing her cheer uniform in public. It was thrilling. The short white skirt felt so odd and freeing compared to the below-the-knee uniforms from Richmond High. Hemlines were creeping up, that was true, but their high school advisor would never have allowed them to show so much leg! As she had pulled the sweater over her head and looked into the mirror earlier, she couldn't quite believe it. She was actually that Husky songleader in the reflection! There was the braided purple and gold W wrapping itself over her shoulders and ending in a V in the back of the sweater. It was like a dream.

She grabbed her pom-poms and ran down to take her place with Billie and Patty at the end of the lines. Unless they had a huge tour group outside, the three of them wouldn't take anyone. They would "float" and try to meet as many girls as they could, and they would do their routine to "Bow Down to Washington" for the party's entertainment. They waited silently inside the double doors for Molly to signal the exact moment for them to send up their opening cheer. Checking her watch, Molly held up three fingers, counting down to one. The foyer erupted into noise as she and her assistant swung the doors open and ran with the two lines of Del Phis following them to meet the waiting group.

The butterflies in Kathleen's stomach disappeared the moment she saw the nervous looks and tentative smiles of the rushees as they were hustled through the clapping, bouncing lines and into the living room. She remembered her uncertainty and Mary's gentle ridicule of her ignorance about Rush, and her heart went out to these girls. She went around and talked to as many as possible, but as the day wore on, it became more and more difficult to think of something new to say. She remembered how tired she had grown of being asked her major and her high school. By the end of the last party, Kathleen was exhausted.

"I'm boiling. I think I should burn my sweater," she told Mary. "I wore a men's T-shirt underneath to keep the wool from scratching, like Billie said, but it's drenched!"

"Well, so is my blouse, and I haven't even done one routine," Mary said, pulling her blue sweater over her head and fanning herself with it.

"OK, everyone, upstairs and change so we can eat and get started with our hash session right away," Molly announced to the room at large. "You can shower later."

Hope Chest

They assembled in the dining room to a pick-up meal of sandwiches, fruit, and chocolate pinwheel cookies and took their places at the long tables facing Molly and the alumnae advisors. Lisa Baxter, the membership chairman, sat at one end behind a large box of files and papers.

"OK," Molly said. "For you sophomores who haven't done this before, here's what we do so we can all get out of here before midnight. I will read off the list of rushees from the first tour group and the name of the Del Phi who signed her nametag. That girl will give a brief description and her recommendation as to whether we carry or drop her. If anyone else has a comment, raise your hand. First girl, Patti Grendahl from Lincoln of Tacoma."

"I had her," said a voice behind Kathleen. "She wore a red plaid skirt and had a kind of messy ponytail. I say no."

"Wait a minute," said another voice. "I went to school with her. She's really tops."

Kathleen tried to remember if she had met Patti Grendahl, but the whole day sort of ran together. There were hundreds of girls with red plaid skirts and ponytails.

"Did anyone else talk to her?" Molly asked.

"I remember her," another girl said. "She's just OK. Put her on the maybe list. She might be worth looking at again."

"OK, the maybe list," Molly said. "All in favor?"

There was a chorus of Ayes. Molly read the next name, and the next. They went over each girl. Sometimes no one could remember anything about a particular girl, not even the Del Phi who hosted her and signed the nametag. Other times arguments broke out.

"Sandy Hollis."

"I had her. She's a drop."

"Wait a minute. She's really neat."

"You can't pledge her anyway." This from one of the alums. "She only has a 2.3 G.P.A. Sorry, but you know the rule: we carry no one under a 2.8. Someone with low grades like that could ruin your chapter average."

"Plus we don't have a recommend on her anyway," said the membership chairman, ruffling through the box in front of her.

111

"But she was homecoming queen. She is *darling*! I'll write a recommend."

"Recs have to come from alums. Sorry."

"Besides we don't need any 'darling' dummies," said the first voice. "Drop her."

The fact of recommendations had floored Kathleen. No one could be pledged without one, she found out. The alumnae had to verify grades and activities for each of the 900-plus rushees. They also had to determine if the family could swing things financially.

Even with the alum advisor's patient explanation that, after all, the house was a business and they had to be assured that each pledge could make it for the full four years, both scholastically and financially, Kathleen felt there was a violation of sorts. She imagined what people must have said when she had blundered so naively onto the scene. And where they had dredged up a recommendation for her still remained a mystery.

The discussions dragged on and on. Rushees she thought were wonderful were reviled by others. "How can they be so sure after two minutes of conversation?" she whispered to Mary. "Maybe they just didn't know how to dress for tours. I certainly didn't."

They also were reminded that they could pledge only two nursing majors, because they had to move out after two years to continue their program.

Hash lasted until 11:30, and then there was a long line for the showers. Kathleen didn't get to bed until nearly 1 o'clock. Her legs and arms ached. She longed to stay in the pounding shower forever but got out quickly so the rest of the girls could have their turns. It seemed as if she had barely climbed under her quilt when the alarm rang and it was time to do the whole thing over again.

This day was even warmer than the day before, but somehow the excitement she had anticipated yesterday came back to her, and she joined her Del Phi sisters when the doors swung open in singing their clap song at the top of her voice. The rushees seemed more relaxed as well, and conversation seemed to flow more naturally. Throughout the day she whirled through ten presentations of "Bow Down" and waved her pom-poms good-bye to 500 more smiling faces beside the willow tree. This time, in spite of Molly's warning, she ran to the shower before dinner and slipped much more comfortably into her muu muu for hash. She even put a couple of rollers into her damp hair and donned her ruffled roller bonnet so that she could wear her hair up to hash. All the perspiring was causing her curls to electrify, and she hoped the extra time in the large rollers would ease out some of the frizz.

Now that she had an idea what the inside of Rush was all about, she made it a point during the day to remember the names of girls she particularly liked, jotting a note or two to herself and cramming it into her message box by the phones just before each party. Two girls from Richmond had come through the house today, and she wanted to be able to vouch for them if anyone had questions.

They raced through hash, despite several quarrels, so they could set up the house for the ski party. Even so, it was nearly 11:30 again when they straggled out of the dining room to begin decorating.

"Where are all the fabled frat boys when you need them?" she asked Mary as they lugged skis and poles up the stairs from the luggage room.

"Smoke and mirrors, dear girl, smoke and mirrors. But actually some of the girls are out 'night gardening' with some of the guys from next door so we can have greenery for the railings."

Kathleen and Mary carted in firewood that someone's parents had donated for the fireplace and laid the fire for the morning. "We'll probably really need this fire, Kath, since it's going to be a mere 75 degrees tomorrow and we'll be wearing only a few layers of ski clothes," Mary grumbled.

One group was cutting out nametags and threading them with silver pins. Still another group counted the tags into piles of 35. They wouldn't know exactly how many would be in each party until the next morning after the rushees marked their acceptance cards and they got the computer lists from Panhellenic. Then there would only be time for last-minute shifts. The house manager inspected the powder room and put up a sign that read "NOBODY uses this bathroom. NOBODY!!!"

"I don't have time to keep running in here and checking for water spots and empty toilet paper rolls," she announced to everyone in earshot. "This has to be clean for the rushees. Go upstairs if you have to go!"

The parties passed in a blur of names and skits and decorations. Hash sessions lasted forever and continued to be painful. There were girls she loved whom other people didn't like and vice versa. There were girls she never even met whom others argued over for hours. There was one girl everyone liked, but some alum had sent in a negative recommend on her, so she had to be dropped.

"Why do we have to do what some old biddy wants?" Kathleen asked Mary, not daring to question the alums directly in hash. "It's been centuries since they were in school."

"I don't get it either. Especially that one tonight. They said she had a bad reputation. To them that probably means she wears a half-slip instead of a full one."

All of Rush faded for Kathleen, however, when it was time for the first Husky game. She and Billie and Patty met in the foyer and checked that they had everything—gloves, pom poms, tights, jackets, and yellow mums for their hair, which Patty had picked up earlier from the florist on the Ave. They ran to the Sigma Chi house to meet the rest of the squad, including the six men on the yell squad and the president of the Sundodgers. All fifteen of them poured into the Sundodger jalopy, an ancient convertible painted vaguely purple and gold, and headed down 45th toward Husky Stadium. They sat on seats, laps, and the folded-down convertible top.

Fans had already started to stream in from the parking lots, outnumbering the ubiquitous seagulls that circled the old garbage dump at the far north end of the parking area. They waved and flashed victory signs at the rally squad, and Kathleen waved her pom-poms back. She was sure there was not enough room in her chest for all the happiness she felt. It was the most thrilling thing she had ever done. Even Trudy, wedged into the space next to her, didn't diminish anything.

They drove right to the east end of the stadium and piled out of the car. As the people in the stands caught sight of them running in on the track, a loud roar built. The visiting high school bands picked up the excitement and responded with drum cadences, several different ones, and the yell kings plied their megaphones to try to make some coherent cheer out of what was simply noise.

The six bands rarely were in time with one another, so the girls' carefully practiced routines suffered greatly in the translation. They roasted in their wool sweaters, and the dust from the cinder track coated their sweat-glistening legs, which seemed to bother Trudy even more than the uncoordinated music. Kathleen's hair turned to frizz, and her flower lost most of its petals. But the Huskies won, and it was glorious, beyond anything she had imagined it to be. The response from the fans was heady, and she hugged Billie as they all jogged back to the car.

"I never realized how fabulous the card stunts looked," Kathleen said. "You can't tell when you're in the stands holding those unwieldy colored cards that the people across the way can actually see a picture of something. It was incredible seeing them from the field."

"Well, it's sort of a trade-off, don't you think?" Billie responded. "We can see the card stunts from here, but we can't see the game."

"That's true," Elspeth joined in. "Why does the team have to stand on the bench all the time? There's no one in front of them. It's like looking at a purple brick wall."

"As long as we can see the end zones, ladies, and all those lovely touchdowns," Max, the yell king, added, "that's the important part."

"And that there wasn't one of those lovely touchdowns right after those cards were passed out," Gabby, the Alpha Gam from Mary's school, added. "Last year it seemed to happen at every game, and everyone would toss those heavy cards into the air, and you took your life in your hands, hoping not to get hit by any of them. My roommate got clobbered at the USC game."

They all squeezed happily back into the jalopy, and the breeze when they finally stopped inching their way through the wild crowd felt wonderful against Kathleen's face. They passed several rushees whom Kathleen recognized and waved at. The sight of them reminded her that they had to hurry back to shower and change for two more parties that evening. She was exhausted, but she felt wonderful. She even hugged Trudy when they all split up back at Sigma Chi and smiled at the quizzical look on her face.

Finally it was preference night, and thankfully most of their first choices were at the last party, with more than a few happy tears blotted by tissues that magically appeared from the boxes stowed for that purpose by the alumnae volunteers. The Del Phis closed their doors for the last time and whooped at their success.

The next morning the stress of Rush was forgotten when the Panhellenic lists finally arrived and they found out just who had accepted their bids. Girls with crossed fingers shrieked and hugged one another as a favorite's name was read. Then new Big Sisters took long-stemmed yellow roses and dashed for the HUB as the frenzy of moving the new pledges into the sorority began.

Mary helped Kathleen set up the dining room for the pledge meeting.

"It seems like yesterday that we were sitting in this meeting in the last pre-girdle moments we would ever know, and now you're the bad guy!"

"Thanks, pal," Kathleen said and straightened her notes for the third time. She was going in to give the same instructions on manners and house rules to the new pledges that Linda had given to her class last year. "I just hope I'll have the same effect that Linda did. She seemed so perfect, and I'm . . ."

"So much shorter, I know. But don't worry, you're bossier."

"Thanks, friend. How did I manage before I met you?"

"I wondered that myself."

Kathleen's nervousness vanished when the lovely and eager pledges filed into the dining room. It was thrilling to be able to do for these girls what Delta Phi Tau had done for her.

"Hi, I'm Kathleen Andrews, your social chairman," she said when they got settled, "and what we're going to be doing over the next few weeks is giving you the tools to make your life at the U and after you graduate smooth and comfortable in all social situations."

Hope Chest

When classes began, Kathleen was instantly immersed in her course work with Professor Hawkins. She couldn't help with the Saturday workshops as she had last spring because of the football games, but Hawk had assured her she could resume her old tasks next quarter. She had loved working with the grade-schoolers as Hawk spun her magic with them and was relieved that her professor wanted her back next quarter. In the meantime, Kathleen was taking more courses in children's literature. She spent long hours in the children's section of the library searching for new or obscure stories that would lend themselves to imaginative play.

And she worked on routines. After the disastrous music of the opening game, having the Husky band was ambrosia. The throb of the drums seemed to well up from the very ground. They not only sounded fabulous, but they seemed to have a new song every week. The director had pulled in all kinds of music, from "Peter Gunn" to the hopeful "California, Here I Come." While they had made up several routines during the summer to a tape the director had supplied them with, these new songs meant lots of work between the games, creating and polishing the new repertoire.

The crowd responded enthusiastically to their efforts, making it all worthwhile. And the purple and gold umbrellas they decided to use in their "Singin' in the Rain" routine did double duty at the one game when it really *did* rain. Kathleen and Billie even got their picture in the Sunday paper holding their umbrellas over the Husky mascot to keep him dry. And after a one-field-goal loss, the team won and *won*. It looked as if they would be in the Rose Bowl again for sure. The band started playing "Everything's Coming up Roses."

Putting the exchanges together with the social chairmen from the fraternities was also turning out to be fun. More than one of the guys called her for dates after the exchanges, much to her mother's delight.

"Normally, I wouldn't tell her about too many of these casual dates," she told Mary, "but I thought it might take her mind off the election. She's really upset that Kennedy is President."

"You're kidding. Why? I think he's wonderful."

"So do I. I would have voted for him if we were old enough to vote. She has a thing about Catholics and thinks the Pope will be running the country now. So I tell her about my dates. Actually, no one is making my heart do flips, but at last I have some choices to ask to the Pledge Dance besides poor old Jake."

Pledge dances and final exams and Presidential election results faded into insignificance after the final game, however. The Huskies had done it again: they were Rose Bowl bound! The stands exploded as the final whistle blew, and the band with the rally squad at the head swept around the track to a now positive "California, Here I Come."

"I'm so proud of you, Kitten," Kathleen's father said later when she finally got a free phone to call home.

"I didn't have anything to do with it, Daddy."

"Nonsense. Who cheered them on? It was all your doing, I tell you."

Kathleen laughed and felt wonderful. "We get to perform at Disneyland and Marine Land and Knott's Berry Farm. And I think there's some kind of big rally on New Year's Eve. But the most exciting thing is that we get to ride on the float in the Rose Parade."

"They have everything planned out already? They must have been pretty confident."

"Billie and Patty got to go last year, and that's what they did. I'm sure it will be pretty much the same. I can't wait!"

"We'll look for you on television. Be sure to wave when you see a camera."

The day after Christmas the rally squad and the Husky Marching Band boarded the charter plane for California. Kathleen was nervous as they rose through the thick clouds that blanketed Seattle. It was her first flight, and all the thumps and bumps caused her to grip her arm rests tightly. Billie noticed and patted her hand.

"Those noises are supposed to be there. Relax and enjoy it. We could have been on a bus."

One of the yell leaders had brought a banjo, and soon the sounds of "Leland Stanford Junior Varsity Farm" and "Tom Dooley" chased her anxieties away. They sang their way to California and were soon on land again and ensconced in the spartan dormitories of a nearby college.

One of the female trumpeters from the band played "Reveille" up and down the halls every morning at 7 a.m. When the brass notes bounced off the concrete walls of the dorm, further attempts at sleep were fruitless. But it didn't matter to any of them. The weather was perfect all week. They practiced their routines in shorts on the beach, laughing when their bare feet refused to spin in the wet sand and they went sprawling. They marched down Main Street at Disneyland and had a pep rally on the stage at Marine Land where the seals usually performed.

There were Husky fans everywhere in purple and gold who flashed them victory signs and applauded their entrances. There were Minnesota fans, too, who gave them good-natured thumbs-down signals—and a few serious boos.

Early in the morning on game day, they gathered to board the Husky float, slipping on the tightly packed beds of chrysanthemums and grabbing for the wire supports at each station where they were to stand.

"Can you even bear it?" Cindy, the cheerleader from Bellevue, said to Kathleen as they arranged themselves in the supports. "We are in the *Rose Parade*! I could just die!"

"Me too," Kathleen said, looking around her at the throngs of uniformed band members, drill teams, exquisite floats, and horses, all quivering in place like heat waves, unable to move anywhere. "Pinch me to see if I'm really here!" They laughed again and swatted at each other with their pom-poms.

Even Trudy was silly, Kathleen noticed, practicing her "queen wave" and then giggling hysterically. The sharp smells of the crushed mums underfoot swirled around them as they waited their turn. Finally, their tall, handsome drum major raised his long silver baton in both hands high over his head, blew the familiar one long and four short blasts on his shrill whistle, circled his baton in a huge arc, and pointed them all toward the parade route. With a slight jerk, the float slid into place behind the perfect lines of the Husky Marching Band as they struck up "Glory of the Gridiron." Goose bumps rose on Kathleen's arms. She and Cindy waved to the cheering spectators packed along the sides of the street. It was starting.

Along the route they picked out a few people they knew who shouted to them by name, but most of it was a blur. Then she spotted Jake, frantically waving both his long arms and whistling.

"Hey, Jake!" she shouted back. "Cindy, there's Jake." She pointed with her pom-pom.

He flashed them a victory sign and nudged the fellow next to him. Kathleen looked to see who it was and caught her breath. There was Paul Gordon, the handsome friend they doubled with last summer. His arms were crossed, and he was smiling the slow, superior smile she remembered. He lifted his chin to her in greeting as their eyes met, and then the float moved past them. Cindy had noticed him too.

"Who was that with Jake?"

"A friend of his from Dartmouth. We doubled last summer to a Rush party."

"Maybe I should transfer to Dartmouth."

"Save your money, Cindy. He thinks he's God's gift."

"Could be he is. He sure looks like it."

The parade moved on, and Paul Gordon faded from their attention. They arrived at the Rose Bowl and wound their way through walls of people to the gate. Then they were inside. Their squad had only gone to two away games this year, and all the stadiums they'd been in, including their own, had at least one open end. Here they were encircled. Kathleen's pulse throbbed with the pounding drums as she ran down the track to the Husky section. The fans roared. The sun was wicked on them at the base of the bowl, but Kathleen didn't mind. The poor mascot with his heavy coat of fur was panting, his ears and tail drooping piteously in the sun. It was not a sign of defeat, however. The Huskies burst into the stadium and passed and marched their way to a 17 to 7 victory.

Pandemonium continued as victory-crazed fans mobbed the field and tore down the wooden goal posts. Amazingly, Kathleen saw Jake in the throng, and he picked her up and spun her around.

"Here, Kath. A souvenir." He broke off a splinter of the goalpost he had snagged and handed it to her.

"Hey, thanks!" she said, thrilled with her treasure. Then she glanced around, but Paul Gordon was not with Jake. Just as well, she thought, surprised to feel disappointed. Jake would probably have had to remind him who she was anyway. She hugged Jake and ran off with her scrap of goalpost to show the others and to board the buses for the airport.

Chapter 5

April 1961

If Kathleen expected a letdown after the excitement of football season, she was mistaken. No sooner had they returned to campus when basketball season started with a bang, and there were sometimes several games a week. She had to have someone stand in for her on exchanges more than once because of a game. In her classes, her professors seemed to specialize in term papers, and she practically lived in the library. But her hard work was worth it. She got her first 4.0.

"Dean's list, Daddy," she told her father at dinner when her grades arrived in the mail during spring break.

"Not surprising, Kitten." He kissed her on the cheek. "We're very proud of you, you know."

"It's not good to appear too smart, Kathleen," her mother said.

"Oh, Joan, she appears to be just about perfect, and any man would be a fool not to see that. Just be yourself, honey, and there's nothing better."

"Well, men don't like to feel that a woman knows more than they do, I can tell you that for sure." Mrs. Andrews blotted her lips and rose to clear the table. Kathleen moved to help her. Her mother's cooking was infinitely better than the food at Delta Phi, but Kathleen was happy to head back to the sorority.

Back in her room, Kathleen heard her name over the intercom. "Kathleen Andrews, line two."

She went to the phone booth in the hall and pushed the flashing button.

"Hello."

"Kathleen Andrews?" said a deep, unfamiliar voice.

"Yes, this is Kathleen." She thought it was probably the call she was expecting regarding the next exchange.

"I don't know if you remember me or not, but this is Paul Gordon. Jake's friend from Dartmouth."

She couldn't speak.

"Kathleen?"

"Yes, Paul. Of course I remember you. How are you?" *How are you?* She closed her eyes. Who would not remember him? And who would sound so stupid? "Are you calling from Dartmouth?"

"Yes, I am actually, but I'm coming to town in two weeks for my mother's birthday, and Jake tells me the Rogue formal is that Saturday night. Would you like to go with me? It might be fun."

He was calling LONG DISTANCE! Her mind raced. "I . . . why, yes, I'd love to."

"Wonderful. I was hoping you'd be free. It was fun to watch you at the Rose Bowl—somebody down there I actually knew. I'm looking forward to getting to know you better."

Her stomach was aflutter. She slid down the wall of the booth and sat on the little bench.

"I'll call you when I get to town and tell you when I'll pick you up. I'll have to get all the particulars from Jake, but I wanted to be sure you were available."

"Yes, I'm available." She felt so muddled; everything she said seemed to come out wrong.

"All right, then. I'll call you when I get in."

"Yes. OK. Bye."

"Good-bye, Kathleen."

She hung up the phone and just sat in the booth staring at it. Then she ran down the hall yelling for Mary.

"I've never seen you in such a twit," Mary said. "Who is this man? You've never even mentioned him."

"There was nothing to mention. He never even gave me a second look when Jake and I doubled with him last summer. Besides, he doesn't even go to the U."

"I saw him at that party," Billie said. She'd followed Kathleen into Mary's room when she heard the noise and came to see what was happening. "He's pretty gorgeous, all right. I do remember that."

"What does he do? Who are his people?" Mary joked.

"He goes to Dartmouth, and he's a Rogue, and Jake's mother and his are friends." Kathleen realized that besides that, she really knew nothing about him.

"Do you even know what year he is or what he's majoring in?"

"No."

"Great credentials. Call Jake and get the details." Mary pushed Kathleen out the door and down the hall to the ironing room. "In the meantime, let's check out formals that will appeal to this Adonis."

Kathleen tried on all of her dresses, and all of Mary's. Nothing seemed right. Billie volunteered a lovely beige strapless that fit perfectly, but the color made Kathleen look ill.

"We'll go shopping," Mary said, "after you find out from Jake if this guy's worth the investment. Go call him now."

She went dutifully to the phone booth and came back to Mary's room a short time later with a look of amazement on her face. "I never put the name to it, but his dad owns Gordon's!"

"Oh, my Gawd," Mary yelped. "*The* Gordon's. The very place I was going to take you to find the perfect formal? The tastiest dress shop in the whole city? That Gordon's?"

"Yes. And he's majoring in business because he's going into the family store as soon as he graduates this spring."

"Not possible, gorgeous and filthy rich. And an older man. The gods are smiling on you, Kathleen, old girl. All these lonely months of penance at all those exchanges and all those hymns and prayers at Fishers have brought you to this glory."

Kathleen laughed at Mary. "I hope those gods bring me a dress to wear, or I won't have to wait until midnight to be seen in my rags."

The two weeks sped by in a flurry of shopping and trial hairstyles and nervous anticipation. Paul called her on Thursday when he got in to tell her he would pick her up at six on Saturday for dinner before the dance.

At five o'clock, Mary zipped Kathleen into the long white sheath she finally found at a small shop on the Ave that specialized in wedding gowns and formals. It was a sleeveless silk organza that had a cropped top above a tight black insert at the waist. Horizontal pleats that began at the neck continued below the waist to the hem. The only other decoration was a tiny black bow above the right hip. Mary lent her some rhinestone and jet earrings.

"Understated. Elegant. Boob-enhancing. It's perfect," Mary said. They both examined the reflection in the full-length mirror behind the closet door. "Now sit and let me do your hair." She began pulling the rollers out of Kathleen's hair and tossing them into a sack. Then she brushed out the roller marks and smoothed the back into a French roll.

"I still don't think it's long enough to stay, Mar."

"Not to fret. I'll put a thousand pins in it and spray it to death. A tornado won't dislodge it." She pulled curls down around Kathleen's face and ratted the top to give her some height. "Now hold your breath."

Kathleen put her hands over her face as Mary mercilessly sprayed her hair. Finally, gasping, Kathleen ran into the hall to take deep breaths of clear air. "That stuff will kill us all!" she said.

"Yes, but we'll go out looking great."

Mary arranged to be on "door duty" so she could get a look at Paul without having to hide in the coatroom. Kathleen waited with her in the powder room, nervously checking her lipstick and the contents of her beaded bag for the millionth time. She had a small comb that would be utterly useless if her hair didn't hold, her lipstick, a clean hanky, and a dime for the phone, as her mother always admonished. Her hands were damp and her heart was pounding. Mary had done miracles with her hair and makeup, and the dress was fabulous. Why did she feel so inadequate? Especially when she had been so scornful of Paul Gordon at the Rogue party last summer. Could it have been because he hadn't paid any attention to her then?

The doorbell rang. Mary threw her a look and went out to the foyer to answer it. She came into the powder room rolling her eyes. "He's beautiful!" she declared. "See if we can have him bronzed."

Kathleen laughed, then sobered as she took a last dissatisfied look at herself. Grabbing her black evening coat, she took a deep breath and went to meet Paul as calmly as possible.

He stood when she came into the living room and smiled at her the way he had when Jake had introduced them last summer. She had forgotten how tall he was. His tan was gone now, and his hair was darker without the sun-streaks, but his eyes were as blue as she remembered. He looked like a movie star in his tuxedo.

"Wow," he drew out the word. "You look fabulous. I wasn't sure what color your dress would be, but I knew these would go with your hair."

He handed her a box with a beautiful corsage of dark red roses with black velvet leaves and ribbon.

"It's perfect, Paul. Thank you. I'll put it on when we get there so it doesn't get crushed." She knew if she tried to pin it on now, her trembling hands would give her away.

He helped her with her coat and guided her to the front door, his hand at the small of her back. They went to dinner at Canlis, where the maitre d' knew Paul and seated them at a window table himself. Kathleen had never been to such an expensive restaurant before, although she knew her mother claimed it was her favorite.

"Do you mind if I order for us?" Paul asked her.

"Please." She was relieved that she would not have to decide what would be acceptable to order from the high-priced items on the menu. From what Jake said, the Gordons had money, but she didn't want to order the wrong thing and have him think she didn't have good taste or worse that she would pick the most expensive thing.

He ordered the special Canlis salad, which Kathleen noted was not part of the dinner and was quite expensive. Then he ordered a filet mignon for her and a New York steak for himself. "How do you prefer your steak, Kathleen?"

"Medium rare, please."

"The lady will have her steak medium rare," he told the kimonoed waitress, "and I'll have mine rare. And please bring us an order of scallops first."

Kathleen's heart stopped. She had been sitting there entranced at his command of the moment and the good choices he had made as if reading her mind, but she hated scallops. She had never tasted them before joining Delta Phi Tau. They had them on Friday nights at the house occasionally, alternating with dreadful fish sticks and tuna casserole. The scallops were like erasers, they were so tough. Once, because the housemother didn't attend Friday dinners, they had a contest to see who could bounce them higher off the plates.

"Wait until you taste these scallops, Kathleen. They're the world's best."

She smiled what she hoped would be a bright smile. The scallops soon appeared, looking not at all like the small, breaded things she knew. These were large and flat and coated in a light, crispy crust with slivered almonds on them, and they smelled of lemon. Hesitantly she took a bite and could not believe the tender, delicious morsel in her mouth.

"They're wonderful!"

"I told you they would be."

"I'm sure they wouldn't bounce at all," Kathleen said and started to laugh. "You have no idea how I was fearing them."

Paul raised one eyebrow at her, and she told him the story. "I was set to be polite," she said, "but these are magnificent."

"Perhaps this will teach you to trust me," he said, and they laughed together.

After dinner they drove to the country club where the formal was already in progress. Jake flagged them down as they came in.

"We saved you a place at our table," he said. "Kath, you look terrific."

"Doesn't she?" Paul said.

She warmed at Jake's compliment, but the tone of Paul's voice made her stomach do an elevator dip. Jake introduced them around the table. His date was a girl Kathleen knew slightly from Rush, a cute blonde Pi Phi. She wondered how long they had been dating. Jake hadn't mentioned her before. She made a mental note to ask him when they danced.

The band played "When I Fall in Love," and Paul held out his hand. "Shall we?"

They made their way to the dance floor. Paul was a superb dancer. Kathleen could follow his strong lead easily. While many of the couples were simply swaying in small circles, Paul spun her expertly around the floor.

"You follow beautifully," he said, smiling down on her.

"You lead beautifully," she responded. The perfume from the roses at her shoulder mingled with the faint scent of his aftershave. The nervousness she felt before dinner had completely dissolved. He was surprisingly easy to be with. That he could dance so beautifully was a bonus.

The music switched to a swing number, and she expected Paul to lead her back to the table. All during high school, she and her friends raced to be home every afternoon by 4 o'clock to watch *American Bandstand* and bemoaned the fact that no local boys could dance like the boys on that program. At slumber parties and cheer practice the girls would jitterbug with one another, practicing new moves they had seen Kenny and Arlene do, but at school dances they were resigned to sitting out the fast ones.

She hesitated just a moment, waiting to follow Paul back to their seats. To her great surprise, he wrapped his arm around her waist and began to dance exactly as she and her friends had longed to. They spun and twirled and separated and came back together as if they had choreographed the number. Several other dancers made room for them and stood at the edge of the dance floor to watch. When the number ended, people clapped.

"I can't believe you can dance like that," Kathleen said. She felt warm and short of breath and deliciously happy. "Is that a Dartmouth thing, or were you born that way?"

He threw back his head and laughed. "It's a my-mother-made-me-take-dance-lessons-at-her-club thing. And now I think I must thank her."

They danced most of the dances, including a rumba, which Kathleen had never done before.

"It's easy," he said. "Just like the waltz. A box step with a different rhythm. Just follow me."

It *was* easy. One-two-*one*, one-two-*one*. He gave her a gentle push on the back and guided her under his arm in a slow circle. One-two-*one*, one-two-*one*.

"We're like Arthur and Kathryn Murray," she said. "I should have bought a Ginger Rogers dress." Suddenly she blushed, realizing she had admitted to buying a new dress for the occasion.

"I like the one you have on," he said smoothly.

They traded partners with Jake and his date once, a slow dance.

"Looks like someone's having a swell time," Jake said.

"He's really something," Kathleen admitted.

"It appears the feeling is mutual."

"I don't know, Jake. He's so smooth, he probably makes all his dates feel that way. And how about you? Have you been seeing this one very long?"

"Only a few weeks, but she's pretty neat. Besides, if you're going to be unavailable for my functions, I've got to have some reserves."

Kathleen laughed, but wished she could get the subject back to Paul's feelings for her. She had changed the focus herself, and now she didn't know how to undo it without seeming too interested. She waited for Jake to say something else, but he didn't, and soon the song was over and they went back to the table.

Finally it was the last dance. Paul held her close and pressed his lips to her hair. She was afraid he could feel her heart pounding. She didn't want the music to end.

He would be going back to school tomorrow, and she might never see him again. The last note of "Goodnight, Sweetheart"

Hope Chest

swirled around them, but Paul didn't release her. They stood there, looking at each other. Then the lights came on and the orchestra started packing up. They chatted with Jake and his date for a few more minutes and then headed with everyone else for the parking lot.

They drove back to the sorority the long way, along the lake and through the Arboretum. The pink of the spring blossoms stood out even in the darkness. Paul held her hand as he drove, but they didn't talk. Finally at the house, he parked the car and turned to her. "I wish I didn't have to leave tomorrow. I really want to get to know you better. May I write to you?"

"Of course. I'd love that."

"I'll be finished this June, and then I'm coming home for good."

Kathleen nodded, but she couldn't think of a thing to say. He was talking about the future, but she wasn't sure he meant to include her in it, and she didn't want to imply that she thought he had. She just smiled.

He reached across the back of the seat and drew Kathleen to him. Lifting her chin with his fingers, he kissed her softly on the lips. "You are really something. What an unexpected surprise."

She wondered briefly what that meant. Compared to the girls at Dartmouth perhaps? Were there girls at Dartmouth? She didn't even know. And with his lips on hers she didn't even care. Nor did she care that it was against the rules to kiss so near the front of the house. She was not going to let this moment pass. But then she saw the clock on the dashboard. It was nearly 2 o'clock. She couldn't be late.

"I have to be in in three minutes or I turn into a pumpkin."

He furrowed his brow at her. "House rules," she explained. "We're locked out after two."

"Good," he said and bent to kiss her again.

"Be serious, Paul. I'll be campused from now until you graduate if I'm not in."

"I wouldn't want you to be in trouble," he said, removing his arm and putting his hand on the door handle. "I just wish we had left the dance earlier." He came around and helped her out of the car. He kept his arm around her shoulders as they walked up the front steps.

"I'll write you when I get back. I hope you'll write me. And when I'm back this June, perhaps we'll see what the Arboretum looks like from the water." He bent to kiss her again, but she stepped back slightly, reluctantly. He raised a questioning eyebrow.

"Sorry," Kathleen said, "no kissing on the front porch."

"Oh, more house rules." They both laughed, and the awkwardness of the moment passed. Then he took her hand and raised it to his lips, never letting his eyes leave hers. He kissed her hand slowly and then covered it with his other hand. "I hope there's no rule against that."

She was melting. She could barely speak. She didn't want to go inside. She wanted to stay here forever, but just then another couple dashed up the steps to beat the curfew. Paul still held her hand in both of his.

"I had a lovely time, Paul. I hope you will write."

"Count on it, Kathleen."

He held the door for her and waved a sort of salute as she turned to look at him one more time. The standards chairman was shooing her inside so she could lock the door. Kathleen watched as Paul went down the stairs. She hung up her coat and then headed up the stairs with her hand pressed against her cheek. Mary sat on the top step in her pink chenille robe.

"Well?"

"Oh, Mar. He's just fabulous. He took me to Canlis, and they knew him there, so we got special service. And he can dance like Fred Astaire. We even did the rumba! Can you stand it?"

"I'm not sure I can—not for any length of time anyway. This sounds too good to be true. What's wrong with him? Anything?"

"Not that I could see. He asked if he could write to me. Can you believe it? He *asked.* Like I'd say no or something."

"He's smooth."

"We drove along the lake. The water was like glass. It was so beautiful. The whole night was so *perfect* I could just die!" She took Mary's hands and pulled her up and spun her around down the hall.

"It's going to be a long spring quarter," Mary said.

Her words proved to be prophetic in a different way. Kathleen pinned her corsage carefully on her bulletin board. The first week she figured it would be too much to expect that he would write so soon. She could still smell the fragrance of the roses in her room as she sat at her desk and tried to study. Her mind would not stay on her books. A hundred times she relived the moment on the porch when Paul kissed her hand.

The second week she dashed back to the house to check her mail every day, trying not to be too obvious if the phone-duty pledge hadn't sorted it yet. She would slowly sift through the envelopes as if she had nothing better to do. But there was no letter.

By the third week the flutter in her stomach as she thought about Paul became a sort of ache. The roses on the bulletin board curled to black.

"Maybe you're right, Mar," she said at dinner. "He was too good to be true. But what a night it was."

"Why can't we trust guys who are that gorgeous? Is it like those brightly colored fish that are lethal, do you think?"

Kathleen laughed and felt better than she had since the formal. Al least she might be able to concentrate on her studies. Paul was exactly what she expected to find at college, but now he was like a dream that had to be put away. She was disappointed, but she wasn't broken-hearted. There hadn't been time for that.

She hadn't told her mother anything more than that she had gone to a formal with one of Jake's friends. Her mother hadn't even asked any questions, which Kathleen had counted on. Once Mrs. Lavik had bragged about one of Trudy's dates, but when Kathleen's mother heard that the boy of Trudy's dreams was in Jake's fraternity, she refused to be impressed. By the same token, any friend of Jake's must be unimpressive. If Kathleen had told her Paul was heir to Gordon's, she would have become insufferable. Waiting to hear from Paul was bad enough. With her mother calling every day, it would have been a nightmare. Things had a way of working out.

Besides, she had tryouts coming up, and she hadn't even started to work on her routine. There were other things to think about besides a man she had only one date with. One good thing was that her preoccupation with Paul had served to make her far less nervous for tryouts than she had been last year. There were as many girls trying out, but the numbers didn't feel as overwhelming. Billie had been elected captain, and Kathleen as well as Trudy and Gabby made it easily onto the next year's squad. They were the only ones returning. Elspeth had gotten married just before Christmas, laughing that she had a Rose Bowl honeymoon; Penny and Cindy were both engaged, and Patty was graduating.

"Let's hope we get another Rose Bowl!" Billie said as they ran back to the house with Patty, who as a senior helped with tryouts.

"Wouldn't that be something!" Kathleen agreed. She was thrilled and happy and for the first time since the Rogue formal, thinking about something besides Paul. On the way up to her room, she glanced automatically at her mailbox, and there it was. The handwriting reminded her of the way architects wrote on the plans at her father's office, straight up and all capitals. She ripped the envelope open.

Dear Kathleen,

This is the first time I've regretted choosing Dartmouth. It seems so far away now. It was a great night, but too short. (And you should talk to the girls in your house about those rules!) Next time we'll start earlier. Drop me a line if you have a minute, and I'd love to have a picture of you in your cheerleading outfit. It's how I remember you from when I watched you at the Rose Bowl.

Soon,
Paul

She folded the letter and carried it with her for days. He had said "next time." When she finally read it to Mary, however, all Mary heard was the part about "in your uniform."

"Might that be so he can show his frat brothers he dated a 'someone' way out here on the frontier?"

"Come on, Mary," Kathleen had argued, stung because she had had the same fleeting thought when she read it. "He said it's because it reminds him of seeing me at the Rose Bowl."

"Humph."

Kathleen sent Paul a funny card a week later, so she wouldn't seem too eager, thanking him again for the nice time at the formal and mentioning looking forward to summer. She pushed the small voice that echoed Mary's concern far down and set her sights toward June and the "next time." She didn't mention to him that she had been chosen for a second year on the rally squad, and she didn't include a picture.

On Saturday she took the bus downtown by herself to visit Gordon's. She had shopped there before, but this time she really wanted to look at the place where Paul would be spending his future. She felt terribly self-conscious as she stepped out of the revolving door and into the store, as if the employees would know why she was there. She told herself she was being stupid, but her heart was hammering just the same.

She walked slowly around the counters on the first floor. Summer necklaces festooned driftwood displays. Large button earrings in hot pink and yellow and red clipped themselves onto tiny beach umbrellas, and large matching bangle bracelets circled the handles. The cosmetic area behind the jewelry featured the newest colors for summer from Revlon and Max Factor. The air was heavy with countless mingled perfumes.

The entire back wall was filled with shoes, sandals, and woven straw flats with miniature bunches of fruit on them. She picked up a stunning pair of *peau de soie* evening pumps with pointed toes and slender, champagne-glass heels. For a minute she was tempted to try them on, but she wasn't here to buy.

She smiled back at the many well-dressed sales ladies who asked if they could help her and murmured, "No, thanks, I'm just looking."

She took the elevator to the second floor. Even though they had only three floors and three elevators, Gordon's, like the much larger Frederick & Nelson, had attractive elevator operators who wore matching outfits in the latest styles. Today they wore cotton piqué sheaths in a pale yellow with white piping around the neck and sleeves with black patent-leather pumps that featured the same skinny heel Kathleen had just admired.

"Two, please."

"Second floor: Sportswear, daytime dresses, lingerie." The elevator girl pulled back the handle as they came to a stop. "Here you are," she said with a smile.

The second floor mannequins that greeted Kathleen as she stepped out of the elevator wore brightly colored bathing suits with matching cover-ups and played a frozen game of beach ball on a bed of white sand. Kathleen needed a new swimsuit, but she certainly couldn't show up in one that Gordon's had on display if she and Paul went to the beach. On the other hand, how would it look for him to see that she bought her clothes from the competition? And what if they never went to the beach?

Suddenly she had to get out of the store. She turned and waited for the second elevator to come so the same operator wouldn't see her leaving so quickly. She hurried outside. Paul must be enormously wealthy, and he would know so much about her from the simplest thing she wore. She'd always paid attention to how she was dressed before, but now it was different. She felt the way she had during Rush when she realized she had worn the wrong outfit on the first day.

June 1961

He called her at home two days after he got back to Seattle. She sat down when she recognized his voice. How lucky that she had answered and not her mother.

"I wasn't sure how to reach you. No one answered at your sorority, but Jake bailed me out with your number. I really owe him. Are you free Saturday night?"

"Yes," she said too quickly.

"Great. I'll pick you up around seven. I'm already at the store, so Saturday is a work day."

"How does it feel to be a college graduate?"

"Actually not much different. I've worked for my dad ever since high school, so it sort of seems like nothing's changed. But

I've got some ideas I'm trying to talk my dad into. I'll tell you about them Saturday. And stay hungry. We'll go have dinner."

She waited until Friday to tell her mother. "I won't be here for dinner tomorrow, Mother. I have a date."

"A date? With whom? You haven't mentioned anyone."

"His name is Paul Gordon. He just graduated. From Dartmouth. I met him last summer." She decided to leave Jake out of it for now.

"Dartmouth! Well, for Heaven's sake. Who is he?"

"You'll meet him tomorrow. I only went out with him once when he was in town. I think you'll like him."

"Well, what is he going to do? What did he graduate in?"

"He graduated in business and is going to work with his father—in retail."

"Retail what, Kathleen? There's lots of retail."

"They own Gordon's, Mother." There. It was out.

"Gordon's. My, my. That's quite a good store. I can't believe you didn't mention him."

"Well, I only went out with him once, and I wasn't sure I'd ever see him again, so I didn't see the point."

"What are you going to wear? If he's in the fashion industry, he'll have a sharp eye for appearance. Let's go see."

She put down the knife she was using to chop walnuts and whisked Kathleen down to her room and peppered her with questions about Paul and his family that Kathleen couldn't answer. Pulling things out of Kathleen's closet, her mother went on, "At least wear something classic, dear. You can never go wrong with the classic. And have your hair done. I wonder if you can even get in on a Saturday. Well, I'll call and see."

By Saturday night, Kathleen didn't know if she was more nervous from anticipating seeing Paul again or worrying about how her mother would act toward him. She wore a black linen dress with her gold circle pin and black pumps. Her mother had managed to get her in to the hairdresser, who had done a good job of taming her curls. The doorbell rang exactly at seven.

When she opened the door, Kathleen was again struck by Paul's fierce good looks. He wore a summer tan suit with a blue oxford-cloth shirt and a navy and camel striped tie. He took her in with his eyes and then smiled approvingly.

"Come in, Paul, and meet my parents."

"Mrs. Andrews, how do you do?" he said. "I can see where Kathleen gets her beauty."

"And I'm where she gets her brains and good sense—and her tuition." Her father rose to take Paul's hand while Mrs. Andrews smiled broadly and tucked an imaginary strand of hair back into place.

"It's a pleasure to meet you, sir."

"Do sit down, Paul," Mrs. Andrews said.

"Thank you, Mrs. Andrews, but we have reservations at 7:30."

"Of course," she said, and then, as Kathleen knew she would, added, "And where are you going for dinner, may I ask?"

"I thought we'd go to The Outrigger. I guess it's now called Trader Vic's. It's one of my favorites, and I missed it while I was back East."

"Well, have fun you two," her father said.

"How could they not at that restaurant? It's one of my favorites too," her mother said, smiling again at Paul as he told them it was nice to meet them and ushered Kathleen out the door.

The restaurant was dimly lighted, and soft Hawaiian music played. The gardenias floating in exotic drinks mingled their heady fragrance with that of the straw matting on the walls. Paul and Kathleen were shown to a booth in the back that was flanked with fish netting and Japanese glass floats. The salt and pepper shakers were Polynesian figurines with short legs and fat bellies.

"What would you like to drink?" Paul asked when they got settled.

"I'm not twenty-one yet, Paul. Sorry." She felt embarrassed.

"I thought all you sorority girls carried fake I.D."

"No, I don't. With my luck, I'd get caught."

The waiter came just then. "I'll have a Fogcutter," Paul told him, "and the lady will have a Wahini—without the alcohol—but with the gardenia."

The waiter smiled and vanished.

"I hope you don't mind my ordering for you, Kathleen, but you can't leave here without a gardenia. My reputation would be shot."

"We wouldn't want that. Besides, I love gardenias, and I thank you for being so clever in getting me one." She didn't mind his ordering for her at all. She loved it. No one had ever made her feel taken care of before. She remembered he had done the same thing at Canlis the night of the formal.

The drinks arrived, and Paul raised his rather large ceramic container to her. Kathleen lifted the pottery coconut shell and breathed in the creamy scent of the flower floating in it.

"To this summer and getting to know you better," he said, looking at her as he took a drink. She took a quick sip of her sweet drink through the straw and then studied the menu intently. Finally, as she had been trained at the sorority, she asked, "What do you suggest?"

His answer would give her a clue as to how much he was prepared to spend, and if she didn't like what he chose, she could find something in the same price range and be safe.

"Have whatever you like. Their steaks are especially good because they have that incredible Chinese oven. But the Oriental stuff is good too. What looks good to you?"

"I think I'll have the sesame chicken." It was sort of in the middle of the price range and sounded delicious.

The waiter returned and took their orders from Paul. As they sipped their drinks, Kathleen breathed in the perfume of the gardenia. Finally she took it out of her drink. With her cocktail napkin, she blotted the stem and the glossy green leaves that were stapled to the cardboard circle around it. Then she tucked it behind her ear.

"It suits you," Paul said. "You should always wear flowers in your hair."

"You said you were going to talk your father into some new ideas for the store," she said, feeling uncomfortable and wondering if she should have left the flower in her drink. She didn't know exactly how she looked. Maybe he was being polite.

"What a memory! Yes I am. What size do you wear?"

"Excuse me?"

"I mean are you an 8 or a 9?"

"Usually an 8, but sometimes they're too big. I wish there were something smaller."

"That's my point. We carry some size 6 dresses, but the only companies interested in the smaller sizes are the people like Lanz and Jonathan Logan who are coming in with junior lines. I can picture a whole department just for petite ladies like you."

"I've never thought of myself as petite before. Maybe short, but not petite."

"Trust me. I've danced with you, remember?" He gave her a wink and smiled his slow smile. "Petite is not a bad thing."

She laughed a little self-consciously. "Do you think enough girls would need to wear junior sizes to justify a whole department?"

"How about a whole store? Believe it or not, there are some girls even smaller than you. We'd corner the market in Seattle if girls knew they could find really stylish clothes at Gordon's in their size."

"That's brilliant, Paul. How did your father react? Was he excited?"

"Actually, yes, he was. I think it's appealing to him that after sending me through college, I appear to be able to think. I'll be spending the summer here at the store, and then in the fall, I'm going to San Francisco to work at my uncle's store and get some more buying experience."

San Francisco? Her heart plummeted. He was leaving? "You'll be moving?" Her voice was nearly a whisper.

"No, no. I'll just be gone for a couple of months. I'll be back for the Christmas crunch. My dad says they can most afford to have me gone after back-to-school and before Thanksgiving. I'm not moving!" He put his hand over hers on the table. "Were you worried?"

She hoped in the darkness of the restaurant he could not see her blushing. She pretended to dab her eyes with her napkin. "I was devastated, Paul. I didn't know how I would even be able to eat my dinner," she teased. "Fortunately, now that I know you'll be back, my appetite has returned. Plus, I'm starving."

He laughed and squeezed her hand. "Lucky for you, here come the salads."

She listened to Paul's many ideas for the store during the salad and the main course and the changes he would implement if his dad didn't "go stubborn" on him. He was incredibly clever, she thought. His ideas were well thought out and logical. She was growing more impressed by the minute. She nursed her drink while Paul ordered another Fogcutter.

"It sounds like you've plotted this whole thing out, Paul. The store must be very important to you."

"I've thought of little else since I started college. When I was young, it was just the place where my dad worked and my mom got her clothes. But then when I started studying it, I realized there's a fortune to be made if you do it right. Even though Dad seemed to like my ideas, he's been happy enough with the status quo, but I know that we could capture that market if we focused on younger styles for smaller sizes. I'll just have to convince him."

"Well, you've convinced me. He can't help but notice how committed you are. Besides, Gordon's is one of the leading stores in town already, so your dad can't be too closed to good ideas."

"Thanks for the vote. I may bring you in to back me up if the old man needs a woman's touch."

He finished his drink and signaled to the waiter for the check. "Let's see what else is happening in this town, shall we?" Then he paused. "Oh, I forgot. No I.D. In that case, let's just stay right here."

Kathleen felt uncomfortable. "I'm sorry, Paul. But I love it here."

"You're right. Here's perfect. How about some dessert?"

The waiter appeared, and Paul asked to see the dessert menu. He ordered coconut ice cream for Kathleen and another Fogcutter for himself.

"Don't you want any dessert? I can't have one all by myself."

"I'm having dessert. These're mostly fruit juice." He held up his drink.

"OK I'll give you a bite of mine."

The ice cream came on a large scallop shell with a chocolate mint on the side. It tasted the way Kathleen imagined her gardenia would if it could be made into ice cream, smooth and thickly sweet. It was delicious. She offered Paul a bite, but he laughed and said it didn't quite go with a Fogcutter. Eventually Paul ordered coffee for both of them.

"I want to be able to drive you home." He laughed, but suddenly he said, "What are you doing tomorrow?"

"Going to church is all. Why?" The evening had been a success. He was asking her out again. She rattled her coffee cup as she replaced it in the saucer.

"I thought we might take a ride somewhere. Does your church last all day?"

"No, silly. I'll be home before noon."

"I could be up by then, I suppose." He winked at her. "Let's get out of here."

He paid the bill and led her out to the car. They drove north and up Queen Anne Hill on the steep street still called the counterbalance by the natives, even though the streetcars that carried folks up and down the hill had long since vanished. Paul turned into the small park that overlooked Seattle and Puget Sound and turned off the motor. The scent of gardenia filled the car. A ferry blew three sharp blasts. There were no other sounds. The lights of the city and of West Seattle directly across the water from them winked in the blackness.

"Do you know about lighthouses, Kathleen?"

"Do I know what about them?"

"Each one has a different timing. That's how mariners know where they are. Watch the Alki light over there. It flashes its own code, and no other lighthouse has the same rhythm."

"I'm impressed. Are you a sailor?"

"My dad got a boat a few years ago. With the store open on Saturdays, he never felt he had the time for one, but I guess I begged him long enough that he finally broke down when I was in high school. Now he loves it. It was always on the top of my list." He took her hand and began tracing the lines of her palm with his finger. "What's on the top of your list?"

"I don't really know. I can't even decide what to major in." Little shivers ran up her arm where he touched her.

"I thought you were in education, like most girls."

"I probably will end up there, but I'm not sure. I love working with the kids in my creative dramatics programs, but I don't think there are too many jobs in that field."

"You could become a professional cheerleader."

"Right. There's a lot of future in that."

"Well, how about being a Rockette? New York can be wild."

"I'm too short."

"Pity. As I recall, you have the legs for it."

"Thanks, but they're not long enough to qualify." They both laughed. "Besides I don't really want to leave here. I love this city. Look at it." She pulled her hand away from Paul's and made a sweeping motion. "And imagine what's ahead of Seattle with the World's Fair coming in a year and a half."

"I'm counting on it. When people come out here and see what we have, there'll be such a population explosion. And I aim to put Gordon's right in the middle of it. I can see opening a couple more stores, maybe more."

"You certainly are focused, I'll say that for you. And I believe you'll accomplish anything you want to."

"I usually do, Kathleen, but thanks for the vote. Again." He took her hand back and pulled her gently toward him. Kathleen knew he was going to kiss her. A thousand things ran through her mind. She'd let him kiss her after the formal, so this wasn't really a first. And they did have a date for tomorrow, so maybe it would be all right to let him. But before she could reach any rational conclusion, Paul was kissing her, as lightly as he had kissed her fingertips after the dance.

He tasted of the Fogcutters. His lips were warm on hers. He never increased their pressure and then pulled slowly away and looked at her. Though she opened her eyes quickly, it embarrassed her that he had seen that they were closed. She longed to be sophisticated for him so he would be impressed. She hadn't been able to order a cocktail, and they couldn't go someplace after dinner for drinks because of her. She was afraid he would be bored with her and silently prayed that he wouldn't be.

"You are really something, Kathleen Andrews. This is going to be a great summer." Then he yawned an enormous yawn. "I guess I'd better head back to the barn. It's been a long week."

"Yes, you poor thing," she agreed. "Sleep in tomorrow."

"While you're doing your prayers. Say one for me, and I'll give you a call when I wake up." He started the car and backed smoothly out of the parking area. They were back at Kathleen's house in just a few minutes, but Kathleen could tell Paul was having trouble keeping his eyes open.

"Are you sure you'll be all right driving home?"

"I'll be fine, don't worry." He helped her out of the car and walked her to the door. She handed him her key, and he unlocked the door for her. Then he kissed her lightly once more and gave her a crooked smile. "No rule about kissing on the porch here is there?" He kissed her once more and then said, "Call you tomorrow."

"Thank you for a lovely dinner, Paul. Please drive carefully."

"Always."

She watched his car drive away and spun into her bedroom. She wished she were at the sorority so she could share the evening with Mary. Paul Gordon! Imagine. And she was going to see him again tomorrow. She took the gardenia out of her hair and held it to her nose, breathing in the perfume and the night's new memories. Then she crept quietly to the kitchen and put the flower in the fridge.

Her mother quizzed her endlessly during breakfast. Kathleen told her about most of the evening, but something kept her from sharing that Paul was going to call today. When he did, she would simply act surprised.

By dinnertime, the phone had rung what seemed like a million times, but none of the calls was from him. Perhaps he had tried when the line was busy. Maybe when she was talking to Mary, but she'd kept all her calls short to keep the line free.

"What's the matter, Kitten?" her father said at dinner. "I thought you had a good time last night. Are you so smitten already that you can't eat your mother's delicious roast?"

She smiled at her father. How sweet he was. "I think I'm still full from last night, Daddy." She made an attempt to put another bite into her mouth when the phone rang again.

"I'll get it." She tried to move nonchalantly to the phone.

"Hi. You still wearing your gardenia?"

"Not at the moment, but it still smells like heaven. You just get up?" She hadn't intended to say that. It just came out.

He laughed. "No. I've been up for hours. What have you been doing? Heard any good sermons today?"

Had he forgotten he said he would call her when he got up? Or maybe she was being too literal. After all, here he was, calling her, even if it wasn't earlier.

"As a matter of fact, yes. I heard one just this morning. How about you?"

"Right. I heard two. Want to go get a burger?"

"Sorry, Paul, I'm just eating dinner right now. I wish you'd called sooner."

"Well, save room for dessert. I'll pick you up in half an hour, and you can watch me eat. OK?"

She hesitated only a moment. "See you then."

"Was that Paul?" her mother said when Kathleen returned to the table.

"Yes. He's picking me up in half an hour for dessert."

"You accepted a date at this last minute?" Her mother's voice was high.

"Of course not, Mother. He asked me last night if we could do something today."

"Oh. Well, that's different."

"How is that different, Joan?" her father asked. "I swear I will never understand you women."

"If she had been too available, it might appear that she had no other plans and was simply waiting for him to call."

"But she didn't, and she was."

Her mother gave an exasperated sigh and turned her attention to Kathleen. "It sounds as if you made quite an impression on him, hmm?"

"Well, we'll see. It's only been one date."

They went to the Burgermaster drive-in near the University. She had a chocolate shake while Paul devoured a deluxe burger and fries. "I really missed this place when I was at Dartmouth. There are no burgers like a Burgermaster."

On impulse, Kathleen reached across him to the tray the car-hop had affixed to the driver's side of the car, stole one of his fries, and then dunked it into her shake.

"We used to do this in high school to make people sick, but it actually tastes pretty good." She popped the dripping fry into her mouth.

"No, it actually does make people sick. I can't believe you really did that."

"Want me to make you one?" She giggled and reached across him again for another fry.

He grabbed her wrist, laughing. "No wasting of fries. That's a rule. I think you're in need of fresh air. Finish up, and let's walk around Green Lake."

They parked by the boat rental place and walked down to the path that circled the lake. "Looks like a lot of people had the same idea," Paul said, eyeing the crowd of bicycles and pedestrians moving along at various speeds in front of them.

"You can't blame them, Paul. It's a perfect evening. Come on, it's not that crowded."

The warm air was heavy with the smell of the lake and the damp, weedy shore. A canoe and some kayaks broke the smoothness of the water with their slow wakes. A small cloud of gnats pulsed crazily near the water's edge, a pointillist's tornado. Serious walkers passed Paul and Kathleen several times along with bikers shouting, "On your left!"

Paul took her hand, and it was as natural to walk holding his hand as if she had always done it. She noticed the admiring looks of other girls as they saw Paul. The shadow of envy she read in their quick glances or blatant stares pleased her. It was a new feeling, and she liked it. It felt wonderful to appear to belong to someone as handsome and in command as Paul. She prayed it would last.

And it did. They saw each other every weekend, with occasional casual dates during the week when Paul was not too exhausted from the store and she didn't have cheer practice. Kathleen's every moment was filled with thoughts of him, and more than once she'd found herself daydreaming at work instead of adding up columns of figures. He brought her flowers for her hair, a daisy or a carnation, and chocolate Frango mints from Frederick & Nelson when he discovered they were her favorites. They explored the zoo and the art museum and countless places she had been to hundreds of times before, only now each place became special, a stitch in the tapestry of dreams she was weaving for the two of them.

She had been terrified the day Paul took her to meet his parents. Their home was imposing, with a huge circular driveway curving around the front. The gardens were in full and glorious bloom. Kathleen tried to breathe normally as Paul helped her out of the car.

"Don't look so gloomy," he said, giving her shoulders a squeeze. "They'll love you."

"I hope so."

Paul's father met them at the door. "Kathleen," he said with a smile that was the twin of his son's. "So you're what's been keeping my son so busy this summer. Now I understand why." He gave Paul an exaggerated wink and led Kathleen into the house.

Paul's mother appeared from the dining room and held both her hands out to Kathleen. "It's delightful to meet you, my dear. Let's go out onto the patio and enjoy this magnificent summer we're having."

The house was what was magnificent, Kathleen thought as she followed her hostess across the white terrazzo floors. Dark red and blue Oriental carpets defined seating areas, and polished antique furniture that Kathleen could appreciate but not identify was interspersed with modern pieces. A live orchid plant bloomed on a small lacquered table.

The patio was more like a terrace, edged in a low box hedge. The ground cover between flowering plants and the large, flat stones of the patio was a profusion of tiny wild strawberries. From inside, Kathleen had not been aware of the way the house was situated, but as they stepped outside, Lake Washington sparkled in uninterrupted beauty at the end of a long sweep of lawn.

"How lovely," Kathleen breathed.

"Thank you," Mrs. Gordon said. "We moved here to Mercer Island from the city when Paul was nine, and I've never regretted it. I could look at the lake forever."

"You must come for the hydroplane races next Sunday, Kathleen," Mr. Gordon said, moving to stand beside his wife. "We have a terrific party every summer for Seafair. This is the best spot for watching the Gold Cup on the whole lake."

She looked hesitatingly at Paul, wondering if that was all right with him, but he was smiling, so she replied, "I'd love to."

"I understand you're a friend of Jake's, Kathleen," Mrs. Gordon said. "His mother and I have been friends for ages."

"That's what he told me."

"I owe him," Paul said. "It goes far beyond Rogue loyalty for him to introduce me to Kathleen."

"Did Paul tell you I was a Rho Gam too, Kathleen?" his father asked her. "Class of '39. Got out just in time to tour Europe, compliments of Uncle Sam. Did your father serve?"

"In the Pacific. He was stationed in Hawaii where my parents met."

"Would you care for a drink, Kathleen?" Mrs. Gordon asked.

"She doesn't drink, Mother. She's underage."

Kathleen felt her cheeks redden, but Mrs. Gordon stepped smoothly in. "I didn't mean **liquor, Mr. Smarty. How about some lemonade or iced tea, dear?"

"Thank you, Mrs. Gordon. Iced tea would be great."

"I think I'll have an iced beer. How about you, Dad?"

"Happy to join you, son."

༺༻

"He took you to a party at his parents' house!" Billie said at the practice following the Gordons' Gold Cup party. "This is getting Serious. How were they? Do you like them? Do they like you?"

"I think they like me. Their house is unbelievably beautiful, and I must have met everybody who ever worked at Gordon's or who was related to them or who had been a Rogue with Mr. Gordon."

"They invited all their employees?"

"And their families. It's a tradition. Everyone goes there to watch the Gold Cup races. There was a ton of food and drink."

"Well that seems like some sort of statement or something then, you being there on the arm of the heir with all and sundry as witnesses."

"He has to have brought dates to this event before, Billie. I'm sure no one even noticed. I tell you, there was a crowd there."

"I don't know. It sounds pretty serious to me."

"Do you think so? I keep pinching myself to be sure I'm not making all this up. He's so wonderful. I just can't believe he's as interested in me as I am in him."

"Nonsense. You? A big-time Rose Bowl songleader? He should be so lucky."

Kathleen felt relieved that Billie, who was a senior, was saying the very words she needed to hear. Even though she and Paul had spent so much time together during the summer, she wasn't sure of his feelings. She told herself that he wouldn't have seen her so regularly if he didn't have some serious intentions, but she didn't quite believe it. Hearing Billie reaffirm her hopes made them seem more real.

Once again, school began in a frenzy of Rush and the opening football game. Paul's family had season tickets on the fifty-yard line, so when the squad went to cheer on the other side of the stadium, she knew where to look for them in the stands. They all met under the scoreboard after the game, which the Huskies won handily, and she could tell Paul was proud to introduce her to his parents' friends.

"We're sorry you won't be joining us for dinner, Kathleen," Mr. Gordon said.

"I'm sorry too," she said. "I have to be back at the sorority for two more Rush parties tonight."

"Can't you miss them?" he prompted.

"No. There's a huge fine for missing any part of Rush. We can't even be excused if we have a job."

"Sound pretty serious," he said, looking over her head to Paul. "Well, we'll miss you."

"Thanks, Mr. Gordon. I really wish I could join you."

"I'll have something chocolate for you," Paul told her.

"Thanks a lot. We'll probably have a pick-up dinner of leftovers."

After Rush was over, Paul came to the house for Stock Show, and Kathleen showed off the new pledges—lined up like bonbons in their pastel formals—to him and Paul to her sorority sisters. He looked handsomer than ever in a dark blue suit. All the fraternity men were in their standard navy blazers and grey pants, and the contrast made Paul seem even more sophisticated. The Del Phis gave her approving looks whenever he wasn't looking. She could hardly hold all of it in. Life was perfect.

Even her classes were wonderful. She had another Children's Theater class with Professor Hawkins and Children's Literature 244, which featured young adult books that Kathleen lost herself in. But the best was a puppetry class that she couldn't wait to go to every day, where they were studying the history of puppetry from all parts of the world. Kathleen had no idea there were so many kinds of puppets with such noble pedigrees. When they tried their hand at marionettes, Kathleen managed to tangle hers nearly beyond salvation. She took it back to the house and spent an hour that night undoing her mess. But this quarter nothing seemed like homework.

But would her terrific classes and cheerleading fill the time when Paul would be in San Francisco? He hadn't even left yet, but she already missed him. They talked nearly every day. How could she bear not to hear his voice? Of course, he might call her long distance, but that was so expensive, she was sure he wouldn't do it often. He was leaving next Friday and would be gone until just before Christmas.

"Can't you even come home for Thanksgiving?" she asked.

"The day after Thanksgiving is the biggest shopping day of the year, Kathleen. I'll have turkey with my uncle's family."

She wasn't thinking of turkey, and she had forgotten about the day after Thanksgiving. She figured since it was a holiday, he could come home for the long weekend, and then the wait until Christmas might be bearable. Suddenly she found herself identifying with the tearful heroines in the young adult novels she was reading in her Children's Lit class.

Thursday night before Paul left, Kathleen signed out for dinner and went with him for what he called The Last Supper. They went to his favorite Mexican restaurant near the university. Kathleen had no appetite and swirled a warm chip around in the guacamole.

"Cheer up, Kat. I'll be back before you know it."

"I know, Paul, but it seems like such a long time until Christmas. I wish you could have waited one more month so we could have gone to the pledge dance. I'll miss you."

"I'll miss you too," he said, taking the chip out of her hand and popping it into his mouth. Then he took her hand and looked at her. "I mean it, Kat. I will miss you."

The serious look on his face and the way he said he'd miss her made her stomach flip. It was the closest he had ever come to some kind of declaration of his feelings, and it made her giddy.

The portly waiter broke the spell with platters of food, but she couldn't eat. Paul, however, had no trouble polishing off the enchiladas and chili rellenos. He paid the bill and they left.

"Cheer up, Kat. I'll write, and I expect volumes of mail from you," Paul said once they were in the car. He pulled her toward him and looked at her again the way he had in the restaurant. "You *will* write?"

"Of course I will, Paul. I'm sorry to be so sad, but I can't bear to think of you gone for such a long time." She felt tears stinging her eyes and willed herself not to cry.

"It will go by faster than you know. Just don't forget me." He wrapped his arms around her and drew her as close as she could get, kissing her on each eye and then on the lips. She wrapped her arms around his neck and kissed him back as if she would never kiss him again.

"I wish I didn't have to take you back to the house so soon," he murmured into her hair, "but I have to pack. My flight leaves early tomorrow."

A new pang of disappointment went through her. She thought at least they would spend some private time together before he took her home. She never wanted to stop kissing him. The clock on the dashboard showed it was only 7:45. She started to protest but didn't want to come across as clinging or worse. So instead she smiled and said, "Of course, Paul. You don't want to arrive at your new adventure exhausted."

"I knew you'd understand. You're the best." He kissed her briefly again and then started the car. At the house he walked her to the door. Kathleen fervently hoped he would break the rules and kiss her, but he didn't. He took her hand in the way that touched her heart and kissed her fingertips as he had the first time.

"I'll miss you so," she said again.

"Write to me. I'll send you the address."

And he was gone. Kathleen went slowly up to her room and sank onto the daybed. She had work to do, but she felt too numb to accomplish anything. A grey raccoon hand puppet lay on the pillow, and she slipped her hand into it.

"What do you think, Rackety? Am I a fool or what?"

"Definitely a fool if you think a puppet is going to answer back." Mary popped into the room and flopped down on the daybed beside Kathleen.

"Don't be so mean," the puppet said to Mary. "My friend here has a broken heart."

"Your friend has an addled brain. He's only going to San Francisco, and it's only for a few weeks. If you want to pity someone, Mr. Raccoon, pity those of us who have to suffer while she's like this."

"I know I'm being silly, Mar. It's been only a few months, but I really think I'm in love."

"And what about him? Has he said anything?"

"No, not really. He did say he'd miss me."

"Well, that's something. Cheer up. It'll be Christmas before you know it."

Hope Chest

Kathleen smiled at her friend and put the raccoon puppet back on his pillow. She put a Tony Bennett album on the stereo and changed into her blue Del Phi muu muu and slippers. At 10 o'clock she gave up trying to read and grabbed her coffee mug. The cook always put a fresh pot of coffee out at ten. At the kitchen door she ran into Billie, who was just coming in from outside.

"Hey, I just saw your Paul drive away. Did you go out like that?' Billie said, motioning toward Kathleen's fuzzy turquoise slippers.

"Of course not. We had dinner, but he had to go home early to pack. I've been back since eight."

"Oh," Billie looked away from Kathleen and took off her coat. "It must have been someone else then. I just got a glimpse of him."

"It must have been. He's been home for hours. I'm sure."

"Well, I just thought I saw him when I crossed the street. Must be some other handsome guy running around loose."

"Must be."

The days dragged by, even though they were full. The Husky band was better than ever, and the pep squad spent extra hours making up new routines to the exciting music they kept coming up with. The fans responded with whoops of approval, but under all the excitement was Kathleen's wish that Paul could be there to see it.

He was very busy at the store, he wrote, in the few cards he sent her. She treasured all of them as if they had been love letters. She wrote back immediately after receiving one, but pressure from Mary helped her resist the impulse to write every day.

"You have to be a little hard to get, Kath. Don't write him unless he writes you first. Didn't you mother ever teach you anything?"

"Not about anything like this, Mar. Who could imagine anything like this?"

"Oh, for Pete's sake. If you ask me, he could write a bit more often if he's missing you so terribly. I just don't trust this guy. He's too gorgeous to be anything but a cad."

"Don't be so grumpy. He's wonderful, Mary. And he's terribly busy at the store. I think he's writing quite often considering the workload he must be under." She wouldn't let herself remember the daily disappointment when there was nothing in her mailbox. The days when he did write erased all the others.

She went to Fishers once a week as usual and felt a closeness that the meetings always brought to her. She wondered to herself how she could have been so smitten by Guy. He seemed so unsophisticated compared to Paul. The thought immediately filled her with guilt. Guy was the kindest man she knew. She closed her eyes tightly as he asked everyone to join him in prayer.

Her puppetry class was the one thing that managed to keep her from thinking about Paul all the time. It was magical. They explored all kinds of folk tales from every country and then made puppets and wrote scripts to act them out. She and her group did an Uncle Remus tale with papier mâché hand puppets and a backdrop that dripped with Spanish moss. Professor Hawk had arranged for the various groups to perform their plays at nearby grade schools, and the children's squeals and joyous laughter made her heart swell. She had chosen her major well. This was what she wanted to do. And she could always fall back on it after her children were grown. Her mother was always telling her to take more secretarial courses, just in case, but Kathleen could not see herself in an office. This kind of joy could never be found behind a typewriter.

Georgia, one of the other girls in her group, left class with Kathleen after one of their "shows."

"Isn't this fabulous? Who would think you could have this much fun with puppets? The girls in my house think I'm crazy."

"My roommates laugh at me, too, but they just don't understand," Kathleen said.

"Where are you headed?" Georgia asked her.

"I thought I'd go over to the Commons and get a cup of coffee. I have about half an hour before my next class. Want to come?"

"Good idea."

They walked across the damp path where slick yellow maple leaves stuck fast to the pavement. The air was heavy with the scent of wet grass. Someone had attempted to mow it but had succeeded only in creating great green clumps everywhere.

Hope Chest

The Commons was full and smoky. The two girls found a table in the corner that some bridge players had just vacated, and Georgia claimed it while Kathleen went for their coffees.

"That is such a cute outfit," Kathleen said as Georgia struggled to drape her coat over the back of her chair. "I meant to tell you that earlier. That shade of blue with that soft grey is terrific on you."

"Thanks, but I can't take any credit. It's my roommate's. She works at Gordon's, and with her discount, she has all these fabulous things. Fortunately we're the same size. Lucky me."

At the name, Gordon's, Kathleen's stomach did a little flip flop. "Gordon's. They have darling clothes."

"She loves working there. Probably because she's dating the owner's son."

Kathleen heard a ringing in her ears. Her cheeks grew hot. She tried not to let Georgia see her react. Surely she had not heard right. "She's dating the owner's son? Isn't that kind of dangerous? How long has she been doing that?" Her voice was calm. It was like talking through her puppet.

"I think she met him during the summer. He works there too. I don't really know. He's gone to San Francisco for a while now, so no one's the wiser. It's not going to be her career, so if she has to quit, she'll just get another job. She's gaga about him."

"Are they serious?"

"She is. I don't know about him. Every day she runs to the mail to see if he's written, but mostly he just sends her those goofy contemporary cards. She acts like they're love letters. He is quite handsome, though. He's been to the house a bit this quarter, and all the pledges just stare at him and giggle."

Kathleen attempted to drink her coffee, but her hand shook when she tried to lift the heavy white mug, so she set it down and wrapped both hands around it, barely feeling the scalding porcelain.

"It went pretty well today, don't you think?" Georgia asked, mercifully changing the subject. "I was afraid second graders might not get some of the subtleties, but they did all right. They're so cute."

Kathleen looked at the clock. She had to get out of there. "Sorry, Georgia. I think I need to head to class. I just remembered I have to ask my prof something about my term paper before class starts. I'll see you tomorrow."

She fled up the stairs and out into the cool air. Her mind was a jumble, playing back the whole summer. Suddenly the fact that she only saw Paul one night on the weekends took on a whole new meaning. She believed him when he said he was working, or that he was too tired to do anything. True, they hadn't agreed not to date other people, but their time together seemed so special, and he was so attentive and so romantic. It just didn't seem possible that he would even be thinking about anyone else, let alone dating. It hadn't occurred to her. Not once. He had called her every day. Why would she think there was someone else? How stupid she must have seemed to him! And that night Billie thought she had seen Paul. He had left her at eight o'clock to go out with someone else! And Georgia's description of her roommate's ridiculous reaction to Paul's letters. She could have been describing Kathleen.

Kathleen almost ran back to the house. Mary was in her room typing. Kathleen slammed her books onto the daybed and started pacing.

"No mail today?" Mary said, finishing typing a word and then looking up. "Whoa, what happened?"

"He's seeing someone else! All this time, he's been dating someone else at the same time he's been dating me."

"How do you know?"

Kathleen slid down the wall and sat on the floor. "A girl in my puppetry class. It's her roommate." She told Mary the story. "Was I born stupid, or could it be the water here?"

"I knew he was too pretty to be nice. I could just smack him."

Chapter 6

November 1961

"Oh, come on, Kath. It's been nearly a month. You can't just spend the rest of your life moping. What have you got to lose?"

"Mary, the last thing, the very last thing I want is to go out on a blind date."

"You can't miss the pledge dance, you'll get fined. Besides, Patrick is very nice. Much nicer than some I could name."

"Please don't do this, Mary. I'm not interested in dating anyone. Ever."

"Well you have to do something. That poor Tony Bennett album is going to warp any second, and my dad's buying stock in Kleenex. Don't let that turkey ruin your life. He's not worth it."

"I know you're right. But what kind of a date would I be? Why make someone else miserable?"

"It'll be fun. We'll double. Mark says he's told Patrick all about you, and he's interested. And you don't have to marry him, for

Pete's sake. It's just for one dance. Then you can mope forever. But you can't skip the pledge dance."

"Wanna bet?"

"Well, he's going to call you, so be polite at least. He's Mark's best friend, and I don't want to lose points for having a mean sorority sister I'm just trying to cheer up."

Mary had been seeing Mark since their coffee date in the spring, but Kathleen did not recall her mentioning a Patrick before.

"Is he a Beta too?"

"Well, good. There's a spark of interest. No, he goes to Seattle U."

"He's Catholic?"

"Some people are, my dear."

"I didn't mean anything. I didn't know Mark was Catholic."

"He isn't. Some people aren't. Look, you're not getting engaged, Kath. It's just a dance. And besides being Catholic, he's smart and funny and not a two-timer."

Kathleen shot a look at Mary.

"Sorry. But wouldn't it be nice to go out with someone with some standards? You're the one who's up to her ears in Fishers, for goodness' sake. Have you even talked to the Crown Prince? Does he know that you know?"

` "No. He sent me a card last week, but I haven't written back. When I got it, I wondered if he had sent one to her at the same time. And what would I say? 'I heard that you were two-timing me.'"

"That does it. You are going to the pledge dance with Patrick if I have to tie you up to get you there. Come on." She pulled Kathleen off the daybed and pushed her out the door and down the hall to the ironing room where the formals hung.

"Wear your black sheath, Kath. You'll wow him."

"I don't think I'll wow anyone, Mar. But black might be appropriate."

"Oh, brother. Bad suggestion." Mary ruffled through the many gowns on the formal rack. Most were hanging in clear plastic cleaners' bags that rustled as the hangers skritched along the steel bar. "How about the hot pink? You haven't worn this one yet. The tags are still on it."

Kathleen had been hoping to impress Paul with the pink dress and had been waiting for a chance to wear it for him. She didn't want to wear it for anyone else. She bought it for him. She didn't want to have a picture taken in it with some stranger. She would save it for when . . . she felt the prickle of tears starting. Save it for what? There would be no "when."

"No, I'll wear the black. And don't worry, I won't embarrass you. I'm in drama, remember."

"Yeah, *children's* drama. That fills me with confidence." Mary took down the black sheath and her own new dress. "Come on, Smiley, this could be Mr. Right. Or you might even meet someone else, you never know."

"Why do people always say that? Have you been talking to my mother? When has anyone on earth met someone else while on a date? This will be a disaster, Mary, and you can't blame me for it. I warned you."

The next night, the intercom blasted Kathleen's name. Her heart started to beat as she rushed to the phone. Please, please be Paul, she whispered.

"Kathleen, this is Patrick McHugh," came an unfamiliar voice. In her spiraling disappointment, she didn't connect the name.

"Yes?"

"Mark's friend. He and Mary gave me your name."

"Oh, yes, Patrick." She couldn't think of anything else to say. There was a long pause.

"It seems Mary and Mark have decided that we should go to your dance together, but I thought I should see if that's all right with you. I know how determined those two are, and it sounds like a good idea to me. I just wanted to make sure you had a vote."

"Yes, that . . . that would be fine." Her brain was not sending any messages to her mouth.

"Well, good then. I'm looking forward to meeting you. I'll see you Saturday night."

"Yes, Saturday night." She hung up and walked slowly back to the room. This was not starting out well. Not well at all.

On Saturday night, girls in merry widows and rollers dashed to and from the bathrooms. The noisy splash of all three showers

Hope Chest

going at once filled the halls. Steam billowed out every time the bathroom door opened. The air smelled like a perfume counter.

Kathleen fastened her nylons. She had given up the panty girdle of her freshman year for an elasticized garter belt that smoothed down over her hips but didn't bind her legs. It was much more comfortable, but sometimes the bumps of the garters showed if she was wearing something jersey. She checked herself in the mirror and was happy to see that nothing showed through the heavy brocade of her dress.

"Can you zip me?" Mary said, backing into the room.

Kathleen zipped Mary into her new purchase. It was ice blue lace with the pattern of the lace creating the neckline and hem. Mary twirled slowly, arms extended. "What do you think?"

"You look stunning, Mary. Mark doesn't stand a chance."

"Thanks, Kath, I hope it's worth the investment. This dress was a fortune. Fortunately, it was on sale."

"It really makes your eyes look blue. He's doomed."

"Is that the voice of my old friend coming back a bit? We may have fun yet. Now sit down while I draw a face on you. You can't wear black and no makeup, you'll look the way you've been acting this past week or so."

The intercom voice announced, "Mary and Kathleen, you have guests."

"Come on, smile. We'll have fun." Mary gave Kathleen a push toward the door, and they went downstairs together.

Patrick and Mark were sitting on the green sofa. They both rose when the girls came into the room. Patrick was slightly taller than Mark's six feet. He had pale blond hair parted on the side, worn a bit longer than the short look popular on campus. He was not bad-looking, but he would never turn heads the way Paul did. His sport coat hung loosely on his thin frame. Kathleen's heart sank. How could she have let Mary talk her into this?

"Wow. You two look gorgeous," Mark said. "All you need are flowers." He handed Mary a corsage box. "Patrick McHugh, you lucky man, this is Kathleen Andrews."

160

Hope Chest

Patrick smiled shyly at Kathleen and handed her a white box like the one Mary had. "It's nice to meet you, Kathleen. I hope you like gardenias."

"Thank you, Patrick. They're my favorite flower." She took the box and slipped off the gold elastic. The sweet smell of the waxy flowers brought an instant memory of Paul. She bent down quickly to put the corsage box on the coffee table in front of the sofa so no one could see her face. Taking a deep breath, she removed the two perfect blossoms from the nest of shredded green in which they lay.

"Want us to help you pin them on?" Mark asked innocently.

"No," Mary shot back at him. "We'll carry them until we get to the dance, silly. They'll just get smooshed under our coats."

They went out to Mark's car. Patrick helped Kathleen into the back seat. Mary and Mark kept up a running banter in the front, so Patrick and Kathleen didn't have to say much.

At the dance, the girls went into the ladies' room to pin on their corsages.

"Well?" Mary said.

"He's kind of quiet."

"Give him a chance, Kath. He's a doll."

"Don't worry. I won't embarrass you or ruin your chances with Mark." She took a deep breath and followed Mary back out to their table. The band was playing "More," a song that reminded her of Paul. Well, she thought bitterly, every song would remind her of Paul. Deliberately she looked at Patrick and gave him her brightest smile. "I'm glad you could come with me tonight. Tell me about Seattle U."

"There's not a lot to tell. We don't have a football team or any fraternities, unless you count the Jesuits."

He didn't crack a smile, but Kathleen saw a twitch at the corner of his mouth and they both started to laugh.

"Would they appreciate your humor?" she asked him.

"Oh, sure. They're the first to make jokes. There are some fantastic teachers at Seattle U, even if you don't major in theology."

She looked at him closely. There was the twitch—he was teasing again. "So what are you majoring in then? I thought theology was all that was offered there."

"Ah, touché. Actually, Seattle U is just like a real university. You can major in practically anything you want. I'm in business with an accounting emphasis. How about you?"

"Education with an emphasis on children's theater. I don't really want to teach, but it's the only way I can get a degree in anything related to what I want to do."

"You want to act in children's theater?"

"No, I want the children to act. They're so creative, it's magical to watch them."

"How old are they? Can they read yet? I mean, how do they manage a play?"

"We do creative dramatics with them. We talk about a situation, or I read them a story, and then they act it out. You should come to one of the workshops. You'd be amazed at what they can do." What did she just say? She had invited him to see her again. She was getting stupider every day.

"I just might do that. I like theater, but I don't think I've ever seen this kind of thing. Sister Mary Ignatia wasn't much into letting us out of our seats long enough to do a play. Would you like to dance?"

The band was playing another slow song, and Patrick led her out onto the floor. His thin shoulder felt strange under Kathleen's hand after Paul's solid one. Yet he was a strong leader, and they danced smoothly around the floor.

"You're a good dancer," he said.

"Thank you, but you're the one leading, so the credit goes to you." How easily that had come out. She hadn't intended to say anything like it. He wasn't Paul. Why was she complimenting him?

"No, if you can follow me, you're good. Trust me."

They danced the rest of the number without talking. The song ended, and the band began a Latin number that quickly cleared the floor of all but three couples. Mark and Mary joined them back at the table.

"How you two doing?" Mark asked.

"You were right, pal," Patrick said. "We don't have dances like this at SU. Or too many ladies like these, I might add."

Mary lifted an eyebrow, and Kathleen studiously avoided looking at her. She didn't want Patrick to be interested in her. She simply wanted the evening to be over so she could go home. They danced to the slow songs. Kathleen attempted to make small talk while they sat out the fast ones, but mostly they just listened to the music. Now and then she noticed Patrick rubbing his forehead.

"Is the music too loud?" she finally asked him.

"No. Sorry," he said sheepishly. "I guess I left my contacts in too long."

"How long is too long?"

"Two weeks." He smiled at her.

"Are you crazy? I thought people were supposed to take them out every night."

"They are. I just forget when I'm studying and fall asleep. I'll be fine."

Kathleen shook her head. Maybe that was why he was so quiet. Paul didn't need glasses, she thought, and then shook her head harder to chase those thoughts out.

"Why don't you take them out now?"

"I forgot the case."

"I thought accountants are supposed to be good at details. This bodes ill, Patrick."

He laughed. "I agree. But I do pretty well when the details are on paper in front of me. It's the other stuff I lose track of."

He had a nice laugh. Kathleen found herself relaxing finally. Why should she let Paul ruin this night? She had to get on with her life without him, and here was a perfectly nice guy, and she was practically ignoring him. She tried even harder to get him to talk about himself. "Do you have any brothers or sisters?"

"I have three brothers and two sisters," he said. "I'm the youngest of the boys."

"Six of you?"

"Good Irish Catholics, my dear. My dad was one of ten."

"I or six siblings! Do you get along?"

"Oh, sure. We have great times. The family get-togethers are like conventions. We have to rent a hall for Thanksgiving dinner."

She saw the twitch again, and this time she laughed first. They danced the last dance as the band played "Good Night, Sweetheart," and it was finally time to leave. They followed Mary and Mark to the car and climbed into the back.

"Anyone feel like stopping somewhere?" Mark asked.

Kathleen glanced at Patrick. He was frowning slightly. "I think Patrick needs to go home. He's having trouble with his contacts."

"You leave them in again, Pat?" Mark said.

"Is this a regular thing?" Kathleen asked Mark.

"Stop picking on me, you two. If you want to go get something to eat, I'm game."

"Rhymes with 'in pain,'" Mark said.

"I think we'd better just head back to the house," Mary decided. "It's late enough, and my feet are killing me. If we stopped somewhere, it would have to be a drive-in, because I think I have just enough energy to make it into the house where I can burn these shoes."

"I'm sorry about the headache," Patrick began as they walked to the door, "but I'm not sorry we went to the dance. May I call you?"

"Of course," she said automatically. She wondered if anyone had ever said "please don't" when a date asked her that. It hadn't been the terrible evening she had envisioned, but she really didn't want to date anyone. Patrick was not bad looking and had a good sense of humor. If she had met him before Paul, she might even have been interested. But she hadn't, and her heart wasn't in it. When Patrick called, she would just be busy for all the things he asked her to. After the second call, he'd get the picture. She'd be polite, but not available.

"There now, that wasn't so bad, was it?" Mary asked as she followed Kathleen into her room.

"He's very nice, Mar. I just can't get excited about anyone right now."

"You are impossible. He's better than 'very nice.' He's funny and smart and I think quite taken with you—what little of you was actually on this date tonight."

"Come on, Mar. I made conversation. I danced. I laughed."

"Good thing he doesn't know you yet, so he couldn't tell what he was missing. Next time, shape up."

"Don't count on a next time. I don't think I could go through this again."

On Monday there was a letter in her box when she and Mary came back to the house for lunch. With pounding heart she reached up to pull it out. Not from Paul. The address was written in thick, black, gorgeous italic script. It looked almost as if it had been printed on a machine, but it was definitely done by hand, and hand-delivered—there was no stamp. She opened the envelope and read:

Dear Kathleen:
   Again let me apologize for not being quite myself Saturday night. I have taken a pledge to remove my contacts religiously (and this from a Catholic) every single night, so that if I am lucky enough to be in your most charming company again, I will be far worthier than I was.
   Now, if I might be so bold, I have two tickets to the Cirque Dinner Theatre for next Friday night. Might you be interested in seeing grown-ups act? I'll give you a call.
                                                               Yours hopefully,
                                                               Patrick

In spite of herself, she smiled. Could he have managed this artful penmanship by himself, or had he found someone to do it for him? She couldn't imagine an accounting major being so artistic. Maybe there was more to this man than she had let herself notice.

"Oh, no, a letter from Him?" Mary said.

"Which 'Him' would that be," Kathleen said, raising her left eyebrow.

"Oh, sorry. I thought you were my friend Kathleen. Excuse me, you look just like her, but she thinks there is only one man on the entire planet, so you must be someone else."

"Actually, it's from Patrick. Look at this handwriting. Have you ever seen anything so gorgeous?"

"Wow. Maybe he's going to be a monk. All that's missing is the big gold capital letter with Adam and Eve cleverly intertwined. What did he have to say?"

"Here, read it. It's really quite funny."

Mary read it and handed it back to Kathleen. "Well, well. A second date. I guess he did have a rotten time at the formal, after all. Hmm. You were right."

Kathleen swatted her with Patrick's letter. "If he's practicing to be a monk, maybe I shouldn't accept."

"Folks, she laughs. She makes jokes. Could this mark the return of Kathleen, the normal person?"

"Who could be normal around you? Let's go eat."

"But wait. A question hangs in the air. Are we going to say yes to this gorgeously written invitation?"

"Probably. I guess you've been right all along, Mar. I have to get over Paul sometime. I know that finally, and Patrick was very nice."

"There you have it, folks. She's back from the curse of the zombies. Kill the fatted calf."

"What is she talking about?" Billie said, joining them as they walked to the dining room.

"Pay no attention to her, Billie. Our Mary is a very strange person."

Patrick called the next night.

"Did you really write that?" Kathleen blurted out when he identified himself.

"With my very own quill."

"We wondered if you were studying to be a monk."

"We?"

"Oops. I'm revealed. Mary was with me when I got the mail. We were both quite impressed. Sister Ignatz must have given you an A in penmanship."

"That's Sister Mary Ignatia, and yes, she did. I hoped it would serve some purpose someday. If you can make it to the play Friday, all the hours of drawing curves and loops will have been worth it."

"I'd love to, Patrick. It will be novel seeing adults on stage, and I've never been to the Cirque. I'm looking forward to it."

"So am I. I'll pick you up at six."

She wasn't nervous. Maybe anxious was a better word. She hadn't heard from Paul, and she fought with herself every day in drama class to keep from asking Georgia if her friend had gotten a card. Never mind. A date with someone else would be fun. She'd had a good time with Patrick at the pledge dance, and she was very impressed with his medieval script in his clever letter.

Kathleen carefully brushed the roller marks out of her hair, hoping the larger rollers she bought would straighten her insistent curls, and put on her mascara. She wore her red wool sheath and gold earrings, which she hoped wouldn't pinch her ears too much before the night was over. Mary was already out with Mark, and her roommates were gone as well. There was no one around who could approve or disapprove of her image in the mirror. Oh, well, the dress looked all right. Lipstick helped. She dropped the tube into her evening bag and headed downstairs to wait for the doorbell to ring.

Patrick was exactly on time. He looked appreciatively at her and let out a slow whistle. "Red is your color, Madame," he said and produced a single gardenia from behind his back. "Your favorite, I believe."

"Thank you, kind sir, for the flower and for remembering. I'll be right back."

She ran upstairs thinking how thoughtful of him. She found a bobby pin and fastened the flower over her right ear. She looked at herself in the mirror again. Better.

"What do you think?" she said, coming out of the door.

"I think the gardenia is much improved." He helped her on with her coat, and they headed out the door. Patrick's car was an old yellow Mercury with one blue fender.

"Your chariot, Madame," he said as he held the door for her.

"It's colorful, Patrick."

"Two-toned. That costs extra."

Their table at the theater was near the stage, the food was excellent, and the play, a light comedy by someone Kathleen had never heard of, was hilarious. She found herself relaxing more and more as Patrick made humorous comments about everything from the shape of the green beans ("They leave them whole so that not many will fit in the can, and you'll have to buy two") to one actor's use of his hands ("I think he really wants to be a windshield wiper"). Except when she went to the ladies' room and saw herself wearing the gardenia, she hadn't thought of Paul once. Perhaps she was healing.

After the play, Patrick drove her home. At the house he turned off the engine, but didn't move toward her. Kathleen was prepared in case he tried to kiss her or hold her hand, but he didn't. Instead he looked at her and said, "So what do you like besides cheerleading and the theater, Kathleen?"

"Oh, lots of things. I love to dance, and I love Chinese food, and parades, especially parades with bagpipes, and reading, and picnics, and lots of things."

"I choose Chinese food," he said. "When?"

Kathleen couldn't help but laugh. "How about next Saturday. I'll be starving after the game. In fact, if you can get a ticket, why don't you come?"

"I'd love to, but I work Saturdays counting shekels for a grocery store. But I'll be starving too. A whole day of adding figures, well, you can imagine how famished that would make a person."

"Saturday, then. What time are you off work?"

"I can be here by five-thirty. Can you last without food until then?"

"I'll try."

On Wednesday there was a square brown box addressed to Kathleen sitting on the mail shelf below their mailboxes. The letters C.A.R.E. were stenciled on it.

"What in the world?" she said to Mary as she unwrapped it. Inside was a can of peanuts, two Hershey bars—one with almonds—a package of sliced Italian salami, and a box of Animal Crackers. The note read: "In case you can't make it to 5:30."

"I don't get it," Mary said as Kathleen began to laugh.

"It's from Patrick. A C.A.R.E. package so I won't faint from hunger before we go to dinner Saturday. Honestly, he's something else. What a nut."

"Told you so," Mary said softly.

Kathleen reached into her box for the rest of her messages, and there was a card from Paul. She caught her breath.

"What now?" Mary asked. Then she said, "Oh, no."

Kathleen opened the blue envelope. It was another contemporary card with a baseball player on the front. Lines indicated he had just swung at the ball that was thudding into the catcher's mitt. Inside was printed, "Missing you." Paul had added, "Boy, am I swamped. Saw that the Huskies won last week. Don't cheer too hard. Love, Paul."

Mary took the card from Kathleen. "Wow, this guy is really romantic. Save this, and maybe you can publish all of his letters someday. You know, like Elizabeth Barrett and Robert Browning."

Kathleen shoved the card back into her box but took the C.A.R.E. package with her into the dining room to show it to Billie. She felt in better spirits than she had in a long time.

She saw Patrick every weekend from then on. They went to movies and odd little inexpensive places she had never heard of that Patrick somehow knew about. He took her to a Middle Eastern restaurant near Seattle U where there was no silverware. They used their hands to eat a buttery chicken served on a brass tray. They drove forty-five minutes north of Seattle to a place in Marysville that had pies with meringue nearly six inches high. They shared peanuts with the bears at the zoo. One cold sunny day they rented a canoe and paddled around the Arboretum, their frosty breath streaming behind them like vapor trails.

The house closed for Thanksgiving, so the girls all went home for the long weekend. It was nice to be in her own room for a change and to have dinner with her family. Gran and Grandpa Andrews were there asking her many questions about school. They listened attentively as she described her classes.

"Are you still hearing from that nice Gordon boy?" Her mother interjected. Then turning to Gran she explained, "Kathleen is dating the son of the Gordon's department store family." Kathleen had avoided mentioning Paul, but now everyone was waiting for her answer.

"He's been gone since September. He's at a store in San Francisco, but I get a card once in a while."

"Well, I hope you don't write back too promptly. It would never do to seem overly eager. He's from a good family, so I'm sure he'd be aware of that. But you don't want to be standoffish, either. Men only like the chase if it's not too difficult."

"Oh, so that's the game, is it?" her father said.

"You just finding that out, son?" Grandpa Andrews asked.

"Well, I'm dating someone else too." There she had plunged in. Her hands shook a little as she refolded the napkin on her lap.

"Oh?" Her mother stopped with her fork midway to her mouth. "Does he go to the University?"

"No. He goes to Seattle U."

"Kathleen, surely you're not dating a Catholic!"

"Mother, I'm not marrying him. We've just gone out a couple of times. He's really quite nice."

"Nice is not the same as suitable, my dear. The world is full of nice people that you wouldn't want to have anything to do with. What if you get serious about this boy? That church takes over your life. You have to sign over your children to it. Are you aware of that, Kathleen?"

"Oh, Joan, for Pete's sake. No one is talking about children here," her father said.

"No one does at this stage, but it is precisely at this stage when Kathleen must be clearheaded about her future. Fish every Friday. The Pope dictating your every move. It's unthinkable. We've tried so hard to bring you up right, Kathleen. What are you thinking?"

"I'm sure he must be a nice young man if Kathleen chooses to go out with him, Joan," Gran said in her soothing voice. "I'm sure you'll have many beaux before you settle down, my dear. Now's the time to enjoy yourself."

"Besides, Joan," her grandfather said, "the Catholic Church isn't all that different from the Episcopalian one you go to, is it?"

"I should say it is," her mother sputtered. "Night and day different."

"Well, I think I'll have some more of that delicious turkey, Joan, if you would, please. It's about the juiciest I've ever tasted," her grandmother winked at Kathleen. "And maybe a bit more gravy, too, while you're passing things this way."

Thank you, Gran, she said to herself. Why had she even brought it up? Now if she ever dated Patrick again, she would have to keep it secret from her mother, and she had never done that before. She felt confused and angry. And her anger spread to Paul. If he had just been honest, none of this would have happened. There would have been no Patrick and no argument with her mother. Suddenly she hated him for going out on her, and she hated herself for still caring. Well, she would *absolutely* date Patrick again, and anyone else who asked her out. Besides, Patrick didn't seem very religious. Maybe she would invite him to Fishers.

She didn't answer Paul's card, and she wondered if he would notice. She was aware that he would probably be home for the holidays, but she didn't have much time to spend thinking about him. Football season was over. The team had just missed going to the Rose Bowl, and now the cheer squad was busy getting ready for basketball season. There were two major papers she had to write, and she had signed up with Fishers to be in a choir that would carol at hospitals and nursing homes for the holidays. They started evening practices once a week. And she was seeing a lot of Patrick.

Things were still pretty casual. He always kissed her good night, and sometimes they held hands in the movies. He sent her poems in his beautiful script. Or wacky cartoons. Once she got a bright orange leaf. But there had been no serious necking, and she was grateful.

They also never talked about religion, and Kathleen had not given it a thought until she'd mentioned Patrick to her mother. Now her mother's niggling voice surfaced at unexpected times. So far she was managing to ignore it. She thought about asking Patrick to come to Fishers with her, but they didn't see each other during the week, and she thought he might be too busy.

"Do you sing, Patrick?" she asked him finally.

"Only when the moon is full. Why?"

"I thought you might like to join our caroling group at Fishers."

"Fishers? Sounds like a restaurant."

"No, silly. I suppose they don't have one at Seattle U. It's a nondenominational Christian group I belong to. We're going to sing Christmas carols at hospitals. Interested?"

"Do I have to convert?"

"Do you sing different versions of Christmas carols?"

"Ours are all in Latin."

Kathleen poked him. "Will you be serious? It would be fun. We rehearse at seven on Wednesday."

"Sorry, I'm working on Wednesday nights, but how about if I come to the caroling party and promise not to sing. I could carry the jingle bells."

She talked to Guy at the next rehearsal. "He says he doesn't sing, but I'd love to have him see what fun we have."

"Are you getting serious about this fellow, Kathleen?"

"Not terribly serious, Guy, but I do like him."

"Well, let me caution you a bit. It is very difficult for many Catholics to become Christians. The structure of their church doesn't have much room for the kind of personal relationship with the Lord that we have. He may not understand. In fact, he may not even be allowed to participate. They can't be part of other church services, you know, except weddings and funerals, of course."

"I don't think he's particularly religious. At least he's never said much about it." Kathleen had not expected this turn of the conversation. It was almost like talking to her mother. She wished she had never said anything to Guy. Things were becoming extremely complicated, and she wasn't even in love with Patrick. What would Guy have thought of Paul? He wasn't Catholic, but he was hardly what Guy would call a Christian.

"As a famous Catholic bishop once said," Guy continued, "'Give me a child for the first seven years, and I'll give you a Catholic for the rest of his life.' But we could pray about it, if you'd like."

Not knowing what else to do, she nodded. Guy took her hands and bowed his head. "Lord, let this be an opportunity for Kathleen to spread the word about Your precious Son to this young man. Guide her speech that she might bear witness for You and keep her feet on the true path to righteousness for Your sweet sake. We ask this in Jesus' blessed name, Amen."

She thanked Guy and made a quick exit. As she walked home, she thought of *Alice in Wonderland* that her kids were reading : curiouser and curiouser. She had been head over heels about Paul, and being with him felt absolutely right. Yet nothing was as it had seemed with him. Dating Patrick, on the other hand, should be simple. It was just dating. They had a lot in common and laughed a lot. Plus, he was the most honest person she had ever met. There should be no problems here, but now even going out with him was getting complicated. She never brought up religion around Paul, whom she was crazy about. Now it loomed like a shadow with Patrick. She liked him a lot, but not in the way she had felt about Paul. Curiouser and curiouser, indeed.

That weekend, she and Patrick went to Alki for fish and chips. It was cold and windy. Kathleen watched the waves hurl themselves against the high bulkhead. She was still feeling uneasy about her conversation with Guy. Catholics had statues of Jesus everywhere. How could they not be Christians?

She and Patrick sat on a slatted bench facing the Sound and ate hot fries with frozen fingers. The garlic vinegar they sprinkled liberally on the once-crisp fish stung her nose and made the batter turn soggy, but it was delicious.

"Where are you?" Patrick asked. "Your mind seems to be dining elsewhere."

"Sorry. I guess I was worrying about my two term papers I should be working on." How easily she lied, but she didn't want to discuss religion right now, and that was the only thing on her mind. The black water of the Sound roiled about with whitecaps everywhere. The last of the pale winter sun was just slipping down

Hope Chest

behind the craggy peaks of the Olympics. Here was God's majesty undivided. Why did people splinter it and make everything difficult?

"Want to go back?" He didn't even mind. He was obviously concerned for her. Suddenly she looked at him. With the sun's rays in her eyes it was hard for her to see his features. The light was behind his tousled hair.

"Thanks, Patrick. That's so sweet of you. You really are special."

"I know," he said, grinning at her, "and you don't really deserve me, but you are luckier than most."

She threw her French fry at him, and he caught it in his mouth. They both laughed. It felt good to laugh like this. It felt so good to be with someone who really cared about her. Suddenly she stopped laughing. He had stopped too. With one motion, he pulled her toward him and kissed her, really kissed her. To her great amazement, something inside her quivered. This was not like his good-night kisses. She leaned into him and kissed him back.

As they finally separated, he said, "Nice perfume. Eau de garlic?"

They laughed again, Kathleen a little nervously. They finished their meal and threw the last scraps to the hovering seagulls. One caught a fry before it hit the ground and swooped off with it to the raucous protest of his companions, who circled in for their share. What had just happened, she wondered, stealing looks at him as they drove home.

From that point on, things were different between them. There was still the light banter, the playfulness, the envelopes in her mailbox, but beneath that there was a growing warmth that pushed away all thoughts of Paul and any desire to discuss religion.

Chapter 7

November 1961

School was flying by. Suddenly the holidays were just around the corner. Kathleen had a breezy note from Paul saying he would be staying in San Francisco through January to see how the holidays were handled there instead of coming home. She felt only relief that she wouldn't have to face him. She hadn't written him since she found out about the other girl he was seeing, but he didn't seem to have noticed. Kathleen was happy to discover she had no customary reaction she had once had to seeing his handwriting on the envelope. She wondered briefly if he had sent a similar note to the girl in Georgia's house, but even that possibility didn't ruffle her.

She had other things on her mind, like finals and whether to get Patrick something for Christmas. She wanted to get him something light or even funny, but something that had a bit of meaning as well. She and Mary took the bus downtown to see what she could find, but nothing struck her as right, and they came back to the house empty-handed.

"Thanks for making the trip with me, Mar," Kathleen said as they walked the few blocks from the bus stop on the Ave, their breath clouding around them in the cold.

"My pleasure, my friend. I'm only too happy to assist you in what has definite signs of turning into a wonderful relationship. And I might add, *finally*."

"Well, I guess thanks for that too. Without your pushiness, I would never have met Patrick and would probably be found floating Ophelia-like in some stream by now. I can't believe how stupid I was to waste all that energy . . ."

"Not to mention all those tears."

"Not to mention all those tears, on Paul."

"Just look upon the experience as training wheels, Kath. Now you can appreciate what a really nice guy Patrick is. Before, you had no low to measure him against."

౸

As soon as finals were over, everyone packed to go home for the holidays. Kathleen still hadn't found a gift for Patrick, but now she would have time to shop without worrying about studies.

She and Patrick joined the group from Fishers and caroled at several hospitals. As promised, Patrick refrained from singing, but jangled the sleigh bells forcefully during "Jingle Bells" and "Winter Wonderland." He shook hands with Guy and seemed to get along with everyone. Kathleen had only one moment of discomfort when Guy led them all in a prayer before they started.

"Sweet Jesus," Guy began, "please guide our voices tonight that we may bring hearts and souls to Your dear Self, that those who are sick and suffering may know Your healing presence. We ask this in Your precious name, Lord, Amen."

Kathleen glanced at Patrick, who had bowed his head with the others. At the "Amen" he crossed himself. While she was not surprised, she looked quickly around to see if anyone else had noticed or might remark, but everyone's eyes were closed. She added a little prayer of her own that religion might not become a problem.

She finally finished her shopping by getting Patrick a leather-bound copy of Shakespeare's sonnets. Patrick had attempted a couple of sonnets to her in his weekly shower of poetry, so she knew he would appreciate this volume.

Christmas Eve, Patrick surprised her by asking her to come to midnight Mass with him.

"I did the caroling thing with you, so you need to come to Mass with me." She could tell he was smiling on the other end of the phone.

"They're hardly apples and apples, Patrick, but I'd love to." Midnight Mass. It sounded vaguely romantic. They had midnight services at her church on Christmas Eve, but they never went as a family. Both her parents agreed that it was just too late.

"I'll pick you up around nine then, and you can meet my family."

Then as she hung up the phone, Kathleen realized with a jolt that he would finally be meeting *her* family as well. Her heart did a little lurch as she imagined her mother's reaction to him. Then she wondered what Patrick's family would be like. Funny, she thought, when she went to meet Paul's family, she was terrified they would not like her, but she had always known her mother would be enchanted by Paul. Now things had reversed themselves somehow. What would her mother think of Patrick, Catholic Patrick, who was neither as rich nor as handsome as Paul? Then she worried about what she should wear on her head to church. Certainly not the terrible Rush hat, which was the only one she owned. She would just have to make do with her lace scarf. The romance of midnight Mass evaporated with the reality of the events that loomed just a few hours away. Then she smiled in spite of herself, imagining her creative dramatics kids acting out "The Meeting of the Families." Maybe it wouldn't be too bad.

The doorbell rang right at nine.

"That must be your young man," Gran said. "I'm looking forward to meeting him."

Avoiding her mother's eyes, Kathleen went to the door. Patrick stood on the porch holding a red poinsettia. His hair still had comb marks in it, and he was wearing a navy V-neck sweater over a white shirt and grey slacks. He was more dressed up than she had seen him except for the dance they had gone to. She was touched that he had made such an effort. Or was he simply dressing up for church?

"Come in," she said. "They're all inside."

Her father and Grandpa Andrews stood as they came into the living room. Kathleen made introductions, and the men shook hands. "This is for you, Mrs. Andrews. Merry Christmas." Patrick handed her the plant.

"Thank you, Patrick. That was very thoughtful," she said, and set the plant on the end table. Kathleen thought her mother looked rather surprised. What had she been expecting? Kathleen wondered.

"Will you have a cup of eggnog with us?" Mr. Andrews asked Patrick.

"I'd love one, sir."

"You twenty-one yet, young man?"

"Yes, sir, but I like eggnog plain."

"Good man," her father said with a smile, slapping Patrick on the shoulder. "I wouldn't want to get arrested on Christmas for supplying liquor to a minor."

"Have a seat by me, Patrick," Gran said, patting the sofa cushion next to her. "Kathleen says you're going to be an accountant. Never could do figures much myself."

"I find them fascinating," Patrick responded to her. "I love the challenge of making everything balance out."

"It's a challenge, all right," Gran said.

"And what do you intend to do after you graduate?" It was from Kathleen's mother.

"I hope to get a job with one of the large accounting firms for a while, until I learn the ropes, and then go into business for myself."

"You've got the right idea, son. Nothing beats being in business for yourself," her father put in, "unless it's getting a regular paycheck from someone else who has to do all the worrying."

They all made small talk for what seemed to Kathleen like hours, when Patrick said they had better go if they were going to meet his family and get to Mass on time. "It's pretty crowded for this service, as you might imagine."

She went in to get her coat and her lace scarf as Patrick said how nice it had been to meet them all.

As Kathleen bent to kiss Gran good-bye, Gran whispered, "This is a nice young man. I like him, honey."

A wave of love for her grandmother swept through Kathleen as she led Patrick to the door. The careful composure of her mother's face couldn't dim how Gran's words made her feel.

"Nice people, Kath," Patrick said once they were in the car. "I especially liked your grandparents. I wish mine were still around. Your Gran's Scottish accent reminded me of my grandmother's, except hers was Irish, of course."

"Of course."

Patrick turned into a long street of large, two-story houses built around the turn of the century. It had begun to rain lightly, and the Christmas lights that shone from every window made the spattered windshield a kaleidoscope.

"Well, are you ready to meet my tribe? We're almost there."

He pulled over in front of a large white house. They parked the car and Patrick helped her out, holding his raincoat over her as they dashed to the front door.

"Hey, Patrick, 'bout time you showed up. But, my, no wonder you're late!" A taller version of Patrick with the same blond hair met them at the door and took Kathleen's hand. "I'm Patrick's handsome older brother, Michael. And you must be Kathleen."

"Now stop it at once, Michael McHugh," said a small woman who was obviously their mother. "Welcome, Kathleen, and pay them no mind. I admit to being their mother, but I'm not responsible for any of them. They all take after their father's side."

"And that's a compliment sure," said Mr. McHugh, taking Kathleen's hand out of his son's. "We McHugh men have fine taste in women, and I'm pleased to see that my youngest son hasn't lost the touch."

He led Kathleen into the living room. A huge fire blazed in the fireplace. A tall, bushy Christmas tree stood in the corner between two mismatched wingback chairs that once must have been plush. A mostly red Oriental rug lay haphazardly on the floor, dappled by a row of wood chips from another door to a pile of split logs on the hearth. Everything appeared jumbled together but very comfortable.

Patrick introduced her to his other brother, Peter, and a sister, Katie. She also met a messy brown dog named O'Grady and two fat grey cats named Wattle and Daub.

"You named them, didn't you," Kathleen asked Patrick.

"Oho! She really knows you, little brother," Michael crowed as Patrick reddened.

"Behave, Michael, it's Christmas," Mrs. McHugh said. "I thought we could sing a carol or two before we leave for church. Sort of get us in the mood. Come on, Katie."

Katie sat on a battered piano stool, the kind with crystal globes in brass claw feet, and began to play "Oh Come, All Ye Faithful." Everyone gathered around the piano and began to sing, except Patrick, who held the music open for his sister. Their voices blended and filled the room with gorgeous harmony. It was far lovelier than Kathleen's group had sounded in the caroling group with Fishers.

"You are wonderful," she exclaimed when the song finished.

"Just like the von Trapps, but we don't look so good in those leather shorts," Michael said.

"And it's too hard to travel with the piano," Patrick added.

"Such kidders," Mrs. McHugh said. "Have I mentioned there's not a drop of Sullivan blood in them? They are totally their father's."

Kathleen laughed with them and felt wonderfully included. They were strangers, but they wrapped her in as if she were one of the family.

They sang a few more carols until Patrick suggested they'd better leave for church. "We'll walk, Kathleen, if that's all right with you. It's just a couple of blocks, and this is about the closest parking place we're likely to find."

"Good news, it's stopped raining," Michael announced from the front porch.

"I wish just once we could have a white Christmas," Katie said, closing the lid of the piano and stacking the caroling books neatly.

"You need to live in Minnesota for that, I'm afraid," Mr. McHugh said. "I don't think there's ever been a white Christmas in Seattle. At least not in my lifetime, which is a darn good thing too. People don't know how to drive in the snow around here."

"Oh, Pa. Don't be so practical. It would be beautiful."

"Not only that, it would be a miracle. Let's go so we can get a seat."

They walked in a group to the enormous white church. Inside it was dim and holy. Candles twinkled in myriad alcoves beneath statues of saints. An organ played, and the sharp and faintly cloying odor of incense and the smell of beeswax assailed Kathleen. She stood uncomfortably while the McHughs dipped their fingers in the font of holy water and crossed themselves. She and Patrick followed them as they walked up the long aisle to find a pew that could accommodate all of them. Everyone but Kathleen knelt quickly in the aisle and then slid into the pew and knelt again to pray. She sat instead, feeling a bit awkward.

There were hundreds of people there, many kneeling on the prayer benches, a few with rosaries glinting in their hands. The sanctuary was packed with red poinsettias against tall fir trees. Everything was red and green and bathed in golden light. It was beautiful. Kathleen studied the large crucifix above the altar. The agonized body of Christ hung above the decorations celebrating his birth, the red of his blood matching the flowers below.

She had never thought much about the Catholic Church or any church for that matter until she went to Fishers. As far as she was concerned, differences between churches were more about architecture than philosophy. Her mother's disparaging comments about Catholics over the years, which her father always laughingly disputed with a "Now, Joan," were as much conversation about religion as she'd ever had. There was also the huge flap about

Kennedy as a Catholic President, but so far her mother's prediction that the Pope would run the country hadn't come to pass.

Guy's explanation that Catholics could never really experience a personal relationship with Christ because of all the layers of priests and popes they had to go through just to pray had made sense to her at the time. Yet here was Patrick's entire family kneeling and praying together. It didn't quite add up. They were all praying without a priest. Did God not hear their prayers? Just then the organ music swelled and everyone rose. The priest and several others in robes came slowly up the aisle behind a small boy carrying a tall golden cross. "Just follow me," Patrick whispered, "and it's OK not to kneel."

Had Patrick sensed her uneasiness? The Mass began, but she couldn't follow the Latin. The priest would say something unintelligible, and the altar boys would respond in low voices, their words blending into a sort of murmur.

The sermon was short, far shorter than she was used to, and mercifully in English, all about the glorious birth of Christ and the unquestioning belief of the shepherds, whom it would be wise to emulate. Then incense roiled about the altar as the priest swung something from a long gold chain.

"What's that for?" Kathleen whispered to Patrick, hoping his family couldn't hear her.

"Helps the prayers go up and deodorizes the church."

She elbowed him in the ribs as he smiled broadly.

Finally the priest turned his back to the congregation and removed a golden object from a small box-like stand on the altar. A golden goblet was handed to him, and other priests or helpers with their backs to her, poured water and wine into it. Then the priest raised a round wafer above his head and held it there for a moment before he lowered it again. She couldn't see what he was doing, but she presumed he was eating it. She had studied the sacrament of transubstantiation in her Western Civ class and could not imagine how anyone could believe that the bread and wine actually became flesh and blood in the mouth. It made her shudder. Communion in her church meant that Jesus was spiritually present but not physically in the host. Surely they realized that Christ was speaking metaphorically and that Communion was symbolic.

A great shuffling began next, as people edged to the aisles. Patrick remained in his seat while the rest of his family went up to take Communion.

"Aren't you going up with them?" she whispered.

"No. We don't like to leave visitors unattended. Sometimes they bolt."

Kathleen poked him again and then concentrated on the activity at the altar rail. People disappeared from her line of sight as they knelt. The priest placed a wafer into the mouths of the kneeling parishioners, who then rose and walked back from the altar with hands pressed together in front of them. In Kathleen's church the minister just placed the host into her cupped hands as she knelt, and she put it into her mouth herself. Then the wine was offered from a chalice if you wanted to take a sip. In a way there was a majesty in all this Catholic ritual that fascinated Kathleen. If she had been there merely as an observer, it would have been quite interesting. But because Patrick and his family were a part of it, she found it unsettling.

Afterwards, they walked back to the house together, and Kathleen said her good-byes all around. All of them said how delighted they had been to have met her and insisted that she come back again soon. She waved happily as Patrick helped her into the car.

"They loved you, Kath, in case you couldn't tell."

"I liked them too, Patrick. They seem to have such fun together." She was thinking of her own family gathering again.

"I have a present for you." Patrick said. "Open the glove box."

She did and found a small, flat package, strangely similar in shape to the one she had put into her purse in case there would be an opportunity to give it to him. Smiling, she unwrapped the silver paper.

"Oh, Patrick. It's perfect." It was a small volume of the complete sonnets of Elizabeth Barrett Browning. "And you will see why." She handed him the package from her purse and watched as he ripped through the paper.

"Sonnets from Shakespeare. Great minds," he said with a shake of his head. Then he leaned across the seat to kiss her. "Merry Christmas, Kathleen."

"It is, Patrick. It truly is."

And it was. Even the Christmas card she got from Paul before she'd moved home hadn't produced the same effect on her. The sight of his handwriting on the envelope had merely triggered suspicion as to what glib thing he would say this time. He'd wished her a Merry Christmas and said he didn't know when he'd be home. She had sent him a card, but she merely signed her name in it.

March 1962

By Spring Quarter she and Patrick both knew their relationship had become more serious. In the Del Phi world, a girl didn't go exclusively with one fellow for more than six months without becoming pinned, but in Patrick's case, with no fraternities at Seattle U, he had no fraternity pin to give her. He had, however, begun to make small, light allusions to marriage.

He would graduate at the end of summer, so he could participate in the flood of spring interviews on campus to land a good accounting job. All the major firms sent representatives to the colleges to grab the brightest and shiniest. "And since there's no one shinier than I am, I should have my pick of jobs, and I'll be quite wealthy by the time you graduate the next spring. I know the style to which your mother would expect you to become accustomed."

Kathleen would smile and joke right along with him, even though the occasional allusions to her mother made her nervous. She had taken to going home on the weekends less and less often so that Patrick could always pick her up at the sorority and she wouldn't have to deal with her mother's questioning—and usually disapproving—looks.

"How many kids should we have?" he would tease.

"Two, like normal Protestants," she would retort.

Then one night she said in the same spirit of play, "And, of course, they won't be brought up in the Catholic Church."

"Why not?" he said after a moment's pause. "Are you really that opposed to it?"

"Only to bringing up my children in it, Patrick. You can still go to Mass," she said, starting to laugh. The look on his face stopped her. They had bantered like this on many occasions when she would try to get him to Fishers or he would invite her to Mass. They had never really argued. Usually he would smile and avoid comment, or he would laugh and call her a bigot. Once, in mock sorrow, he said he would light large candles for her in hopes she would come back to the True Church. This time there was no lightness.

She quickly changed the subject and pretended she had not noticed anything, but the incident jarred her. What if his church really meant as much to him as hers did to her? Since he didn't attend regularly or talk about his faith much, it hadn't occurred to her that he might be as strong in his beliefs as she had come to be in hers. They always had so much fun together she hadn't really let herself think about any problems that might loom in the future. It seemed too far away.

She busied herself all week with schoolwork and kept her mind anywhere but on Patrick. Then late one night the following week, Kathleen sat with Mary on the back hall stairs talking about Mary's future.

"What do you think, Mar?" Kathleen asked her. "Do we have a pinning coming up? Does Mark talk about it at all? Even little hints?"

"I can't figure it out. Neither of us is seeing anyone else, but he doesn't say anything."

"How long has it been?"

"Nearly eight months. I really expected something at Valentine's Day."

"What did he do?"

"He got me a huge box of chocolates and a long-stemmed red rose."

"That's pretty romantic."

"I thought so, too, but he never said anything else."

"How did he sign the card?"

"He always signs 'Love,' but he never says it. I don't know what to do."

"Well, give him until after finals, and then, if he doesn't say something, tell him you've decided you both should date other people, since things don't seem to be going anywhere."

"That's what I thought I'd do. But what if he says OK?"

"Don't be silly, Mar. He's not stupid. No one would let you run around loose. He knows what a good deal you are. Maybe he's just slow."

"Yeah, maybe. What about you and Patrick?"

"I don't know. We always joke about our relationship, but the other night he got a little serious, and I didn't know what to say. I just pretended he was still joking. With Paul I was so smitten, I would have run to Mars with him. But with Patrick, it's just been so comfortable. I haven't worried about commitment and I-love-you's."

"But it's been nearly six months," Mary reminded her. "That's a long time to be with just one guy without some idea where you want things to go."

"You're right, but maybe that's why his sort-of-serious response was so, I don't know, so scary."

"Are you getting serious about him at all?"

"I think so. This church thing is really big though. I've tried to talk to him about how I believe, and he's been to a Fishers' activity with me, but his whole family is really involved with their church. I just don't know how that would work. Not to mention the fact that my mother would die if I married a Catholic."

"Yeah, so would my Lutheran-forever folks. Some people can make religion pretty sticky. How serious are you about Patrick? I mean is this religion thing going to cause trouble? Because if you're not serious about him, is it fair to keep stringing him along? Mark says Patrick's never been like this with anyone before. And you have to admit, he's a pretty special guy."

"He's the best, Mar. Even not compared to Paul."

"Compared to Paul, Jack the Ripper was a saint. Patrick's in a whole different league!"

"But I don't think I'm stringing him along."

"Are you falling in love with him?"

"I don't know. Sometimes there's chemistry, but most of the time it's like good friends."

"What's wrong with that?"

"That's the question, isn't it? I wish I still had my Magic Eight Ball. We could ask it what to do."

"On the big questions, mine always said 'Ask again later.'"

"Come to think of it, so did mine. I guess what will happen will happen."

"I hate that. I want to know right now."

"So do I."

Kathleen welcomed the interruption in her worries about Patrick when it was again time for cheerleading tryouts. This year she would be helping judge with Billie and the others on the squad who would be graduating. It seemed strange not to be trying out herself, especially since Trudy and one other junior were trying for a third year. She knew her mother was a bit disappointed, but only after Mrs. Lavik mentioned that not many girls were on the squad for three years. Kathleen explained that she felt she needed the time for her senior year to concentrate on her major, so her mother was a bit mollified, sniffing, "Of course, your studies have to come first."

A freshman Delta Phi made the final cut, and Kathleen and Billie jumped off the stage at the announcement to congratulate her. Trudy and the junior also made it, and Kathleen hugged them both, feeling a bit sad that she wouldn't be cheering next year. It had been such a part of her life for so long. But at the same time she was secretly glad she wouldn't have any reason to be with Trudy anymore. As Gran would say, there's always something good in everything if you just look hard enough.

"Won't you miss it?" Billie asked her as they all walked back to the house.

"Of course I will," she replied. "I'm just getting so involved with the children's theater thing that I don't think I'll have that many free Saturdays next fall."

"I can't imagine going to the games next year and sitting in the stands. And on the adult side! What a change. It makes me feel so old." Billie shuddered.

"Yes, you are ancient. You're probably even eligible to vote. But look at it this way, you can finally use your own I.D. in a cocktail lounge."

"Ah, yes. The privileges of old age."

༺༻

The spring formal was coming up. Kathleen couldn't believe all that had happened to her since last year's Rogue formal. She had floated through that evening with Paul. And headed for the biggest thump when the balloon burst, she thought. This year she would be with Patrick. There were no butterflies about inviting him, no worrying about what he would think when she called. She knew what he would think; he was in love with her and had finally told her so. His poems had gotten more and more romantic, and finally one night he had recited one to her from her own Browning book.

"I love that one," she had told him.

"I love you," was his reply.

She had been surprised and a bit stunned and hadn't known what to say. But then he smiled at her and melted her heart. It felt so much better being with someone who cared and wasn't afraid to admit it, someone she could trust. Patrick would never cheat on her. It wouldn't occur to him to be dishonorable. Of course, she had trusted Paul in the same way, but that was before she found out what he was really like. How naive she had been, and how clever Paul had been to use that. Really, it was her blind trust that enabled him to cheat on her, she admitted to herself. She never even suspected.

Well, that was all behind her now. Her time with Patrick was special and wonderful, and she rarely gave Paul a thought unless it was to thank God that she found him out when she did.

The night of the formal, Patrick arrived with Mark to pick her and Mary up.

"You look so beautiful," Patrick said, handing her gardenias when she came out to meet him.

"So do you," she replied. He looked remarkably handsome, a word she had not used to describe him before. Except for the pledge dance all those months ago, she realized that she had rarely seen him dressed up.

"Gee, maybe I should wear a tuxedo every day."

"I don't know, pal," Mark said. "I don't think I'd want my taxes done by a guy in a tux. Smacks of high overhead."

"Nonsense," Mary said. "I think guys should wear tuxedoes all the time. They look fabulous in them."

"Yeah, especially playing basketball. Tails would be the order of the day then, I would think," Mark added.

"Would the numbers go on the tails or on the cummerbund?" Patrick examined Mark's tux like a tailor.

They all laughed and headed out to Mark's car. The dance was at a near-by country club with beautiful gardens. The dinner was delicious and the music was excellent. After a particularly long set of dancing, Kathleen and Patrick went outside to get some air.

"Look at those stars!" she said. The absence of lights around the golf course revealed more stars than could ever be seen in town.

"They came out to see you."

She looked at Patrick with a smile and saw that he wasn't smiling back. He led her to a bench, and drew her down beside him. "Kathleen," he said, taking both of her hands in his, "I've been thinking a lot about our last conversation. What if you didn't have to convert? What difference would it make if I stayed a Catholic and you stayed a Protestant?"

"Patrick, what are you talking about?"

"I'm talking about us, Kathleen. I don't think you know how much I love you. I want to spend the rest of my life with you.

Forever. I meant what I said before. By this time next year, I should be well established in my career, and we could get married when you graduate next June."

"Married?" Her face was suddenly tingling, and she felt light-headed. Music from the ballroom floated out around them. It was a perfect night for this. Hollywood couldn't have set it up better. He was proposing. Why was she reacting like this?

"You sound surprised. You must know how I feel. Am I alone in this?"

"Of course not, Patrick. I love you too." Well, she did.

He smiled at her then with such eagerness that he looked fourteen. He pulled her to him and kissed her. Then holding her close, he pressed his forehead to hers and smiled again.

"Would your folks come to an Episcopalian wedding, do you think?" She said it in the old way that they had always bantered, but his smile stopped.

"We could have both my priest and your pastor officiate. I've given it a lot of thought. I even talked to my priest about it. He wouldn't mind if your pastor served with him." He had released her and was now holding her hand.

"You spoke to your priest? About us?"

"Well, yes. I thought it was important."

"It is important, but why didn't you say anything to me about it first? Why would you go to your priest?" Her voice had a shrill edge, she realized.

"Kathleen," he began in bewilderment.

"Did you have to get permission to ask me to marry you? Do you have a special dispensation, perhaps?"

"Of course not. I just wanted to . . . " He dropped her hand and ran his fingers through his hair.

How could this be happening? They had been having so much fun. This was not how it was supposed to go. Why couldn't she get her lines right?

"I care about you, Patrick, it's the Church. People should be able to talk to God any time they want, without going to some priest. I can't imagine bringing up children that way. I mean, it's no one's business what we do or think, but you have to tell your priest about every little thing. You talked to him before you even talked to me. Is that how our lives will be?"

"Kathleen, I don't have to go through a priest . . . I mean, the priest isn't . . ." And then they were both crying. Kathleen clung to him, burying her face in his shoulder. This could not be happening. All the lightness of their relationship seemed to have been a protective shield against this moment.

Patrick took a handkerchief out of his pocket and handed it to her. She took it and dabbed at her eyes, trying not to smear her makeup. Then she wiped his cheek. They both tried to smile and failed.

"We'd better go in before we both look too terrible to face anyone," he said, taking the hankie back from her. He kissed her gently on the forehead and drew her to her feet. "I should have picked a better time. I'm sorry, Kathleen. I just couldn't wait."

"I'm sorry, too, Patrick. It's just that I was so surprised."

"How could you be surprised? We've talked about this for a long time."

"I thought you were teasing. I mean, next year seems so far away. And you know how I feel about my beliefs."

"I'm not asking you to give that up, Kathleen. It's one of the things I love about you."

"Patrick . . ."

"Shh," he said, placing his fingers on her lips. "I should have knelt. My fault."

Kathleen felt miserable watching him try to make her feel better. He had proposed to her in this romantic setting. That's how it was supposed to happen. Why wasn't she happy? She didn't know what to think. She wished she were somewhere else. Making another attempt at a smile, she took his arm and they walked back into the building.

The glare of the lights in the lobby made her blink, and she was thankful that the lights were dimmer in the ballroom. Somehow they made small talk with the others at the table and danced the rest of the dances, holding each other tightly.

As they walked to the car with Mary and Mark, Kathleen avoided Mary's eyes. She could tell her friend sensed something was wrong, and she knew if she looked at Mary, she would burst into tears again.

When they got back to the house, Patrick gave a quick goodbye to Mary and Mark and took Kathleen's hand. Mary looked questioningly at Kathleen, and said, "Good night, you two. See you upstairs, Kath," then went up the stairs to the front door.

"I parked my car about a block away," Patrick whispered. "Please walk with me."

They walked in silence. The night smelled like lilacs and dew-wet grass and her gardenias. Patrick held the door for her when they got to his car, and she slid in. He went around to his side and got in.

"Kathleen, I don't know what to say. I . . ." And then he was kissing her, over and over again, as if his kisses could change everything and make it right between them again. She responded with a rush of passion she had never felt before with him.

"Oh, Patrick, why does this have to happen? Why can't we just go on like before?" Without preamble, tears streamed down her face.

"Because I want to marry you, Kathleen. I want to live with you and have children with you and show the world that we belong to each other. I'm tired of taking you back to your sorority at night when my whole body is aching to have you and not even be able to kiss you good night at the door. No, we can't just go on like before. I know it'll be at least a year of waiting, but I could do that if you were at the end of that wait. Please, you must decide."

She had to be in soon. There wasn't time for what had to be said. All she could do was cry.

"I guess I'd better get you back," he said, looking at the clock. "Please think about it, Kathleen. I want to marry you whenever you'll have me." He started the car and drove the block to the sorority. At the door he kissed her hand and held it in both of his. The pain in his eyes broke her heart again. What was wrong with her? He was a wonderful man who wanted her to be his wife.

The door opened at that moment, and the housemother said, "One minute, Kathleen. You'd better come in now."

Patrick squeezed her hand and turned to walk down the stairs. Keeping her head down so Mrs. D couldn't see her tears, she rushed into the house and up the stairs. As she expected, Mary was waiting for her in her room.

"OK, kiddo, what's going on?" Mary said.

"I wish I knew, Mar. I think I am about the rottenest person on the planet."

"No, you broke up with that person a long time ago. But what makes you so bad?"

Kathleen told Mary what had happened and then burst into tears again.

"Well, it seems to me, if anyone wondered, that the brief encounter I had with your Fishers group claimed that it doesn't matter what church you go to as long as you have some sort of 'relationship' with God." She handed Kathleen a tissue. "Patrick certainly seems to have a relationship with God, and a rather strong one at that. How come he can't join your club? What's the deal here?"

"Oh, Mary, Catholics aren't really Christians. They have this whole hierarchy of priests and saints and statues and whatnot. And you have to bring your kids up to believe all that stuff. And they can do whatever they like and then just confess it to some priest and then they do some penance, and poof—sin's all gone."

"That sounds pretty good to me," Mary said.

Kathleen sat down on the bed with a thump. Why was she being so obstinate? Before her experience with Fishers, she rarely gave the Catholic Church a thought. Only her mother's disapproval whenever it was brought up caused her to be aware of it at all, and she certainly didn't share her mother's objections, which were purely social.

Since Fishers, she had tried to define what she believed. Guy and the others there seemed so happy and so confident. She wanted to be like them. She studied her Bible, underlining passages that seemed significant. She prayed for God's guidance, especially during the heartbreak with Paul. But there was no priest who could arbitrarily tell her if her decisions were right or wrong. She just had to take her chances and trust her faith to see her through.

She knew from her experience with Paul that she wanted someone who believed the way she did to share her life with. But why, then, did she have such feelings for Patrick? Paul had teased her about Fishers, changing one of her favorite hymns into a cha cha. Yet she had not minded Paul's nonreligion. Why did she mind so much Patrick's faith?

"I don't know what to do, Mar."

"Yes, you do, Kath. If this were Paul last year, you would have been floating around here and been perfectly unbearable. If you aren't having that reaction now, you must not really love Patrick."

The panicked feeling in her stomach fought its way to her throat. Had she realized this would happen from the beginning and just ignored it, playing at love?

"And if you don't love him, you certainly can't think about marrying him. You have to let him know."

"How can I tell him, Mary? He's the most wonderful man I've ever known. I can't hurt him like that."

"You'll hurt him more if you play him along, my friend. He deserves better than that. And you need your head examined."

Monday night at chapter dinner there were two candles passed. The buzz around the tables was that one of them must be Kathleen's. The more she denied it, the more people tittered and accused her of bluffing. When one candle bouquet was finally brought to her table, the girls there rolled their eyes and nudged each other. They were completely surprised when one of the freshmen blew it out and announced that she and her high-school sweetheart would be marrying in June. He was still in California, so there would be no serenade after dinner.

The other candle belonged to a sophomore who was not getting married for a year. Her fiancé was an Alpha Delt, and Mrs. D dismissed everyone to go upstairs and "freshen up" for the fraternity's imminent arrival.

"We thought for sure it would be you, Kathleen," her tablemates said as they left the dining room. "You and Patrick seemed pretty much in a world by yourselves at the formal."

Kathleen could barely smile back at them. It would be lovely to blow out the candle with a beautiful diamond ring attached to it and stand with her intended in the living room to be serenaded by her sorority sisters. She couldn't imagine actually planning a wedding, yet she'd had her wedding colors all picked out since high school. Most of her friends had. They spent long hours at slumber parties discussing it. If her wedding was in the fall, she'd have her attendants carry sheaves of wheat with yellow and rust-colored mums. If the wedding was in the winter, they would carry muffs with red roses and holly on them. If spring, she couldn't decide between tulips or lilacs, but the color scheme could be nearly the same. What they hadn't discussed was the groom part. They had all just assumed that piece would fall into place so they could proceed with their wedding plans. And there were sure to be lots of potential grooms when they got to college.

Kathleen could never have imagined that being proposed to could make her this miserable. Was Mary right, then? Did she truly know what to say to Patrick? The looks on the faces of both newly engaged girls at dinner were the complete opposite of the look on the face staring back at her from the mirror now. The girls were radiant, stretching out their slender hands to show off their new rings.

She thought she loved Patrick. Certainly when he kissed her the way he had Saturday night, she felt waves of passion for him. Wasn't that a sign? She looked at the picture of the two of them at the pledge dance that sat on her dresser. He was nice looking. He was bright. He loved her. Was her objection just to the Catholic Church? Or was that a smoke screen to hide, as Mary said, that she didn't really love him enough? Could she come to love him more in time?

She had thought that she could never be as miserable as she was when she discovered Paul was two-timing her, but this was worse. She knew what it felt like to be in that kind of pain; inflicting it on someone she cared about was much worse.

She heard the Alpha Delts arriving, lots of shuffling feet on the porch below her window, male voices joking and laughing, the doorbell ringing. She just couldn't face it. She stepped out of her heels, and pulled her dress over her head. Putting on a skirt and blouse and her flats, she grabbed her notebooks and headed down the back steps so she could leave the house unnoticed.

The night was warm and still fairly light because of daylight saving time. She headed for the library on campus. Maybe her paper on the Whitman Massacre for her Washington State History class would take her mind off herself for a while. Surely her troubles were minor compared to what the early missionaries had gone through.

When she came back to the house at ten, there was a message from Patrick waiting for her, but all three lines on the phones were busy until after eleven, and she knew that if he'd tried to call again, he couldn't have gotten through.

On Tuesday, there was a poem in her box in his beautiful script. It was light and sweet, and it didn't even allude to their conversation, except with a postscript that read: "I had a wonderful time with the loveliest girl at the dance. Maybe I will invest in a tuxedo!"

Kathleen smiled in spite of herself. Maybe things would be all right.

But they weren't. The unresolved issues lay like pentimento just under the surface, no matter how hard they tried to paint over them. Patrick was as attentive and sweet as ever, which broke her heart. The more thoughtful he became, the more she tried to respond. She was miserable, and she suspected he was too.

At Fishers one night in May, Guy talked about Christian marriage. It was as if he were speaking directly to her.

"Well, now, here we are in one of the most gorgeous springtimes God ever blessed us with. And y'all know where a young man's fancy turns to in spring. And a young lady's as well, I would imagine. So tonight I want to talk about love, the earthly kind for a change."

There was bright laughter from the crowd.

"God has given us a wonderful gift in creating us with the capacity to love. A relationship based on God's love is—well, it's just about the best thing there is. Imagine being able to pray together over your disagreements and really feel the Lord's answers in your hearts. There's something to that old saying that a family that prays together stays together.

"It's like God has given you a compass, and anytime y'all feel even a tiny bit lost, why, all you do is check that compass—together, mind you—and you're right back on the true path, sure as rain. But if you both don't share that same faith, if you both don't know the love of Jesus in your hearts, then the compass doesn't work. One of you may be turned to the Light, but the other might not see. Then it's like that old Tower of Babel where nobody could understand what the other was talking about.

"The love of God is complete. And when two people who have the Lord's love in their hearts find one another, well, my friends, it doesn't get any better than that. I'll grant you that sometimes a sweetheart might come to the Lord when he sees the Power working in your life, and we all know what a glorious thing it is to bring someone to the Lord, but guard your hearts from the beginning. The shared love we feel tonight in this room—well, take hands around and just feel it."

Kathleen joined hands with the two girls on either side of her. Guy's words dropped like stones on her heart. She did love Patrick, but she could never share the love with him that she felt coursing through the room just now. She thought of the Mass she had attended with his family. She hadn't felt God's love in Patrick's church the way Guy explained it. But, then, she hadn't understood much about the service, let alone the Latin. Her head began to ache.

"Let us pray while our hands are joined," Guy continued. "Dear Lord, guide the wonderful young people here tonight to walk ever with You, to be guided ever by You, and to seek true earthly love with one who knows You. May they ever fix their course on Your true compass that their way may be unfaltering and filled with Your love as they look for a love that lasts not only for this lifetime, but through all eternity with You.

"We ask this in Jesus' precious name, Amen."

Kathleen didn't stay for coffee. She walked slowly out into the still-light evening. Was tonight a sign? Was God speaking to her through Guy? Patrick was the sweetest, finest man. She couldn't imagine that a life with him would be difficult. He loved her and told her so not only in words, but in everything he did for her. Wasn't that enough? She had prayed for an answer, but was this it?

The Del Phi willow tree was still pale green, but all the branches had softened into a veil of new leaves. She touched their softness and slipped behind them. She wished she could just stay there in this safe, green place and never have to come out.

Chapter 8

June 1962

Moving home for the summer did nothing to lighten Kathleen's mood. If her mother answered the phone when Patrick called, she handed the receiver to Kathleen with a look of utter disapproval. Kathleen always kept the calls short. Patrick had begun his new job in a large accounting firm that had hired him even before he graduated. When he picked her up at home, Kathleen made it a point to be absolutely ready when he arrived so they could zip out of the house and not have to sit around and chat.

Back at her old job at her father's company, Kathleen was grateful for the tediousness of the tasks she had to perform. Today she had already finished the filing and was now replacing pages in various catalogues with updated information. The jobs were mindless and difficult to do incorrectly, so even in her muddled state, she was able to do the tasks without making mistakes.

"How about lunch today, Kitten?" Her father's voice startled her, and she dropped the staple remover.

"Love to, Daddy," she managed to say.

They went to the familiar diner, but her father directed her to a booth rather than the counter where they usually sat. After they gave their orders to the waitress, her father took her hand.

"What's going on, Kitten? You seem upset. Anything you want to share with your old dad?"

"Oh, Daddy, is it that obvious?"

"Well, you don't seem like your old, cheerleading self. At first I thought I'd just been given a reprieve because you were finally over making up those routines, but it seems like more than that."

"I don't know what to do, Daddy. It's Patrick. He's so wonderful and so serious, but he's also so . . . so . . ."

"So Catholic?" he finished for her. She nodded her head miserably. "Now look here, young lady. I've tolerated your mother's snobbery about Catholics as long as I've known her because she didn't harm anyone directly with it, and we both know that's just how she is. Her folks were the same way, so I guess you can't blame her. But that Patrick fellow is one nice young man."

"I know. He's the best."

"But what? Don't blame his church if that's not what this is all about."

"No, it's not just the church. I certainly don't feel the way Mom does. With me it's more that we don't share the same beliefs."

"Nonsense, you've gone to church since you were a little girl."

"I know, Daddy, but since I've been to college and gone to Fishers, I've come to believe that being a Christian is more than just going to church. They say going to church doesn't make you a Christian any more than going into a garage makes you a car."

"Well, shutting people out for their beliefs doesn't seem very Christian to me. The Catholic Church is paved with Christian stuff. How can you think they're not Christians?"

She didn't want to get into it. The words sounded hollow, and she feared that her father would think them silly. She wanted him on her side. She wanted him to fix things as he had always done when she was a child. But she knew, deep down, that she had to do this one herself.

"I know it doesn't make sense, even to me. That's why I'm so confused."

"Well, maybe you should spend a little less time with those Fisher people. They seem to be muddying up your good sense. Look at Patrick for what he is, not for what he isn't or what you wish he could be. If what he is doesn't suit, then you have a case. But you can't change people, Kitten. Your mother can tell you that." He smiled his warm smile at her and squeezed her hand. "But different isn't always bad. Just think about what I said, will you?"

"Thanks, Daddy, I will. I love you."

"I love you too, Kitten.

The summer rain that always fell in June finally segued into glorious sunny days, and Kathleen's mood brightened as well. She and Patrick saw each other often, but he didn't bring up marriage again. Things seemed light and fun once more. They did zany things and laughed a lot. Once they took a banana cream pie to a drive-in and devoured it while they watched the movie. Another time they wandered around the Public Market just to watch the street performers, or sometimes they drove around exploring antique shops in small towns. At one shop Patrick bought her an ancient lace-edged handkerchief with her initial embroidered on it in blue. She somehow seemed to have taken her father's advice and was fretting less about Patrick. He *was* a wonderful guy, and she was being silly.

In August, she and Mary got together with their sorority sisters to plan the details for Rush. Neither of them could believe they were going to be seniors and that this would be their last Rush.

"In a couple of weeks we'll be moving into the house for the last time!"

Mary said as they cut out tiny silver stars for the name tags. "It seems like yesterday we stood outside the Ice House together, doesn't it, Kath?"

"With me so ignorant of Rush and sorority life, and you having to fill me in on everything. I thought I would die when you said houses could actually drop you."

"What did you think happened?" asked a sophomore on the committee.

"I didn't have any idea. I thought you just picked the one you liked and that was it."

"Boy, were you naive," Mary said. "It's a good thing you were with me. You'd be living in the dorms now for sure."

"I know you're joking, but isn't it funny to think where we'd be right now if we hadn't pledged Del Phi? Our whole lives would be different."

"Absolutely. You'd be completely lost if you hadn't met me. And you wouldn't be planning your future with Patrick." She gave Kathleen a pointed look, which made Kathleen's stomach clench.

At that very second, Kathleen knew with absolute certainty she had to break up with Patrick. So many people expected her to be with him. Even her father. But she knew that she had been kidding herself. She cared deeply for Patrick, but she was not in love with him. Something Mary had said once came back to her with stunning truth. If Paul had proposed to her, she would have been ecstatic. When Patrick proposed, she withdrew. How much more of a sign did she need, a burning bush? The prospect of hurting him again sickened her, and she focused intensely on the silver paper in her hand.

She felt rotten. What kind of person was she, anyway? Fall in love with scoundrels, break up with saints. She laughed aloud at the irony of her Catholic allusion to Patrick.

"What's funny?" Mary asked.

"Nothing," Kathleen said, embarrassed that she had made a noise. Improvising quickly she said, "I was just thinking about how many stars we must have cut out over the last three years." By the time Kathleen got home, she was more miserable than ever. Her mother met her at the door with a broad smile.

"You'll never guess who called you tonight."

Kathleen knew from her mother's pleased expression that it hadn't been Patrick.

"Who?"

"Paul Gordon! I thought you weren't hearing from him."

Paul called her? Paul? What could he possibly want? Why was this happening? Wasn't she confused enough? She couldn't even remember how long he'd been gone. Was he back from San Francisco?

"I told him to call back after nine or so, and he said he would. He has such a nice voice."

"Did he say what he wanted?" She was numb.

"I imagine he wanted to talk to you, silly. I let him know you were at a sorority meeting."

The phone rang. Kathleen tried not to run to answer it. She knew her mother was watching her every reaction. It was Patrick.

"Hi, I thought I'd call you on my break. How was your meeting?"

"Fine, Patrick." She tried not to sound disappointed. "I can't believe this is our last year to plan for Rush."

"Don't worry, you'll have other things to plan for next year."

It was a typically light allusion to their future together, and it nearly broke her heart. How could she tell him? Well, not on the phone and not with her mother listening. They chatted a few minutes more, and then he had to go back to work. She hung up the phone and tried not to listen for it to ring again.

It didn't. At eleven o'clock she went to bed. Perhaps Paul had tried to call when she was talking with Patrick. Was this another sign? Just when she decided to break up with Patrick, Paul phoned. After all this time. She tried to recall the hurt she felt when she found out Paul had betrayed her, but it eluded her. She remembered instead what it felt like to be with him. It was well after one before she fell asleep.

The next day at work was like moving in a fog. She remembered nothing about it except making a frantic call to Mary at her job.

"We have to have dinner tonight. I absolutely need your advice."

"Wedding plans?"

Kathleen only groaned. "Please, Mar. It's way more important than that."

"Oops. Sounds serious. Pizza or Chinese?"

"Chinese. See you at the Hong Kong at six."

Kathleen didn't even go home. Her father's office was near Chinatown, so she worked a little longer and then walked over to the huge restaurant. She sat in the black and red waiting area watching waiters scurry around with steaming plates of mysterious food. The place was fragrant with ginger and garlic and the smell of things frying in very hot oil.

After what seemed like forever, Mary plopped down beside her.

"OK, what gives? I know that neither of us vestal virgins is pregnant, so what could be so terrible?"

The smiling hostess started to seat them at a table, but Kathleen asked for a booth. Mary raised an eyebrow and followed Kathleen to the back of the room.

"I can't marry Patrick, Mary. I realized that last night. You've been right. I don't love him enough. And I know I'll hurt him terribly." She fussed with her napkin, trying desperately not to cry. Tears had threatened all day. "It just struck me last night at the meeting, and I knew."

Mary tried to interrupt, but Kathleen plunged on.

"And then when I got home, my mom told me that Paul had called. And that's not the reason I'm doing this. I knew before. But when I heard he had called, my stomach went crazy. I knew if I really loved Patrick, I wouldn't have had any reaction to Paul's call. It's like a sign."

"A sign? Boy, you do need to talk to someone. How about the waiter? He's fast approaching, and we haven't even decided."

They studied the menus quickly, decided to split moo goo gai pan and some fried rice, and waved the waiter off.

"OK, Kathleen. First things first. You say you had this epiphany at the Rush meeting that you had to break up with Patrick? How? What happened?"

"You said something about how I would never have met him if we hadn't pledged Del Phi, and suddenly I just knew. There was no preamble."

"Not good enough. You must have been thinking about it."

"I guess I just wanted to keep the relationship going as it had been. Just sort of fun. In retrospect, I guess I've been dreading this since the formal when he proposed. I thought if we just ignored it, it would go away."

"So you always knew you didn't want to marry him, and you kept on dating him anyway?"

"I sound like a rat, don't I?"

"There are some similarities."

"I didn't know I didn't want to marry him. He's so dear. I guess I hoped that somehow magic would happen, and then I'd be sure. I thought love would grow, I guess.

"But it didn't."

"No, not enough. Oh, Mary, what am I going to do? I can't just tell him, sorry, I changed my mind."

"What else is there to say— hope we can still be friends? You need to level with him, my dear. What is it about him that you don't like? Are we still on the Catholic thing?"

"That's part of it, although I think I have been trying to overlook the reality of it. It's nothing I can point to. He's wonderful. I think I have honestly been trying to fall in love with him. And some of the time I actually thought I had."

"But then Paul called."

"No. I don't think this has anything directly to do with Paul, but when I was with him, I was sure of my feelings. It's not that way with Patrick."

"Do you think he was just a replacement for Paul?"

Kathleen looked up to see if Mary was actually gathering information or making a judgment. "I don't think so. At least I hope not. It's not as if I needed someone to keep me company in my mad social whirl, you know. I was used to dragging good old Jake to functions."

"Well, what are you going to do about Paul now?"

"Who knows? Who knows if he'll even call back?"

"My point exactly. If Patrick said he'd call, you could count on it. With Mr. Wonderful . . ."

"I know. You don't have to remind me. But I can't help how I feel, Mary, or how I *don't* feel."

The waiter came with their dinner, and Kathleen busied herself with dishing up. She took a couple of bites, but the fried rice was like sawdust in her mouth.

"Look, sweetie," Mary said at last. "You can't just marry someone because you feel sorry for him. How horrible would that be? And how unfair to Patrick. Are you sure this isn't about Paul?"

"Paul had nothing to do with it, Mary. Honest. It didn't help that he'd called, but I came to this decision at our meeting."

"You heard voices, maybe? Like Joan of Arc?"

"Something like that. I just knew. Boy, whoever said knowledge is power can keep it. I don't feel powerful at all. I just want to wake up from this nightmare and have everything be fine."

"Remember how we used to moan and groan because there were no men in our lives? Maybe this is one of those be-careful-what-you-wish-for moments."

Kathleen finally managed a smile. "I knew talking with you would help, old friend."

"Glad to oblige. Besides, it was time for Chinese food anyway. I haven't had any in ages."

Back at home Kathleen did feel better, but her heart ached at the thought of what she still had to do. She wouldn't see Patrick until their usual Saturday night date, so she had a couple of days to plan what to say. She had to be honest, he deserved that, but she didn't really know how to describe what she felt. She did love him in a way, but not in the same way he loved her. How could she tell him that without sounding conceited?

The phone rang in the midst of her musings.

"Hi, Kat. Remember me?"

Her stomach lurched. Paul! She had actually forgotten about him until that moment. Kathleen held her breath.

"Hello, Paul." She tried to keep her voice from giving her away. Her heart was pounding.

"I'm finally back from San Fran, and I wanted to see you. It's been too long."

"You stayed longer than you expected." How inane did that sound?

"Yeah, we—that is my uncle, Dad, and I— thought it would be useful to have me experience the whole retail cycle from the holidays through summer fashion. I learned a lot, believe me. San Francisco is booming."

She didn't know what to say. What did he want? The silence was lengthening.

"So, are you busy this weekend?"

"Sorry, Paul, I'm busy Saturday night."

"How about Sunday?"

Say no, every voice in her head was screaming. "Sunday?"

"Yeah, if it's nice we can take the boat out. I really want to see you."

"Well . . ."

"Of course, after church. I know you don't like to miss that."

Kathleen heard herself say, "All right. How about noon?"

"Pick you up at noon on the dot. Till then."

She hung up the phone and stared at it.

༺✦༻

By the time Patrick picked her up Saturday night, she was a wreck. Her mother had quizzed her mercilessly about Paul, throwing in thinly veiled remarks about what a better catch he was. It took all her determination to stay focused on what she had to do, rather than deciding to stay with Patrick just to prove her mother wrong.

As usual, she was ready when Patrick drove up, and she dashed out the door before he even had time to get out of the car.

"Now that's what I like, a woman who can't wait to see me." He leaned over and gave her a kiss on the cheek.

His words sliced into Kathleen. How could she tell him when he was so happy?

"I thought we'd grab a pizza and then take advantage of this gorgeous weather to walk around Green Lake. What say you?"

"Sounds great," she managed to respond.

At dinner she felt as she had as a child trying to "run in" during jump rope. She weighed each moment to see if it was just the right time, and then the rope circled again. How could she tell him now when they were gooey with cheese? So she waited. After they ate, Patrick paid the bill and they were back in the car. The parking lot with people coming and going was not right. She waited again, praying that the right moment would be plainly evident.

There were people everywhere at Green Lake enjoying the glorious summer weather. Picnics and volleyball games filled the grassy area. Bicycles wove in and out around hikers and dogs. Kayaks and paddle boats dotted the lake. Music from the show at the Aqua Follies at the south end of the lake drifted out. Patrick took her hand and they began the three-mile circle around the lake.

Couples strolled hand-in-hand, just as they were doing. Just as she and Paul had once done. Were any of them less happy than they appeared? Would someone seeing her and Patrick together be envious of their relationship? Did it look perfect from afar?

Her head began to throb. They were a little over a third of the way around the lake. If she said something now, it would be almost as long if they turned back as if they went on. How could they walk that far if she told him now? Maybe she should wait until they were nearly back to the car.

"Penny for your thoughts," Patrick said.

"They aren't worth that much."

"Is something wrong, Kath? You don't seem yourself."

There was an empty bench facing the lake. "Could we sit a minute, Patrick?"

"Sure. That was a lot of pizza. We should rest every few feet."

In spite of herself, she smiled. He was so sweet. Shaking her head, she said, "Patrick, I've been giving us a lot of thought, and I just can't . . . I mean, I . . ."

She saw the hurt gather in his eyes. His smile faded. "Don't do this, Kathleen. Please."

"I'm so sorry, Patrick. I never want to hurt you. I really do love you, just . . . just not enough. I can't marry you."

"What did I do?"

"Oh my God, Patrick. You didn't do anything. You're practically perfect. It's me. I'm the one. I'm just not . . . that is, I can't . . . "

He took her hands in his and brought them to his lips. She felt the tears stinging her eyes. The late sun was still warm and the green smell of the lake broke through her fog. A cloud of the ever-present gnats swarmed up near the shore. She heard the crunch of the cinder path as two bikes sped by. It was as if time on their bench had stopped while the rest of the world spun on.

"Come on," he said, pulling her to her feet. "This isn't the place."

Kathleen couldn't answer. She nodded. They held each other's hands tightly and walked the long way back to the car.

They drove in silence, still holding hands. Patrick stopped the car near a small park a few blocks from Kathleen's house. He turned the key with his left hand and then drew her to him. "What happened, Kathleen? Please, tell me."

"I don't know, Patrick. I just know I can't marry you." She was crying again.

"Is it the church thing?"

"Mostly."

"I told you, you don't have to convert."

"But the kids would have to." Tears streamed down her cheeks.

"Kathleen, why would that be so bad? Didn't I turn out all right?"

"Oh, Patrick, you're wonderful, but you aren't free from that terrible fear that if you don't do what they say, you're doomed."

"Aren't you sort of in the same place, though? What would happen if you switched to my church? Hellfire and brimstone?"

She didn't want him to make sense. She wanted to be home. She wanted this whole scene to be over. She wanted to stop crying and feel good about herself again. She wanted Patrick not to be hurt. Why was everything so hard?

"I can't force you to love me, Kathleen, and I love you so much, I can't stand to see you so unhappy. Maybe we should take some time apart and see what happens." He smiled at her a little crookedly. "Maybe I'll make a novena."

"What's a novena?"

"When you want something really bad, you pray for it for nine days. And then it might happen." He pulled back to look at her. "But maybe I won't do it. If it didn't work, I'd have a double loss." His eyes filled with tears then, and terrible sobs broke from him. Kathleen put her arms around him and drew his head down to her shoulder. There was nothing to say. She laid her tear-streaked cheek on his hair and felt like the worst person on earth.

"I'm sorry," he said finally, straightening up and reaching for his handkerchief. "I'd better take you home before we look even worse. We look pretty cute, both of us."

"Patrick, I . . ."

"It's OK, sweetheart," he said, wiping her tears. "You have been the loveliest thing that ever happened to me. You're a part of my heart, Kathleen. That will never change."

He kissed her when they got to her house, finally, a hard lingering kiss. She didn't let him walk her to the door. It didn't help at all that she felt she was doing the right thing. Her heart was breaking.

After a sleepless night, Kathleen lay in bed knowing she should go to church, but she felt too unworthy. The memory of Patrick's tears broke her heart again and again. As she turned to bury her head in her pillow, she suddenly remembered that in just a few hours she would see Paul again. She pulled the pillow over her head. It was too much for one weekend.

Finally, she got out of bed and put on her robe. She rolled up her blinds and blinked at the brilliant early morning sunshine. It was going to be a beautiful, sunny day. Paul mentioned going out in the boat if the weather held. Whatever did she have to wear? Paul was so up on fashion, no matter what she chose would probably be wrong. She rummaged through her drawers and her closet. Nothing looked right. Giving up, she went into the bathroom to take a long shower. She'd washed her hair yesterday, so she wrapped it tightly in a towel to keep it from frizzing.

It didn't help. The steam in the bathroom wreaked havoc with her hair as soon as she removed the towel, so she pulled out her biggest rollers and set her hair anyway.

Finally she had no more busywork to divert her thoughts from Paul. What would she say to him? What could he say to her? His silly cards from San Francisco had come less and less frequently, and she stopped being excited when one appeared in the mail. She still couldn't believe he had called after all this time. She hadn't told her mother about the date. She could just imagine the look on her face when she saw Paul. What on earth should she wear? It suddenly hit her that she had never agonized this way over Patrick. He always thought she looked beautiful no matter what she wore. Once again she was awash with guilt.

She tied a scarf around her head and went into the kitchen, rollers still in her hair. She didn't need to cover them up at home, she realized. Her mother had seen her in rollers forever, but her Del Phi training had become habit. Her mother was making waffles, and the smell of bacon and fresh coffee filled the room.

"You're up early, Kathleen. Why are you doing your hair on a Sunday morning?"

"I have a date today, Mother." Why couldn't she say it was with Paul?

"You just saw Patrick last night, Kathleen. I don't think it's healthy to spend so much time with just one young man. Play the field before it narrows itself down. This is your last year at college. Make good use of it, for heaven's sake."

"I'm not going with Patrick, Mother."

Her mother's hand stopped beating the waffle batter. "Oh?"

"I'm going boating with Paul."

"Well," her mother said, resuming a brisk stir. "That's a happy surprise. I'm delighted. What are you going to wear?"

Coming from her mother, the question that had plagued her all morning sounded shallow. "Probably shorts and a top."

"Why not that cute shift with the white piping I bought you? It makes you look fuller on top than most of your outfits."

Her mother had never offered any suggestions for her dates with Patrick. Kathleen had forgotten about the blue shift. For once she agreed with her mother. It was flattering, and it would be perfect for whatever they did on this sunny day. She sighed and poured coffee into her stoneware mug. It seemed she'd been up forever, and it was only 9:30.

When the doorbell rang finally at noon, her hands were shaking so badly she grabbed the doorknob with both of them and squeezed with all her might. Then, taking a deep breath, she opened the door. There he stood with his dazzling smile, and it was as if no time had passed since their last date. He swept in, kissing her lightly on the cheek before turning the full force of his charm on her mother.

"You're looking well, Mrs. Andrews, as always."

"Why, thank you, Paul. It's so nice to see you here again. I understand you've been in California."

"I have. It was a wonderful experience, but there were a great many things I missed about home." He looked at Kathleen then, but spoke to her father as Mr. Andrews entered the room. "Hello, sir," he said, and crossed to shake hands with him.

"I understand you're going boating," her father said. "Perfect day for it. Have fun, you two, but don't get sunburned."

"Don't worry, sir, I'll watch out for her."

"See that you do, young man," he bantered, smiling in his daughter's direction.

Kathleen stepped quickly to her father and gave him a kiss. The turn of the conversation made her uncomfortable. "See you later," she said to her parents and steered Paul to the door.

In the car, Kathleen seated herself halfway between the door and Paul.

When they were dating, she had sat next to him on the wide front seat. Now it felt awkward, but it would be too weird to sit next to the door as if it were a first date or as if she were making a statement or something. She turned to face him and put her arm up on the back of the seat.

"You look terrific," he said when he got into the car. "I've really missed you."

Is that why you never wrote or called, she thought, but didn't say. Instead she said, "Tell me about San Francisco."

"It was something. I worked my tail off, but I have so many ideas for the store here. San Francisco is light years ahead of Seattle in women's fashion. You should see how they dress down there. It's so classy."

Kathleen unconsciously smoothed her dress. How did it compare to what the sophisticated ladies he was used to wore, she wondered, feeling frumpy and inadequate.

"I got some incredible ideas for our store, though. Really incredible. Do you remember my idea about a whole department of just junior sizes?"

Kathleen nodded, but Paul went on without looking at her.

"I plan to put the whole emphasis of the store into juniors. We'll blow Frederick's and Best's right out of the water in the young women's market."

"What's so special about junior sizes? I mean, why would that make such an impact?"

He did look at her then. "Don't you see? The sizes are smaller, the look is fresher. Women will feel smaller."

"What if they aren't small, though? If someone wears a twelve, she's not going to fit into an eight."

"But she might fit into an eleven. It's only a half-size smaller, but it's psychological. And for the first time, really tiny girls can find stylish clothes for themselves somewhere besides the kiddies' department. Think of it."

She could sense his excitement and his exasperation that she had asked questions instead of just being excited with him. Her mind raced to say the right thing. "I'll bet your dad is thrilled with your idea."

"You'd think so. I've still got a lot of convincing to do with old dad, but I'm sure he'll come around. He's run the shop the same way all these years, but we're just a smaller version of the big stores. This way—my way—we'll be in a niche all our own. The big boys would have to follow us for a change."

"You've sold me."

He smiled at her. "Well, that's a start, isn't it?"

Her stomach fluttered wildly. What was the matter with her? Why didn't she just come out and ask him what had been going on for the last few months? And what about his other "pen pal"?

When they got to the marina, he took her hand as he helped her out of the car, and held it while he moved to open the trunk. "Rations," he said with a wink, lifting a large basket from the trunk. "Come on, the water's waiting."

The boat was huge, all white and wood. The name on the stern said "Fashion's Lady."

"Corny name, isn't it? Dad said it was appropriate since fashion allowed him to buy the boat. But she's a beauty despite the name. Come aboard, Mademoiselle."

"Paul, you could live on this," she breathed. The carpeted salon had plush furnishings in muted shades of grey and blue. There was a full-sized refrigerator and an oven in the galley. Kathleen ran her fingers along the carved teak railing leading down to the next level.

"Glad you like it, Kat. It suits you." She watched as he expertly freed the boat from its moorage, undoing the lines and settling himself behind the wheel. They slid slowly out into Lake Washington. Mt. Rainier stood out in clear relief to the south.

"Feel like a snack," he said, motioning to the basket. She lifted the lid. He had packed some red apples and green grapes, a box of crackers, some cheddar cheese, and a six-pack of beer. "Put the beer in the fridge, would you. It's probably still cold, but why take a chance? Want one yet?"

"Paul! It's practically still morning."

"Nonsense, it's way after noon. How about opening one for me."

She looked around for an opener and found it in the top drawer. "Where are the glasses?" she asked.

"Glasses? Oh, that's right. Sorority girls never drink out of cans or bottles, do they?"

Kathleen turned so he couldn't see her blush. She didn't like beer and, even if she did, would never even consider drinking out of a bottle. Why did he make her feel silly about that? She opened a bottle and handed it to him.

He took a long swallow. "Ah, still nice and cold. Want to help steer?"

She moved beside him, and he put his arm around her. "I thought about this a lot in San Fran. There's plenty of water and thousands of boats, but looking at Alcatraz isn't quite the same as seeing this mountain. And you were never there."

"Paul, be serious." She pulled herself out of his embrace. "You haven't written or called. I can't imagine that you spent any time missing me. It certainly didn't seem like that from here."

He raised an eyebrow at her. "I wrote you a lot. Didn't you get my cards?" He managed to look concerned, she thought.

"I got them." She didn't care that she sounded like a shrew. It felt good to tell him finally what she had been thinking.

"I was so busy learning the ropes at my uncle's. But I was learning more than just the retail business. And that's what I wanted to talk to you about."

He cut the motor and let the boat drift. They were out in the middle of the lake with no other boats near. He turned to her. "I had a lot of time to think down in California. I spent a great deal of time with my uncle and his wife. You'd like her— she's a lot like you." He smiled at that but didn't wait for Kathleen to respond. "She was his right hand. They're quite a team."

"Does she work at the store?"

He laughed. "She doesn't work, Kat, at least not at the store. I'm talking about the entertaining they do. They're on the opera board and the symphony. She always knows people's names and how to make them feel important. And she's genuine about it."

"Oh, of course." Naturally Paul's aunt wouldn't have to work.

"I saw lots of other women every day, and the more I saw of them, the shallower they seemed. Yes, they were sophisticated, but they weren't real. They weren't like you. No, don't look away. I mean every word."

She forced herself to look at him again, but her pulse was racing, and she knew he could read in her face everything she had tried to hide. "I don't trust you, Paul."

"Why don't you trust me, Kat? What am I missing here?"

"I found out about the girl you were dating when I thought we had an exclusive relationship. How do you explain that?" She couldn't believe what she heard herself saying. Her heart was pounding.

After a long silence, he set down his beer and took her hand. "I assumed you were dating other guys too, Kat. I was too stupid to see what was right in front of me. That's what I'm trying to tell you. All that happened before I saw where I wanted to go in this world. Everything was a game to me. Now I know where I'm headed—and I know who it is I want to be there with me."

Here he was, standing right in front of her and saying all the words she had longed to hear him say, but she was determined to hold her ground. "I can't go through what happened before ever again, Paul. So why should I believe you this time?"

"I was a fool, Kat. You were right not to trust the old me. But I'm trying to tell you what I've come to know. I know how special you are, Kat. You are everything real and true and solid in this world, and I was a fool not to recognize that before."

Then he kissed her, and she felt herself spinning out of control.

༄

Mary was furious with her. They had moved back into the house two weeks after she had seen Paul again. Kathleen had no free time during Work Week or during Rush, so tonight was the first time she could go out with him. Mary plopped down on the daybed in Kathleen's room.

"How can you even consider dating that man again, Kathleen Andrews? He has proven himself to be a genuine creep. What are you *thinking*?"

"It's hard to think when I'm around him, Mar. I can't help it. And I told you, he's changed since last year. I believe the time in San Francisco really made him settle down. I told him I wouldn't put up with things this time, and if he wasn't serious, it was over."

"And what did he say to that?"

Kathleen was trying to do something with her hair. Paul was coming at seven, and she was attempting to put it up, but no matter how many pins she used, it kept falling out. She was still letting it grow, and she wasn't used to the new length.

"He told me he would prove how serious he was."

"Hmph," Mary said and snatched the brush out of Kathleen's hand. "Sit," she ordered and began to redo Kathleen's hair. She swept it up from her neck in a classic French roll, but feathered the sides so that they curled in tiny wisps in front of each ear. The effect was startling. Kathleen looked glamorous!

"Wear this," Mary ordered and handed Kathleen her new red outfit, a matching skirt and soft sweater. "They'll go with your new shoes."

Mary redid the makeup as well, adding some grey eye shadow to Kathleen's usual mascara-only look.

"Now you look like something. Make him eat his rotten heart out. But be careful of yours, my friend. From what I recall, there's not much left."

"Don't worry, Mom. He's changed. Really. You wouldn't believe how different he is."

"You got that right. Just remember, my shoulder is still waterlogged from the last go round, so try not to be stupid this time. As a favor to your old friend if not for yourself."

Chapter 9

February 1963

The white candle rose from the center of a nosegay of lavender Sterling Silver roses and darker purple ribbons. A large solitaire diamond, attached to one of the roses with white florist's wire, winked in the candle light as the girls passed the bouquet slowly from table to table.

"Whoo, that's some rock," one was heard to say.

"I'll say! This is the size I'm holding out for."

When it was returned to Kathleen's table she passed it by the first time around. When it landed in her hand a second time, she blew out the flame. Shrieks and applause filled the dining room as her sorority sisters gathered around her. With shaking fingers she undid the ring from its wire holder and slid it onto her left hand.

"How clever, Kath, to have a ring you could also use as a coffee table," Mary said, waving Kathleen's hand around for all to see.

"When did you get it?"

"Yeah, how did he ask you?"

"When is the wedding?"

The questions spun around her. Finally, someone tapped a glass for quiet and Kathleen had the floor.

"Paul put it in a box of chocolates on Valentine's Day. It was in one of those foil-wrapped chocolates, and he insisted that I try that one first."

There were murmurs of How darling, and Isn't that sweet. Then someone asked, "Where were you?"

"He took me to Rosellini's 410. And the wedding is in July."

"Are the Rogues coming to serenade tonight then?"

"No, Paul went to Dartmouth, you know. Except for Jake, I don't think he even knows too many of the guys in the house now."

"OK, no Rogue serenade, but we can sing, can't we girls?" Mary stood and brandished her knife like a baton. On cue, they sang the sorority's engagement song, "The Love of Delta Phi Tau."

Kathleen had sung that many times over the last four years, but this time, hearing it sung for her brought tears to her eyes. Mary hugged her and said, "I'm glad I was wrong this time. I hope you'll be very happy."

Kathleen hugged her friend back. "You're my maid of honor, Mar, so I'm glad you finally approve."

She looked around at her smiling sisters and then down at her beautiful ring and felt that life truly couldn't get any better.

༄

Spring quarter was a blur. Finishing her final courses and planning a wedding at the same time was a sort of madness. Paul was busy at the store, and they had so little private time together. They were only really alone when Paul was able to take the boat out. She couldn't wait until they were married, and they could make love any time they wanted, and she could wake up next to him every morning, instead of getting dressed and going home to her parents' house.

She and Mary went to every bridal salon to try on dresses. Then she went back again with her mother.

"It's a summer wedding, Kathleen. Don't even think about those long pointed sleeves. To the elbow at the most. Shorter if we can find them."

She tried on satin and lace and more lace. At a salon called Arthur's, the salesgirl ushered her into a pink satin room with mirrors on every wall. In the center of the pink carpet was a stand about six inches higher than the floor. After each dress was eased over her hair and buttoned carefully up the back, Kathleen slid her feet into white satin pumps and mounted the stand. The salesgirl then twirled about the hem of the dress, fluffing and straightening and then finally lifting the train and letting it float into place.

She brought in veils of various lengths and styles, placing them on Kathleen's head as if it were a coronation.

"All I'm getting is confused, Mother. What do you think?"

"Well, we haven't found it yet. We need something more regal," she said to the salesgirl. "After all, you only get married once, so the gown should be magnificent."

The girl smiled knowingly and disappeared behind a mirrored door. In a few moments she came back. "I wasn't sure when you first came in, but now I know this is the dress for you. Not everyone could wear it, but with your coloring and the kind of wedding I now understand you'll be having, I think this is perfect."

She held out a cloud of silk organza.

"Well, that's more like it," her mother said. "Try it on, dear.

Kathleen stepped into the additional crinoline the salesgirl handed her.

"I don't think you'd want to wear a hoop—they're hard to manage if there's any kneeling—so you'll want to add a few more petticoats to make this dress really stand out." She eased the dress over Kathleen's head and did up the row of covered buttons down the back. "Don't look until you're all together."

Kathleen finally stepped up onto the little stand and looked into the mirror. The dress could have been made just for her. The bodice was all lace embroidered with pearls. The pattern of the lace formed the neckline in a shallow V that made her neck look longer. At her waist, the lace continued into a kind of peplum in a matching V. The full skirt, dotted with tiny pearls, floated out from under the peplum and ended in a short train in the back. She turned slowly, watching the organza of the skirt billow and sigh as she moved. The pearls gleamed richly whenever the light struck them.

"What headpiece do you suggest with this one?" Mrs. Andrews asked.

The clerk smiled again and pulled a veil from a short rack. "This is called a Juliet cap, and I think with her curls poking up around it, it will be stunning. Note the repeat of the pearl motif."

For the first time Kathleen didn't hate her hair. The little criss-crossed pearl strands sat perfectly atop her curls, while the veil poofed out from the back and fell to her shoulders.

"What do you think, Mother?"

"I think it's perfect. I can't believe they didn't bring this one out first."

"How much is it," Kathleen asked.

"The gown is only $175."

Kathleen gasped. That was nearly double what most of the gowns she'd tried on. She looked at her mother.

"That sounds right," Mrs. Andrews said smoothly. "And the veil?"

"The veil with the cap is only $65. And of course we rent you the crinolines. No need to buy them. It looks like this is a perfect fit for you, Miss Andrews, so there probably won't be any alteration cost. Will you be wearing heels this high?"

Kathleen nodded.

"Well, there you are. It won't even need hemming. You're a perfect eight, my dear. A true eight, I might add, not those silly half sizes they're trying to foist off on girls nowadays. Which is lucky, since we may have been in a time crunch if you'd needed a lot of alterations."

Kathleen took off the dress and handed it to the salesgirl, who went to get her order book.

"Mother, isn't it too expensive?"

"Now don't you worry about that. The Gordons know fashion, Kathleen. They will recognize the quality of this dress. Besides you look lovely in it. We just won't tell your father."

Kathleen and Mary went to Arthur's after class Monday, and Mary agreed that the dress was perfect. The same salesgirl helped Kathleen try it on, and then turned her focus to Mary, the maid of honor. The salesgirl had never heard of Kathleen's favorite Sterling Silver roses that the bridesmaids would be carrying, but she said she had many dresses in shades of purple that would be perfect with lavender roses. She popped out and returned shortly with several bridesmaid dresses—long, short, full, straight.

"Will these go with your flowers?" she asked.

"They're perfect," Mary and Kathleen said together.

Mary tried each one on. The salesgirl left to bring in more.

"I want to find something you can all wear again," Kathleen said.

"You're dreaming," Mary said. "We graduate in a couple of months. We'll never go to a formal again. Where are we going to wear these? Let's just pick something we all look gorgeous in for the pictures."

"I have a suggestion," the salesgirl said, entering the pink room with several zippered bags over her arm. "This dress is stunning on just about everyone, and it comes in several shades of each color." She pulled the first dress out of its bag.

"Hey, maybe we've got something here," Mary said. She slid the lavender organza dress over her head. "Wow, whadda ya think?"

The dress had a V neckline similar to the bridal gown and capped sleeves. The full skirt was ballerina length.

"I look tall," Mary said. "Let's get this one."

"Well, the beauty of this one is this," the salesgirl said, unzipping the rest of the bags. Each dress was a different shade of purple, running from the lightest shade that Mary had on to a deep plum. "You can go from light to dark or dark to light as each attendant comes down the aisle. I would suggest having the lightest shade on your maid of honor—especially with her blonde hair—since she will be next to you at the altar, and the dresses will go from your white one through to the darkest."

"I'm sold, Kath. How about you?"

Kathleen held her breath. The dress was lovely, and she could envision how they would all look in the stately Episcopal church. It would be wonderful.

"How long will it take to get the dresses," she asked.

"If you order them this week, we can have them to you in plenty of time for the wedding. How many bridesmaids will you have?"

"Five, including Mary."

"Oh, by the way," Mary said, "how much?"

"You're lucky. These are only $49.95."

Kathleen swallowed. That was a lot of money to ask the girls to come up with. Then there would be the shoes dyed to match. The salesgirl gathered up some discarded dresses and slipped discreetly out of the room.

"That's not bad," Mary said.

"It isn't?"

"Heck, my prom dress was more than that four years ago. We can get shoes at Leed's or Chandler's for around fifteen bucks. Let's do it. I love this dress!" She twirled around once more. "What about headpieces?"

As if she had been listening, the salesgirl reappeared with several headpieces. "These can be made up in the right colors, but I thought you'd like to see what there was to choose from."

Mary tried on several, making silly faces at most of them. "They're too fussy, Kath. I'm not the picture-hat type. How about this one?" She placed a headband topped with a simple flat bow on her head.

"That works," Kathleen said. "All of you have bangs, so that would look good on everyone."

"It's a very popular style," the clerk said. "And elegant with the simplicity of this dress. Very Jackie Kennedy."

"All right, we'll have everyone come in on Saturday to get fitted. I think this will be gorgeous." Then she paused for a moment. "I hope my mother likes these dresses. I'd better get her in here to see them too."

"She'll like them, Kath. They look expensive."

"Very Jackie Kennedy."

Laughing, the two friends changed back into their street clothes and headed off for Frederick & Nelson.

"We're having a hard time picking out a china pattern, Mar. Come tell me what you think."

"What's the problem?"

"Well, Paul says we have to have Lenox china, but I found some other dishes I like better."

"And you want me to cast the deciding vote? No, thank you! Besides, what's that ad in every *Seventeen* magazine, 'You get the license, I'll get the Lenox'?"

"I just want your opinion. Here, look." The Lenox was a plain off-white plate with a double gold band.

"It looks fine to me. What don't you like about it?"

"I don't like mixing silver silverware with gold dishes. I think it looks strange. I never wear gold and silver jewelry together, do you?"

"No, but I never thought about it for dishes."

"Actually, that makes two of us. I never thought about any of this before, except of course from those ads in *Seventeen*. We have 'good dishes' at home, but I don't think they're anything special. I think my dad got them during the war or something. And they don't have either silver or gold on them. Come see the pattern I like," Kathleen said. "What do you think of this?" The dishes were a stark white with a raised design around the rim of the plates and cups.

"I see what you mean. These are pretty. What does Paul care—you're the one who'll be cooking the food that goes on them and washing them up afterwards. Get the ones you want."

"Oh, Mary, I can't just do that. I wish I had some inherited pattern the way Barbara did. Remember when she got engaged our freshman year?"

"Yeah."

"She said that when she was born, her grandmother bought her a plate or something from the 'family pattern' and every year she got another piece for her hope chest. By the time she got married, she had practically the whole set. And silver."

"Do you have a hope chest?"

"Not an actual one, but my gran has given me pillowcases that she's embroidered over the years. Stuff like that for when I get married."

"I have a chest my grandmother brought over from Sweden, but it's full of junk! I don't have a single spoon!"

"Neither do I, which is probably just as well. Paul and I don't agree on a silver pattern either. He's meeting me here on his dinner break tonight, so maybe we can reach some sort of compromise. But enough of this. Let's go get something sweet."

After they had a cup of coffee and split a piece of chocolate cake, Kathleen walked Mary to the bus stop and then went back to the bridal registry. She had some time before Paul could join her, so she immersed herself in this new world of china and crystal and silver. Marrying Paul would put her into a position where things like the right table settings were important. She was anxious about liking the right things.

There were so many choices—plain or ornate, flat plates or ones with rimmed edges, delicate cups or modern mugs. She lifted coffee cups to see how the handles felt in her hand. She imagined everything from roast beef to spaghetti on the plates. She compared covered vegetable dishes and platters for style and shape. She grew more confused by the minute, but she knew with even more certainty that she didn't like the china Paul preferred.

She walked into Gordon's a few minutes early. The sweet smell from the cosmetic counter engulfed her as she entered. People were strolling around the circular racks of clothes as well-dressed salesgirls offered assistance. A thrill went through her, banishing all her silly anxiety over dishes. In a few short weeks, she would be a part of all this. *Mrs. Paul Gordon.* She had practiced writing it a hundred different ways. *Kathleen Gordon. Mrs. P. Gordon. Paul and Kathleen Gordon.* She still could not believe that he had chosen her. He was older. He was from a wealthy family. He had a degree of sophistication she couldn't hope to match. Yet he had asked her

Hope Chest

to marry him. She must have done something right to be so lucky. She shook her head.

"No, what?" his familiar voice came from behind.

She turned and saw him smiling at her. He was so handsome, and he was hers. He gave her a kiss on the cheek, and Kathleen saw one of the older clerks smile.

"I was just thinking how lucky I am, Paul. All of this seems like a dream."

"It is a dream, darling, and we're never going to wake up, I promise. Did you and Mary find a bridesmaid dress?"

"The perfect one. You'll love it. The wedding is going to be beautiful."

"I have no doubts. Let's go. I don't want to be gone too long."

He took her hand and led her out of the store. At Frederick's, they stopped first at the main floor silver department.

"I've been looking at patterns, Paul, and I really like this one." She didn't want to pick something Paul hated. Somehow she felt it would reflect on her. She held up a tapered but deeply patterned spoon labeled "Medici" by Gorham.

Paul took the piece from her and turned it over. "Well, not too bad. It's heavy enough and elegant. I think you've found our silver, Kat."

Relief flooded over her. She hugged him briefly and beamed up at him. "I love the 'our' part, Paul. I can't wait until we're married. I can just imagine having people over and setting the table with this beautiful pattern."

He kissed her on her nose. "Now if we can agree this easily on the china, we might just make it to our golden wedding anniversary."

On the escalator she broached the subject of the china she liked. "I had some time before I went to your store this afternoon so I did China 101. I found a beautiful pattern I think you'll like."

"I thought you liked the Lenox we looked at." He raised an eyebrow at her.

"It's OK, Paul, and I know Lenox is a big name, but I just don't like the gold band. But maybe we could look at it again. It's just a feeling I have about gold and silver together."

Hope Chest

They walked into the china department and she led him to the dishes she had shown Mary. "What do you think of these?"

"You like plain things, don't you Kat?" He made it sound like it was a failing.

"These aren't plain, Paul. There's a design on every piece—it's just not gold or silver."

He took the dish from her hand and turned it over. "Let's go back and look at the other one."

"OK."

They placed the dish Kathleen liked next to the Lenox. The comparison made the Lenox one look even worse to her. She liked the sharp whiteness of her choice so much better than the yellowish hue of the other, but she waited to see what Paul would say.

"Hmm. This one is whiter. Interesting."

"That's what I thought. And with plain white, Paul, I can do so many things with a table setting. But there are lots of other styles here. Do you want to look some more?"

"Nah. I think you're pretty good at picking out things for our house, Kat, so I'll let you just keep going. After all, I've done the hard part."

She looked at him questioningly.

"I picked you."

Her heart swelled with love for him.

❧

All that remained before the wedding was for her to have her premarital physical and get on the birth-control pills. She especially wanted to make sure she wouldn't have her period on her honeymoon. She made an appointment with a doctor on campus rather than with her family doctor. This was one thing she didn't feel like sharing with her mother.

The doctor was a short woman with sensible shoes and a New York accent who introduced herself as Dr. Stern. She was brusque and all business, and Kathleen thought she was aptly named.

Hope Chest

"Have you had a pelvic exam before?"

"No, but I'm getting married in June, and I need a prescription for the pill." Kathleen shivered in her thin gown. Her bare feet were freezing.

"All right. Let's have a look. Feet in the stirrups please and scoot down here."

The metal stirrups were colder than her feet, and the starched white cover on the examining table resisted slightly as she tried to position herself.

"You still a virgin?"

"No." Kathleen surprised herself at how matter-of-factly she responded. "But I am getting married."

"I'm not judging you, dear. I just needed to know for medical reasons. This may be a bit uncomfortable."

"Oh." Kathleen braced herself as something hard and cold was pushed into her and spread. Then she felt several dull pokes.

"Your cervix is a bit inflamed. How have you been protecting yourself from getting pregnant?"

"Um, we . . . I mean my fiancé . . . we . . ."

"Condoms?"

"Yes." Kathleen had never felt more uncomfortable in her life. Feet in the air, with this woman poking her physically and emotionally. She wanted the whole thing to be over. "Is there any chance you might be pregnant? When was your last period?"

Kathleen froze. "Pregnant? Am I pregnant?"

"I'm merely asking about the possibility. You gave a urine sample?"

"Yes."

"We'll run some tests. Condoms have been known to fail. Your last period?"

"I can't remember. I'm not very regular. I think it was a month or so ago."

"Your cervix seems a bit abnormal. I'm going to have another doctor check you just to be sure."

Kathleen's mind was reeling. Abnormal. Was that a sign of pregnancy or cancer? She couldn't speak.

"You'll need to make an appointment for Dr. Ryan. He'll be in Monday. It might be nothing, so I hope you won't spend the whole weekend fretting about it." She smiled then for the first time. "You can get dressed now."

Numbly Kathleen put her clothes back on and made an appointment with the receptionist. She walked back to the sorority house in a daze. She wanted to talk to someone, but there was no one. She couldn't share her fears that she might be pregnant with anyone. Certainly not her mother, and certainly not Paul. She would never alarm him over something this serious that might prove to be nothing at all. She even avoided Mary, spending the long weekend by herself, willing Monday to come sooner. She couldn't decide which would be worse, pregnancy or cancer.

She and Paul had not had the opportunity to make love very often. The first time had been on the boat after he asked her to marry him. They had petted seriously before, but she had known that time would be different. They were engaged, not just dating. They hadn't used a condom, but Paul hadn't been inside her more than a few seconds before he'd pulled out of her and pressed himself against her, gasping and moaning. She felt a hot liquid pour onto her stomach. She was surprised that it was over so quickly when Paul went to get a towel.

"Sorry about the mess," he'd said without a hint of the embarrassment she was feeling. "Next time I'll get a condom. We don't want to risk anything."

Then he'd wrapped his arms around her and told her he loved her. She felt safe and incredibly happy. The scruples and her mother's admonitions she had thrown aside when he asked her to marry him ("No one will buy the cow if he can get the milk for free!") no longer played in her head. She belonged to him now. He would take care of her, and she would do everything in her power to make him happy.

For a few days after that first time, she had worried about getting her period, but it came the following week. Since then, the few times they had any privacy, Paul had always used a condom, and like the first time, he was never in her very long, and the condom had never come off. She hadn't given any thought to pregnancy or anything besides wishing they had more time together so their lovemaking wasn't so hurried and counting the days until the wedding. Now the doctor's words terrified her. Could she have gotten pregnant even with a condom? If she was pregnant now, it would be so unfair and so awful. How could she tell her mother? How could she face her father?

On Monday she was back in the freezing exam room staring at the menacing stirrups while waiting for the new doctor to come in. Dr. Ryan was a tall, thin man in his late 50s, who smiled warmly at her over his half-glasses. To Kathleen's surprise, he was accompanied by a young, blonde nurse. Having an audience made Kathleen even more uncomfortable than the previous exam had been. Once again she was poked and probed. Finally the exam was over.

"Well, young lady, I'm happy to announce you are perfectly normal. Your cervix is a little irritated, but nothing to worry about. It's also a bit more open than usual, but there is a great variance from person to person. You are just fine."

Kathleen let out a huge breath she didn't realize she was holding. "Then I'm not pregnant?"

"Pregnant? No. The urine test was negative, but that's not even what we were looking for. Dr. Stern was concerned about your cervix, but everything there is quite within the range of normal."

"Thank you, Dr. Ryan," she managed. "So there should be no problem with my taking birth-control pills?"

"None whatsoever. However, I won't be able to prescribe them for you. I'm Catholic, and I'm afraid I don't believe in that sort of thing. But I'm sure Dr. Stern will be able to handle that little detail for you. She should be in tomorrow or the next day."

With that, he and the nurse left the room. The terror she had felt all weekend evaporated in intense relief. She was not pregnant, and she didn't have a fatal disease. She could get her prescription and start on The Pill. For a brief moment, Kathleen thought of Patrick. If she had married him, she mused, would she have been able to take the pill at all? She felt a moment of sadness at the memory of how much she must have hurt him, but the feeling was eclipsed by the thrill she felt to be marrying Paul.

Hope Chest

She got dressed and stopped at the reception desk to make another appointment for the first doctor so she could get her prescription. Nothing was wrong with her. Everything was going to be perfect.

◦◦

There were three bridal showers. Mary gathered all the bows from the gifts at each shower and threaded them through a paper plate for Kathleen to carry as her "bouquet" at the wedding rehearsal. Dark-green Frederick & Nelson trucks made their endless way to Kathleen's parents' home, dropping off gift after gift. It was like Christmas. Kathleen would wait impatiently until Paul arrived after dinner, and they would open the packages together.

The gifts piling up in her mother's living room were amazing. There were enough place settings of her everyday and good china to serve at least eight. They had only enough silver so far for six, but there were so many of their crystal wine glasses that Kathleen was sure she could trade many of them in and fill out the missing pieces of silver. And the presents were still pouring in. There were three fondue sets, two electric coffee pots, an electric griddle, two sets of monogrammed towels, seven silver Revere bowls—all the same size but two with clear-red liners—and countless other vases and kitchen things. There was even an electric, silver French bread warmer. Her favorite gift, however, was from Mary: a pair of carved stone lovebirds. She ran her hand over their smooth, fat little bodies and placed them carefully together in front of all the other gifts.

There was a flurry of final fittings, and meetings with the florist, and photos in her gown to be taken for the newspaper to run after the wedding. And she and Paul had to find an apartment.

They spent weekends looking at possible places, but Paul didn't seem to see exactly what he was looking for. The ones with views or fireplaces seemed terribly expensive to Kathleen, at least $165 a month, but Paul just waved her objections aside.

"We can't entertain in a hovel, Kat. We have to have a proper setting for all those silver bowls, now don't we?"

"But can we afford that much, Paul? I really don't mind working after we get married. I'm sure I could get a teaching position."

"I'm sure you could, too, sweetheart, but there's no need. I make enough money for both of us. And I want you home and pretty at the end of my long day. Besides, how would it look? People would think I couldn't support my wife." He took her in his arms. "I want to take care of you, Kat. Did that ever occur to you?"

All she could do was smile. Surely there wasn't anyone luckier in the whole world.

They finally found a beautiful place on Queen Anne Hill, near the Seattle Center. It had a large sandstone fireplace and a big kitchen with a dishwasher. Best of all it had a view of the Space Needle and the downtown city behind it. Their apartment was on the ground floor, so it had a little yard in front of it with several rose bushes and large rhododendrons and a back door in the kitchen that led out to a small patio. It felt like a house, and Kathleen loved it. Even her mother approved.

"This is just what I hoped you'd find," she told Kathleen. "Quietly elegant. Paul must be doing *quite* well to afford something this nice. Your father and I would like to buy you your sofa for a wedding present. A place like this deserves something special."

Kathleen had never seen her mother so excited.

There were some problems with the guest list. Her mother insisted that she invite Trudy Lavik and her parents, even though Kathleen really didn't want to. She didn't bother arguing though. Trudy wasn't even engaged yet, and Kathleen's mother was finally getting a piece of her own back from Mrs. Lavik. But Kathleen was worried about the ever-growing numbers and what the whole thing was going to cost her parents. She had pared down the Del Phi list and invited only a couple of her high school chums. Jake was Paul's best man, and her closest sorority sisters and special cheerleading friends were bridesmaids, so that narrowed things down a bit. But with the Gordons' huge circle of friends, they were over the 200 mark.

"Don't you worry about the cost, Kitten," her father reassured her. "I have only one daughter, and I'm going to do her proud."

She and Paul had to go to two sessions at her church for premarital counseling. Paul said he didn't see the need for some minister to poke around in their business, but said if that's what they had to do, that's what they had to do.

The Reverend Johns had been at the Episcopal church since Kathleen was little, but she had never really had occasion to speak with him on personal matters before. To her he was the man who gave the sermons. She and Paul went into his spacious office and sat beside each other on a small sofa. Father Johns settled himself in the chair opposite. He asked them how long they had known each other and whether they felt they were prepared to take on this "awesome responsibility."

"I don't feel it's a responsibility, Reverend," Paul replied with a huge smile. "I feel like the luckiest guy in the world." He squeezed Kathleen's hand, and she felt a warm flush rise to her face.

"I'm sure you do, young man, but there will be times when you both will be tried. There will be disagreements, bound to be, even in the best of marriages. I trust that at those times you will turn to God together and ask His divine guidance to get you through the rough spots. He's got a lot of experience, you know." He smiled at Kathleen.

"When my wife and I were in our first years of marriage, we had a way of working things out whenever I couldn't convince her I was right. We'd head out the front door together and take off in opposite directions and walk around the block. Of course we'd have to pass each other, and it usually didn't take more than a couple of turns before we realized how silly we must look to the neighbors. We'd take hands and walk back to the house together—usually in the direction she was already going, but not always! And then when we'd cooled down, we'd thank the Lord for our many blessings and get on with being happy."

She was reminded of Guy's sermon at Fishers so many months ago. Would she and Paul pray together about anything? Ironically it wasn't something they had talked about. Paul teased her about her church, but declared that he wasn't very religious. "I'll let you do the talking to God, Kat, and I'll take care of things down here." But they loved each other so much she couldn't imagine a situation that would be so dire that they couldn't work it out. Since Paul had come home from San Francisco, he had been tender and attentive. He was a different person from what he'd been when she first met him. As she had assured Mary, his experience in California had changed him. He seemed so much more mature. She had no complaints and no worries.

She held tightly to his hand as Father Johns held his hands over their heads and prayed a blessing on their marriage. Her heart was full.

"I've known Kathleen since she was in kindergarten, Paul. I trust you to take very good care of her."

"You have my word on it, sir. I know what a prize I have."

When they got into the car, Paul was laughing. "Can you just see us walking around the block? Our neighbors would wonder what kind of people they had let into the neighborhood."

"I thought it was rather sweet, though, didn't you?" She was surprised by his response.

"Sweet? Well, maybe for a religious guy. If there's something we disagree on, we'll just talk it out." He took her hand. "Besides, what could ever be so terrible? If things ever got really bad, we could just go to bed. We know how to 'work things out.'" He leered at her, and she ended up laughing with him.

It rained on the Friday night of the rehearsal, a heavy, unseasonable downpour. Everyone dashed from the parking lot to the church and then back to their cars to go to the rehearsal dinner. Kathleen and Paul sat at the head table flanked by their parents. The attendants seated themselves down the sides of the U-shaped table. When the champagne had been poured, Mr. Gordon rose to propose a toast.

"To my son and his beautiful bride-to-be. We loved Kathleen from the first time Paul brought her home, and we are delighted to welcome her into our family. May your lives together be as happy and as full of love as mine has been with my dear wife."

Everyone raised the bubbling glasses and drank to the couple. Then Mr. Andrews rose and delivered his toast.

"This is a lovely dinner and a special night. Thank you, Gordons, for hosting us here. It seems like just yesterday that my little girl was bringing me things she found outdoors like bird nests and butterfly wings or very often things that needed fixing. Or screaming for me to come save her from a spider! She's been a source of joy and real pride to her mother and me, and we're very much going to miss having her home. But we know that she's found someone she truly loves. We welcome Paul and the Gordons into our family. To Paul and Kathleen, long life, love, and happiness."

Everyone drank again, and Kathleen rose to give her father a kiss. The waiters began bustling around serving delicious-looking salmon. Kathleen gave her bridesmaids necklaces to wear at the wedding, a single pearl drop on a fine gold chain. Paul gave each of his attendants monogrammed silver jiggers. Then he reached into his suit pocket and pulled out a long slim box.

"Here, sweetheart. I want you to wear this tomorrow."

Kathleen opened the box and saw a strand of luminous pearls. She felt tears prickle her eyes as she lifted the necklace from the box. People began to clap, and her mother gave Kathleen a satisfied smile as Paul secured the clasp behind her neck.

"Paul, they're beautiful. I have something for you too." She had planned to give him his gift later, in private, but it seemed now was the time. She took a square box out of her purse and handed it to him.

"Wow!" he said as he removed the watch from its box. It had a plain black face and a small diamond at twelve o'clock. He fastened it around his wrist and gave her a kiss. "I bet this is so I won't be late for dinner," he said to everyone's laughter as he held up his wrist.

She had been so nervous about his gift. What if he hadn't liked it? She was relieved to see a look of appreciation on his face, but she felt so unsure of herself when it came to choosing something for him. He seemed to have so much more taste and sophistication than she did. Yet she had never been happier. This was the last night she had to go home to her parents' house. Tomorrow night she could sleep with her husband.

~

She was up at six, although she hadn't slept much. To her enormous relief, the downpour of yesterday was gone, and the sun was already up and shining. It was going to be a beautiful day. It was as if yesterday's rain had happened to make everything sparkle for her wedding.

The beauty salon had agreed to take her and the bridesmaids at 7:30 so they could be finished and at the church by 9:30 for pictures. Kathleen's mother was horrified that the groom might see the bride before the wedding, but the photographer convinced them that he would keep Paul in a separate room while he took Kathleen's shots. The only pictures they would take after the ceremony would be of the couple together and a few of the combined wedding party and the families.

She took a long bath doused with Estée Lauder Youth Dew from a sample she picked up at a bridal show. Her mother had given her a whole set at one of her showers, but the travel flagon was already packed and the rest was at her new apartment. She loved the spicy fragrance that rose with the steam as she settled herself into the tub. She'd done her nails—toes included—yesterday, so all that remained was her hair and then getting into her gown. It was today! Finally!

All her bridesmaids joined her at the salon where they were shampooed and rollered and dried and sprayed and turned out gleaming and lovely. The beauticians affixed all the headpieces except Kathleen's and artfully arranged curls around the bows. Their dresses and Kathleen's veil were already at the church, pressed and waiting.

They piled into two cars and headed for the church. Mary stood lookout when they got there to make sure Paul was nowhere in sight and then signaled for Kathleen to make a dash to the dressing room. The bridesmaids helped her into her slip and the stiff crinolines and carefully lowered the voluminous wedding gown over her newly coifed hair. Mary fastened the tiny buttons down the back while the rest of the girls got into their gowns.

"How are we doing on time, Mother?" Kathleen asked.

"It's only 9:15, dear. We're fine. Don't rush or you'll perspire and your hair will frizz."

Billie fluffed out the veil and handed it to Kathleen. She placed it on her head and fastened the comb that held it in place. "Can you see the bobby pin?"

"No, it looks perfect."

"Well, you all look gorgeous. Billie, that shade of purple is so pretty with your red hair!"

"Yeah, who would have thought?"

"I wish there were a mirror in here. How do I look?" Kathleen lifted the front of her dress and twirled slowly around.

"Here, there's a mirror on the back of this door. We wanted to wait until you were all assembled," Mary said. "Voila!"

Kathleen couldn't believe her eyes. The dress was stunning. Her hair curled softly over the jeweled cap and framed her face in soft points. The pearls Paul gave her were the perfect complement to the pearl detailing on the dress. Even her shoes weren't hurting—yet.

"It's good, isn't it?" she said.

"Better than that, sister," Mary said. "You look gorgeous!" The other girls clapped, their white-gloved hands muting the sound.

"But look at you!" Kathleen said. The bridesmaids' dresses were also gorgeous. The variegated shades flowed from one girl to the next, and the effect was stunning.

"You look pretty sharp yourself, Mrs. Andrews," Mary said.

"Yes, Mother, you look beautiful."

"As always," Billie added, bringing a smile to Mrs. Andrews, who wore a pale pink silk suit and matching pumps. "That color is great with our dresses."

"Where are the flowers?" her mother asked, just as a knock on the door announced the florist's arrival, and right on his heels were Gran and Paul's mother.

Kathleen gave each of them a hug and then stood back to be examined.

"Oh, my," Gran said. "You're the picture of loveliness, my girl."

"I'll second that," Mrs. Gordon said. "And I have something to add, if you'll permit me." She took off a thin gold bracelet with tiny turquoise stones on it. "You need 'something borrowed' to wear. This was Paul's grandmother's, and she had me wear it when I married her son. I'd be honored if you would wear it when you marry mine."

"Oh, I'm the one who would be honored. Thank you so much." She slipped the bracelet over her hand and kissed her future mother-in-law on the cheek.

"It's even 'something blue,'" Gran added. "What a precious thing."

"Here," Kathleen said to both of them. "Let me pin your corsages on you."

"We'll take these boutonnieres out to the men," Kathleen's mother said. "Then the boys can have their photos taken, and we'll come get you when the coast is clear."

The bridesmaids' bouquets were topiary balls of the lavender roses with sprays of ivy, suspended from satin ribbons that matched each of the dresses.

"These are spectacular, Kath. I've never seen anything like them," Mary said, walking around the room doing the hesitation step and letting the flowers sway.

Kathleen's bouquet, which Paul had picked out as was the groom's duty, was a cascade of white orchids and stephanotis with slender ribbons that ended in pearls. Kathleen was enchanted with it.

Mrs. Andrews poked her head into the room and said the men were finished, so they could go into the sanctuary. The white carpet had been rolled out down the center aisle. Large standards of purple gladiolas interspersed with roses flanked the altar behind spiral candelabra. The altar arrangement was stunning. Kathleen paused to take it all in until her mother reminded her that they had to finish before any guests arrived.

Her father came around the corner and then up the stairs to join Kathleen.

"Oh, Daddy, you look so handsome!" Kathleen said to her father. He was resplendent in a cutaway and striped trousers.

"But no one will be looking at me, Kitten. You look beautiful."

"Thanks, Daddy." As she kissed him on the cheek, she saw the flash of the camera and hoped this shot would turn out.

They finished their photo session and then went back into the dressing area to wait. The photographer knocked on the door and came in to take a few staged photos of the girls getting ready, of Mary helping Kathleen put on her blue garter, of Gran fluffing the veil, of the bridesmaids crossing their fingers as Kathleen put a sixpence into her shoe.

Billie went out for a drink of water and came back smiling. "If you think your dad looks handsome in his tux, wait until you see the groom! He looks like a movie star, Kathleen. I peeked in on them. I just wanted to prepare you so you don't embarrass us when you come down the aisle."

"I'm so nervous right now, I can't promise you what I might do. I just hope I don't trip on this dress or drop my bouquet! I wish I could sit down for a minute, but I don't want to wrinkle."

"You'll do fine. We beauties will set the stage, stunning them all as we float down the aisle. They'll take little note of you, wrinkled or not." Mary and Billie struck a model pose.

Suddenly they heard the organ begin, and Kathleen knew it would just be a matter of minutes. She checked her lipstick in the mirror one last time and pulled the veil over her face.

"OK, kids," Mary said, "it's showtime."

They lined up from dark to light purple. Mr. Andrews appeared and offered Kathleen his arm.

"You ladies look splendid," he told them. "And I'm mighty proud to walk the loveliest girl in the world down the aisle. I can't say as I'm happy to be giving you away, though, Kitten. No, can't say as I am."

Kathleen felt tears threaten, and she held tightly to her father's arm.

The wedding coordinator from the church was there to send each bridesmaid down at precisely the right moment. Mary gave Kathleen a wink and then disappeared around the corner. Then the coordinator signaled for Kathleen and her father to approach. Kathleen heard the seven high notes struck on the organ and then the swelling sounds of "Here Comes the Bride." She and her father moved to the doorway. Everyone rose and turned toward them. They were a hazy blur through Kathleen's veil. She couldn't even see Paul.

"Here we go, Kitten," her father said, and they stepped off.

Kathleen was vaguely aware of smiling faces on either side of her until Paul came into view, and everything else faded away. Her eyes could not take him in. He did look like a movie star. When she reached the steps that led up to the altar, he moved toward her. She let go of her father's strong arm and placed her hand in Paul's, but before she could move entirely away, her father lifted her veil slightly and placed a kiss on her cheek. She felt the tears start again.

"Dearly beloved . . ." The words of the age-old wedding ceremony began at last, and she and Paul faced Father Johns together. She moved through the ceremony as if in a dream. She gave her bouquet to Mary and held her hand out to Paul as he took the ring from Jake and slid it onto her finger. He looked deep into her eyes as he said his vows. She had trouble putting the ring onto his finger, but managed to get it on as she finished her vows. At long last, she heard the magic words, "I now pronounce you husband and wife."

Paul gently lifted back her veil and kissed her, a long kiss that caused a few titters from the guests. Father Johns smiled at them and said, "Ladies and Gentlemen, allow me to present Mr. and Mrs. Paul Gordon."

Kathleen thought her heart would burst. She put her arm through Paul's and retrieved her bouquet from Mary. The organ swelled into the recessional, and she walked with her husband down the aisle through the smiling crowd.

They went into the office to sign the license with Mary and Jake while the church emptied so they could go back in for the final photos before they went on to the reception.

"Well, sport, you did it. And you owe me big time for introducing you to this prize lady," Jake said. "Do I get to kiss the bride?"

"Oh, Jake," Kathleen said, "how can I ever repay you? This is the happiest day of my life!"

"How about dinner at your house—and maybe I'll bring my laundry while I'm there."

"How about if you wait until we're back from our honeymoon, sport," Paul punched Jake lightly on the shoulder.

"I can't believe it," Mary said. "My best friend, an old married lady. I won't have anyone to play with!"

"Don't worry, Mary," Paul said, putting his arm around her. "I've seen the two of you together enough to know that a little thing like marriage won't have a great deal of impact on your time together—at least not on the phone!"

They took the formal photos quickly and folded Kathleen and Paul into the back of Jake's car, nearly shutting the door on her veil, for the short drive to the Tennis Club for the reception. The Gordons had sponsored her parents for the reception at their club, and now as they drove into the entrance, Kathleen realized she would be a member here.

As she and Paul walked in, the guests sent up a cheer and raised their champagne glasses. Mrs. Andrews quickly organized the wedding party into a receiving line and the handshakes and introductions began.

"You look lovely, my dear."

"Such a beautiful gown!"

"What a handsome couple you make."

"I never thought you'd bite the bullet, old man. She must be pretty special."

Kathleen introduced Paul to her family and friends, and he did the same for her. Guests streamed through nonstop. Kathleen had no time to see who was coming next. Consequently when Mark stood in front of her, she gave a start. She hadn't seen much of him since she broke up with Patrick, although she knew Mark would be here as Mary's escort. Paul was still chatting with the previous guests.

"Congratulations, Kathleen. Or I guess 'best wishes' is what I'm supposed to say to the bride." He smiled and gave a quick look in Paul's direction. Noticing that he was still occupied, Mark leaned close to Kathleen. "Patrick told me to tell you he wishes you all the happiness in the world. This is from him." And he kissed her on the cheek.

"Thank you, Mark." She couldn't think of anything more to say. Fortunately at that moment Paul turned to them and offered his hand.

"Hey, Mark. I saw you kissing my wife."

My wife. Kathleen savored the sound of it on Paul's deep voice. Mark shook Paul's hand and moved on to hug Mary, and Kathleen was instantly caught up again in the stream of well-wishers.

After what seemed like ages, the last of the guests went through, and the wedding party could take their places at the head table.

The room was perfect. Each table had a small bouquet of roses, and the large standards from the church had been positioned behind the head table. The sun glinted off the lake just outside the huge picture windows of the club, and everyone was happily chatting.

"Looks like all the work you did on the seating chart paid off," she whispered to her mother as she paused behind her chair. "No long faces anywhere. Oh, Mother, everything is wonderful. Thank you." She hugged her mother tightly.

Mrs. Andrews had attacked the plans for the reception like a general preparing for battle. Kathleen knew her mother was pleased with the results.

After the meal, Jake rose to give the toast.

"I've known this guy since we were kids and he had all the girls. And I've known Kathleen since kindergarten. How many guys can say they were best man at the wedding of their two best buddies?" There was a pause for laughter. "But seriously, Paul and Kathleen, may your lives together be filled with happiness and joy forever. To the new Gordons!"

Everyone saluted them. Then Mary gathered the Del Phis together in a semicircle in front of Kathleen. They sang their special Delta Phi Tau wedding song in sweet harmony, and everyone clapped.

The band played "When I Fall in Love" as Paul took Kathleen by the hand and led her onto the dance floor. She melted into his arms and they slowly circled the floor. Then the wedding party joined in, and soon Paul's father cut in on them to dance with Kathleen while Paul twirled off with his mother.

"Welcome to our family, my dear. We couldn't be happier."

"Thank you, Mr. Gordon."

"Mr. Gordon? No, no. You must call me Ted. None of this Mr. business now. We're family."

"Thank you, Ted," Kathleen replied. The name felt strange on her tongue, but exciting at the same time.

Then she danced with her father while Paul took a turn with her mother.

"How does it feel to be an old married lady, Kitten?"

"You're the second person to call me that!" she pouted, but then broke into a smile. "This is such a whirl, Daddy. I can't take it all in."

"Well, that's what honeymoons are for, so you can recover from the wedding." He gave her a broad wink that made her blush.

"But I'm so happy. Isn't Paul wonderful, Daddy? I just feel so lucky."

"He seems like a real nice young man, Kitten. And I like his people too. For all their money, they seem like genuine folks. I just wish you all good things, honey."

"Thank you, Daddy. I think I have them all right now."

They cut the cake and threw the garter, which, to his horror, Jake caught and then tried to give to another groomsman. Then the bouquet, which Mary caught and waved over her head while looking at Mark. They danced some more and chatted with guests, and then it was time to change into their going-away clothes.

The honeymoon was a gift from Paul's parents. They flew to San Francisco, getting free champagne on the flight from the stewardess, who recognized them as newlyweds from Kathleen's corsage and the stray grains of rice that fell out of her hair at awkward moments. They had a lovely room at the St. Francis Hotel, and after the bellboy delivered their bags, Paul took her into his arms and kissed her.

"How does it feel to be married?"

"Wonderful, Paul. It's like a dream. Being on an airplane with you, and now this beautiful room. We have to thank your parents. This is like something out of a movie."

"Let's go have dinner—a quick one—and hurry back to this nice bed." He kissed her again and they went down to the restaurant.

Paul ordered a bottle of champagne. The waiter discreetly filled their glasses and then disappeared. When he returned a short time later, Paul ordered Chateaubriand.

"The lady will have Roquefort dressing on her salad," he told the waiter, "and so will I."

"Very good, sir," the waiter responded.

Kathleen was thrilled. Paul knew just what to do and just what she liked. He was totally in charge. She felt so cared for.

It was exciting to have the steak carved and presented at the table. It was tender and delicious. The waiter kept refilling Paul's champagne glass. Kathleen sipped at hers.

When they got back to the room, there was another bottle in an ice-filled bucket waiting for them.

"From my folks," Paul said, reading the card.

"Let's save it, Paul. We can have it tomorrow."

"But tomorrow won't be our wedding night, Kath." He expertly opened the bottle and poured two glasses. "To us, Mrs. Gordon." He touched his glass to hers and downed its contents.

Kathleen sipped hers, as she had done at dinner. *Mrs. Gordon* gave her more tingles than any champagne could ever produce. Paul poured himself another glass.

She wanted to say something, but she didn't want to spoil things. Still, he had drunk so much today. There seemed to have been champagne flowing all day.

"I think I'll go change," she said, and went into the bathroom to put on her new lace nightgown. She had spent such a long time choosing just the right one. It felt cool and sexy against her skin. Then she brushed her teeth, sprayed a light mist of Youth Dew between her breasts, and went to the bathroom, leaving the water running to cover the sound. Then she smoothed her hair as best she could without completely undoing it. When she came out, Paul was stretched out on the bed, sound asleep.

Uncertain what to do, she knelt beside him and kissed him on the cheek. He turned toward her and pulled her down beside him.

"Paul," she tried again, "take off your clothes, and let's get into bed."

"Mmmf." He settled himself against her.

She shook him gently and then took off his shoes and tie. He woke up as she was struggling to get him out of his jacket.

"Well, what have we here?" he said, cupping her breast as she leaned over him. "Are you trying to have your way with me, woman?"

"I'm trying to get you into bed."

"Isn't that what I said? I think I can help you." He pulled her over him onto her side of the bed and started to undress himself. He stood up to unfasten his pants and fell back onto the bed.

"Are you all right, Paul?"

"Never better, my dear. Never better." He struggled out of his clothes finally. Kathleen pulled back the covers. Paul climbed onto the bed and with one motion pulled her flimsy nightgown over her head. "No one should wear clothes to bed on the wedding night. Isn't that what you said, Kath?"

Before she could reply, he was on top of her. "Let's consummate this marriage, shall we? No need for condoms now, thank God. Like taking a shower with a raincoat on."

He thrust his way inside her before she knew what was happening. And then, as before, it was over in less than a minute. Paul slumped heavily on her and was fast asleep. She turned him gently off her and pulled the covers over him. She slipped out of bed and went into the bathroom to clean up and then crept back to the bed. She hesitated before sliding in beside him. Should she put her gown back on or not? He hadn't even noticed it. She picked it up off the floor and laid it across the chair. She arranged Paul's clothes that he had dropped on the other side of the bed neatly on the sofa. Then she climbed under the covers and snuggled up to the warm body of her new husband.

In the morning she woke before he did and went into the bathroom to brush her teeth and use the toilet. Her hair was a disaster, and she pulled the pins out of it and brushed it furiously. Giving up, she went back to bed. She looked at Paul's handsome profile as he slept. The wedding ring glowed softly on his hand. Last night hadn't been what she expected, but after all, it had been an unusual day. There wouldn't be nonstop champagne forever. Overflowing with love for him, Kathleen leaned over and kissed him on the cheek and then slid down beside him and laid her head on his shoulder.

He finally stirred and put his arm around her, drawing her closer.

"God," he said, finally. "My mouth tastes like the bottom of a bird cage."

"I'm not surprised, after all that champagne."

"Well it hasn't damaged the rest of me. Come here, wife."

He pulled her to him and made love to her much more gently this time. He stroked her and traced each breast with his fingertips, sending shivers down her back. This time when he finally entered her, she was ready for him. Again it seemed to be over before it began, but Kathleen was thrilled with the feeling of him inside her. They were married at last, and they could do this any time they wanted without worrying about having to get home or fumbling for condoms or trying to find any privacy. They could be naked in front of each other all day if they wanted. She put her arms around his neck and hugged him tightly.

"I'm so happy, Paul. I love you so much."

"I love you too," he said. "Now let's get dressed, and I'll show you San Francisco." He got up and padded into the bathroom. She heard the shower running. She had to pee again, but she couldn't quite bring herself to go into the bathroom until he was out.

When she had finally showered and they'd had breakfast, Paul showed her all the places he had discovered during his year there. They toured the waterfront, rode the streetcars, visited his uncle's store, and danced at the Fairmont. He was greeted by name at more than a few of the places they went to, and she felt proud to be with him. He was completely in charge, and she loved it. She didn't even mind too much that he seemed to order a lot of wine or cocktails whenever they ate. "C'mon, Kath, we're on our honeymoon! This is the time to celebrate."

When they'd gone to their last night's dinner at the Blue Fox, the maitre d' had welcomed them effusively and shown them to the best table in the dark restaurant. Paul had whispered to her that he'd learned an important tip from that man.

"He doesn't even look at what dress a woman is wearing. He can tell if she has style or not from her shoes and her handbag. He claims anyone can buy a stylish copy of a dress, but the shoes and bag tell everything."

Kathleen was glad she had on her new lizard going-away ensemble. The pointed-toe pumps and matching clutch purse were expensive, so she felt they should measure up. Paul had approved of them when she came out at the reception, and more and more his approval seemed to validate her. How could she ever have been so lucky as to have married him?

Chapter 10

September 1963

The thank-you notes were all written. Every piece of china and crystal was put lovingly away. Odd-colored towels and extra toasters had been exchanged for more practical items. Wedding photos were fretted over and finally selected. The sofa, a gift from her parents, was perfectly positioned to take in both the view and the fireplace. Mary's lovebirds graced the new end table they had bought with some of the wedding money. Kathleen surveyed her apartment with quiet joy. It was lovely.

She spent each day poring over her Betty Crocker cookbook and exploring local supermarkets to make delicious meals for Paul when he came home at the end of his workday. She baked cakes and pies. She did laundry. She weeded the tiny garden and planted a few flowers.

Most of their neighbors were away during the day. The only other person who seemed to be at home was Mrs. Ferguson, an elderly widow. They met in the laundry room on the first day

Kathleen went to do the wash. She discovered the tiny, grey-haired lady struggling with a large laundry basket and an unwieldy door.

"Please, let me help you with that," Kathleen said, as she held the door open.

"Thank you, my dear. This horrible door always snaps shut on me." Mrs. Ferguson slipped into the laundry room and plunked her basket down in front of the first washer. Kathleen moved to the one farther down.

"That basket is almost as big as you are," she said to the tiny woman.

"It does seem large for just me, but with sheets and towels, it holds them all. You must be the newlywed."

Kathleen blushed and introduced herself.

"I'll just get this load started, and you must join me for a cup of tea. It's so nice to meet you."

Kathleen started to protest but realized she didn't have anything to do until her wash was finished, so she accepted. It was nice to have someone to talk to.

Mrs. Ferguson's apartment was smaller than Kathleen and Paul's, and faced away from the view, toward the parking area. It had no fireplace, but it was sunny and light, and smelled faintly of lavender and camphor. Mrs. Ferguson bustled about making tea and serving it in fragile cups with faded gold rims.

"These are lovely, Mrs. Ferguson."

"They were my mother's. Haviland. She gave them to me when Alfred and I married. And looking at your fresh, young face makes me realize how long ago that was. We were married 47 years when he died, and he's been gone nearly 12 years now."

"Do you have any children?"

"No. The Lord never saw fit to bless us with any, but I have several nieces and nephews. And how about your young man? I see him leaving sometimes in the morning. What does he do?"

"He and his father have a clothing store downtown. Gordon's."

"Oh, my, yes. I know Gordon's. My nieces all shop there. And such a handsome young man too. With such a good future. How very fortunate you are."

"I know. I feel so lucky to have married him."

"That's how I felt about my Alfred. He was in insurance. He always took such good care of me."

Kathleen felt her heart squeeze. She forced herself not to think about what it might be like to lose Paul. It must be unbearable pain. She reached over and patted the old lady's hand.

Mrs. Ferguson smiled back at her. "How are you taking to married life, my dear? It was quite an adjustment for me, I must say. I couldn't boil water!" She laughed and put her hand to her cheek.

"I've never cooked much before. I baked cakes and cookies, but I never made real food. My mother did all that."

"Mine did too. And she was quite a cook. But my Alfred was very patient. I remember making pork chops one night right after we were married. My grandmother had always said to be sure to cook pork thoroughly or you'd get worms—they didn't know what it was called back then—so I fried the life out of those things. Oh, my. But Alfred just ate them as nice as you please and told me they were delicious, God bless him. They were as crisp as burnt toast, but he never let on. And I learned over time."

"I hope I will. Actually, I really enjoy it. I have this Betty Crocker cookbook that I got as a shower gift, and it's really easy to follow."

"What are you making tonight?"

"Sort of a pot roast. My girlfriend gave me this recipe. You put half a package of onion soup mix on some foil and then put the roast on that and top it with the rest of the soup and seal it tightly. Then you bake it for hours at 250°. She says it's yummy. I have my fingers crossed."

"I'm sure it will be wonderful. I never heard of wrapping meat in foil. I guess it's like cooking with the lid on though, wouldn't you say?"

"I'm the wrong one to ask!" Kathleen replied with a laugh. "But I'll let you know how it turns out."

"I hope you will, dear. It's lovely to have someone to chat with."

"It's been nice for me, too, Mrs. Ferguson. Now that the apartment is somewhat in order, I find some time on my hands occasionally."

"Well, you just pop over any time at all. But right now we'd best be seeing about our laundry."

Hope Chest

Kathleen carried the cups into the tidy kitchen, and the two women went into the laundry room. Kathleen transferred her things to the dryer. She thanked her new friend again for the tea and went back up to her apartment.

It was nice to spend time talking with someone during the day. Mary was working full-time, as were most of her friends. She called her mother occasionally, and Gran, of course, but after the bustle of finishing school and planning the wedding and then moving into the apartment, her life seemed to have slowed down considerably. It was way too soon to think about children, but she wasn't used to having no deadlines.

She set the table with their everyday dishes and some plaid placemats with matching napkins. There were daisies blooming in the back, so she picked a large bouquet and arranged them in a blue vase. She even put candles on the table on either side of the vase. She couldn't wait for Paul to get home to see how pretty the table looked. And the roast smelled wonderful.

At 5:30 she pulled the pan out of the oven. When she peeled back the foil, a pungent cloud of steam rose from the meat. The roast had shrunk, but not disastrously so, and it was swimming in a lake of dark brown liquid. She cut a tiny sliver off the roast and tasted it. She couldn't believe she had made it! It was the most tender, delicious thing she had ever had. Smiling, she put the meat onto a platter and put it back into the oven. Then she pulled out her cookbook and looked up gravy. She followed the directions exactly, and the result was a glossy puddle of perfectly seasoned sauce—with not a lump in sight, she noted, unlike her first attempt some weeks ago. She mashed the potatoes and pulled the green salad out of the refrigerator. By 5:45 everything was ready. Paul should be home any minute.

At 6:15 she put the salad back into the fridge, covered the potatoes with foil, and put them into the oven with the meat. She turned the thickening gravy off and covered it as well. By 6:30 she was frantic. Paul was usually home by six at the latest. The store closed at 5:30, and it only took him ten minutes to drive home.

What if he had to stay late? What if there had been a traffic jam? What if he'd been in an accident? Then the phone rang.

"Hi, Kat. Sorry I'm going to be late. I'm having dinner with a new buyer we just hired in the junior department. I need to go over some things."

"Paul, dinner is all ready." She tried not to sound whiny, but it just came out.

"Sorry, honey. Put it in the fridge. We'll have it tomorrow night. I won't be too late. Bye."

She put the phone back into its cradle and looked at the table. Tears pooled in her eyes, making the daisies swim and the candles blur. Then she went down the hall.

"Why, Kathleen, how nice. How was that pot roast?" Mrs. Ferguson looked delighted to see her.

"I think it's going to be delicious, but Paul has to work late. Have you eaten? I'd love it if you could join me."

"I was just going to heat up some soup, but I'd much rather try this mysterious meat in tinfoil. Thank you, my dear."

Kathleen tucked the afghan around her as she stared at the television. It was nearly 9:30. Her delicious dinner, so carefully and hopefully planned, was put away without a trace. She returned the candles to their box and removed the place mats. Mrs. Ferguson had been effusive in her praise of Kathleen's cooking and decorating skills. It was good that she invited her neighbor after all, but now that the kitchen was cleaned up, time seemed to crawl by. How long could Paul's dinner last?

Finally she heard his key in the door.

"Hey, there's my girl," he said as he came in.

"Hey," she returned.

He came over to the couch and gave her a kiss. He smelled of cigarette smoke and tasted like scotch.

"How was your dinner?" she asked.

"Productive, really productive," he said, pulling off his tie and draping it over a chair. "I think she's going to be a great asset."

"'She?'"

"Yeah, didn't I tell you? Brenda Ward. I talked dad into hiring a separate buyer for the new junior line—finally! She worked for my uncle in San Francisco. I tell you, Kat, this new department is going to be something. The store's just going to take off. I can feel it!"

He'd had dinner with a woman? Her stomach did a strange dive. But he told her about it. And it was business. And he was so excited about it, she couldn't whine.

"She just got in today, and dad and I wanted to go over our plans with her."

"Your father joined you?"

"Of course. This is a big step. He wants to be in on everything."

She let out a breath she didn't know she'd been holding. Hearing that the senior Mr. Gordon had gone with them made Kathleen feel better.

"Well, you missed a really good dinner here."

"I'm sorry, hon. It couldn't be helped. We had to go over the plans," he said again.

Paul sat next to her on the sofa and began kissing her neck.

"How interested are you in that TV program?" he asked, running his hand up her thigh.

"What program?" She slid her arms around his neck.

"Let's go to bed, then. I have plans for you too."

⁓

She talked to Mary almost daily, but they didn't see each other much. Mary was working full time, so if they did get together it was on Saturdays. Paul usually worked at least the morning, or he played golf, so Kathleen was free for the day. Sometimes she and Mary would meet downtown and shop, or they would just have coffee at Kathleen's.

This Saturday they met at their regular first stop, Frederick's Tea Room.

"Well, what's new? Any babies yet?" Mary asked.

"Don't be silly. It's really hard to remember to take my pill every night, though. I'm so afraid I'll forget."

"Would that be so terrible?"

"Oh, Paul would kill me if I got pregnant so soon."

"Really? I thought he liked kids."

"Be serious, Mar. We have to save up and get a house first. Could you see a child in our apartment? I don't even think they allow children there!"

"I think I would like three kids."

"Nice, Mar, but don't you think you should think about getting married first?"

"Oh, that. Didn't I tell you?" Mary pulled off her glove and wriggled her left hand under Kathleen's nose. A sparkly solitaire graced her ring finger.

"You rat! Why didn't you tell me?"

"I'm telling you."

"I mean before. How long have you known? When did Mark ask you?"

"He surprised me with the ring last weekend. I knew I couldn't pass the candle at Frederick's, so the glove removal trick was all I could think of."

"When's the wedding?"

"After the holidays. I'm in the market for a matron of honor. Know anyone who isn't pregnant who wouldn't mind buying a bridesmaid dress?"

Kathleen hugged her friend. There were tears in her eyes. "Do you have a dress?"

"I thought we could go look today. You're such an old hand at weddings and all."

They finished their coffee and headed down the escalator to the bridal department.

"Who else is going to be in the wedding?" Kathleen asked.

"My sister, of course, and a cousin you haven't met, and you." She paused and then looked at Kathleen. "Patrick will be the best man, Kath."

Kathleen caught her breath for a brief second. "Of course he will."

"You OK with that?"

"Why shouldn't I be? Patrick is a wonderful person, Mar. And Mark's best friend. I'm sure it will be fine. Maybe a bit awkward at first, but fine." Then, after a moment, "How is he?"

"He's great. He got a super job with a Big Eight accounting firm downtown."

"Is he going with anyone?"

"I don't think so. You ever tell Paul about the two of you?"

"Not really. When I dated Patrick, Paul wasn't even in town. And I'm sure he did his share of dating while we were apart. I never saw any need to go into details."

"That makes sense to me. Do you ever think about him?"

"Not in the way you mean. He was very special, but I never loved him the way I love Paul. I think I always knew that. Besides, we could never have made it work."

"Oh, yeah, the church thing. I thought of the two of you when I was in a high-school friend's wedding last summer. She married a Catholic but didn't convert, so they had to get married sort of in the aisle. They couldn't go up to the altar."

"Really?"

"Yeah. And at the rehearsal, they had to figure out the seating for her parents because they were divorced and the dad had remarried. I heard the priest mutter something about it was a good thing they had plenty of pews. I don't think he was all that happy to be enlarging his flock with this particular family."

"How sad."

"Do you and Paul have problems with religion? I mean, he doesn't seem like one of those Fishers guys you were so fond of."

"No, he's not. But he's not that committed to any particular religion the way Patrick is, so it works. I wish we went to church together, but somehow on Sundays we just spend the whole morning making breakfast and sharing the paper. It's such a special time—maybe because it's the only morning he's really home. I don't mind it at all."

"I don't think I would either! I can't wait until Mark and I can finally be together without roommates and Lutheran parental scowls."

"Well, here we are at Bridal," Kathleen said, laughing at her friend. "Let's go get you a drop-dead-beautiful gown."

After countless disappointing gowns and veils, Kathleen suggested they go back to her apartment so Mary could try on

Kathleen's dress. It fit Mary perfectly, despite a slight difference in their height.

"It looks gorgeous, Mar. I'd be honored if you'd wear it."

"Are you sure?"

"When am I going to wear it again? Please. By the way, I'm giving you a shower over the holidays," Kathleen said as she replaced her gown onto its padded hanger and zipping it back into its garment bag. "What kind do you want? Kitchen? Personal? China?"

"I don't care. I don't have anything yet, so whatever would be super. Everything I have in my apartment is someone's discard or my roommates'. It all goes when Mark and I have our own place."

"OK, it'll be a general shower then. Are you registered yet?"

"I think God is punishing me for making fun of you when you and Paul couldn't decide on china. We've looked a couple of times, but we haven't chosen anything yet."

"Well, get on the stick, or people won't know what to get you. I want this shower to be fabulous—and I can't wait to show off my holiday decorations."

"Aha! I'm just a shill for you to be Mrs. Homemaker-Showoff."

"You bet. You'll love the ornaments I've made. I spent hours on them.

"As long as there's food, Kath."

"And presents. We'll have fun. Be sure to give me an invitation list."

Mary hugged her friend and left with the garment bag draped gently over her arm.

Kathleen had made beaded ornaments for the Christmas tree, working on them while Paul was at the store. She carefully hid everything before he got home, not wanting him to see them until they were all finished. Sometimes she took the whole box of sequins and ribbons, pins, and tiny glass beads over to Mrs. Ferguson's and worked on them there. The older woman exclaimed over Kathleen's ideas and skill in combining colors.

"You husband will be so proud of you when you show these to him," she said. "My Alfred used to love it when I made things like this. He thought I was terribly clever. He would have admired these."

Kathleen could hardly wait until it was time to get a tree. When the holidays finally arrived, she asked Paul when they could go get one.

"Oh, God, Kathleen. I'm so sick of Christmas decorations. The store has been nuts trying to gear up for the season. Can't you just go get us a tree? I trust your judgment."

"But Paul," she began. "This is our first Christmas together. I don't want to go by myself. We could start our own tradition, find our favorite tree lot. Then we could come home and make a fire and put up the lights and snuggle."

"You are such a romantic," he said, but he smiled as he said it, and Kathleen felt better.

"Please, Paul, it's no fun alone. Besides, I have some surprises. Please? After dinner?"

"All right, after dinner."

She had looked at the standard Douglas fir that her family always had, but Paul went straight for the higher-priced section of the lot. The noble fir he selected seemed too expensive to her, but Paul waved her objections away. She had to admit this tree had perfectly spaced branches that would show off her ornaments better than the other kind.

"Our first Christmas tree, remember. Besides, we may have people over."

She smiled as Paul and the attendant hoisted the tree over to the area where they made a fresh cut on the trunk. The sharp Christmas smell of pine and fir was everywhere in the busy lot, and she couldn't breathe in enough of it. She loved Christmas, and this would be the best one since she was little and got her beloved bride doll.

She'd bought a tree stand and some tiny white lights earlier in the week, as well as some red and silver ball ornaments. She couldn't wait to see what Paul thought of the special decorations she had made. They would be the perfect counterpoint to the plain glass balls and give the tree its personality.

When they got home and unloaded the tree, Paul had trouble getting it into the stand.

"Hold the thing straight while I try to screw these things in, Kat."

"I am, Paul. It looks straight from here in the mirror."

"Well, it looks crooked from down here. Lift it up about an inch or so."

Kathleen tugged on the tree. It was heavier than it appeared, and she had trouble pulling it out of the stand.

"Here," Paul said, grabbing the trunk out of her hands. "Get down there and screw in the deals when I tell you to. I'll hold it steady."

She crouched down under the damp branches and tried to turn the metal screws into the base of the tree. It was hard to do, but she kept turning and turning the round end of the fastener.

"Shall I do all of them, or do you want to?" she asked.

"If I let go, it'll go crooked on us again."

"Right." She crawled around to the other side and began working the second screw into the unyielding bark. There was a knot or a place where there had been a branch right next to where she was trying to sink the screw.

"I can't get it to work, Paul. There's a bump on this side."

"Oh, for heaven's sake." He sounded exasperated. "Come up slowly and hold the trunk. I'll fix it."

They traded places in slow motion. Kathleen felt the tree shift and tried to right it.

"What are you doing? Now the damn thing's all screwed up again."

She felt tears prick her eyelids. This was supposed to be wonderful. "I'm sorry, Paul. It shifted when you moved."

Paul let out a frustrated breath and twisted the trunk furiously again. After several long minutes, the tree was finally standing, and Paul emerged from beneath the branches.

"I've never done this part before," Kathleen said, almost in apology. "My dad always just stuck our tree in the stand, and it stayed. I didn't realize it was so hard to do."

"Do we even have anything to decorate it with?" Paul asked, wiping his hands on his pants.

Kathleen managed a smile. "Actually, we do. I got some lights and some ornaments, and I told you, I have a surprise."

She went to the hall closet and brought out the decorations. "Put the lights on first," she said, handing them to Paul. She went to their stereo and put on an LP of Christmas carols. Paul wound the strands around the trunk, handing them to Kathleen to arrange among the branches. Regaining some of her excitement, she plugged in the lights. Nothing happened.

"Shit!" Paul exploded. "What kind of lights are these?"

"Maybe it's just a loose bulb. I'll check them." One by one, she turned each tiny bulb into its socket, and finally the whole strand burst into light. "There, see. It was just one."

She turned to see Paul's reaction, but he had gone into the kitchen and was pouring himself a scotch. She heard the ice cubes clink into the glass.

"Want a drink?" he called.

"No thanks."

"I didn't think so." He came back into the living room.

Kathleen felt she had disappointed him somehow, but she rarely drank. He had known that from the beginning. Plunging ahead, she pulled out the box of ornaments she had made. "Tah dah!"

"What are those?" he said as she held two of the glittery balls up for him to see.

"Our first ornaments. I made them."

He took a long drink of his scotch.

"You hate them."

"I don't hate them, Kat, but I think our tree should be more sophisticated, don't you? Like all silver with the white lights. Wait until you see the store—that's how we did it this year, and it looks terrific."

"I thought you were sick of decorating the store."

"I am. It's taken so much time. But it looks really classy."

She couldn't stop the tears. She had worked so hard on her ornaments. How could she have judged Paul's reaction so far off the mark? She was hurt, but she was embarrassed too. She wanted him to be proud of her. Now she only felt foolish.

"Hey," he said, finally noticing her tears. "Hey, come on. No need to cry." He came over to her and put his arm around her shoulders. "We'll just go get some other stuff and put it on the tree together. It'll be great."

She moved away from him and went to get a tissue. Then she pulled the plain red and silver balls out of the sack. "Is this what you had in mind, Paul?"

"Yeah. Now those are more like it. Tailored. You were just kidding about those other things, weren't you?"

He wasn't looking at her any more. He sat down on the couch and sipped his drink. She blew her nose and stuffed the tissue into her pocket. "Aren't you going to help put these up at least?" she asked.

"Sure. Bring me a box of those silver guys, and I'll put the hooks on them."

☙

Kathleen threw herself into planning Mary's shower. She sent out the invitations and pored over her cookbook to find something special for her best friend. She thought the apartment looked wonderful, even if Paul hadn't appreciated her artwork. She pulled out their largest silver wedding-gift bowl and piled all her precious ornaments into it. Then she arranged evergreen branches and pine cones down the center of their dining table and put the bowl in the middle. She placed their silver candlesticks with red candles in them on either side. It looked beautiful, she thought, and she didn't ask Paul for his opinion.

She decided to serve creamed chicken with pimento and peas on puff-pastry shells from Frederick & Nelson, with cranberry sauce in lettuce cups. She would order a cake from the Danish bakery nearby, white with raspberry filling. Mary's colors for the wedding were going to be pink and red, so that's what Kathleen would have them do the roses in for the decoration on the cake.

She'd planned the shower for a Saturday when she thought everyone could come and Paul would be at the store. It would be the first time she really got to use her sterling silver and her good china, except for their one-month anniversary when she'd made a special dinner. She lit a Pres-to-Log in the fireplace and turned on the tree lights. Then she lit the candles on the mantel and surveyed her handiwork. Everything looked perfect.

Mary and her mother were the first to arrive. Kathleen took their coats and gave Mrs. Bergstrom a tour of the apartment.

"Hey, Kath, where'd you get these gorgeous ornaments in the silver bowl?"

"Et tu, Brute?"

"What?"

"Paul hates them too."

"I was serious. They're beautiful. Look at these, Mom."

"Kathleen, they're lovely. Wherever did you find such things?"

"I made them, Mrs. B. Do you really like them?"

"Oh, my, yes. They're perfect in that silver bowl, but I would hang them on my tree if I had them."

Kathleen laughed to herself and hugged Mary's mother. She wished Paul were there to hear all this.

The holiday season seemed particularly stressful for Paul, Kathleen thought. He was late every night. She gave up trying to wait dinner and just ate when she got hungry. She made casseroles that she left warming in the oven. Finally, on Christmas Eve the store closed at six, and Paul came home on time. She had wrapped all his presents and arranged them under the tree. He came into the apartment with two sacks with the familiar Gordon's logo on them.

"Ho! Ho! Ho! Merry Christmas, little girl." He put the bags down near the tree and swept Kathleen up into his arms. She giggled and wrapped her arms around his neck. She could smell liquor on his breath.

"Party at the store?" she said with a smile.

"We sold everything but the fixtures, Mrs. Gordon. Old Dad broke out a bottle of champagne, if you can believe it, to salute our record sales. It looks like it'll be the best damn Christmas we've ever had. And much of it due to yours truly's juniors' department. Thank you very much, ladies and gentlemen."

"Oh, Paul, I'm so proud of you!" She looked at her handsome husband, and her heart swelled. "Merry Christmas, darling."

Chapter 11

January 1964

Kathleen waited until after the holidays to return the outfits Paul had given her. She felt terrible that the things he had obviously spent so much time picking out hadn't worked. She dressed carefully but went into Gordon's knowing she looked just like what every clerk dreaded after Christmas: a woman with bulging Gordon's shopping bags signaling "returns."

"May I help you?" came a pleasant but professional voice.

Kathleen turned to see a striking blonde woman in a stylish grey suit. The skirt was just to her knees, the jacket cropped at her tiny waist.

"Thank you," Kathleen responded with a smile. "My husband bought me these for Christmas, but they don't seem to fit. I don't think I'm built for junior sizes—I'm too long-waisted and broad-shouldered. I can't move when I have either of these on. And I can't raise my arms."

"What size are you usually?" the clerk asked, taking the bags from Kathleen.

"I'm an 8. These are just 9s, which should be bigger, but they don't work."

"Well, let's have a look, shall we?" The young woman removed the outfits from their bags and laid them out on a nearby counter. "Oh, my," she said.

"Is there a problem?" Kathleen asked.

"I might have one, I'm afraid. You must be Paul's wife."

Kathleen was startled. *Paul's* wife? "Yes, I'm Mrs. Gordon," she said, choosing her title intentionally.

"I'm happy to meet you. I'm Brenda Ward, the buyer here for Juniors. I'm afraid these are my fault."

"I beg your pardon."

"Your husband asked me to choose some outfits for you for Christmas. He said he thought you were about 110 pounds and my height, so I figured size 9. Would you mind trying these on so I could see?"

Numbly, Kathleen took the outfits into a dressing room. This was Brenda? And she did Paul's—*Paul's*—shopping for him. For *her* Christmas presents! She stepped out of her dress and looked at herself in her slip. She was trim. She'd weighed the same since high school—except right after her freshman year when she'd discovered to her horror that she'd put on nearly ten pounds and promptly dieted them off.

She pulled the first dress on and zipped it up. It was a sleeveless wool sheath with a matching jacket. It was very smart. Kathleen could imagine Brenda in it.

There was a tap on the dressing room door, and Brenda peered in. "Well, that looks darling! What's wrong with that one?"

"Nothing if I don't try to raise my arms. Look how the armholes are cutting into me."

As Brenda came closer to her, Kathleen could smell her abundant perfume. From its cloying sweetness, Kathleen guessed it was Jungle Gardenia. Not at all like the flower it was named for, Kathleen thought.

"Hmm. You do have broad shoulders. OK. I see the problem. Be right back."

Kathleen examined herself again. Her curls looked unruly and not at all chic. Fortunately she had worn her going-away slip, but she didn't feel like the stylish wife of the storeowner's son. She felt frumpy next to Brenda, and she wondered what the buyer Paul thought so highly of was thinking about her. Kathleen had intended to replace the outfits she'd imagined Paul fussing over with identical ones in a larger size so he would never know, but now she didn't really care. She'd just try to find something she liked that fit and that made her feel stylish. Brenda knocked again.

"Try these," Brenda said. She hung several dresses and a pant suit on the hook. "I brought some different sizes so we could see if it's just the brand or if it's really the size. Sometimes different lines fit differently. Try the Jonathan Logan on first. It's so darling. And I think these pants with matching jackets are going to be a very big look this year."

Kathleen tried on the blue and red shepherd's-check pants. They fit perfectly, and amazingly didn't even have to be shortened. The jacket was almost tunic length with gold, rather military-looking buttons. She could move her arms in it, and she reluctantly had to agree with Brenda's assessment about the pant suit. It was wonderful.

The dresses were shorter than she was used to, but as Brenda had said, they were darling. The first one didn't fit at all; the waist circled her rib cage. The next one she tried on was a bright-green wool chemise with full sleeves that fastened at the wrist. It had a scoop neck with a blue-and-green-striped turtleneck insert that could be worn with it or not. It looked wonderful and felt even better. The last one was what was called a poor-boy knit, a softly ribbed jersey in a heather blue. It fit too. She was turning to see how it looked from the back when she heard Brenda's tap.

"How you doing?" Brenda said, opening the door slowly. "Oh, good. I brought you a smoke-ring scarf for just that dress. Try this with it." She slid a filmy dotted circle of silk over Kathleen's head and stepped back to appraise her handiwork. "Oh, that's great on you. You have good legs for that length."

"This, the pants, and the green one all seem to fit fine. This other one hit me about a mile above my waist."

"It's the junior size. I found these other three in the regular sizes. I hate to say it, but junior sizes really aren't right for you. I'm surprised. Juniors are designed for someone your height generally, but they don't work for everyone. Fortunately we have great clothes in all our departments. That green dress is by Ladybug. It's made for you. Have you decided which you would like?"

Kathleen thought for just a moment. She didn't know what Paul had paid for the original things, but then he probably didn't either. Besides, he got a discount on everything, so why should she care? "I'll take all three. And the scarf. Thank you."

She got dressed and went out to the cash register. Brenda had the clothes wrapped in tissue and put into bags. "Here you are, Mrs. Gordon. I'm happy to have met you. I don't usually work the floor, but when you come in again, please let me know, and I'll pull some outfits for you. Now that I know what to look for."

Kathleen took the bags and left the store without going to Paul's office.

As she drove north out of downtown, she found herself going to the university instead of going home. She parked on campus and walked briskly toward her old mentor's office. She didn't expect to find Hawk there, but the cold felt good against her hot face and the grey sky matched her mood. She didn't really feel like being in the apartment just now. Her steps echoed against the worn stone stairs as she climbed to the third floor of the familiar building where she had spent so much undergraduate time. It smelled of dust and damp coats.

To her amazement, when she knocked on the closed door of Hawk's office, her professor's voice said, "Come in."

When her former teacher saw Kathleen in the doorway, she bounded out of her chair and embraced her. "What a happy day this is after all!" Hawk said. "What brings you to your old haunts, my dear?"

"I was just in the neighborhood and thought I'd see if you were about. How are things going in the drama world?"

"I am beyond busy. But how about you? Old married lady and all. Are you working?"

"No. I'm just a housewife."

"Oho, that old word 'just'! I would imagine your days are pretty busy keeping up a house, aren't they?"

"Well, the holidays were pretty hectic, but now I seem to have a lot of time on my hands."

"Want to put them to good use?"

"What do you mean?"

"Well, I just can *not* believe you walked in here right now. This week I got the OK to hire someone and was going through my roster to see if I have any students who could help me out. But I don't have anyone who could do the job as well as you, Kathleen. And pop goes the weasel, in you walk!

"I'm so swamped here I could spit. If you're at all interested, I could use an assistant. Someone to take over the details of our creative dramatics program with the young kids. You know, the way you used to."

"Are you serious?"

"As dirt. But, oh, that means you'd have to be here on Saturdays. What would hubby think of that?"

"He works every Saturday. I'm sure he wouldn't even know I was gone."

Kathleen felt a surge of excitement. She hadn't admitted even for a moment that she was restless with nothing to do all day besides shop and plan dinners. She truly loved their apartment and loved doing things for Paul, but except for Mrs. Ferguson and occasionally her mother, Kathleen had no company until Paul came home. The possibility of working with Hawk again in the field that she loved seemed like a miracle.

"What do you need me to do?"

"You know the stuff, contact the schools to tell them about the program, register the kids, take attendance, set up the classroom, help plan the program, spin straw into gold. Same as always."

"I would love to. When would you need me to start?"

"Take off your coat and you're on! I have extra classes this quarter, so I just didn't know how I was going to manage everything. Kathleen, you are a godsend. Plus, I even have some money to pay you. It's not much, but it's something. And it's only part-time."

"Oh, Professor Hawkins, I'm so excited."

Hope Chest

"Do you need to ask your husband?"

Kathleen paused. What would Paul say? He never said she couldn't work, just that she didn't *have* to. As long as there was clean laundry and dinner on the table, she didn't think he would mind. "No, I'm sure he won't have any objections. He knows how much I loved working with the kids. And I really can start right away. I'm so happy I stopped in just now."

"There are no accidents, my dear. Didn't I teach you that?"

Kathleen left the university in such good spirits she drove over to see her mother. They had spent a part of Christmas Day with her parents and grandparents before she and Paul went to the Gordons' for dinner. Her mother was thrilled with being Paul Gordon's mother-in-law, so Kathleen's dealings with her had been much easier since the wedding. Consequently, Kathleen had been surprised when her mother expressed extreme displeasure when she heard that Mary was going to wear Kathleen's wedding gown.

"I'm happy she wants to wear it, Mother. Don't you see it as a compliment?"

"Compliment? Do you realize what we paid for that dress, Kathleen? What if she spills something on it?"

"Oh, for heaven's sake, Mother. It's not as if I'm going to wear it again."

"Of course not, but what if you should have a daughter? What then? Might she not want to wear her mother's gorgeous gown? Really, Kathleen. You must think ahead."

"I'm sure Mary will be very careful, Mother."

Except for a couple of phone calls, Kathleen had not seen her mother since then. But right now she felt that nothing could burst her bubble. She grabbed her packages and headed up the stairs to her parents' home.

"Anybody home?"

"Kathleen, is that you? To what do we owe this honor?"

"I wanted to show you my new outfits, Mother. What do you think? I'm getting very modern. Look at the new length." She held the dresses up to herself one at a time.

"These are quite nice, Kathleen. Where would you wear that pants thing, though?"

"Paul's new buyer assured me that it's the latest style." How easily she talked about Brenda. There was no indication in her voice of what she was feeling. Her mother never even moved her eyes from the clothes. "It'll be great for going over to friends' for dinner or even to the movies. I think it's cute. And for once I don't have to hem the pants."

"Well, come into the kitchen, and I'll put on the coffee pot. Have you had lunch?"

"Not really. What's in the fridge?"

"Look and see while I do the coffee. I think there's some tuna salad, and I have some fresh bread."

"I just talked with Professor Hawkins, and she offered me a job."

Her mother stopped in mid-motion. "A job? You never mentioned looking for a job."

"I wasn't looking, Mother, that's just it. I happened to go visit her, and she just happened to be shopping for an assistant. I'll be working with the school-age kids again."

"You accepted this job before you talked with Paul?"

"He won't mind, Mother," she said. Hawk had asked the same question. She hadn't even thought about asking Paul first. "It's only part-time, so he won't even know when I'm gone."

"But how will it look? What if people think Gordon's is not doing well enough to support you?"

"All they have to do is go into the store, Mother. I was just there. It's two weeks after the Christmas return rush, and the store was as busy as ever. Paul said they had their biggest season yet, partially because of his new ideas. The juniors' section has really taken off."

"Just the same, you should really consult your husband before you do something this major, Kathleen. It's only proper."

"I'll certainly discuss it with him, Mother." Kathleen didn't want to talk about Brenda or Paul or Gordon's, so she switched to a subject she knew would command her mother's full attention.

"I told Gran that Mary was going to wear my wedding gown. She thought it was a wonderful idea."

"Of course she would. Your grandmother would think it was wonderful if you jumped off the Space Needle. She and I have never quite seen things the same way. I hope at least that you have told your friend there can be absolutely no alterations done."

Kathleen smiled to herself and started making the sandwiches.

She stopped at the grocery store on the way home and bought the ingredients for beef stroganoff. It was one of Paul's favorite dinners. She got salad makings, even choosing an out-of-season and fairly expensive green pepper because he liked them. Even though Paul gave her a generous allowance each month for household expenses, Kathleen had become adept at finding bargains. It was the only way she could accumulate extra spending money. She knew she could have whatever she wanted if she asked, but if she wanted to surprise him or do something for herself, she didn't want to have to ask. She'd always had her own checking account since college, but now Paul handled the checks and gave her cash. She didn't want him to think she couldn't manage.

It was only three o'clock by the time she got home. She hung her new clothes in the closet and changed into some wool slacks and a sweater. In the kitchen, she turned on the oven and pulled out her wedding-present mixer to begin a chocolate layer cake.

By the time Paul arrived a couple of hours later, the whole place smelled deliciously of chocolate and the stroganoff bubbling on the stove.

"What's for dinner," he asked as he came through the door. "Smells great, and I'm starving."

"Beef stroganoff. Take off your suit and we'll eat."

Paul came into the kitchen a short time later, dressed in his jeans and an old sweatshirt. He dipped a spoon into the stroganoff and promptly burned his mouth.

"It's almost ready, Paul. Go sit down."

He went to the cupboard over the refrigerator and took down a bottle of wine. "Want some?"

"Sure. That would be nice with dinner," she responded. She didn't really want any, but she didn't want to make a scene just before she told Paul about her job. She hadn't been anxious about it at all until she spoke with her mother. Should she have accepted Hawk's offer before she talked to her husband? It hadn't occurred to her. What objections could he have? It wouldn't affect his home life, and she would be bringing in extra money. How bad could that be?

She dished up both their plates and brought them into the table.

"Heard you were in the store today. You didn't come up."

"I didn't want to bother you while you were working, Paul. I exchanged those outfits for some that fit me better. There was quite a selection. I thought that after Christmas things might be a little picked over, but there were some really cute things."

"Yeah, Brenda is doing quite a number in juniors. She was exactly the right choice for that job. I'm sure there are tons of things you'd like in that department."

"Well, actually, she helped me, and even she agreed that I'm the wrong shape for junior sizes. But I got some darling things from the regular department. I'll show you what I bought after dinner."

Paul put down his fork. "What do you mean? Everyone your height can wear junior sizes."

"Not everyone, I guess. They're cut a little smaller in the shoulders and higher in the waist. But the stuff I got today fits perfectly."

"So when I turn the whole store into junior sizes, my wife will shop elsewhere?"

"Paul, why would you turn the whole store over? There must be at least three other women in the world who can't wear a size 9. Wouldn't you be better off appealing to more people?"

"Boy, it's a good thing you don't run the store. You can't please everyone, Kat, so to succeed, you have to specialize. I want to target the younger, more stylish girls. Let the old ladies shop at Frederick's and I. Magnin. I've done my homework. If we are the biggest and the best in appealing to the younger group, the other stores will have to play catch-up, and we'll spend all our time counting our dough."

"I never looked at it that way, but it makes sense. You really are good at this business, Paul. Your dad is lucky to have a son who can not only carry on his business but improve it in ways he never even imagined."

Paul looked at her and gave her one of the smiles that had caused her to fall for him in the first place. "I wish he shared your opinion."

"He will, Paul. He won't be able to help himself. Give him time. He built Gordon's after a certain pattern. It's worked for him all these years. Change is hard for men his age, especially when what you want to change is still producing."

"I guess you might have something there. It's so frustrating to talk to him though. He's so stubborn. But the numbers this quarter will make him look again."

"Speaking of changes," Kathleen began nervously, "My old professor offered me a job today."

"A job? As what?"

"Remember the creative dramatics workshops for kids I used to do? Well, they need an assistant to help put them together and run them. It would only be part-time."

"I don't think so, Kathleen. You don't need to work."

"I know I don't *need* to, Paul, but I just loved those workshops. I think it would be really fun. Until we have kids, I have a lot of time every day that I could spend on this project. It wouldn't take away from anything I do here."

"Did you already tell him you'd take the job?"

"I told *her*, Paul. You remember Professor Hawkins—Hawk. I talked about her all the time, and she came to the wedding."

"There were lots of people at the wedding, Kat. Anyway, I don't think it's a good idea." He took another bite of stroganoff. "If you were working, who would make these delicious dinners?" He smiled again.

"I didn't get home until after three today, Paul. And I even had time to make you your favorite dessert. Honestly, you wouldn't even notice I was away." She hated the pleading tone her voice had taken on. Could he forbid her to do something she wanted to do?

"Well, I'll have to think about this."

"Paul, there's nothing to think about. I can't just sit home day after day cleaning the bathroom and having tea with Mrs. Ferguson. I'm really good at working with kids, so I've taken this job. If it turns out that it interferes with our lives, then I'll quit. But until then, I'm doing it. Please don't be upset."

Suddenly Paul smiled again. "Well, maybe it's a good idea. I don't want you sitting around here and thinking about having babies until we're ready for that."

"We need to get a house before that, Paul. I thought we could start looking once the weather got nicer." She looked up and smiled at him, but he was busy with his plate.

Chapter 12

February 1964

January did an about-face as soon as Kathleen started to work. What had begun as long, slow days now became a whirl of activity. When she wasn't at the creative dramatics lab, she was at the library searching for new ideas for "her kids." She brought piles of books home—fairy tales, story poems, Greek myths. And when she wasn't doing that, she was at Mary's helping with wedding plans.

Amazingly, she loved her bridesmaid dress, a red velvet sheath with a broad V-neck and long sleeves and red satin buttons at the wrist and down the back. It was a dress she actually might be able to wear again, and it wasn't too expensive. To save money she had her wedding shoes dyed to match. Funny, she thought as she handed them to the shoemaker, even though she knew she would never wear them again, it made her a bit sad to break up a part of her wedding ensemble. But although her mythical daughter might wear her wedding dress some day, she very probably would want her own shoes.

The wedding would be at Mary's Lutheran church in Ballard, so the rehearsal dinner was to be held at the nearby Windjammer restaurant in Shilshole Bay. It would be the first time Kathleen would see Patrick since they broke up. Even though she'd assured Mary that she had absolutely no qualms about seeing him again, as the date grew closer, she began to wonder. Did he still care for her, or was she being totally conceited to even think he might? It had been nearly two years. It was silly to think he would still be carrying a torch.

She heard Paul's key in the door and gave dinner one last stir, happy to have her thoughts interrupted. She went to kiss him hello and took his overcoat to hang it in the hall closet.

"Cash registers still ringing?"

"Like music, Kat, beautiful music. What's for dinner? I'm starving."

"Spaghetti. Go wash up and come sit down."

She dished up their plates and set them on the table. Paul poured himself a glass of wine, sat down, and sniffed appreciatively.

"You are becoming quite a cook, wife of mine. This smells great."

She smiled and sat down across from him. The spaghetti did smell good. It was a new recipe, the first one she had had time to try in a while. Her schedule lately had forced her to rely on her limited dinner repertoire, but she was starting to feel guilty about feeding Paul the same things, so she had taken her cookbook to work with her yesterday and looked for something new and easy while she ate lunch.

"By the way, you're included in the rehearsal dinner next Friday," she said.

"What rehearsal dinner?"

"For Mary's wedding. It's next Saturday."

"This coming Saturday?"

"No, a week from this Saturday."

"Sorry, hon, I'm going to be in New York."

"New York? Why? You never said anything about a trip."

Hope Chest

"Buying trip. I guess I forgot to mention it. I leave that Wednesday after work and come back Sunday."

"Paul, you can't miss Mary's wedding! Can't you go later? Or can't someone else go instead of you?"

"Sorry, honey. I'm taking all the department heads, and I want to supervise what they choose. I've wanted to do this forever, and I finally talked my old man into the merits of my idea. Frankly, I think he only agreed because we had such a good Christmas, but it means he's finally starting to recognize that I might have a head for this business after all. Besides, you'll be so busy you won't even know I'm not there."

"But, Paul, I'm so disappointed. It won't be the same without you."

"I'll be home the next day, and you can tell me all about it."

༄

She took a long time getting ready for the wedding rehearsal. She wished she could have had her hair done, but since they would all have theirs done the next day for the wedding, it wasn't possible. She would just have to struggle with it herself. Then she couldn't decide what to wear. And on top of it all, she was feeling guilty. Would she be acting like this if Patrick weren't going to be there?

As she drove to the church, her stomach was aflutter. What would she say to him? This was ridiculous. After all, she was happily married. And she knew Patrick would be a perfect gentleman. He was too kind to be otherwise. She parked the car and took a deep breath before she pulled the key out of the ignition. She gathered her purse and the bouquet of bows from the shower for Mary to carry, but before she had walked more than a few steps, she saw that she had left her lights on and had to go back and turn them off. She shook her head and double-checked to make sure she hadn't forgotten anything else.

The church, when she finally got inside, was dimly lit and smelled faintly of old flowers. Mary's mother greeted her at the door. It seemed that Kathleen was among the last to arrive. She walked up the side aisle and waved to Mary.

"About time. Some matron of honor! I thought I'd have to rehearse without a bouquet."

Kathleen relaxed and hugged her friend. This wasn't about her, she suddenly realized, feeling totally selfish and more than a little bit foolish. Who cared what Patrick and Kathleen were feeling? This was the time to celebrate Mary and Mark. She hugged Mary again for good measure and felt instantly better.

"Hey, Kath," Mark called out and came to give her a hug as well.

"Hello, Kathleen." It was Patrick. They stood apart for a few seconds, neither appearing to know quite what to do. Then Patrick stepped quickly toward her and gave her a brief hug. Only their shoulders and arms touched, but she was aware of the remembered scent of his aftershave.

"It's nice to see you again, Kathleen," he said, smiling at her. "How are you?"

"I'm fine, Patrick. And you?"

"Great."

"That's good. Your family?"

"Everyone's fine."

"Good, that's good."

"And your job?"

"It's good. Getting busier now that taxes are approaching."

"Oh, yes. I guess it would."

Mercifully the minister began giving them directions at that moment, and the bridesmaids went to sit on the left, the groomsmen on the right. Kathleen didn't hear much of what was said. Her face was warm, and she felt incredibly awkward. What a dumb conversation! She was not the sophisticated married woman she had hoped Patrick would see. She was as awkward as she had ever been on a Del Phi exchange. Well, at least Patrick might feel better about her marrying someone else—if he had ever felt bad at all.

They lined up and went through the processional, each bridesmaid waiting until the preceding one reached the sixth pew before beginning her own hesitation step up the aisle. As matron of honor, Kathleen went next to last, and Mary's sister Julie, the maid of honor, walked down just before the bride. The minister told Mary and Mark what he expected of them, when Mary should hand her bouquet to Julie, when Mark should get the rings from Patrick, when they would kneel. The soloist went through "The Lord's Prayer" and "Because," the silver notes of her clear voice echoing magically in the empty church. Then they turned and followed the bride and groom back down the aisle. Mary's sister took Patrick's arm, and Kathleen fell in with the next groomsman.

"OK, everyone. I think that was perfect. Let's go eat!" Mark's father wrapped an arm around his son and his future daughter-in-law, a broad smile causing his eyes nearly to close, just the way his son's did when he smiled. He was still a handsome man, and it was easy to see what Mark would look like at that age. They had the same broad shoulders and crisp, wavy hair—only Mark's was not yet streaked with gray. At six feet, Mark had an inch on his father, but they both had such erect bearing, they seemed even taller.

"Anybody need a ride?" Patrick asked.

"I do," Mary's cousin Kristin said, smiling at him. She was an attractive blonde, just like most of Mary's Scandinavian relatives. Kathleen fished for her car keys in her purse and went out to the parking lot. Wouldn't it be something if Patrick and Kristin hit it off? He deserved to find someone wonderful. Then he could be as happy as she was. Paul hadn't called since he left for New York, but long distance was expensive, and she didn't expect to hear from him. Still, whenever the phone rang, she hoped it would be his voice.

Kristin sat next to Patrick at the dinner. Kathleen glanced at them from time to time, and they seemed engrossed in conversation. Patrick threw back his head once and laughed heartily.

There were the usual we-are-so-thrilled-to-welcome-Mark/Mary-to-our-family toasts, and a delicious salmon dinner, which the restaurant was known for. Mary and Mark beamed at their guests from their seats at the head of the U-shaped table and looked the way brides and grooms should. Mary gave her bridesmaids beautiful beaded satin purses to carry tomorrow. The groomsmen got gold cufflinks, each monogrammed, but with the wedding date as well engraved on the underside. Then it was time to go. Kathleen watched Patrick help Kristin on with her coat. They left the restaurant together.

Mary and Kathleen headed for the ladies' room.
"I love this purse, Mar. I really needed one, and this is gorgeous."
"I knew you didn't have one. I just hope no one else did either."
"Who cares? You can always use another elegant thing."
"How was it?"
"How was what?"
"Patrick."
"Oh, fine. What did you expect?" Kathleen looked at herself in the mirror. Her curls were moderately under control. The hairspray had held, she was happy to see.
"Well, you were both quite civilized. I just suspected you might be a teensy bit wiggly at seeing him."
"Not wiggly at all, my friend. Unless they have gotten extremely fat, old married ladies don't get wiggly around ex-boyfriends."
"That's good. It looks like my cousin is quite taken with him. Did you notice?"
"No, not really," she lied. "She's awfully pretty though. I wouldn't blame Patrick for being interested. You all ready for tomorrow?"
"I think so. My mom has everything in alphabetical order. You know her!"

The two friends laughed and left the powder room. Kathleen made the rounds of farewells among those who remained and then drove home. It hadn't been too bad seeing Patrick. Awkward at first, but not too bad. He looked the same, and she had no regrets, but she wished again that Paul could be there tomorrow night. She missed him. It seemed strange sleeping in their king-sized bed all alone. She checked the lock on the door several times each night before she went to bed, especially since after the first night alone, Mrs. Ferguson had rung her doorbell the next morning to tell Kathleen she had left her keys in the door.

"You must be more careful, my dear. Anyone could have come in!"

Kathleen met Mary and the other bridesmaids at the beauty parlor the next day. Mary's mother was there as well. They all chattered merrily and teased Mary somewhat less vigorously than they might have had Mrs. Bergstrom not been there. The owner of the shop congratulated them on having the foresight to wear blouses that buttoned down the front so they wouldn't have to ruin their hairdos getting them on and off and hustled them all into various chairs.

Kathleen hadn't gone to this salon before and couldn't believe what the tall young man had been able to do with her hair. With dark combs, he pulled it back slightly from her face, leaving wispy curls in front of her ears. Then he let the rest of the back curl as it wanted to up and over the red satin bow the bridesmaids were wearing. The bow pushed her hair up at the crown, giving her height. The result was stunning. She barely recognized the attractive girl looking back at her from the mirror. How she wished Paul could see her.

"Whoo-ee! Who are you? And where's my matron of honor?"

"You should talk!" Kathleen said, looking at a whole new Mary. Her blond hair was swept back from her face into a smooth French roll. Tiny strands of hair accentuated her cheekbones.

"You look like Grace Kelly, Mar! Mark is going to positively faint."

"I told you this salon was fabulous. Wait till you see my mom. She's almost finished so we can head to the church and draw on our faces."

"How you holding up?"

"I'm fine. I'm also very glad you're driving."

The bride's dressing room at the church was the Sunday school classroom closest to the lavatory. They put on their makeup under hideous fluorescent lights and then went back to the room to dress. All the gowns were hanging on a portable rack, and the room smelled of roses and damp florist's paper and very new shoes. The bridesmaids slipped into their red dresses. Then Julie and Mrs. Bergstrom carefully managed Kathleen's freshly pressed gown over Mary's hairdo.

Kathleen then began the long task of fastening the tiny buttons up the back. Mrs. Bergstrom unhooked the veil from its hanger and turned to put it on Mary's head when she stopped in midmotion.

"Oh, my, Mary," was all she could say before she began to cry.

"Oh, Mom, don't start on me now."

"You look so lovely."

"Mom, you're going to ruin your makeup," Julie said. "We can't do you and Mary at the same time."

"Besides, I'm sure it's the dress, don't you think?" Kathleen teased, causing Mrs. Bergstrom to laugh. Mary bent her knees so her mother could put the headpiece in place. Julie fluffed out the veil, and they all stood back. Mary did look beautiful. Kathleen was so happy Mary had chosen to wear her gown. Again she found herself wishing that Paul were there to see it and they could relive their memories together. Oh, well, she would certainly have a lot to share with him when he got home.

The photographer tapped on the door and hustled them out to the sanctuary for the photos at the altar. Mary decided to have them all taken before the ceremony to save time, so when the groomsmen came in with Mark, Kathleen watched his face as he saw Mary for the first time. Kathleen smiled to herself as Mark gazed in awe at his bride, his handsome face creasing finally into a huge smile of his own.

Patrick came up behind Mark, and Kathleen was reminded of how he had looked in his tuxedo for her formal at what seemed so long ago. He, too, looked very handsome. He smiled at her and gave a thumbs-up. She smiled back with a nod.

Finally they went back to the dressing room to wait until the signal for the ceremony to begin.

It was over before Kathleen's shoes had even begun to pinch. The happy couple beamed at the assembled guests, and they all filed out to a vigorous Mendelssohn piece, played, Mary's father said, as only a Lutheran organist could play. At the reception, the wedding party arranged itself into the receiving line, Kathleen

Hope Chest

standing between Julie and Kristin. They all introduced one another to the polite strangers who commented on how lovely everyone looked and hugged and squealed with the Del Phis who came through. The groomsmen mingled with the guests. Kathleen noted that they didn't keep bringing Mark drinks as they had for Paul at her wedding. Finally, the last of the guests came through, and they could finally sit down. Kristin and Patrick sat together.

When it was time for the first dance, Mark led his bride onto the floor as the band played "More." Kathleen watched her dress swirl around the ballroom and wondered if she had looked so happy in it. She was sure she had. Why wasn't Paul here, she thought for the hundredth time. He was missing so much.

Then the wedding party joined the bridal couple on the dance floor in the same pairings as they had come down the aisle: Patrick with Julie, Kathleen with Mark's fraternity brother. They danced for a few bars, and then Mark and Mary traded partners with her parents. Soon everyone was switching partners, and Kathleen found herself in Patrick's arms.

"You look beautiful tonight, Kathleen," he said, holding her loosely and smiling.

"You look pretty beautiful yourself," she teased back, determined to keep the conversation light.

"Tuxedoes make the man, you always said. But red is definitely your color."

"Thank you, Patrick." She couldn't think of what else to say. They danced in silence for a few more bars.

"You look very happy too," he said.

"I am, Patrick. Very happy."

"I was hoping to meet the lucky guy. Mark said he's out of town."

"Yes, buying trip to New York. He'll be back tomorrow though." Why did she say that?

Then before she could say anything else, they switched partners again, and Kathleen found herself dancing with Mark's father.

"I must say my son has very good taste in women. You all are just about the prettiest group of girls I've seen in one place for a long time!"

"Thank you, kind sir. Not to mention the handsome groom, who looks very much like his father."

"Too kind! But I'll take it and repeat it to my wife whenever she looks unappreciative."

The song finished when she was dancing with Mary's father. He escorted her back to the table where she and Julie then plotted to gather up the Del Phis and serenade Mary.

The cake was cut and passed, the bouquet and the garter tossed, and it was finally time to help the bride change into her going-away clothes. Kathleen put her gown into its zippered bag to take it home, but Mary took the bag from her and handed the dress to her mother.

"We'll have it cleaned and boxed for you," her mother said. "That way it'll be perfect for when your daughters need it."

The two friends looked at each other and giggled at the thought.

"I felt beautiful in your dress, Kath," Mary said, hugging Kathleen. "Thank you so much for letting me wear it."

"You *looked* beautiful, Mar. I'm so glad you chose it!"

Then they were at the door flinging rice at the fleeing couple. The groomsmen had decorated the car with streamers and shaving cream, and everyone laughed gaily as the newlyweds drove off with a rattle of cans tied to the rear bumper.

Kathleen went back inside to gather her things from the dressing room and then headed to her car. Someone held the door for her, and as she turned to say thank you, she saw it was Patrick. She had not danced with him again after the first bridal party dance. He had spent most of the evening dancing with Kristin.

"Looks like you have your hands full."

"Yes."

"Mark said that was your wedding gown. It looked like you. I'll bet you were a beautiful bride, Kathleen."

"Mary looked beautiful in it, don't you think?" She said quickly, uncomfortable with Patrick's comment.

"Yes, she did." He glanced away and then looked at her. "It was good to see you again. I'm glad you're happy. I really mean that."

"Thank you, Patrick. That means a lot to me."

"Shall I walk you to your car?"
"No, thanks. I'll be fine."
"All right then. Good-bye."
"Yes, good-bye."

She walked through the darkened parking lot to her car without looking back. If Paul had been here with her, they could have danced and had a wonderful time tonight. Instead she had sat for most of the evening when she wasn't chatting with her sorority sisters or Mary's family. Now with her lovely dress and fabulous hairdo she would go to an empty apartment and get into bed alone. She didn't feel like going to bed. She felt like talking to someone about the evening. She couldn't wait until Paul got home tomorrow.

When she woke up, she thought fleetingly about going to church. As long as Paul was not home, she could go without intruding on their Sunday morning time together. She looked at the clock. If she showered quickly, she could just make it to the 9:30 service. The 11:00 service would get her home too late to get the place ready for Paul. She was going to bake him a pie—both because he loved pie and because it would make the apartment smell wonderful for his homecoming.

She looked at her hair in the bathroom mirror. It hadn't survived being slept on, but she knew if she just didn't wear a shower cap, all the curls would spring back from the steam of the shower, and she was eager to try the trick with the combs to see if she could do it herself. Amazingly, when the mirror unfogged after the shower, she was able to recreate the hairdo almost exactly. Even without the bow to give her some height, she managed to tumble the curls on top of her head. She couldn't wait for Paul to see the new her.

Smiling, she slipped into her easiest dress and hose, hastily downed a glass of orange juice, and drove to her old church. She hadn't been there since the Christmas holidays. Now the familiar sounds of the organ and the smell of the hymnal as she opened it washed over her. She wished Paul would be more interested in going with her, but it didn't really matter. She was so happy. She thanked God for her wonderful luck in marrying him and said a prayer that Mary and Mark would find such happiness together.

The sermon was about counting one's blessings, and Kathleen hugged herself, knowing that she was indeed truly blessed. The priest's words seemed like a validation. After the service, she went directly home, not going to the coffee hour. She wasn't sure when Paul would be back, so she wanted to get started with dinner.

Once home, she changed out of her dress and tied an apron around her waist. She made the piecrust, just has Gran had taught her, with milk. "Those folks who use ice water don't know what they're doing," she would say. "That little bit of extra in the milk makes the crust so flaky it just floats away." She peeled the apples, trying to take the skin off in a single spiral, thinking she had learned that, too, from Gran. Another blessing to be counted, her grandparents.

Finally, the pie was in the oven and the mess tidied up. She set the table with their good china and put new candles into silver holders. Everything looked perfect, and the buttery cinnamon smell of the apple pie was starting to drift out of the kitchen. It was only a little after noon, so Kathleen made a fire with a Pres-to-Log and sat down to read the paper. It was so cozy in their apartment. This summer they would probably go house-hunting so they could start thinking about a family, but for now, this was as wonderful a home as she could ever have imagined.

The phone rang, and she jumped to get it, hoping it would be Paul. It was her mother, however.

"How was Mary's wedding?"

"It was lovely, Mother. She looked like a movie star in my dress."

"And did the dress survive?"

"Without a scratch. There wasn't even any red wine served—and no ketchup either."

"Don't be sarcastic, Kathleen. I was just curious. Is Paul back yet?"

"No. I don't expect him until late afternoon."

"It's a pity you couldn't have gone to New York with him. It's such an exciting city."

Hope Chest

"Well, maybe next time. I couldn't very well miss the wedding. But he *is* there on business."

"Business doesn't take 24 hours a day to transact. You could have had some lovely dinners or seen some of the Broadway plays. And you could have shopped while he was busy."

"Just the same, this time I couldn't have gone. I told you, he took all the department heads with him, so I don't think anyone's wife went along."

"You aren't just anyone's wife, Kathleen. If the owner wants to include his wife, he jolly well can."

The same thought had flitted through Kathleen's mind when Paul announced he was going, but she had blocked it as quickly as it had appeared. She felt the same momentary unease at her mother's comment, but quickly changed the subject. She didn't want to argue with her mother when part of her was in agreement with her. "Mary's going to have the dress cleaned and boxed for me, Mother. Isn't that nice?"

"Well she should after the money you saved her. She didn't have any alterations, did she?"

"Not a button."

Kathleen hung up a few minutes later. Despite her mother's approval at her marriage to Paul, it was still difficult to have a conversation with her. She wished she could share more things with her, but she knew she was better off keeping things to herself. No telling what her mother would do if Kathleen ever had a serious problem that she needed to discuss with her. That's what friends like Mary were for.

Finally she heard the key turn in the lock, and she ran to open the door.

"Welcome home, darling. I've missed you so much!" She started to hug him, but he had lifted his suitcases as the door opened.

"At least let me get inside, Kat."

She took his briefcase from him and carried it into the bedroom. Paul plopped the suitcase on the bed and took off his overcoat.

"What a trip. I'm beat." He undid his tie and pulled it off, tossing it on top of the suitcase.

"Why don't you take a shower while I finish dinner?" She moved to put her arms around him.

"I ate on the plane. I think I will take a shower, though." He dropped a kiss on the top of her head.

"Is that all I get after five days of missing you?" She smiled up at him, thinking if he went directly to the shower she could unset the table before he saw it. Her disappointment about dinner was overshadowed by just having him home. At least she hadn't started cooking. They could have the chops tomorrow.

"Sorry, Kat. Come here." He drew her to him and gave her a brief kiss. "God, that flight took forever. And getting to the airport was nearly fatal. It snowed like crazy in New York this weekend. You couldn't believe the streets!"

"How was the buying? Did you find some good stuff?"

"Did we ever. Brenda has such an eye for trends. Wait till you see the line for summer. We are going to kill the competition. She found all these four-piece outfits with skirts and tops and jackets and pants. They're separates, but they all coordinate. Girls can buy one piece or all four."

Brenda? Kathleen hadn't considered that Brenda would be going. He had said department heads. Were buyers considered department heads?

"What did the other people come up with?"

"What?"

"The department heads. Shoes? Jewelry?"

"Oh, well, at the last minute the old man decided it was too much to have all his top people gone at the same time, so . . ."

"So it was just you and Brenda?"

"Yeah. We decided to concentrate on just the junior lines, and that's her specialty. It was a good trip."

She felt the blood leave her face. She felt hot and cold at the same time. She sat down slowly on the edge of the bed next to the suitcase.

"Just the two of you?" she heard herself say in a small voice.

Paul stopped taking off his shoes. "Come on, Kat. You're not jealous. She's an *employee*."

"I know that. It's just that you said there would be a group of you going."

"Look, Kat," he came to the bed and stood over her. "This wasn't a vacation. We worked our butts off. Just getting a taxi in that blizzard was next to impossible. We went a million places and scoured a million more stores to get ideas. It was work. It was *my* work. This is what I do."

"I know, Paul. It's just that I missed you so much at Mary's wedding. It was so lovely. She looked beautiful in my dress, and it brought back such memories."

"If I can make this spring's sales do what I think the junior lines will do, my dad will have to agree that Gordon's can go in the direction I know it must. The other lines are on their way out, Kat. It's juniors all the way. We'll make a killing! And then I'll take you to New York and we'll do the town, just not in the middle of a blizzard and not when I have to run around like crazy."

He put a hand on each of her shoulders and smiled his most winning smile.

"Maybe we'll go for our anniversary. How would that be?" He kissed her this time as if he meant it. "And I missed you too. Wait, I'll show you."

He opened the suitcase and pulled out a flat turquoise box with a white ribbon.

"A present?"

"No, my laundry. Of course a present. Open it."

She undid the bow and opened the Tiffany's box. Inside was a gold bangle bracelet. She slipped it on and held up her wrist to show him. It was cold from being in the car.

"It's beautiful, darling. Thank you." She kissed him and felt relief wash over her as fear had a few moments before. How could she have doubted him? His enthusiasm for Gordon's was one of the things that had attracted her to him from the very first date. He had drive and passion.

"I was thinking of you all the time, you silly thing. Now, I'm going to take a shower. Oh, and I put all my laundry in the top part of the suitcase."

He took off his jacket, shoes, and pants and hung up his suit.

"Is that apple pie I smell?"

"Of course."

He kissed her lightly, and walked into the bathroom. Kathleen went to put away the table setting, and then she would do the unpacking. She turned the bracelet on her wrist as she walked into the kitchen. It was no longer cold.

Chapter 13

June 1964

Even though Kathleen still was officially only part-time, she was at the university nearly every day. Hawk had sectioned off a portion of her office for Kathleen, and she had her own key.

With working so much, she had less time at home to cook and clean. Some days, by the time she stopped at the grocery store and then picked up Paul's shirts at the cleaners, she barely had time to make dinner before he got home. Then there were dishes and endless other little things to do every night before she could get to her precious children's books. Once in a while Paul would tell her to leave everything and he'd help with the dishes, but then he'd start watching television with a glass of wine, and she would slip into the kitchen and clean everything up.

She didn't mind. She loved being his wife. It gave her a thrill when Paul told her he liked something she had cooked. She loved to fold his laundry and put it into the drawers for him. She'd ironed his shirts when they were first married, but he made such fun of the way she did it that she'd taken them to the cleaners ever since. Now she was glad of it, although sometimes getting to the laundry was a hassle.

She still looked at her handsome husband with a sort of awe that he had chosen her. Once he had said to her in a teasing way as they both shared the mirror while getting ready to go to a party, "You know, Kat, I'm handsomer than you are pretty."

He'd said it as a joke, she was almost sure, because she still had rollers in her hair and no makeup on when he said it, but it was undeniable. He was stunningly good looking. She'd spent extra time that night on her makeup.

And even though they were not making love as often as they had the first few months, Kathleen was content to simply curl up beside him at night, reveling in the lean body next to hers. When they did make love, it was still with a minimum of foreplay. Paul would kiss her deeply. Then he would caress her breasts a couple of times and perhaps kiss them and then enter her and reach an almost immediate climax.

One night he said, "How come you never have an orgasm with me, Kat?"

She didn't know what to say. Paul was the only man she had ever made love to. He had sometimes brought her to orgasm after he withdrew from her, but it sometimes took her a long time, and she felt guilty. "I don't need to, Paul. I just love to be close to you. That's enough for me."

"I don't think you're trying," he'd said once. But she didn't know how to try. And besides, it was usually over before it began. She was sure, however, that she could never tell him that. She knew without ever being told that it would not do to criticize a man for his lovemaking skills. She tried instead to say the right things to him while they were making love, about how good it felt, even though she really didn't feel anything other than the weight of him and the quick thrusts inside of her that soon stopped. But it really wasn't important. Lying next to him and watching him as he slept was as fulfilling as anything she could imagine.

She felt another kind of fulfillment in her work. She loved the children, and they seemed to love her. Hawk was letting her do

Hope Chest

more and more of the hands-on interaction, and for the summer she would have her own group to plan, direct, shape, and control. Hawk was teaching a class for teachers on how to incorporate creative dramatics into the curriculum. Kathleen would prepare the students for the teachers to observe. She was excited and nervous at the same time.

"I'll give you the fifth- and sixth-graders, Kathleen. They are still malleable and not self-conscious. You'd best have a few different stories ready until we know just how many there'll be in the group—and how many boys."

Kathleen had several ideas. She ran them by Paul at dinner one night.

"What do you think, Paul? If you were a fifth-grader, would you rather be Robin Hood, Bre'r Rabbit, or Tom Sawyer?"

"If you want my honest opinion, Kat, if I were a fifth-grader, I'd rather be playing baseball. You couldn't have *paid* me to spend my summers doing drama. That was for sissies."

"Paul! If you would just come see what these kids can do, you would change your mind. They love our program, even the boys. Please say you'll try to make it this quarter. I would love to have you see what I'm doing."

"You know I can't take work time for something like that, honey. Maybe if you had an evening deal, but not during the day." He smiled at her as if to punctuate the logic of his argument.

"It's pretty important stuff we're imparting to these kids, too, Paul. They learn to get along with each other, how to cooperate to achieve a common goal, and they learn to feel good about themselves."

"How good can you feel if you're a tree?"

"Be serious, Paul. Even those kids who play lesser roles know that what they do is important to the whole. It's something they don't get from doing math—or baseball. Trees don't sit on the bench; they're part of the action."

"Kathleen, you are such a champion. I'm sure your little program does a world of good."

"Well, when we have kids, I hope they get to be in a program like this."

"Only if they're girls, Kat." He smiled again. "Besides, that's a bit down the road."

"We're practically an old married couple, darling. It'll be a whole year next month. You're making such strides at the store, and my job is only part time. Don't you think we should at least go house hunting so we could start *thinking* about a family?"

Paul sat back down and took a large swallow of his wine. "I was going to wait to tell you, but I think I've convinced Dad to open a second store in Portland. So I'm already up to my ears in real estate people now."

"Oh, my. That's a pretty big step."

"And it's about time. I've been tracking the business there, and I think it's perfect for us. The area is really growing. Not as much as Seattle, of course, but still, lots of new houses and apartments going up in that area. It's a natural. But the last thing I want to do right now is work with more Realtors."

No wonder he was staying later and later every night. A second store! She was so proud of him. They'd had dinner at her in-laws' just last week, and his father had praised the job Paul was doing. He was even going to have Paul represent Gordon's on one of the Chamber of Commerce committees.

"We won't have to move to Portland will we?"

"No, our headquarters will always be in Seattle. We'll just hire a manager for there. But for now, Kat, let's just stay in our nice little apartment. OK?"

"Absolutely. It'll be a wonderful base for you to build your empire from."

"You laugh, but Portland is just the beginning."

She went over to stand behind him and wrap her arms around him. "I most certainly am not laughing, Paul. I'm sure it's the beginning of something wonderful."

As summer began, they became busier and busier. They celebrated their anniversary by going out to dinner and sharing the top layer of their wedding cake, which Mary had carefully frozen for them after the reception. It was a bit freezer-flavored, but Kathleen thought it was wonderful. New York was not in the picture. Paul was frequently away to Portland, usually just making the three-and-a-half hour drive in the morning and coming back late the same day. But occasionally he spent the night and came back the next evening. Their trip would have to wait.

Kathleen was busy as well. Her anxiety about her classes had evaporated as soon as she started actually working with the kids, and she loved every unpredictable minute. The teachers in Hawk's class asked many questions, and Kathleen was delighted with the ease at which she was able to answer them.

She and Mary still met on Saturday mornings when Kathleen didn't have a workshop. Now that they were both married ladies, their conversations were filled with recipes and housecleaning tips and things neither of them would have imagined a few years earlier. They shopped for shoes and summer clothes and wistfully went through the children's department and fingered the soft sleepers and lacy bonnets.

"When do you think you'll start a family, Mar?"

"Not for at least another year. We're saving every dime for a down payment. Have you seen the new housing developments in Bellevue?"

"No. Paul can't even hear the words real estate right now with all this going on with the Portland store."

"Well, don't tell him. Come on, I'll show you the model homes. They're unbelievable."

Mary drove Kathleen across the "new" floating bridge. Kathleen dug into her purse for the change for the toll, and then they headed out to an area east of Lake Washington where Kathleen had never been. Every few blocks there was another sort of gate with flags or banners announcing new homes. They pulled into one and followed the signs to the office.

"They have several models. You can choose whichever one you want, and then pick your own colors and Formica and everything."

They parked in a cul de sac and went into the first house. It was a split-level with a living room and dining room on the left and a large kitchen. Up a few stairs were three bedrooms with a bathroom in the master suite. In the basement, there was a laundry room, a large family room with sliding doors to a patio, and an unfinished area that backed up to the two-car garage. Everything was done in pale gold and cream. The appliances were harvest gold.

"How much is something like this, Mar?"

"This one is $26,500. The one I like, of course, is $32,500, but it has an extra room besides the family room that you could do anything with. Come on, I'll show you."

"Do you think you'd like to live all the way over here? What about Mark's job?"

"He can just drive right down the freeway to Boeing. It's closer from here than from where we are now. I just hope we can get one before the prices go up—or they're all gone! We could get one today if the banks would take my whole salary into account for our loan, but since I'm a girl, they'll only count half of what I make."

"Really? Half?"

"They think I'll get pregnant right away and quit working, so they only figure half into our combined income. That means to qualify, we have to come up with a bigger down payment. Mark thinks his folks might help us a bit though. We only need about a thousand more, but it may as well be a million!"

"I didn't realize there was so much to buying a house. Maybe I won't mind waiting. I'd better just bank all my little salary, though."

"Oh, come on, Kath. The Gordons with all their bucks! They'll be able to give you a down payment from petty cash."

"I don't think so, Mar. Anyway, I'd just as soon do it ourselves. I'd better get started. I've been saving some, but I think I need to be more aggressive."

As summer rolled on, Paul began entertaining his business contacts. He invited some members of his Chamber of Commerce committee on board Fashion's Lady to enjoy a dinner cruise around Lake Washington. Kathleen worked for days deciding what to prepare, having many of her suggestions vetoed by Paul. They finally agreed on beef Wellington after Kathleen made a sample one for him and the Gordons the Sunday before the cruise. She got the puff pastry from the bakery, and one of the long-time bakery ladies there told her exactly how to manage the tricky but delicious dish.

On the boat, Paul presided over the bar with a flourish. He made martinis and gin and tonics and poured champagne. The six guests seemed to be enjoying themselves while Kathleen bustled about in the galley, praying that everything would turn out right. Paul had her hire someone to help serve, but she still felt she should oversee the food. While she checked the time on the Wellington, Paul came up behind her and hissed, "Please get out of the galley, Kat. You are the hostess here. And for God's sake have a drink!"

She turned to look at him, but he was already smiling at the wife of one of the Chamber men. Bewildered, she didn't know how to react. If the food was bad, the whole idea of a dinner cruise would be ruined. Didn't Paul realize that? Dave, the person they hired was a waiter, not a chef. He didn't have any idea about the meal.

Shakily, she left the galley and joined Paul at the bar. He was pouring vermouth over ice and then pouring it all out again. "A little trick I learned. Flavor the ice, not the gin." The assisted-blonde woman he was making the drink for pressed her hand to her ample bosom and said, "How terribly clever! I would never have thought of that in a million years. No wonder that was the best martini I ever had."

Paul smiled at her and handed her the drink without moving his gaze from hers.

Then he poured one for Kathleen. She hated martinis but took it from him with a smile and stirred the olive around in the drink. Then she moved on to speak to the other guests who were enjoying the breeze out on the deck. It had been a perfect day,

Hope Chest

sunny but not too hot. The lake was smooth and the sun still high in the sky, even though it was early evening. Daylight saving time was a blessing, she thought. It stayed light here until well after 10.

"This is some little ship you have here, Kathleen," Ron Jordan, the blonde's husband, said. "I'll bet you and that husband of yours spend a lot of time on her."

"Actually not too much," Kathleen replied. "Paul works every Saturday, so we don't have the opportunity to get out very often."

"You ought to tell that guy to slow down. He's always hatching some scheme or another. I'll tell you, if I had a wife as pretty as you, I'd sail away with her as often as I could."

Kathleen felt herself blushing, but she was secretly pleased by the man's compliment. She wanted Paul's associates to be impressed so that he would be proud of her. She had hoped to accomplish that with the meal; she never counted on just herself. Yet she knew how to be gracious and how to move through a crowd of strangers. She and Mary often laughed about that. "Rush prepared us for everything, Kath. Even making endless conversation with someone you have absolutely nothing in common with!"

Kathleen felt she had nothing in common with anyone on the boat. The women were slightly older than she was, and everyone smoked and drank with a flourish. She ate the olive from her drink and then just held the glass while she chatted. Finally Paul cut the engine and signaled that this would be a good place to have dinner. Kathleen hurried to the galley. She was relieved to see that Dave had set out the plates and the utensils Kathleen had wrapped in blue and white napkins. He had also uncorked two bottles of wine and had the wineglasses arranged on a large tray. The fragrance of the Wellington wafted over the cabin as Kathleen removed it from the oven. The pastry was a perfect gold. She dressed the salad and set it next to the plates. Dave would carve the meat.

"My God," the blonde woman exclaimed. "All this elegance and beef Wellington too. I'll come to this restaurant again."

"Any time, Myra," Paul said. "Your presence is always a welcome addition."

People filled their plates and settled themselves around the cabin. Paul sat next to Myra, and Ron Jordan patted the bench next to him for Kathleen to join him. He was a large man who took up most of the space, but Kathleen felt she couldn't refuse his invitation.

"Other than being in the Chamber, Mr. Jordan . . ."

"Ron, please."

"Ron. What business are you in?"

"Newspapers. I have a string of small neighborhood rags around town. I'm always trying to get your hubby to take out a full-page ad, but he's too frugal. I'm working on him though."

"This is delicious, Kathleen," Myra exclaimed. "What caterer did you use?"

"I did it myself."

Kathleen caught a look of annoyance on Paul's face.

"*You* did? I had no idea real people could make beef Wellington. I thought it had to be made by professionals. My hat's off to you. Paul, you have married a gem."

Kathleen looked for Paul's reaction. He smiled at Myra, but he didn't meet Kathleen's look.

Back in port, after everyone had disembarked and said their good-byes, Kathleen and Dave bundled the leftovers into a large basket and wiped down the galley. Paul returned the liquor to its cabinet and paid Dave, who said he'd be happy to help them any time again and left with the garbage sack to dispose of on his way.

"I'd say things went very well, Paul. Wouldn't you?"

"Next time we have it catered."

She was stunned by his tone. "Didn't you like the food?"

"It was fine, Kath. That's not the point. I can't have my wife being the cook when we entertain. It looks cheap."

"Nonsense, Paul. I love to cook, and I thought you'd be proud of me. Besides, everyone seemed really impressed with everything. What's the difference?"

He looked at her almost sadly. "You really don't see it, do you? It's like retail. Everything is in the presentation."

"But if the product isn't good, the presentation is just a lie. And tonight's presentation was beautiful, I thought. We had help. The food was delicious—and elegant. You're right, I don't see why you aren't pleased."

He came over to her and put his arm around her shoulders. "It's probably not a big deal with fifth-graders, Kat, but this is a different world from the one you circle around in. This is the big time. The men we had on board tonight make things happen in this city."

"Well their wives certainly won't be wearing the tiny little clothes from our store, so how do they count so much?"

He dropped his arm and returned to closing up the boat. Kathleen gathered her baskets and headed up the ladder. Her heart felt heavy in her chest. She hadn't liked any of their guests. They were pleasant enough, but not anyone she cared ever to see again. It had been the same with others they had entertained. Paul was acting as if these people were the determiners of their entire future. He practically fawned over them. She didn't like to see him like that, and she didn't like how she felt right now. She had worked so hard to make tonight perfect, and she had thought—fleetingly—that it had been. Once again she felt as if she had failed him somehow, and she was not used to feeling like a failure.

Besides, she was exhausted. She was working more hours than usual with Professor Hawkins in a summer program they had set up. In fact, this evening she should have been with Hawk for a parent presentation, but had to beg off when Paul told her about the cruise. Hawk was understanding, but Kathleen felt she was letting her mentor down. Nevertheless, she had thrown herself into the preparation for this cruise, and to feel that Paul didn't appreciate it was a stunning blow. What did he want from her? What more could she do? She loved him so much, but she hated this feeling of not measuring up.

Her fifth-graders, as Paul referred to them, loved her, and Hawk continuously told her what a wonderful job she was doing. She would come home feeling as if she could fly, but when she tried to share those feelings with Paul, he would turn on the television or skim through the mail. She made special meals for him, or put fresh flowers in the bathroom, or made his favorite cookies. He only commented when she asked about them.

Their apartment was not large, but it seemed to take her hours to do what needed to be done. Before she began working with

Hawk, Friday was the day she'd done most of the big chores around the house while Paul was at work. She'd strip the bed and do the laundry. Then, while things were in the wash, she'd scrub the bathroom and the kitchen, shaking out both rugs and doing the floors. Then she'd vacuum and dust, remake the bed, and start dinner. Now that she worked, she tried to space out the chores, but then the place never felt really all-over clean. As before, she asked Paul to help with a few things, which he always agreed to, but never quite got around to.

One day after the cruise, Kathleen was down in the laundry room pulling what were mostly Paul's things out of the dryer. She was painstakingly turning all his undershirts right side out and folding them smoothly to put them away. Suddenly she stopped. Why couldn't he put them right before he tossed them into the hamper? It was just one more thing she had to do in a growing list of busy days. Fighting a great wash of guilt, she folded the rest of the undershirts inside out and stacked them neatly. On the next load, she did the same with his socks. She bundled them together as she always had, but she didn't turn them right side out.

Paul was coming home later and later after work. The store closed at 6, except for Mondays when all the downtown shops stayed open until 9, and she had been able to plan dinner for 6:30. Lately, however, he stayed to have drinks with some of his "important contacts" and didn't come home until 7:30 or later.

Once she went to the store to have lunch with him. The cloying scent of Jungle Gardenia announced Brenda before Kathleen saw her. How could the flower smell so different from the perfume, Kathleen wondered again as Brenda greeted her warmly and asked if she was shopping.

"No, just popping in to have lunch with my husband." She restrained herself from smoothing her skirt when she saw how stylishly dressed Brenda was. Kathleen had dressed carefully and spent extra time on her makeup, but Brenda made her feel that her yellow cotton dress had been the wrong choice. Maybe she should shop. "If you want to pull some things," she added hastily, "I'd love to try them on when we get back."

"Perfect. I'll do that."

Kathleen took the elevator to Paul's office, smoothing her hair and checking her makeup in the mirror before the elevator girl let her off on Paul's floor.

He looked up in surprise as she appeared in his office. "Anyone interested in lunch?" she said.

"Hey, what a good idea."

"I probably should have called you," she began.

"No, this is great. I'm starving." He led her back to the elevator she had just left.

They went to Pancho's up the street for Paul's favorite French dip sandwiches and salad topped with cheese crackers.

"What brings you downtown, Kat?"

"I just wanted to have a meal with you, honey. It seems we are going in too many separate directions lately."

"I know. But it won't last forever. Once I get the Portland store open, I won't have to spend so much time plotting. You can't imagine what all goes into this venture. I bet I've spent a million hours with the architects alone."

The waiter took their order. A tall redhead at the next table got up to go to the ladies' room. As she passed their table, she turned and said to her husband, "If the waiter comes, order me a Scotch and water, hon."

Paul followed the woman with his eyes. "That shows me a lot of class."

"What? That she drinks? For heaven's sake, Paul, it's only noon."

"It's lunch. Never mind. Are you shopping today?"

"I might." Was there reproach in his voice? Did he dislike her yellow dress too? "I asked Brenda to pull some things for me to try on when you and I got back."

"That's terrific. Brenda has such a great eye. Listen to her. She'll know what to do."

"You never complained about how I looked before we got married, Paul."

"And I'm not complaining now, sweetheart. But we have some top-fashion stuff in right now, styles that weren't even invented a couple of years ago."

"Hawk is talking about opening a children's theater," Kathleen said to change the subject.

"Is that so?" Paul was clearly not impressed.

"It would mean we'd have a place to put on plays for children regularly. Plus there'd be classrooms and offices for our program and other kinds of theater classes."

"Where will it be?"

"I'm not sure. Hawk's looking for space. She may even build a whole new place."

"Where'll she get the money? Just doing the Portland store in an existing space is costing me a fortune. Who'd give her money for a theater for kids? That's crazy."

"It's not crazy, Paul. Lots of parents put their kids into our program now, and the only reason we can't take more is lack of space."

"Yeah, but the U underwrites it, don't they? You use the buildings on campus for free. A new building? She's dreaming."

"Well, as Hawk always says, nothing happens until the dream. It's just like you and Portland. Isn't that a dream?"

"Yes, but it's a dream based on financial feasibility. I know that Portland will give us a return on our investment. What statistics does she have to show that she'll recover a dime with drama classes for kids?"

"I don't know, but she's no fool. If Hawk thinks it can be done, it can."

"Unless she's inherited a wad of money from her folks, that old maid can't begin to put her hands on enough dough to even start such a project. Don't get your hopes up, sweetie. You'll still have your little job right there at the U for a long time."

"Not too long, I hope. We need to think about kids ourselves sometime, Paul."

He looked up sharply. "Not in the middle of this Portland move, Kath."

"I didn't mean now, Paul," she said quickly. "I just meant that I wouldn't be working with Hawk in her new project anyway because we'd probably have children by then." She put her hand over his. "Don't worry, I'm still taking my pills."

He smiled at her then and finished his lunch. "Got to get back." He paid the bill and they walked quickly back to Gordon's.

Brenda greeted Kathleen when they walked into the store. "I've got a room waiting for you. Just follow me."

Kathleen went into a large corner dressing room. Several dresses hung on the brass hooks. "Start with the black and white one," Brenda suggested. "I think it will look fabulous with your hair. I'll be back in a sec."

Kathleen removed her yellow dress and stepped into the black and white. It was sleeveless with a blouson top over a slightly flared skirt. The fabric was a thin cotton that floated as she turned. A large organdy collar framed the scooped neckline and ended in a flat bow in the front. It was wonderful, except the waistline hit her at her ribcage. It wasn't obvious because the blouson part fell below her natural waistline and covered the too-high waist, but it was slightly uncomfortable.

Brenda tapped lightly on the door and then stepped in. "Oh my, that's even better than I thought it would be! Turn around."

Kathleen spun slowly.

"OK. That one's for sure. Try the others." She left, leaving the whole dressing room inundated with her perfume.

Kathleen tried on a few more dresses, all of which fit her wrong. They were all too high in the waist or too tight in the shoulders. She could make do with the black and white dress, however, and knew it would please Paul if she wore it to the next thing they had to go to with his business associates. Brenda tried to assure her that the other outfits were perfect, but Kathleen was not convinced. She carried her Gordon's bag home and hung the dress on the closet door with the tags visible so Paul would see it.

She was making dinner when he came home.

"Now that's more like it," she heard him say from the bedroom. "You approve?"

He came into the kitchen and kissed her on the top of her head. "You'll do me proud in that dress, wife. And you can wear it this Saturday when we go to dinner with my folks and the architects on the Portland project."

When Saturday came, she dressed carefully and had to agree that the dress looked good on her. The slight discomfort around her rib cage would be a small price to pay for Paul's good opinion. She twirled for him, and he pulled her into a hug.

They went to Canlis, and as the maitre d' greeted the Gordons by name, Kathleen recalled how impressed she had been the first time she went there with Paul and the same thing had happened. The two architects spoke earnestly of their project, and Kathleen was delighted to be such a part of Paul's life. One of them made a joke, and Kathleen laughed heartily. At that moment, the zipper of her dress split apart at the rib cage. She grabbed her back and froze.

"Could you come to the powder room with me please?" she whispered to her mother-in-law. She got up stiffly and kept her front to the table as the men rose to acknowledge the ladies' departure.

"What can I do?" Kathleen asked, horrified as she turned to show her mother-in-law what happened.

"Just hold on, dear. This must be one of those new plastic zippers that gives under stress. Let me see."

Mrs. Gordon held the dress together and unzipped it from the top. Then she pulled it back up. It closed normally.

"Oh, thank God!" Kathleen was shaking now. "I didn't know what I would do!"

Mrs. Gordon laughed. "What a moment! I was looking at you when it happened, and I thought you must be about to choke."

"I nearly died!"

The two women returned to the table. Kathleen breathed shallowly for the remainder of the evening and ate very little, although the food was delicious. When they got home, she told Paul what had happened with the dress.

"That's ridiculous, Kat. Did it rip?"

"No. It's apparently a new kind of zipper that's made to give under pressure. When I laughed, it gave." She unzipped the dress and took it off so she could examine the zipper. She zipped it up and then tugged at both sides near the waist. The teeth of the zipper parted easily.

"Are you gaining weight?"

"Paul! No, I'm not gaining weight. You saw what it just did with the least little pressure. I just can't wear those junior sizes you insist everyone can wear. I'm sorry. I tried." She burst into tears.

"Hey," he said, drawing her to him. "There's no need to cry. You looked terrific tonight."

"Oh, Paul, I try so hard to please you, but you just don't seem to even notice me."

"Now that's nonsense. Of course I notice you."

"I used to feel that you were proud of me, and I don't any more."

"If I weren't proud of you, would I bring you along on these important dinners? Think about it, Kat. Would I?"

"You couldn't very well not bring me if your dad was bringing your mom."

"This is silly, Kat. I'm tired and so are you. Let's go to bed. You'll feel better in the morning." He wiped her eyes with a Kleenex and kissed her briefly. Then he took off his clothes and went into the bathroom. She sat down on the bed and unhooked her nylons. She tossed them onto the dresser and put on her nightgown. When Paul finally came out of the bathroom, she went in. She splashed cold water on her face and brushed her teeth. Her eyes were red and her mascara had run. Toweling her skin dry, she turned off the light and got into bed. Paul was already asleep.

Chapter 14

October 1964

"Sit down."

"OK, Mar, I'm sitting."

"You're going to be an auntie!"

"What! You're *pregnant*? When are you due?"

"End of June." The two friends squealed over the phone. "Do you think you could bear to be a godmother?"

"Oh, Mar, I'd be honored. What does Mark think?"

"He's thrilled. Thank God we bought our house when we did. We'd never get a loan now that I won't be working."

"I just can't believe it. We have to do the nursery. What colors?"

"I'm not sure. Probably yellow or green. Something neutral to start with till we see whether it's a boy or a girl."

"You could do primary colors. I always thought it would be fun to do a baby's room in reds and yellows and blues. Maybe balloons or clowns."

"So if you have your baby's room all planned, when are you two going to get started with someone to fill it?"

Kathleen was silent for just a moment, but her friend knew her too well to miss it.

"What's going on, Kath?"

"I don't think anything serious, Mar. It's just that Paul's so caught up in the store that I never see him. The only time we go out is when he has to entertain business associates or architects or someone. He's so tired and cross all the time, and we're hardly ever alone."

"Have you talked to him about this?"

"Well, sure, a little. But I don't want to become a nag. He has enough troubles at work. This Portland project is huge. I'll be so glad when it's finished. It's taken over our lives! Mine anyway. But enough boo hoo from me. Let's have lunch on Saturday and celebrate. Are you fat yet?"

"Not yet, but that's only because I can't keep anything down, I'm sure. Maybe I could manage something by Saturday, though. At least tea and soda crackers. See you then, Auntie Kathleen."

Kathleen hung up the phone and looked around her apartment. It seemed to be growing smaller. She envied Mary her house, although she had been careful not to say too much to Paul about it. Surely they could afford a house by now. The store was doing so well, and she had banked practically all of her salary in what she thought of as her "house account."

Paul hadn't called to say he would be late, so she planned dinner for the usual time. Please be in a good mood, she thought. There was no reason that she couldn't go house-hunting, just to see what was out there. She took special care with dinner and set the table with some wedding place mats that she hadn't used before.

She went over conversations in her head to try to find a good way to bring up the subject. By the time she heard Paul at the door, she was a nervous wreck. She took a deep breath and went to greet him.

"Hi, honey. Dinner's ready."

"Good," he said, returning her kiss absently. "I'm starving. I didn't have time for lunch today. God, what a mess!"

Kathleen looked anxiously around, but the apartment was spotless. Then she realized he must be talking about the store. He'd gone straight to the kitchen to pour himself a drink.

"What now? Is it still Portland?"

"What else? Now it's the elevators."

"What about them?"

"You wouldn't understand. When's dinner?" He swallowed half his Scotch and refilled the glass.

"Right now. Go wash up, and we'll eat."

Kathleen pulled out the plates she had warming in the oven and dished up dinner as Paul came out of the bathroom and flopped into his chair. She set the warm plate in front of him.

"Careful, the plate's..."

"Ow!"

"... hot."

"Did you cook dinner on these plates? Damn!" He stuck his burned finger into his drink.

"Sorry. I tried to warn you." She sat across from him and took a bite of the potatoes. The gravy was as good as Gran's, but Paul didn't seem to notice his food.

"Is it a big problem with the elevators?"

"Huge. I have to go down there tomorrow. I'll probably be gone a couple of days."

"Would you mind if I went and looked at houses while you're gone?" It wasn't how she had planned it.

"Are you going to be on me about that again, Kat? It's the last thing I have the energy to think about right now."

"I know that, honey, but I have time. You wouldn't even have to go. I just want to see what's out there. It doesn't cost anything to look."

"Kat," he said too patiently, putting down his fork, "if you find your dream house, you'll want to buy it. If we buy it, we'll have to move. If we move, you'll start thinking about starting a family. It's not a good time."

"Why not, Paul? I wasn't even thinking about a baby yet, but so what if we did? A baby wouldn't affect your job at all. I'm the one who'd be home with it. I don't understand." She willed herself not to cry. This was going badly, she knew, but she couldn't stop. "Mary's expecting."

"Oh, so that's it."

"No, that's not it! It's just that I rarely see you alone anymore. If we do have a night together without architects or someone, you're exhausted. We don't even make love anymore. I don't understand what's happening, Paul." She bit her lip hard.

"What's happening is that I'm working my butt off to make a go of my business. What's happening is that I'm doing my best to support us. What's happening is I'm dead tired, and I don't appreciate coming home to this."

She had never seen him like this before. She wished she had never said anything. How could it have gone so wrong?

"I'm sorry, Paul. I know you're working hard. I don't mean to nag, it's just—"

"Then don't. I don't need it." He resumed eating his dinner. They didn't speak again. When he had finished, she cleared the table and began loading the dishwasher. He poured himself another drink.

When the kitchen was clean, Kathleen joined Paul in the living room, sitting next to him on the sofa. They watched TV for a while in silence.

"Do you want me to help you pack?" she said finally.

"No, I'll do it."

"There's clean laundry."

"Good."

"I think I'll go to bed."

"Fine."

"You coming?"

"Soon. I'm just going to watch TV for a bit."

"OK." She leaned over to give him a kiss. "I'm sorry I sounded like a shrew, honey. I know how hard you've been working, and I don't want to add to your troubles. I just miss you. That's all."

He kissed her on the cheek. "This'll be over soon, Kat. Then we'll go look at houses."

She smiled and felt her heart lift a little. She got ready for bed and read for a few pages until she realized she hadn't digested a single word. Then she put the book down and pulled the covers over her head. She left the light on so the room wouldn't be dark when Paul came to bed.

He finally turned off the television and plopped his suitcase onto his side of the bed. Kathleen lay there while he banged drawers and rattled hangers. "You sure you don't want me to help?" she ventured.

"Go to sleep."

He finally undressed and climbed in beside her. He pounded his pillow into shape and then settled down with his back to her. She rolled over and tried to sleep.

He'd seemed in a much better mood at breakfast, so the anxiety that had kept her awake most of the night dissipated. He'd kissed her goodbye and said he'd miss her.

She showered and stood in front of her closet. Classes wouldn't start at the U for a couple of weeks, so she was not working. The dishes were done and the apartment tidy. With Paul gone for how long she didn't even know, there were no meals to plan. Maybe she'd go downtown and get a new outfit. She could use something cute to wear around the house. She put on a skirt and blouse and carefully applied her makeup. It would not do to be seen at Gordon's looking less than her best. Maybe she'd take Brenda up on her offer to put some outfits together if she called ahead. She dialed the store number and asked for her.

"I'm sorry, Miss Ward is not in today. May someone else help you?"

"No. I didn't realize it was her day off."

"Well, actually she's on vacation for a few days. I expect her back next Monday. Is there a message?"

"No, thank you." Kathleen hung up the phone. Her face was hot and her heart was racing. Why was she feeling like this? Gordon's employees all took vacations. Why shouldn't Brenda?

Grabbing her car keys, Kathleen practically ran to her car. She drove downtown in a fog and parked the car at the first vacant meter she found, forgetting to put any money in. She walked into Gordon's and took a calming breath, but the cloying scent of the perfume counter reminded her of Brenda's Jungle Gardenia.

She strolled around, greeting employees and pretending to shop. Then she took the elevator up to the office area. The receptionist smiled when she saw her.

"Mrs. Gordon. Good morning. Your husband's not in."

"I know. I was just in the store and thought I'd say hello to my father-in-law. Is he in?"

"Yes. I'll tell him you're here."

A few seconds later, the senior Gordon came into the reception area with his arms outstretched. "Kathleen, what a lovely surprise. What brings you here?"

"I was just downtown shopping and thought I'd pop in to say hi and see if this Portland business is wearing you down too."

"Come on back to my office. No, Portland is going smoothly thanks to your husband."

"I know he's been working so hard on it. I just hope the elevator problem isn't too difficult."

"Elevator problem? I didn't know there was a problem with them."

"Oh, I thought he had to go down there to see about the elevators. Perhaps I misunderstood"

"You must have, my dear. I just met with the elevator people and signed off on everything. Paul isn't even involved with that part of the project." Her father-in-law looked at her kindly. She returned his smile, but her face felt frozen.

"Well, it's hard to keep everything straight. It seems that this business has been going on forever."

"It does, doesn't it? But wait until you see it. I'm surprised Paul hasn't taken you down there. It's going to be magnificent."

"When is the opening scheduled?"

"We hope just in time for the Christmas rush—the day after Thanksgiving. We'll do a big buildup in the newspaper and have a grand opening sale here and in Portland."

"So everything will be done by then?"

"Absolutely. We even built in some slack time in the event of unforeseen problems. So far, we haven't had anything too serious." He tapped his knuckles on his head and laughed.

"Well, I'm glad. I just stopped in to say Hi, so I'd better let you get back to work."

"Delighted that you did, my dear. Delighted. Any time."

There was a parking ticket on her windshield when she made her way back to the car. Numbly she pulled it from under the windshield wiper and stuffed it into her purse. Her first reaction of how she would explain it to Paul faded into insignificance as she sat behind the steering wheel. Why would he lie to her about an elevator problem? Why would he lie to her at all? Why wasn't Brenda at work?

She started the car and drove aimlessly around. The last place she wanted to go was home. Professor Hawkins was at a conference, so the office would be as empty as her apartment. Mary was at work. Her mother wasn't an option. She had never felt so confused or alone. Maybe she had misunderstood. She was so busy rehearsing how to ask Paul if she could go house-hunting that she might have missed something.

Suddenly she turned onto the freeway and headed for the new bridge to Bellevue. She fished into her purse for change for the toll and drove until she came to the developments she had visited with Mary. The office of the first area was open, and the man at the desk told her to wander through the models. He handed her a brochure of all the floor plans.

She went through "The Chinook" first, a compact rambler with one bathroom that opened from the hall and from the master bedroom. It had two other small bedrooms and a large eating area in the kitchen that the floorplan called the family room. The appliances gleamed invitingly with a blue-enameled frying pan on the stove and a matching blue cookie jar on the counter.

The rest of the models were larger. Two had split levels like Mary's, and one had a large upstairs with four cozy bedrooms and a private bath in the master bedroom. Kathleen walked through each of the rooms with a heavy heart. She could imagine them filled with children's toys and books. The kitchen had a small pantry with many shelves and a lazy Susan in the corner cupboard. From the sink she could look out over a large patio into a tidy yard with three young fruit trees. Tears filled her eyes. Would she ever have a house like this? What was happening to her and Paul? Leaving the brochure on the counter, Kathleen got into her car and drove home.

The next two days dragged by; she was in a fog. The only thing she could get down was tea. She went for walks. She cleaned everything in the apartment. She weeded the tiny yard. She went to church, but she couldn't pray. Nothing seemed real.

When Paul came back, she greeted him at the door as usual and took his suitcase from him. "Did you get the elevator problem solved?" She tried to smile but failed.

"What a mess," he said, hanging up his coat and not looking at her. "Those guys tried to pull a fast one, but we got it straightened out. What'd you do?"

"Just the usual. Shopped a bit, made you a pie."

"I'm going to take a shower, then I'll have a piece."

When Kathleen heard the water going, she put the suitcase on the bed and opened it. Mingled with the sharp scent of Paul's aftershave was the unmistakable sweetness of Jungle Gardenia.

Chapter 15

November 1964

"Sorry I'm late, Kath. I had to wait in the doctor's office forever." Her friend maneuvered herself into the booth next to her and gave Kathleen a hug. "In fact, I'm not sure I should have Chinese food because of the salt, but I'm just craving it. Thanks for indulging me."

"You don't look too fat yet, so what's the harm?" Kathleen looked with envy at Mary's barely swelling stomach under her red maternity top.

"So, enough about me," Mary said, taking her friend's hands in hers. "Tell me, Kath, how's it going?"

"Oh, Mar, I don't know. We're going to this 'highly recommended' counselor once a week, but nothing has changed. Paul still seems distant, and I don't know if I can ever trust him again."

"Has he ever come clean about Miss Juniors' Buyer?"

"No. He claims she just happened to be in Portland that week visiting friends and stopped by the project to see how it was coming along. They just had lunch. Period. Ha!"

"But he's willing to go to counseling. That's something."

"It was his idea, actually."

"His idea?"

"He even found the man we're seeing. Paul says I'm the one with a problem because I don't trust him and we need to get this thing solved."

"Well if Mark came home reeking of Jungle Gardenia, I would have a problem too, I'll tell you. Does your mother know anything about this?"

"Are you kidding? Not a thing. That's all I'd need right now."

The smiling waiter came and took their order and left.

"Well, what does this counselor say?"

"That's what's so depressing, Mar. He opened the whole first session by saying that he couldn't promise to solve our problem, but he would make sure that if this marriage didn't work out, he would prevent us from making the same mistake twice. What kind of help is that?" Kathleen felt the tears start again.

"What's that mean?"

"Apparently, or so he says, people tend to make the same wrong choices over and over again. Women who finally divorce alcoholics, for example, end up with other alcoholics. So he's going to make sure I don't marry someone like Paul again, I guess. The thing is, Mar, I don't want to marry anyone else. I'm already married. I don't want to be divorced." The word made her shudder, and the tears wouldn't stop this time, sliding down her cheek.

"What does Paul say during all this?"

"That's part of the problem. He doesn't say anything. There are these huge silences during the sessions where I hope he will say something, anything. Then I end up babbling about how I don't understand why things aren't working, and I sound like a fool."

"Things will work out, Kath. Where's all that faith you used to have so much of in your Fishers years?"

The waiter arrived, set down bowls of won ton soup, and discreetly vanished.

"I've wondered that myself, Mar. It was so easy in those days—so black and white." She retrieved a handkerchief from her purse and blew her nose. "I was even thinking of the terrible conversations I had with poor Patrick about his 'statue worship.'" She managed a smile.

"Poor Patrick."

"He put up with a lot, didn't he? And he was so good. He deserved so much more. I think I broke his heart. And how could I have done that, Mar, when I knew only too well how horrible that feels? And I was so pompous! How could anyone have stood me?"

Mary gave Kathleen another hug. "At least you didn't become a Communist or something more radical like one of Mark's friends. I don't feel very old, but looking back, we seemed very young."

"Spoken like a grizzled twenty-four year old."

"Nearly a quarter of a century!"

Kathleen smiled finally and tasted her soup. She realized she was ravenous. "The Hong Kong was such a good idea, Mar. This soup tastes like ambrosia. I don't think I've been eating much lately."

"I have, but unfortunately I've thrown most of it up. Sorry. Not a good dinner-table topic. But I've got a long way to go until June."

"At least you know what's going to happen in your future. I think that's the hardest thing. I have no idea what to expect. I can't be spontaneous around Paul. If I hug him or give him a kiss or even make a special dinner, I wonder if he thinks I'm trying to make it up to him somehow for not trusting him. I can't be me at all."

"First off, Missy, you have nothing to make up for, so stop thinking like that. What have you done but be the perfect wife he was looking for when he married you? You are attractive, intelligent, and the best hostess he could ever have found to further his ambitions. How many dinners with boring people have you gone to? How many boat rides and cocktail parties? Stop blaming yourself this instant."

Kathleen just smiled. "I forgot you never liked him. Thanks for sticking up for me, but as they say, it takes two."

"Yeah, especially when the other one doesn't play fair. Someone has to be the victim. I just don't want it to be you. You're too special. I can't believe Paul doesn't see that. Maybe this is just one of those bumps we all experience while trying to make a go of things."

"Nice try, Mar. But this is bigger than a bump. I feel as if I've fallen off a cliff, and the worst part is, I don't think I've hit bottom yet."

"Well counseling is a good thing. I'm sure you'll work this out. Paul's not a fool. He wouldn't want to lose you, Kath. You're the best thing that ever happened to him."

"I hope he thinks so, but I'm not sure he does." She took another bite of her soup, but it had lost its savor, and she placed the chipped ceramic spoon on her plate.

෴

Christmas shopping this year lacked all the joy it used to have for her. She bought Paul an expensive cashmere sweater, the first one she came across. She knew he would like it because it was cashmere, so the problem of what to get him was solved. She wanted her gift to be special, but she felt that nothing would be.

The counseling sessions had become unbearable. She had been so hopeful that they would straighten things out so she and Paul could get back to normal, but now she realized that she had no idea what normal was. Had she just been dreaming that this marriage was so wonderful? Looking back, it seemed she'd had stars in her eyes from the very beginning. She wondered why Paul had ever asked her to marry him.

Mary had scolded her on that one, telling her how lucky Paul was to have snagged her, but Paul didn't seem to share Mary's opinion. Kathleen and Paul seemed to be going through a pantomime of what a marriage was like—as if it were an improvisation by two of her students. "Act as if you two are a perfect married couple."

She made dinner, and he praised it. They entertained, and everyone complimented her on the event. His parents loved her, and her parents loved Paul, especially her mother, who never stopped bragging to her friends about her daughter's excellent marriage, especially to poor Mrs. Lavik. Trudy was a stewardess and still not married, a fact that gave Kathleen's mother a great deal of satisfaction.

Kathleen realized that in all the endless high school conversations where she and her girlfriends planned their weddings over and over, no one ever discussed the marriages. Just the weddings. Colors, flowers, bridesmaid dresses (long or short?), and honeymoon destinations. Never did anyone think to say, What happens if your husband fools around with another woman? They giggled about putting beans in a jar every time you made love the first year.

("They say even if you take them out again when you do it after that, you never get to the bottom of the jar."

"No!"

"It's true. I heard that, too, from my sister."

Giggle, giggle.)

No one wondered why. And no one ever said anything about the husband not wanting to do it. Who could have imagined that? Who could have imagined a marriage counselor?

She only hoped she could get through the holidays without thinking about it too much. Maybe things weren't going as badly as she thought, though. Maybe with all the parties and music. Maybe.

She took extra care in decorating the apartment. They went together to pick out the tree, but after Paul put the lights up, he turned off the Andy Williams Christmas album she had on the record player and turned on the television. She hung the ornaments by herself.

They went to several parties and had both sets of parents over for Christmas dinner. During the meal Kathleen watched how they interacted with each other. The Gordons were cordial and pleasant to one another. Mr. Gordon held the chair out for his wife, and she patted his hand as she seated herself. Her own father told the story of their first Christmas during the war and how much he missed his wife in those years. It was all Kathleen could do to keep from crying. Paul was the perfect host, but he added no anecdotes of his own to the conversation.

On New Year's Eve, they went to a party at the Washington Athletic Club with a group of Paul's business associates. She knew that these people were important to him and that most of the wives would be much older than she was. So she went shopping with Mary to find the perfect dress.

"I want to look sophisticated, Mar. I want Paul to be proud of me for a change."

"Then none of this junior stuff, my friend," Mary had said. "We're hitting the big time. And you're not looking at prices."

They found a stunning black silk dress at I. Magnin, with the new slightly shorter hemline right at the knee and a low-cut neck edged with sparkly jet beads. Mary then insisted that they go to Nordstrom and get some "killer shoes" to show off Kathleen's legs. They decided on a very high-heeled sling pump with a peau de soie toe.

"And the sheerest black nylons we can find. Do you have a hair appointment yet?"

"No. It's probably too late now. I thought I'd just do it myself."

"Nonsense. This is war." They went to the bank of pay phones in the lounge area, and Mary called her hairdresser. She hung up and announced that Kathleen had an appointment for a shampoo and set at 5 o'clock on New Year's Eve.

"You must have some influence!"

"I recommend so many people to him, he owes me. Since you don't need a cut, he can work you in. Now, isn't it time for something sweet?"

New Year's Eve, as she looked in the mirror, she was thrilled with what Mary's hairdresser did with her hair. She applied more makeup than usual and then stepped carefully into her new dress. The person looking back at her from the mirror could have been a stranger. She looked sophisticated. She couldn't wait to see Paul's reaction.

"Well, well, well," he said when she twirled into the living room.

"What do you think?"

"Very nice. I don't remember that dress."
"It's new."
"I meant I don't remember it from the store."
"Oh, it's not from Gordon's. I found it at I. Magnin."
"That old-lady store? I can't believe they would carry something like that."
"Does that mean you like it?" The sharp edge of her exhilaration was dulling. She felt invisible. A mannequin. A coat hanger.
"It's very chic. You ready? I don't want us to be late."

Several of Paul's associates were at the party, and many of the husbands asked her to dance. Paul willingly squired their wives, who tittered when he bowed to them. The women raved over Kathleen's dress. Everyone asked if she'd bought it at Gordon's, and with each No, Kathleen realized her faux pas.

Finally it was midnight. The band stopped playing while everyone counted down to "Happy New Year!" and then broke into "Auld Lang Syne." Paul took Kathleen in his arms and gave her a long, sensuous kiss. Her heart bumped wildly as she kissed him back. People were laughing and hugging and blowing horns. She felt giddy as a rush of happiness surged through her. Then she realized two things: This was the first real kiss Paul had given her in a very long time, and he was kissing her in front of people who were important to him. The giddiness subsided. Happy New Year indeed.

Chapter 16

January 1966

"Forgive my saying so, Kathleen, but is everything all right with you?" Professor Hawkins looked concerned.

"Everything's fine," Kathleen responded. "Why do you ask?"

"Well, you seem to be just going through the motions here. It's not quite the you I've come to know. I don't mean to pry, my dear, but you can talk to me if you need to."

"I know that. Thank you. It's just . . . it's, well . . ." The tears washed out whatever excuse she was trying to make.

Hawk put her arms around Kathleen and patted her on the back. "Let's sit down over here, and you tell me what's going on."

Kathleen allowed herself to be guided to the old leather chair in the corner of the office. Professor Hawkins removed a pile of books and papers from the companion chair and sat down. She handed Kathleen a tissue.

"It's Paul," Kathleen managed to say after she blew her nose. "We've been going to a marriage counselor since before Christmas, but now he doesn't even want to do that anymore. I don't know what to think or do. It's so awful. I keep believing there's something that will fix everything, but now I'm not so sure."

"Does he say he wants to leave?"

Kathleen looked up sharply. "Oh, my God! No, he hasn't said that. I haven't even let myself think that. He just doesn't say anything. I've tried and tried to talk to him—and he does listen, but I don't seem to be getting anywhere."

"Do you love him still, my dear?"

"Terribly. I can't even imagine my life without him. The thing is, I don't think he wants to be married to me. I think he's . . . I mean, there's this buyer at the store."

"Ah, the other woman. Are you sure?"

"He denies it, but he seems to have to take so many little trips out of town lately. I'm probably just a fool to hang on, but, Professor Hawkins, to leave him—how could I do that? A divorce? My parents would just die. I don't even know anyone who's been divorced."

"Oh, but you do."

"No, I don't." Kathleen looked at her mentor again. "You mean you?"

"I was married briefly a very long time ago. It lasted almost three years. And look at me now. Do I seem strange to you?"

"I had no idea. I . . ." She didn't know what to say. Hawk, married? It had never occurred to Kathleen.

"I wasn't always old, you know. I, too, was young and foolish once upon a time. And he was young and handsome. My Prince Charming. Not as handsome as your Paul, mind you, but to me he was the sun and the moon."

"What happened?"

"We were living in Los Angeles. I guess we both thought it was the place to be. He wanted to break into film—directing, not acting. I was teaching at a local high school, and whatever he once found attractive in me was soon eclipsed by the many beauties he was surrounded by every day at the studios."

"How awful." Kathleen was no longer crying as she absorbed what her teacher was telling her.

"It got much worse. I was supposed to be at a competition for a weekend with my students, but we got eliminated in the first round, so I came home early and found him in our bed with his latest bimbo."

"Oh, my God. What did you do?"

"It was pretty terrible. I just turned and ran to my car as fast as I could. I had a few things in my suitcase anyway, so I checked into some little motel and stared at the wall for a day. Then I went back to the house on Monday, when I knew he'd be at work, changed the locks, called a lawyer, and here I am a hundred years later, alive, happy, and bearing no telltale scars."

"You just left? Didn't you ever talk to him?"

"Oh, we talked, but no words could erase the picture I had of the two of them. And I never looked back. I could have wallowed in my ill fortune, of course, but chose not to. I moved back to Seattle, got my master's degree and this wonderful job, and that's that."

"You make it sound easy."

"On the contrary. It was the hardest thing I ever did. He broke my heart, but he also unleashed a strength in me I had no idea I had. I thought he would take care of me as soon as he made it big, and I would quit teaching and raise several kids, and we'd all live happily ever after. And you know what?"

"What?"

"He never made it big, so he never would have taken care of me. And I'm living happily ever after now, which I wouldn't have been doing if I'd hung around with him. Don't get me wrong, it wasn't easy. I cried buckets for a very long time, but I came to realize I wasn't so much crying because I lost him. I lost my dream, and that was the big thing."

"What dream?"

"Why, to be a Mrs. Somebody. Isn't that every girl's dream?"

"I guess it is," Kathleen said, shaking her head. "Did you ever think of marrying again?"

"No. I've been too busy." Professor Hawkins laughed, but then grew serious again. "If you are unhappy, Kathleen, and he's not being a loving support for you, then maybe you need to look carefully at what's in front of you."

"That's just it! I don't see anything in front of me without Paul." Kathleen felt the tears prickling again.

"Nonsense. You have a magical life ahead of you. You are the most talented, spirited thing to come along in an age. If that Paul can't appreciate what he's got, don't waste yourself on him."

"You sound like my friend Mary."

"It sounds like you have a good friend. Listen, Kathleen, I'm not suggesting that you rush out and divorce your husband. What I am saying is for you to look beyond what is happening right now. If Paul really loves you and wants this marriage to work, then he will say so and do everything in his power to make you believe him. If he doesn't, well—be careful not to let things get twisted around so that you believe you're the bad guy."

"Bad guy? Me? How could that happen? I'm not the one with a . . . with a . . ."

"Exactly. Neither was I, but by the time my husband got through rewriting our particular script, I came across as a malevolent harpy who never appreciated him or anything he ever did for me. He told everyone I had thrown him out of his *own house* and even changed the locks. His friends couldn't believe how such a great guy could have been put upon by such a dreadful wife. They bought him drinks and opened their apartments for him to have a place to stay. I was shunned by all and sundry. That's when I left for Seattle."

"How awful it must have been for you. But I'm sure Paul would never do anything like that to me."

"I hope not, dear. But as I said, if he wants to salvage this marriage, you'll be able to tell. Haven't I trained you from your very first assignment to observe the things around you?"

"Are you kidding? I still can't look at lawn sprinklers without assigning them personalities."

"That's the ticket. So watch and listen. Don't try to argue it into being. You'll know. The hardest thing to see sometimes is what is right in front of us, especially if we don't want to see it."

Kathleen wanted the words to go away, but deep down she knew Hawk was right. As she drove home after hugging her beloved professor good-bye, she tried to replay the last few months. Had Paul done anything to try to convince her he wanted to stay in the marriage? His Christmas presents had been as generic as hers to him: a flannel nightgown, because she was always cold, and a pair of soft leather gloves lined with cashmere. The only sign of affection she'd had since they began the sessions with the counselor was the New Year's Eve kiss. And that didn't count.

No, she realized sadly, he had done nothing except supply the name of the counselor. And how did Paul even know of such a person? She'd never thought of it before, assuming it was another of Paul's downtown contacts. Had he asked around? Did everyone know they were having trouble? She could never go into Gordon's again. Not that she had since Paul's return from Portland. Kathleen couldn't bear to see Brenda.

Suddenly all the heartbreak of the past weeks metamorphosed into a burning anger. She could imagine a smug look of triumph on Brenda's oh-so-carefully made-up face.

"How could you have done this to me, Paul?" Kathleen shouted to the air. She had been the perfect housewife, doing all the things that were supposed to make for a perfect home. Ha! Professor Hawkins was right. All the information she needed had been staring her in the face from the beginning, while she tied herself into knots to avoid the truth. She parked the car and headed for the apartment.

It was a few minutes to five. She discovered to her chagrin that she had automatically begun to worry about getting dinner ready before Paul got home, a habit she hadn't even realized before. An unnecessary habit, she thought, since recently he was late more often than not. Still, she couldn't quite bring herself to do nothing. She pulled an onion out of the basket on the counter and chopped it furiously. It felt good. She scraped the pieces into her large frying pan. As she worked, Kathleen thought about her professor's amazing revelation. She still couldn't imagine Hawk married. Yet, as miserable as she was feeling about Paul, she couldn't imagine herself divorced. There had to be another way to solve this misery, there just had to be.

The magical fragrance of the onions soon filled the kitchen, and Kathleen began to feel hopeful. She mixed together a casserole and put it into the oven. Then she wiped down the counter, put the few dishes she had used into the dishwasher, and began to make a salad. She wanted to call someone, but she couldn't think of who that might be. How could she tell anyone what was going on? Even Mary. She went through a mental list of people she might just chat with, but as she did so, she realized that the person she really wanted to talk to was Paul.

She finished the salad and set the table. Then she looked around for something else that needed doing. She refilled the salt and pepper shakers and washed the butter dish. The garbage was full, and she knew Paul wouldn't be the one to empty it, so she headed for the large bins outside.

"Hello, dear," came the cheery voice of Mrs. Ferguson. "I haven't seen you in ever so long." Her neighbor was heading in the door just as Kathleen was going out.

"Oh, hello," Kathleen replied. She felt a sudden wash of guilt that she hadn't seen the elderly woman in a long time. "I've been working. How have you been?"

"Oh, just fine. And how about you?"

"Busy. I'm sorry we haven't visited much lately."

"Now, don't you worry about that. I know how you young folks are these days. I see how hard both of you are working. You just come by any time you can. It would be lovely to have a chat with you again."

"Thanks, Mrs. Ferguson. I will." Kathleen emptied the garbage into the bin and went back to her empty apartment. This must be what every day is like for Mrs. Ferguson, she thought. No one to come home to. No one to cook for. No one even to talk to. Was this what lay in store for her? Going out of her apartment only for emptying the garbage or getting the mail? How could she even think of leaving Paul? She wore his ring on her finger. She carried his name. You couldn't just undo all that. Besides, where would she go? Where would she live? How could she even afford to rent her own apartment?

The prospect terrified her as much as it saddened her. She only made $250 a month working part-time. An apartment would cost her at least $110. Her car was paid for, but there would be insurance and gas. And then utilities and phone. Maybe she could get on full-time with Hawk. The professor was always asking her to consider it, but she chose part-time work because she wanted to be able to do things around the house for Paul. Besides, she was planning to start a family soon and . . . The tears came then. Life had seemed so perfect and so easy when she married Paul. Without him, every option seemed impossible. She knew her father would let her come back to work for him, but the windowless office she didn't mind at all during college seemed like a cell.

She wiped her eyes and checked the casserole. It wasn't quite bubbling up enough in the center, so she set the timer for ten more minutes and wiped down the counter tops again. Maybe a fire in the fireplace would cheer things up. She'd bought some real firewood for the holidays, and there was still some left in the basket on the hearth. She balled up some newspapers and stuffed them into the grate. Then she carefully laid some kindling on top of the papers. Finally she added two small logs from the wood basket. Then she pulled a long fireplace match out of the paisley box she had given Paul in his stocking for Christmas and lit the paper.

The flames ignited with a whoosh that made her jump back and then pull the fire curtain shut, but within a few seconds the paper was reduced to ash, and the wood was still untouched. Gathering more papers, she stuffed them in again under the kindling and got another long match out of the box. Four matches and the rest of the classified ads later, Kathleen gave up. She couldn't get the fire started. She couldn't tell when Paul would be home. She couldn't solve a single problem in her life.

The timer buzzed, and she went into the kitchen. The casserole was too brown now and the juices had spilled over into the oven. She set the dish on the burner where the oven vented to keep it warm. It was nearly 6:30. Where was Paul? It suddenly occurred to her that he might have called while she was taking out the garbage. She couldn't hear the phone from there, after all.

So she sat down to read the part of the paper she hadn't burned. Surely he'd be home soon.

At 7:30 she ate dinner alone and put her dish into the dishwasher. Suddenly the place setting left on the table for Paul looked stark and stupid. With a swift motion, Kathleen gathered the plate and silverware and put them away. She took the remainder of the casserole out of the oven where she had kept it warming and put it into the refrigerator. Where could he be? She wanted to worry that perhaps something had happened to him, but she knew that nothing had.

She looked around the apartment. She had worked so hard at turning it into a home that Paul would be proud of. A large poster of Portofino hung on the wall over the dining room table. She and Mary had each bought one and spent a whole day affixing them to boards and then shellacking them with several coats to make them look old. They thought they had turned out wonderfully, and the large picture sort of anchored the long white wall that merged with the kitchen. Paul was unhappy that Mary and Mark had the same picture but finally said it would probably be fine since they didn't run in the same circles. His response had been disappointing, but Kathleen loved how the picture looked.

Above the sofa were two framed floral prints that some friends of the Gordons had given them for the wedding. The colors in the pictures went beautifully with their sofa, and Kathleen had bought some pillows to pick up the shades of green of the leaves.

How could she leave all this? She looked around again. The domed clock—also a wedding present—said 8:15. She turned on the television. It was still surprising to see it come on in color. She remembered coming home from work one day to find Paul opening a huge box in the living room.

"First one on your block to have a color TV, Kat. Wait till you see the picture." He had been as excited as a little kid with his new toy, and Kathleen had loved him for it. His eyes were shining, and he would get up every few minutes to change the channel to see how another program looked in color. The old black and white portable was in their storage unit in the basement.

Everything, every single thing, was making her sad. She couldn't breathe. She switched off the television and went into the bathroom. Maybe a soak in the tub would help. She pulled out her bottle of Youth Dew bath oil and shook a few drops under the running water. The fragrance instantly reminded her of the first time she had used it—the small sample bottle complete with a tiny bow. It had smelled so delicious, she'd decided to try it the night they got engaged. She'd worn it ever since. Was there nowhere she could escape? She quickly undressed and lowered herself into the steaming tub, not bothering to put on a shower cap. Who cared if her hair turned into Brillo? She lay there, trying not to think, until the water turned cool and her fingers were wrinkled. Then she got out, toweled herself dry, and went to bed. It was 9:45. Paul was not home yet. She wondered what story he would tell this time.

༄

"That's it, we're going apartment hunting!" Mary used both hands to push herself out of her chair. Pregnancy became her, and Kathleen noted ruefully that even in her increasing ungainliness, Mary had a certain grace. Kathleen hadn't meant to talk about her problems, but finally at their usual Saturday lunch, everything just blurted out.

"No, Mar. I'm not ready for anything that drastic. I just had to tell someone. I'm sure things will get better."

"When? When have they even been not-so-bad? You told me yourself that Paul's not even going to counseling anymore. You've been walking on your lips for months, and I have bruises on my tongue from not saying anything to you. Come on. Put on your coat. We're on a mission."

She pushed Kathleen out of the restaurant and steered her to the parking lot. "I'm driving while I can still fit behind the wheel, so get in and shut up. I've allowed you to be stupid long enough.

Now what area should we look at first? How about Madison Park? There are tons of apartments down there."

"I can't do this, Mar."

"Nonsense. We're just looking. At this point you don't even know what your options are, so Paul holds all the cards. You need to have a trick or two up your sleeve, old girl. I'm not saying you have to move out today, but you should have a plan. You know, just in case."

Kathleen's eyes stung with unshed tears brought on both because she knew her friend was right, but more so because she knew Mary really cared. The contrast between Mary's concern and Paul's indifference broke down the last shred of hope she had been clinging to.

All right. She'd just see what was out there.

They looked at several places, most of them way out of Kathleen's budget. Finally they followed the street that paralleled Lake Washington. They didn't even bother to look at the quaint stucco apartments that were on the waterfront, but at the end of the street, they came across a sprawling complex of two-story older buildings with a Vacancy sign.

"Hey, I forgot about these," Mary said. "The Edgewater. They're supposed to be really great. Let's go look." She parked the car before Kathleen could say a word.

The manager, Mr. Sivertsen, an elderly man with thick silver hair smiled at them and asked if she needed a two-bedroom. Mary laughed and patted her stomach.

"Don't worry. This kid already has a home. We're looking for my friend here. Do you have any one-bedrooms available?"

"Let's go take a look." He checked a large ledger on his desk, wrote a few numbers on a pad, and then led them outside.

"These lovelies were built before the war, and for my money, you'll not find craftsmanship like this anywhere else in town. The first one I'm going to show you is right here in this building, on the top floor."

They went up the carpeted stairs and into a spacious apartment with gleaming hardwood floors. There was a small foyer with a huge closet and a tiny door right next to it.

"What's this door for?" Kathleen asked Mr. Sivertsen.

"That's where you put your garbage. There's another door in the hall where it gets picked up. You can also have them leave packages in there if you want."

"You mean she doesn't have to take the garbage outside?" Mary said. "How can I get a deal like that?"

Kathleen and Mary went into the large kitchen. It had tiled drainboards just like Gran's house.

"Oh, Kath, look at this stove! It has one of those soup-pot burner things. My mom used to have one of those. I love them."

Kathleen looked. The fourth burner was a flat lid that when removed revealed a deep pot. "I never saw anything like this. Can you really cook in it?"

"My wife makes the best soup you ever had in hers every week," the manager said.

There was a large bedroom and a long hall with two more closets.

"There seems to be lots of storage," Kathleen said. The appliances were vintage, not at all resembling the modern things in her kitchen, but there was more closet space. Not that she'd be needing more once she didn't have to save room for Paul's things. She bit her lip.

"Yessir, and there's a storage unit downstairs in the laundry. Do you need a garage? Costs extra, but I have one available."

"No. How much is this unit?"

"This one and one other like it in the next building are each $110, but heat's included. That's a plus."

Mary and Kathleen looked at each other. It was in her price range, especially if she didn't have to pay for electric heat the way she did at home. At home. The words stuck. What was she doing here?

"May we see the other one?" Mary asked.

"Sure thing. It's just the same floor plan, but it's got a bit of a view."

They walked along beautiful paths surrounded by lush plants. If it was this lovely in January, what must it be like in the summer, Kathleen wondered. Mr. Sivertsen held the door for them to enter a similar-looking building, but when they walked into the apartment, both girls gasped.

"It's right on the lake, Kath! Wow, what a view."

The living room window faced north and east, and not only was the lake right outside, but just to the left in the middle of a large lawn was a huge weeping willow tree. The gnarled trunk was larger than "her" tree at the sorority, and the thin yellow whips of its leafless branches swished like a hula skirt in the wind.

"Oh, Mar. It's lovely. The tree, I mean."

"The whole thing is great. What do you want to do? This one or the other one. I vote for this one."

Kathleen signaled with her eyes that she didn't want to talk in front of the manager, so Mary thanked him and asked for his card. "We'll get back to you, Mr. Sivertsen, but please don't show this unit to anyone else if you can help it."

"Well, now, I can't promise that, young lady, but we have several other vacancies, so it might still be here tomorrow."

Back in the car, Kathleen wrapped her arms tightly about her middle. "What am I doing, Mar? How can I just leave? We've only been married two years—not even two. And my dad spent so much on the wedding. And so many people gave us presents."

"And you are so unhappy! Look at you. Every time I've seen you lately, you've been a wreck. He stays out late, he's on a trip, he's 'maybe' carrying on with someone else. Come on, Kath. Get out of there. Who cares about presents and wedding expenses? You have to think about yourself."

"I am, Mar. I think about how lonely I'll be without him."

"Because you're not lonely enough *with* him? Marriage should be between two people who support each other and stick up for each other and do things with each other. Do you have that?"

"This sounds like the lectures you used to give me at the sorority."

"Yeah, and did you listen then? No. You married him anyway. Well, now you can start over. That great apartment will be just the first step."

"I don't know, Mar. How will I ever tell my parents?"

"That will take some doing, but if you tell them both at the same time, your dad will help things along. He's such a sweetie. The most important thing here is you. They'll understand that."

"He will. My mother is another story. We'll probably have to call an ambulance."

"Mark and I will help you move. You'll see, things will work out in the long run. You deserve someone better than Paul, Kath. You're too special to waste yourself on a guy who doesn't appreciate you."

Back at her own place, Kathleen put the leftovers into the oven. Paul had called and said he'd be home for dinner. While she set the table, her stomach was roiling. She played Mary's words over and over in her mind. Her friend was right, but would she have the strength to leave Paul? She jumped when she heard him open the front door.

"You home, Kat?" he said, as he draped his coat over the chair.

"In the kitchen, Paul." She wiped her hands on a towel and walked to meet him, automatically picking up his coat and hanging it in the closet. "How was work?"

"Same as usual, crazy. The Portland store is planning a big sale with the Rose Festival, so I've been working with the publicity department to plan a huge splash. I'll probably have to spend some more time down there working with the publicity department. I didn't realize what a big deal it is—almost bigger than Seafair is up here. No hydroplane races, of course."

He poured himself some wine and pulled his tie off. With a flick he tossed it toward the chair. It missed by a mile. Kathleen resisted the urge to go pick it up.

"Paul, we need to talk."

"Could we eat first? I'm starving."

They sat down at the table, and Kathleen dished up the leftovers.

"No salad?" he asked.

"No."

"Oh, well. I had one with lunch."

They ate for a while in silence.

"Do you want to get me some more wine?" he said finally.

"Help yourself," she heard herself say.

She could tell he was looking at her, but she kept her eyes on her plate and forced herself to continue eating while he got up and refilled his glass.

"So what is it we need to talk about?" he asked, coming back to the table. "I suppose it's about going house-hunting again. Is that it?"

"Not exactly. It's more than that. We need to talk about us, Paul. Or what's left of us anyway."

"Kat, I have been working my rear end off at the store. Can I help it if I'm putting in lots of hours on something that will make us very rich?

You have no idea how many balls are up in the air right now. If I drop one—even one—it could be a disaster."

"What about our marriage, Paul? *It's* becoming a disaster. Couldn't you put a little of your energy into building what we have? The counselor told us that we had to put each other first."

"That old fart. He had no good advice on anything."

"You found him."

"So now it's my fault. You accuse me of not trying to work on this marriage, yet I found us a marriage counselor when you started to pout. I went to those stupid sessions until I couldn't stand to look at him again. Or to hear you tell him how terrible I was to you, when all I've tried to do was build something for the future."

"*Your* future, though, not ours. Why did you ask me to marry you, Paul? Didn't you love me?"

"Of course I loved you. And I knew you were the kind of girl who would be a good wife."

"A good wife? And haven't I been?"

"Lately it's been tough, Kat. You mope around and follow me from room to room. You're always asking when I'll be home. Hell, I don't know when I'll be home! I'm working like a dog, and when I do get home, I'd like to be able to just rest without the Spanish Inquisition every night."

His words stung Kathleen. He'd never said anything like that in counseling. How long had he been feeling like this? And what did he mean, she followed him around?

"Is it a crime to try to talk to you on the rare moments you're home?"

"I talk to people all day, Kat. All I want when I come home is a little peace and quiet."

"Do you want a divorce then?" There she had said it.

"Can we talk about this some other time, Kat? You're in one of your moods, and I frankly don't have the energy to carry on this heavy a conversation." He resumed eating his dinner. "This is delicious though. I will say that." He smiled at her as if the whole world hadn't just changed forever.

༄

Telling her mother, even with her father there as Mary suggested, was worse than she had imagined.

"What?" her mother shrieked, clasping her throat with one hand and feeling behind her for the chair with the other. "Are you out of your mind?"

"What's wrong, Kitten?" her father asked, immediately putting his arm around her shoulders. "Has he done something we should know about? Do you want to tell us?"

"I'm not sure, Daddy, but I think he's having an affair with someone at work."

He mother threw her hands in the air. "You *think*? You're not even sure? You're making this ridiculous decision based on 'you think'? It's beyond imagining. Paul with a salesgirl? Really, Kathleen."

Kathleen glanced at her mother. She didn't have the energy to go into Brenda's résumé nor to explain the difference between a salesgirl and a buyer. "But even if he's not," she continued, looking at her father, "things are just . . . well, they're just . . ."

"What? They're just what?" her mother said. "Not perfect? Nothing's perfect, Kathleen. You just don't toss away everything and get a *divorce*! My God. It's too horrible to *think* about. How could you do this to me? What will people *say*?"

"Calm down, Joan," Mr. Andrews said to his wife. "There must be something we can do. What does Paul say? Did he admit anything? Does he agree to this?"

"No, he hasn't admitted anything. He doesn't seem to care, Daddy. That's the really awful part. He says I'm imagining things, but he doesn't do anything to reassure me. It's as if everything's my fault." Kathleen fought back the tears.

"Have you two talked to anyone about this? The pastor who married you?" he asked her.

"We went to a marriage counselor, but he didn't help much. I think Paul will be happy to have me move out. I found an apartment."

"Well, that might just do the trick," her mother said. "Once he sees that you're really serious, he may just wake up, and this whole thing will be a bad dream. What did he say when you told him you had the apartment?"

"I haven't told him yet. I keep hoping things will change somehow. I guess I still hope there's magic around somewhere, even though I know there isn't."

"Do you want me to have a talk with him," her father asked. "Maybe man to man he might be able to tell me if there is really something going on."

"Thanks, Daddy, but I don't think so. I don't think anything will help. That's why I decided to move."

"Have you talked to a lawyer?" he asked.

"Not yet. I can't handle that just now. I have to move first. Then we'll see."

"I just can't believe this, Kathleen," her mother said from her chair. "After that huge wedding and everyone giving you so many presents. How can you even think about leaving him? What could be so terrible? All marriages have their ups and downs. You must work through them. Try to be understanding."

"Joan! Leave her be." Kathleen had never heard her father be so stern with his wife before. Her mother looked at him in surprise, but before she could respond, he put both arms around Kathleen. "Don't you worry, Kitten. We'll stand behind you, no matter what. Your happiness comes first. If you think you need to move out, why then, that's what you need to do. And we'll help. Won't we, Joan?" He looked pointedly at his wife. "Do you need any money, sweetheart?"

"No, Daddy, I can manage." She had banked practically all of her small salary in her house account to surprise Paul with a start on a down payment for the house she hoped they would buy. How ironic that she would use it for the first and last month's deposit on an apartment she would be renting by herself. She returned her father's hug, feeling as she had when she was a child, safe and loved. It had been a long time since she had felt either.

As Kathleen drove back home, however, the heaviness that enveloped her daily returned. There were arrangements to make if she was truly going to move. She had to tell Paul her plans.

She picked some straggly white roses that were still blooming in the back yard and put them into a glass pitcher on the table, a pitcher Paul's aunt and uncle had given them as a wedding gift. She wouldn't be taking it.

She set the table and opened a bottle of wine. She looked at the table and reminded herself to breathe. Her stomach was fluttery. What did she hope to accomplish with all this preparation? On impulse, she poured herself a glass and sat down, but she could barely swallow the small sip she took, so she just held the glass and waited. Paul came home on time and laughed out loud when he saw her sitting with a wineglass in her hand.

"Bad day, Kat?"

"Bad month, actually. Dinner's nearly ready." She got up and went into the kitchen, deliberately not noticing what Paul did with his coat. She dished up dinner and then poured a glass of wine for Paul and set it by his plate. The roses on the table were tinged with brown, their stems were spindly, and they had no fragrance. They should have been long past blooming by now, but there they were, Kathleen marveled, despite the weather, the season, and the expectations. The battered, stubborn little roses seemed like a metaphor. If they could make it, maybe so could she.

"What's the occasion, Kat? I know I didn't forget our anniversary."

"We just need to talk a bit, Paul." She took another swallow of her wine, but it didn't go down any easier than before. She took a bite of her dinner, but it seemed dry and tasteless and harder to swallow than the wine. "I've given it a lot of thought, and I just don't think you want to stay married to me." She took another bite so it would be his turn to say something, but he just kept chewing. "So," she said finally, "I've found an apartment, and I'll be moving out."

"You're serious?"

Kathleen looked at her husband for a long moment, reminding herself again to breathe. It had taken all her courage to tell him, but as she nervously waited for his response, she realized his face showed neither shock nor sadness. "Yes, I'm signing a lease," she said at last.

"Where'll you get the money for the deposit?"

"I have a job. You do remember that, don't you?"

"Oh, yes, your little job. How do you expect to pay for everything? I hope you don't expect me to come up with the rent on two places."

Kathleen set down her fork. She couldn't take another bite; her stomach was churning. "I really don't expect you to do anything, Paul." Why had she gone to so much trouble? Had she imagined that he would suddenly throw himself at her feet because of a good dinner and some drooping roses? She looked at him once more, but at the same instant her stomach lurched, and she barely made it to the bathroom in time.

On her knees on the cold tiles, she retched and retched until she thought her insides would come out as well. Finally the nausea subsided. She rinsed out her mouth and brushed her teeth. Paul stayed at the table. She didn't know whether to be glad about that or not. She ran her fingers through her hair and went back to the kitchen.

"You OK now?" he asked. He had finished his dinner.

"Not really. I think I'll go to bed." She started to put things away in the kitchen and then stopped. "I'm going to bed," she repeated. "Please clean up the kitchen."

She couldn't sleep, partly from nerves and partly from staying deliberately on her side of the bed. She was so used to sleeping curled up to Paul's back that she was afraid she would automatically revert to that position if she were not alert. When morning came, she didn't get up to fix him breakfast, and as soon as he left, she took a quick shower and drove first to the bank to withdraw her money and then to the new apartment to sign the lease.

She called the moving company from Hawk's office when she got to work, asking if they could move her the next day, but they were unavailable before Friday. That left her three long days before she could leave.

Hawk was sympathetic. "It always feels worse when you have decided to act and then have to wait. You could go to a hotel if you think that would be better."

"No, I need all the money I have left. A hotel is out of the question. I'll just have to get through it. Maybe he'll come home late every night, as usual. Then it won't be hard at all."

"Don't worry about work. You can have that day off and the following Monday too, if you need it."

"Thank you. I didn't even think about work . . . I mean . . ."

"I understand, Kathleen. Take care of this first. Then everything will seem more possible. Trust me."

She would take only what had been hers before they married or what had come to them from her side of the guest list. That meant that most of the expensive crystal vases and the martini set would stay behind, as well as the color TV and the coffee table. But she would take the sofa her parents bought them and her bedroom set—except for the king-sized mattress Paul had insisted on— and practically all of the kitchen things, including the china and silver, regardless of who gave it to them. She'd be damned if some other woman would use her things for a romantic dinner with Paul. Let him go buy some Lenox. And, of course, she would take her picture of Portofino.

Thursday night on her way home from work, she stopped at the grocery store and filled her car with cardboard boxes. They smelled of decaying fruit. She decided to leave them in the car until the morning. She wouldn't pack until Paul left for work. Ever since she told him she was leaving, they had moved around each other at home like strangers on a train. They were courteous but not cordial, and they didn't say much to each other. She slept as far onto her own side of the bed as possible, and woke up with stiff and aching muscles.

On Friday when Paul put on his coat and walked to the door, he paused and said, "Are you really leaving?"

"I'll be gone when you get home."

"Well, I guess good-bye then." He walked back to where she stood and gave her a soft kiss on the lips. Then he walked out the door. Kathleen waited to feel something, but she didn't. It was as if she were observing the whole thing from somewhere over her right shoulder. As soon as she was sure Paul would be gone from the parking lot, she went to her car for the boxes. The whole car smelled like a garbage can.

She didn't exactly know where to begin. Maybe the kitchen would take her the longest. The movers were due at 11. That gave her three and a half hours to pack. That should be enough. There wasn't that much. Still she just stood in the kitchen, her hands at her sides.

The doorbell pulled her back. What if Paul had forgotten something? No, he wouldn't ring the bell. She didn't seem to be functioning right. The bell rang again. This time Kathleen went to the door.

True to her word, there was Mary to help her move.

"I've got sandwiches for lunch and a pot of spaghetti in the car for dinner. I even brought paper plates and plastic forks in case we can't find your dishes!" Mary announced. "I'm going to be worthless when it comes to lifting anything, and I certainly can't carry anything that requires two arms." She patted her bulging stomach and laughed. "But I'm a terrific wrapper-upper of dishes."

Kathleen was sure she had never been so happy to see anyone in her life. She hugged her friend warmly and marched her into the kitchen. By the time the movers arrived—promptly at 11—everything but the clothes in Kathleen's closet had been wrapped, boxed, and labeled. The movers brought large cardboard wardrobe boxes for the clothes on hangers, so while the two burly men carried out the furniture, the last of the boxes were taped shut.

Hope Chest

"Yer not takin' this nice TV, Ma'am?" the younger of the two movers asked.

"Give a hand here, Hank," the older man said. "The lady knows what she wants us to move."

Kathleen smiled at him gratefully and carried a few fragile items to her own car.

By late afternoon, the movers had transferred Kathleen's belongings to her new apartment and placed things where she and Mary directed. Kathleen thanked them for their help as they brought in the last load.

"Nothing to it, Ma'am. I think you're gonna be real happy here. It's a real nice place." The older man touched an imaginary cap as he left, and Kathleen was moved by his kindness and his obvious understanding of her situation. How many other times had he moved half a household?

Mary went out to her car and came back with a large square box, wrapped in gold paper with a silver bow. "Happy housewarming. Happy new life."

Kathleen unwrapped the box and found four hand-thrown pottery mugs, each slightly different from the others, but all done in an earthy brown glaze.

"These are beautiful, Mar."

"They're also functional. It must be time for tea. If we can find it."

The two friends unpacked boxes while the water in the teakettle, found mercifully in the first box marked "Kitchen," came to a boil. They sat on the sofa enjoying their tea for a brief moment until Mary said, "Up and at 'em, girl. We're almost through."

Mark came later prepared to work. He flattened each box and carried them all outside. Then he hung Kathleen's Portofino picture.

"I figured I should bring a hammer and some nails, just because you never know."

"Mark, you are a find." Kathleen kissed his cheek. The three of them admired the way the large picture warmed up the room. "I'll need to find some more artwork. Without a fireplace, there are really a lot of walls to cover!"

They heated the spaghetti on the big old stove and toasted her "great new home and great new life."

"But especially to great old friends. I don't know what I would have done without you two. I don't even like to think about it!"

By the time she made up a bed on the sofa that night, Kathleen was exhausted, but there were dishes in the cupboard, food in the fridge, towels in the bathroom, and her clothes in the closets. Perhaps it was because she was so tired or because she had been too busy to think, but there hadn't been a single tear.

Well, one, when she ran into Mrs. Ferguson as the movers were taking the sofa out to the truck.

"Are you two leaving, my dear?" The old woman seemed hurt that Kathleen had not come to say good-bye.

"Not the two of us, Mrs. Ferguson. Just me. I'm leaving Paul."

"Oh, my dear. Are you sure? Leaving? Oh, my."

"I'm sorry I didn't tell you sooner. I guess I hoped it wouldn't come to this, but it has. I was planning to stop in before I left."

"Oh, my," she said again. "Moving away. Wait, I want to give you something."

Mrs. Ferguson disappeared into her apartment and came back carrying a small white box. "You admired this the first time you visited me. I want you to have it. It has been a joy to have you as a neighbor. Our tea times brought sunshine into my sometimes long days. Perhaps this will remind you of those happy times."

Kathleen took the box and lifted the lid. It was an Aynsley bowl of white bone china roses. Kathleen remembered exclaiming over it the first time she had been invited for tea. It was lovely. Her eyes filled with tears as she hugged her neighbor. "It may be hard for me to come back here to see you while Paul is still in the apartment, but I will stay in touch. I promise."

"I hope so. I'm so sorry this is happening to you, but be happy, my dear. Remember, when one door closes . . ."

"I know. My gran always says that too."

Thinking of Gran and Mrs. Ferguson, she stretched out on the sofa and fell into a sound sleep.

The next morning she awoke with some aching muscles but amazingly rested. She padded into the kitchen, where the sun poured in through the window, lighting up the whole room. Her other kitchen had never been filled with light like this. It was glorious. Kathleen made herself a cup of instant coffee in one of her new pottery mugs and went into the living room to drink it and look at the lake just outside her window. She would have to get a kitchen table and chairs soon. The dining set had been from the Gordons, so it stayed. She started her list: mattress, kitchen set, lamp for living room, bedroom rug. She had put the old black and white TV on a box that she covered with a bright tablecloth until she could find something more substantial. But all in all, she thought as she surveyed her new home in the bright winter sun, it looked pretty wonderful. She added a note to bring her old bookcases from her bedroom at her parents' house. She could paint them and put one in her bedroom and one in the living room.

She finished her coffee and took a long shower. The heat felt good after all the lifting and stretching. She dressed and headed downtown. The first thing she had to do was to open some store charge accounts in her name and new address so she could buy a few things without the bills going to Paul.

At the first store, a haughty looking woman with a frizzled permanent listened to Kathleen's request and then asked her if her divorce was final.

"I haven't filed yet," Kathleen said, feeling awkward. "I just moved yesterday and have a new address, so I'll need a new account."

"Well, when you and your husband have things figured out, come back and we can talk then. We just can't open and close accounts on a whim."

Kathleen was stunned. She walked away from the window in amazement. She'd had an account there before she was married and had no trouble at all changing it to her new Mrs.-Paul-Gordon name and address. Now that she wanted herself back, it was difficult. Fortunately, her next stop was Frederick & Nelson, and the woman there was gracious and helpful. Kathleen took the escalator to the floor that had the mattresses and box springs, vowing never to shop at the first store again.

Luckily their sheets were on sale, but she couldn't afford most of the furniture at Frederick's, even if she were to charge things. The mattress was expensive enough. Instead she went down to the waterfront to some of the import shops. There she found a charming little table and chairs that would just fit into her kitchen's eating space. The table had a round glass top and wrought-iron legs. The chairs were also wrought iron with woven seats and backs. She found a wrought-iron floor lamp as well that would be perfect with her sofa and would save her from having to buy a table plus a lamp right now. There was also a sale on some colorful woven rugs from India, and she bought a small one for the floor near her new bed.

That was all she could afford this go around. She would still need something for the windows, but there were pull-down shades in every room, so at least she had privacy. Maybe she could get some fabric and borrow Mary's sewing machine if she couldn't find something ready-made.

Kathleen managed to get everything into her car and headed home to see how things looked. Funny, she thought, how quickly "home" had changed in her mind. She still wasn't sad. She felt as though she were on an adventure without a plan or a map. It was slightly scary but not at all the desolation she had expected to feel. And the beautiful sunshine glinting off the lake helped immensely.

In the apartment, the kitchen set was exactly right. She looked around for something to put on the table. Remembering Mrs. Ferguson's china roses, she placed them on top of one of Gran's crocheted doilies in the center of the table. They were perfect. She must remember to write Mrs. Ferguson a note. The lamp was also a good choice, and now she could read in the living room. The rug was a bit slippery on the bedroom's hardwood floor, though, so she made another note to get some sort of pad to put under it. She moved it over under the window where she wouldn't be apt to step on it, yet the colors could still warm the room.

Not bad for the first day, she thought, and was about to make herself a cup of tea when the doorbell rang. She thought it must be Mary again and went to the door with a smile. There stood her mother and father. She could tell from the set of her mother's shoulders that the visit had not been her idea.

"Hi, Kitten," her father said. "We're here to see your new place. And we brought you a present." He hugged her and kissed her on the cheek.

"Come in. I was just about to make tea."

"That sounds good. Your mother brought you some butterhorns from that bakery up the street. It looks like a great one."

"I'd heard about the Madison Park Bakery, Kathleen. Many of my friends get their cakes there." Her mother stepped into the apartment and looked around.

"Here, give me your coats. I'll take you on the tour."

"This is terrific, Kitten. So much light. They don't build 'em like this anymore, I can tell you that."

"Well, at least you still have a view," her mother said. "Don't you miss the wall-to-wall carpeting you had, Kathleen? I should think these floors would be cold underfoot."

"Come see the rug I bought for the bedroom. I need to get a non-slip pad for it, but I think it will be darling." She was trying too hard, she knew, but she was not about to let her mother spoil what had been such a surprisingly good day.

"I see you took the bedroom set with you at least, but where's the bed?"

"My new mattress is coming next week, Mother. I told you, I took what was mine before or what our side had given to us at the wedding."

"That sounds fair to me, Kitten. Although, I don't mind telling you, that husband of yours doesn't deserve one stick of anything after the way he's treated you. You were more than good to leave him with anything."

"I just wanted it to be over, Daddy. I can't even think about fighting over vases and coffee tables."

"Well, we have something that will make this place feel homey." Her father went back out into the hall and came in carrying a tall feathery plant in a shiny brass pot. "How's this? Your mother picked it out."

"It will be perfect, Kathleen," her mother said. "This living room has a lot of space to be filled up, and that will be wonderful right there in the corner." Her father set it down right where his wife was pointing.

"It's lovely, Mother. What kind is it?"

"It's a podocarpus, Kathleen. I felt that you could probably use something tall, but the split-leaf philodendrons are so terribly overused now. I asked the florist to find us something less ordinary. I think it's quite stunning."

Kathleen went over to her mother and hugged her. "Thank you. Thank you both. It makes the room so cozy. I can't believe I didn't have a plant on my list. It was very thoughtful. Let's have some tea with those butterhorns. We can inaugurate my new kitchen set."

"Well, now, this set *is* attractive," her mother said. "Where did you find it?"

"Down at the waterfront. I thought it would be perfect in here."

"I don't remember these roses though." Her mother picked up Mrs. Ferguson's china gift and turned it over. "Aynsley," she read. "Impressive. Was this a wedding gift?"

"No. My neighbor gave it to me as I was moving. Isn't it pretty?" Kathleen set the mugs on the table and got out plates for the butterhorns. She didn't want to talk about moving.

"Kitten," her father said, handing her a folded piece of paper. "I talked with the company's lawyer, and he gave me some names of who he said are really top-notch attorneys you should talk to. The Gordons probably have a whole fleet of legal fellows to choose from, but our guy said you need someone who specializes in this field. Did you know that now you don't have to have what they call 'grounds' to get a divorce in this state?"

"I really don't know much about any of it, Daddy." Moving was one thing. She didn't want to talk about divorce.

"Well, apparently all you have to do now is say you two just can't get along or something. Wait, I wrote it down—'irreconcilable differences'—and if neither of you makes an objection, it takes just 90 days. Anyway, that's what he said."

Her father looked as uncomfortable as she felt, and Kathleen's heart went out to him. She put her hand over his. "Thank you for looking into this for me. I'm not sure what I'm going to do yet."

"Well, don't fiddle around too long, Kathleen," her mother said. "You're not getting any younger, and the sooner you get this all behind you, the sooner you can meet someone else."

"Mother, the last thing I'm thinking about right now is meeting someone!"

"You can say that now, but one day you might just find yourself alone and childless, and then what?"

"Joan, for heaven's sake. This has been pretty upsetting for everyone, Kitten, but most of all for you. You just let me know if you need any money for the lawyer when the time comes. Like I said, we'll help you all we can."

"These are good butterhorns," her mother said, changing the subject. "You'll want to take advantage of that bakery when you entertain, Kathleen." Her mother lifted her mug, looked at it askance, and then sipped her tea.

Chapter 17

March 1966

She'd been in her apartment for two months before she could bring herself to call a lawyer from the list her father had given her. Paul had only phoned once to complain that she had taken the martini set. She told him it was in the cupboard above the refrigerator.

Her mother-in-law called once as well. Kathleen was shocked to hear her voice on the phone. Her in-laws had rarely called when she and Paul were together.

"Kathleen, are you sure you want to do this? We all had our troubles, especially in the beginning, but we persevered until things worked themselves out. We didn't just give up. Why don't you give yourselves some more time?"

"I have. Truly, I have. We even went to counseling, but Paul doesn't seem to want to stay married, so there's not much I can do."

"I can't believe that, my dear. He's just so busy with the two stores right now, it probably seems like he's disinterested, but I'm sure he still cares for you."

"I wish I shared your opinion. Anyway, time will tell."

"But you just can't run away from your problems. You must stand and face them until they're solved."

"Not everything can be solved, I'm afraid."

"Well, I'm sure things will work out. In the meantime, if we call and invite you for dinner, would you come?"

"Of course. You and Ted have been wonderful to me. I hope you know how much I care for both of you. And I'd be happy to see you again."

"Then you will. And you may call me any time. Perhaps we can work something out by putting our heads together."

"Thank you."

As Kathleen replaced the phone in its cradle, she wondered whether she would ever hear from her mother-in-law again, especially if Paul ever introduced them to Brenda. She knew with a certainty that she wouldn't, and she also realized that she suddenly didn't care. Paul had gone through the motions of trying to hold their marriage together, even to the charade of finding a counselor. What a joke, she thought. He didn't have the courage to face her with the truth that he didn't want to be married. Instead he'd made it so miserable for poor, stupid her that *she* finally left *him*. Kathleen wondered if there was a cartoon lightbulb over her head. As Hawk had said, she had been holding on to the dream. The next day she went to the offices of Miles, Phipps, and Stanton, attorneys at law.

Ned Stanton was a man in his 30s with an engaging smile that put Kathleen at ease from the start. He asked her a few questions, and when he discovered there were no children and no property to speak of, he assured Kathleen that the proceedings would be quick and easy.

"I'll just write up the papers and have your husband served, and ninety days from then, you and I will go to court, and it will all be over."

"Will he be in court as well?" Kathleen asked.

"No need. Since it's uncontested, the court part is really just a formality. Both parties can choose to be there, but the one being sued for divorce usually doesn't bother. One thing you will have to do, however," he continued, "is visit the divorce proctor."

"What's that?"

"He's a guy who talks to you—sort of like a counselor—just to make sure you know what you're doing. It's pretty simple. Here's his number. Just call and make an appointment. The whole thing will take about 15 minutes."

Kathleen accepted the card. "Is there a fee for him too?"

"No, he's free." The lawyer smiled.

The divorce, she found out, was going to cost her about $300, more than two months' rent. Her savings were nearly exhausted, but after Paul's comments about her little job and how she shouldn't expect him to pay for two rents, she was determined to pay everything herself. She would manage somehow. And she didn't expect anything from him.

"Do I need to do anything else? Witnesses? I don't know. Records or something?"

"Nope. This'll do it. If both parties agree that the marriage is irretrievably broken and no one contests it, it's done."

"That's it?" Kathleen shook her head. "It was harder to get a driver's license!"

The lawyer laughed again and walked her to the door. "You'll be hearing from me when we get the court date. I'll have the papers delivered to your husband. Don't forget the proctor."

Later that week, Kathleen went to the courthouse to see the divorce proctor. He was a small, balding man with crooked teeth and a bow tie. He stood when she entered and motioned for her to sit.

"Now, Mrs. Gordon, I have to give you the speech I give all young people who are contemplating ending their marriages. Are you sure that there is no hope for your union?"

"I'm very sure, otherwise I would not have filed for divorce." This was ridiculous. Why didn't Paul have to see this man? Why weren't they commanded to be here together if this was a last attempt to save a marriage?

"Yes, yes, but sometimes hasty actions with life-long consequences have been taken for short-term reasons—a quarrel, a difference of opinions."

"Well, this is not the case. My husband doesn't wish to be married to me. I suppose you could say that was a difference of opinion, but it wasn't a hasty thing."

The proctor nodded as if she had said something profound and folded his small hands together on top of his desk. "Well, then, if I may. I'll just give you a piece of advice for the next time."

The next time! Kathleen blinked at him.

"The next time, don't get married until you have known the fellow for at least two years."

"I knew this one for longer than that, sir."

"Oh, my," he said, smiling at last. "There goes another of my theories." He laughed a short laugh and then rose. "I wish you good luck, Mrs. Gordon. I'm sorry I was unable to help you."

Kathleen rose and left the room. What a colossal waste of time! Now she only had to count the days until the waiting period was over, and she would get herself back. She had even told her lawyer that she wanted to take back her maiden name of Andrews. She had had enough of the Gordons for a lifetime.

At the grocery store on the way back to her apartment, she stood in line behind a very pregnant girl about Kathleen's age and her small blond son, who appeared to be around three years old. The little boy leaned out of the grocery cart and managed to snag a package of gum.

"I told you to stop touching things!" the mother hissed at the boy. She snatched the gum from his chubby hand and thrust it back into the display. The boy burst into tears and began to howl. His mother gave him a shake and told him in a loud whisper to stop that crying or she'd give him something to cry about.

Kathleen was furious. How could anyone treat a child like that? And this girl was about to have another baby! Life was so unfair. Here Kathleen was, nearly a quarter of a century old, that expression she and Mary used to find funny, and the life she had counted on living was as far away as it could be. But this young mother was living Kathleen's dream life and not appreciating any of it. She even had rollers in her hair. Kathleen had never gone out in public with her hair in rollers. Never. She had done everything right. She had followed all the rules. Yet here she was in her wool sheath and heels with matching purse, the perfect wife, getting a divorce. It wasn't right. Tears welled up in her eyes. She left her cart where it was and headed blindly for the car.

⁂

Professor Hawkins had somehow managed to expand Kathleen's duties. When Hawk called her in to ask her if she would be interested in full-time work, Kathleen was thrilled. The thought of having to leave the work she loved to find a job that paid more would have been doubly painful on the heels of the other wrenching changes in her life.

The money wasn't terrific, but it was as much as she would have made as a secretary or receptionist, and there were good medical benefits. If she was careful not to be extravagant, she had enough to pay her bills each month with a little left over. It helped that she could take the bus to work, and she brought her lunch, eating outside on the beautiful campus when the weather was nice.

She had tried many times to thank her beloved professor, but Hawk only smiled and said, "Don't worry, Kathleen. I have plans for you, and I don't know if you'll thank me then or not." Try as she might, Kathleen could get no further information out of her, but she didn't take her too seriously. Hawk had hinted that Kathleen should think about getting her master's degree, since working at the university meant she could take some classes for free. It was an intriguing thought. Would she be able to work and go to school? The money she paid out for the moving and the divorce would have seen her through a few quarters without working, she fumed. Paul was certainly not hurting.

"Why aren't you asking for alimony, at least?" Her mother had been incredulous. "With all that money they have, you are certainly entitled to something, Kathleen. I just don't understand you."

It wasn't something she could explain to her mother. She wanted nothing from Paul. If she could erase the whole marriage, she would. She wanted to get on with her life by herself and not be beholden to anyone, especially Paul. She shook her head at all the times before the wedding that she had practiced writing "Mrs. Paul Gordon." It would feel so good to sign her name "Kathleen Andrews" again. The divorce would be final in two days, and she had already ordered her new checks.

Her mother also couldn't understand why Kathleen continued to work with the children's drama department.

"You're not meeting anyone there, Kathleen. You only see children and their parents. Even the faculty are all women. You need a job where you can come into contact with some nice men. If you had listened to me and taken some shorthand, you could have a much better opportunity. I just don't understand you."

"Mother," Kathleen tried, "I would hate working in an office. I worked in Daddy's office every summer for four years. It's not something I like."

"Heavens! Your father's office is hardly what I had in mind. I meant downtown in a lovely tall building with men in suits coming and going. That's where you should be."

"I love my job, Mother. It's a joy to do what I do. And I'm really not looking to meet anyone just yet."

"Well don't wait too long."

※

"Happy Independence Day, old once-again-single friend. How'd it go?"

"It was nothing, Mar. I couldn't believe it."

"Well, save the details. We're going to dinner to celebrate and then to a movie. Mark is treating us. But you have to drive, since I don't fit behind the steering wheel in my present condition!"

"I'll be there in an hour. But promise you won't have the baby until after the movie is over."

"Can't promise, but I'll try."

Mary was due June 30, but the doctor told her it could be any day now. As Kathleen drove to Mary's house, she thought that even though part of her envied Mary, she was surprised to realize that she was enjoying living alone. It was the first time in her life she had ever been by herself. She had lived with her parents until college and then at the sorority with 95 other girls. In both instances, while she had her own part of the house, she wasn't responsible for anything. With Paul, she had what now seemed like double responsibility, cooking and cleaning and planning, as well as picking up after him. Here, in her own cozy apartment, she was free to do exactly what she liked. How she left the kitchen in the morning was how it greeted her when she returned. No surprise dirty cups in the sink or spilled jam on the counter. She could have scrambled eggs for dinner if she felt like it or toasted cheese sandwiches. It was a lovely if lonely sort of freedom.

She thought about how she had felt when she was with Paul. It should have been the answer to her dreams, a beautiful wedding; a handsome, successful husband; and a lovely apartment. Yet that was all on the outside. In the last few months of their marriage, it seemed as if everything she did was wrong. It continually annoyed him that she didn't drink with him. He never quite approved of how she dressed or entertained, even though others always complimented her on both. And why should she want to drink? She didn't like the taste, and besides, she always had fun without it. Once in college, a sorority sister had accused her of being drunk at a party the night before because she seemed to be having such a good time, and Kathleen couldn't convince her she'd been drinking pop all night. "Oh, sure," the girl had said, smiling.

But the most embarrassing memory was of his criticism of her lovemaking. She had no point of comparison; Paul was the first and only. As much as she wanted to make love to him, she had begun to dread it, knowing that he would be satisfied quickly and angry that she had not "been there with him." She felt like such a failure.

Now as she drove to pick up Mary, she had a pang of regret. As her friend's pregnancy blossomed, Kathleen sadly pondered the fact that motherhood for her was at best a long way off. She didn't begrudge Mary's happy marriage, however. Even though Paul thought it was too ordinary for his taste ("They're boring"), their relationship seemed enviable to her. She just wished she could have had the same happiness in hers.

She and Mary went to a restaurant that made great salads. Over dinner Kathleen recounted her day in court.

"It was so weird, Mar. On the way there, Ned, my attorney, briefed me on what the judge would ask me, you know, name, address, and stuff. Then he said the judge would say, 'Why are you seeking this divorce?' I had to think about that."

"Why? Oh, that's right, the judge might not know the famous Paul Gordon."

"Don't laugh. To my surprise, the first thing that came out of my mouth was, 'Because my husband's a rat.'"

"Ha! Good for you."

"Yeah, that made us both laugh. But in the courtroom there were such sad-looking people. I didn't realize we'd all sit in the same room and listen to everyone else's tales of woe until our turn came up. Fortunately, I was about the third or fourth one called. And when the judge said, 'Why are you seeking this divorce?' I started to laugh."

"Oh my God, you didn't."

"I pretended I was coughing, but I couldn't look at Ned at all. I felt so awful! I mean, this was serious. Finally I was able to choke out 'irreconcilable differences.'"

"Hooray! You're on the way to being cured of Gordonitis."

"If you could have seen some of the people in the courtroom, you would have thought I was the most frivolous person alive. But I couldn't help myself. I told you, it was weird."

"Eat up, my weird but liberated friend, the movie starts soon. You should enjoy it. I've heard it's weird too. It's foreign, Czech, I think, but it got great reviews."

Closely Watched Trains had English subtitles and proved to be quite riveting. One of the subplots was about a young man who tried to make love to his girlfriend and failed, and as a consequence, attempted suicide. An older man at the train station where they all worked made arrangements with a mature woman to initiate the young fellow into the ways of sex.

As the older woman was explaining things to the sad and nervous young man, the subtitled dialogue across the bottom read "premature ejaculation." Kathleen burst out, "My God, there's a *name* for it! It wasn't my fault."

"You're going to have to explain this one to me after the show," Mary whispered.

"You bet I will," Kathleen said, and settled back to enjoy what had turned out to be an excellent movie.

Chapter 18

September 1968

"They gave us land? When did you find out?" Kathleen couldn't believe it. Hawk had been working on building a children's theater separate from the university for years. There were many who agreed it was a great idea, but the funds had been slow to come in.

"They just called," Hawk told her. "Now if we can get the city and a few major businesses behind us, well, we're home free."

"You wish it were free! How much do you think it will cost?"

"Lots, but the biggest problem would have been the land, and bless the Carter Trust, we have that now. So we just need a staff—that's us—and building and a sustaining fund and a few odds and ends. Shouldn't be too hard."

"You're amazing," Kathleen said. "Where do we start? Can we continue to use the university facilities while we develop this scheme of yours?"

"Not officially. We'll have to go a tiny bit underground for a while, but once a few things are in place, we'll move you into an office off-site. I'll continue to teach here, of course. Can't afford to lose my retirement, after all, but then we'll have a legit base of operations. What do you say? Are you with me?"

"You bet. This is just fabulous! Imagine how many kids we could reach."

"Well, more than that, we could have real plays for kids with a place for real actors to perform. There used to be a program in this town for school kids. They'd climb on buses and head downtown to one of the large movie theatres for a whole morning of magic. They saw Sinbad the Sailor in real life. And Ali Baba and most of his thieves. The look of rapture on their little faces was worth all the treasure in those enchanted caves."

"Why did they stop?"

"Money. Theaters torn down. Disinterest in the arts in school. Who knows? But we can get it all going again in our very own place."

Hawk's eyes were shining, and Kathleen felt her own heart racing. What a huge project, but she had no doubt that Hawk could pull it off. And she, Kathleen, would be in the middle of it.

In the two years since her divorce, she'd had to refocus her whole outlook on life. From college on, her time had been consumed by wedding plans and apartment-decorating and thoughts of homeownership and eventual motherhood. Then, suddenly, it had all changed. There was nothing familiar in her schedule. Grocery-shopping for one felt strange. It took her months to stop cooking spaghetti sauce in her largest pan. Familiar sizes of cheese that she had plopped into her grocery cart without thinking when there were two of them turned into "science projects" in the fridge before she could eat them. It took her even longer to start lighting candles on the table again just for herself.

She hadn't met anyone special, and sometimes she didn't care, especially after a few disastrous fix-up dates. One was with a lawyer who was given Kathleen's number by one of her mother's friends. He worked with the woman's husband, and she thought he and

Hope Chest

Kathleen would be "just perfect together." He sounded pleasant enough on the phone, so Kathleen agreed to go out with him.

His name was Jud. He was nice looking and well-groomed, and Kathleen thought that despite her misgivings, the evening might be all right. He held the door of his brand-new sports car for her and announced that they were headed downtown to see *Midnight Cowboy*. When they got downtown, however, he spent nearly twenty minutes circling block after block looking for a free parking spot on the street. There weren't any, and the movie had already started.

"Well, we missed the movie," he said finally. "Do you like jazz?"

"Not especially."

"Well, too bad. I thought we'd go hear George Shearing down in Pioneer Square." He headed down to that area, this time found a place to park about two blocks away, and led her into a smoky jazz club. After he muttered about the exorbitant cover charge, which Kathleen figured was only slightly more than the movie would have cost, they were seated near the tiny stage.

To her surprise, Kathleen was enchanted by the music. She had had very little exposure to jazz and had no idea it could be so wonderful. The blind pianist's hands arched and flew over the keys. All too soon, it seemed, the group took a well-deserved break.

"I had no idea this kind of music was so exciting," she said to Jud, who was finishing his drink.

"Yeah, well, let's get out of here," he replied, putting his wallet into his pocket without leaving a tip.

"Don't you want to hear the next set?"

"Nah, let's take a ride."

Disappointed, she followed him out of the club and back to his car. They headed east across the I-90 floating bridge, the lake dark and smooth, the sky without stars.

"Where are we going?" she asked.

"I thought we could take a drive up to Snoqualmie Falls, but on the way I'll show you my house. We go right by it."

Kathleen had no desire to see his house, but it wasn't even 10 o'clock, so she said nothing and studied the scenery that flew by the window. Finally, they turned into a long driveway in a wooded area and pulled into a carport.

"Here we are," he announced, helping her out.

"How long have you lived here?" she asked to be polite.

"My ex-wife and I bought it five years ago. Come on, I'll show you."

It was a low rambler, but Kathleen could make out no distinctive features in the darkness. Jud unlocked the door and turned on the hall light. "Come on in. Want a drink?"

"No thanks," she replied. "One was enough at the club."

"You're not a drinker then. Mind if I have one?"

"Go ahead." Kathleen looked around. The living room had beautiful wall-to-wall carpeting and cream-colored walls. There was a sofa and a leather chair with an ottoman, which Kathleen sat on while her date fixed himself a drink. She noticed there was a wedding picture on the mantle. Kathleen wondered how long he'd been divorced. She wouldn't think of having her wedding pictures displayed. She suddenly desperately wanted to be home.

"Come sit over here," he said, patting the sofa next to him as he sat down with his drink. The ice in it made clicking noises as he swirled it.

"I'm fine here."

"I'm not going to attack you."

"I didn't think you would." She was growing more uncomfortable by the minute.

Jud came over and sat behind her on the leather chair and began to rub her shoulder with his free hand. She stood up and walked over to the fireplace.

"I think I'd like to go home now."

"Why? I'll build a fire and we can just sit here and relax."

"Look, I don't even know you, and I don't feel like relaxing. I feel like going home."

"How long have you been divorced?"

"What?"

"Well, it's been a while, hasn't it?"

"What are you saying?"

"Surely you miss it, don't you?'

"'It'?" She couldn't believe her ears. "Actually, I don't. And if I did, I wouldn't 'relax' with someone I just met. Now, please, take me home."

She was shaking with fury—at him, at her mother for giving her number out, at the situation, at having to date again when all this should be behind her now, at the Fates. Apparently her anger got through to her date, because he changed from his come-hither look to one that Kathleen found appropriately shamefaced. He put his drink down and got his keys.

"Sorry," he mumbled, "but I thought that since you had been married before . . ." He trailed off as he fumbled with his keys.

"I have glands, if that's what you're implying, but I also have standards."

It was the last thing she said to him. They drove in silence back to her apartment. She let herself out of the car before he could come around to open the door and practically ran into her place.

Her mother had phoned first thing Sunday morning. "How was the lawyer, dear?"

"Horrible, Mother. Absolutely horrible. And if you ever give my phone number to anyone again under *any* circumstances, I'll . . . I'll . . . I don't know, but you'll be so sorry!"

"But I was assured he was a wonderful young man, with a very good salary."

"Well, he doesn't waste his very good salary on extravagances like parking lots. We missed the movie because he couldn't find a free space on the street. We drove around and around. And that was the best part of the evening. I mean it, Mother. Never again!"

As soon as she hung up from her mother, she called her friend. "I don't know, Mar," she said. "There aren't any fraternity exchanges in the adult world and no really good ways to meet men. But I'll tell you this, I'm never going on a blind date again. EVER!"

"Was it really that bad?"

"Worse. And to think I even shaved my legs."

"Well, you never know."

"I'm beginning to think I do. I just read an article in *Cosmo* that said I should put all my makeup on except maybe lip gloss or the last stroke of mascara and then greet Mr. Potential at the door with a shriek, saying, 'Don't look at me, I don't have on my makeup!' Then I'm to dash to the bathroom and come out finished. Apparently he'll think I look pretty good raw and be hooked. My God, what if I had done that with this creep!"

"Besides," Mary said, "you can't maintain the makeup forever."

"Oh, they had an article on that too. What you do is keep a mirror, flashlight, and makeup kit under the bed on your side. Then you train yourself to wake up at 5:30 or so and touch up so that when he wakes up, he'll see you in all your natural beauty."

"Mark wouldn't know who was in his bed if I did that!"

"Well, it's all moot because I'm not sure my ship will ever come in."

"Of course it will. There are tons of guys out there."

"If any of them remotely resemble this last one, I think I'll pass."

Her job became the center of her activities. She still got together with Mary, but now they were generally at Mary's house or in a playground with Kathleen's little goddaughter, Kristin. They took her to the park or to the zoo or just walked with her in the stroller by the lake. She was an adorable child, and she loved her Auntie Kathleen. The times Kathleen babysat so Mary and Mark could go out were bittersweet as she watched the child asleep in her crib. Would Kathleen ever get to be a mom? There was very little indication that she would any time soon.

Now the prospect of helping Professor Hawkins put together a children's theatre for the city gave her something wonderful to focus her energies on. It was a field she loved and a cause she totally believed in. These past years seeing the wonder come into children's faces as they either observed or performed characters so opposite from themselves were fulfilling to her, despite her sadness that her life had taken such an unexpected detour from all her planned future. Who knew where this project might lead her? Maybe she'd meet someone on the way there.

Chapter 19

August 1975

"Well, it's now or never, troops." Hawk smiled, but there was a hint of tension behind the smile.

"You ready, Katheen?" Garth Fisher, the promotion director asked. He and Kathleen had worked together from the beginning, Garth coming from two years in sales with a national copy company.

"As I'll ever be." She'd checked the portfolio for the third time that morning to make sure all the drawings were there and in the right order. She went over the time line again and the budget figures, although she knew every date and every dollar by heart. She didn't have a speech. She had all the information in her head, and by the time she began to talk, her speech would create itself. It always did. She still hadn't hit on a strong angle, but she knew even that would come to her.

"I can't believe we're finally taking this to the big guns," Kathleen said.

"We might have done it a long time ago if anyone would have listened," Garth grumbled.

"Patience, my boy," Hawk said. "It wasn't the right time, but now it is. Besides, look at all we've accomplished in the meantime."

A grant from the National Endowment for the Arts had allowed them to open their tiny office in the historic and pleasantly inexpensive Smith Tower in 1972. Hawk still taught at the university, but Kathleen had moved to the office with Garth to start the huge fund-raising task to see Hawk's dream take shape. Hawk had hired another person to take over Kathleen's duties at the university. Kathleen still helped out with the kids in the drama program when she could, but she was usually too busy.

Kathleen loved the Smith Tower with its beautiful brass elevators and friendly elevator operators. It was exciting being in Pioneer Square, which was enjoying a renaissance. Seattle's birthplace, where founding father Henry Yesler's logs were skidded down to the waterfront, had long been crumbling into disrepair. Now the home of the infamous Skid Road was being rediscovered. New and wonderful restaurants opened, and Kathleen tried them all. Galleries and shops bloomed in previously vacant storefronts, and the sidewalks were alive with people. Even her mother, who at first was dismayed that Kathleen would be working in such an "unsavory" part of town, reluctantly agreed, after joining her for lunch at one of the new French restaurants, that the area had style.

Kathleen's duties at first had been mostly secretarial. She answered the phones and helped set up their nonprofit status with the state. While Garth worked the phones, she typed letters to prospective donors. The first list they sent was to the parents of children who had attended Hawk's classes over the years. The professor had kept meticulous records for just this purpose. Amazingly, many responded with generous checks and letters of praise for what the drama program had done for their children. Then she began writing grants to foundations everywhere and struck "silver—not quite gold"—with the NEA.

They were finally able to hire a real secretary, Jenny Perkins, and Kathleen was freed to begin a program of children's plays for the public and for the schools. She coordinated the school programs, contacting individual elementary schools to set up field trips to the performances. Garth, in the meantime, worked to widen their circle of prospective donors, joining Rotary and the Seattle Chamber of Commerce.

Currently the plays were presented in what had been a dinner theater near downtown. It was effective for the field trip showings, because the children could easily sit on the floor in front of the stage. But it was not so comfortable for the adults, who sat on makeshift risers in the back. The plays were so well received, however, that there was little grumbling. Under Hawk's direction, the staff and actors as well as the choice of plays were always top quality. Yet the lack of a proper facility loomed large, and they were all on the constant search not only for money but for a real playhouse.

The impetus to break ground had finally come two years ago. A wealthy family whose grandson had been in Hawk's program called one day to inquire whether or not their organization would accept a donation of an old building near where they were currently located. It had been a warehouse, so it had high ceilings and lots of parking.

"Don't fling me into that briar patch!" Hawk exclaimed, quoting from one of the favorite Bre'r Rabbit stories the kids loved to perform. "Of course we'll accept!"

She and Kathleen did an improvised polka around the office, whooping and laughing until people down the hall came to see what was going on. "Only a miracle," Hawk told them. "No need for alarm."

The building needed extensive work, but with money from selling the Carter Trust land donated in 1968, they could at least get started. It would take additional funds to put in dressing rooms, a sound system, acoustics, new restrooms, a ticket booth, and everything else they needed. So Kathleen had to shift her focus from the schools to helping Garth with the fund-raising. And today she was to pitch the Downtown Seattle Association and the Seattle Chamber of Commerce to outline the dream for the Children's Creative Arts Center. She had to convince the city's most influential businessmen to lend their considerable pull—and their considerable dollars—to the project.

It was imperative that she be taken seriously today. When she turned the dreaded 30, she thought that she would finally have credibility. But for good or for ill, even now at 32, she still looked like a teenager. In an attempt at sophistication, she'd pulled her dark curls back as smoothly as she could from her face and fastened them at the nape of her neck with a flat black bow. She wore a new black and white suit, very tailored, and small pearl earrings, which she kept adjusting.

"You'll be fine. Stop worrying!" Hawk said.

"You look great," Jenny said. "And you have a call on line two. Do you want me to take a message?"

Kathleen looked at the clock. It was still too early to leave. She didn't want to be the first one at the meeting and appear overanxious. "I'll take it in my office." Glancing over her shoulder, she said to Hawk, "I still think you or Garth should be making this pitch. No one can say no to either of you." Kathleen's stomach fluttered again.

"Garth's hit most of them up already, so that's no go, and I don't have the time. You'll be perfect, Kathleen. I have every confidence in you."

Kathleen wished she shared her mentor's faith as she went to take her phone call. "Kathleen Andrews."

"Kathleen? This is Pat McHugh."

She paused and the voice added, "Patrick."

"My God, Patrick!" she finally responded. "I'm sorry I was so slow, but my mind's a million miles away in a major project, and I never thought of you as 'Pat.' It's been forever."

"I'm in town. Are you free for lunch? I realize it's short notice, but I got in early and thought I'd take a chance."

"Sorry, but I have to leave in about two minutes for a speaking engagement."

"How about dinner then?"

"Sure, dinner would be great," she said, hoping he didn't notice the hesitation. "I can't believe it's you after all these years. How in the world did you find me?"

"Mark. I still keep in touch with him occasionally."

Of course, Mark. "Where are you staying?" she asked.

"I'm at the Olympic for a three-day convention."

"Why don't I pick you up there when I get off work. I have to move my car anyway, and you can leave yours parked. About 5:30 OK with you? Will you be through with your meetings by then?"

"Extremely. What kind of car shall I look for? Still driving your mom's Buick?"

"No," she laughed. "Even she isn't. I have a yellow Mustang, and I'll be in the turnaround at 5:30 sharp. I'll make reservations somewhere, all right?"

It was his turn to pause. "Fine. You probably know the restaurants better than I do. And when we get to wherever we're going, you can tell me what you said at your 'speaking engagement.' It sounds quite impressive."

She laughed again. "That's a deal, but if I don't go to it right now, I'll be the Speaker-Who-Failed-to-Show."

"I'm glad I caught you in time then. See you tonight."

Kathleen hung up the phone with a smile. Imagine hearing from Patrick after all this time! She hadn't even asked him what kind of convention he was here for—or where he was "in town" from. They had a lot of catching up to do. She wondered briefly if he was still angry with her. No, that wasn't right. He had never been angry with her, just terribly hurt. Well, he wouldn't be harboring a hurt that happened when they were both so young, she decided. Too much time had passed.

She looked at her desk clock. It was time to go. She gathered the visuals of the proposed Children's Creative Arts Center and headed out of the office.

"Good luck, Kathleen," Jenny said.

"Thanks. Remind me when I get back to make dinner reservations somewhere for tonight. I know if I live through this presentation, I'll forget to do that."

"Why don't I do it for you?" Jenny said with her usual efficiency. "What time and how many?"

"Sixish. Two."

Jenny raised an eyebrow. "Dark booth or view?"

"View would be nice. It's an old friend from out of town."

"Knock 'em dead, kiddo," Garth said. "You look real 'chick' in that suit. They'll be eating out of your hand."

"I want them to be throwing money."

"They will, Kathleen," Hawk said. "Break a leg."

Kathleen forgot about Patrick as she left her office and hurried to the Chamber, searching her mind again for the angle to her approach that still eluded her.

The board room was dark. Its windows faced an alley, so they were covered with heavy, woven fabric that let in an impression of light, but no direct sun. Bullet lights in the ceiling lit only the shiny surface of the oval table, making the area around it seem even gloomier. Along one wall, a buffet table had been set up, and two lines of men were at various stages of filling plates with rice, chicken, salad, and rolls, and taking their seats. Coffee cups, silverware, and squares of chocolate cake were at the twenty or so places around the table.

Kathleen placed her drawings on the easel to the right of the lectern and stashed her briefcase under it, removing Garth's excellent brochures on the Center before she did so. She intended to put one at each place, but then she changed her mind. She would pass them out when she got up to speak, doubling the impact of the message. She hoped.

As she looked around the room and the powerful men in it, she drew a ragged breath. They held the key to months of preparation and hard work. Their funding would enable the center to begin building. She smoothed her skirt, hoping she looked as poised and sophisticated as the saleswoman at Nordstrom had assured her she did when she bought this suit. It had been a major splurge, but so much depended on this presentation. She forced herself not to touch her earrings.

Bill Henry, the chairman of the Chamber's arts and education committee and president of the Downtown Association, was approaching her with his hand outstretched. She had worked with him for most of the past year preparing for this moment. He was as kind as he was influential.

"Kathleen, how pretty you look, as always." He winked at her and took her hand in both of his.

Well, so much for the suit, Kathleen thought. Pretty was the last thing she had aimed for.

They went through the buffet line on opposite sides of the table. She took a little bit of everything, but she was sure her stomach would refuse it all. Bill Henry introduced her to the men around her, many of whom she already knew, and led her to their seats at the head of the table.

Too soon, it seemed, the meal was finished and the business had begun. Her host introduced her as "the lovely and charming children's crusader," and then she was facing them.

"Gentlemen," she began. She looked at the faces above the crisp collars and the similar ties. They represented power, but suddenly she realized that most of these men were fathers, and at that realization, she relaxed. The key she had been looking for was right there in front of her. She smiled at them. "Let me show you what we want to build for your kids."

Back at her office, everyone was waiting when she walked in. Even their part-time bookkeeper, Betty Mullen, was there.

"Well?" Hawk said.

Kathleen tossed the drawings and her briefcase onto her desk and grabbed both of the tiny woman's hands. Twirling her, Kathleen exclaimed, "I think they loved it! Of course, they need to confer with their own boards, but Jim Conkling asked if the auditorium could be named for individual benefactors. I told him of course it could, as could any portion of the Center or the Center as a whole, for that matter. I hope that was all right to say. It seemed like a great idea to me."

"You bet it's all right! And it's a terrific idea."

Cheers rose around the room.

"Well done, my friend." Hawk beamed. "I knew you could pull this off."

"I suppose you'll want to put that suit on the expense account now," Betty said.

"If I had donated its cost, I could have had the auditorium named for me!" That caused more whoops of laughter. "But seriously, Bill Henry said he will champion our cause himself. Your brochure was a hit, Garth. I left a pile of them with 'the boys.'"

"With the Downtown Association on our side and the Chamber, we can't lose," Garth said, wrapping one of his long arms around Kathleen. "Kath, you saucy wench, ya done us proud."

"I suppose you and your silver tongue will take the rest of the day off now," Betty teased.

"Are you kidding?" Kathleen said. "I'm going to send a follow-up to every man in that room. Besides, I have a dinner date tonight, so there's no sense going home first."

"I made reservations for you at The Lakefront, by the way," Jenny said. "That new restaurant on Lake Union by Gas Works Park. Window table. You can tell us if the food's as good as the view."

"Thanks, Jen."

"Dinner date?' Garth asked. "Anyone exciting?"

"Not really. A guy I used to date in college is in town for a convention. He just called out of the blue. It's no big deal. I haven't seen him in ages."

"Well I hope he's prepared for that outfit," Hawk said. "You look like a million bucks."

Kathleen recognized Patrick at once, but he had changed dramatically from the thin, pale college youth of her memory. He was still lean, but broader in the shoulders. His face had filled out too. Funny, she had never thought of Patrick as handsome, especially compared to Paul, but the smiling man heading toward her was most definitely handsome.

He had on a well-cut, three-piece suit with a subdued silk tie and a dazzling white shirt. Maybe that was it. She couldn't remember ever seeing him in a suit and tie. When she'd thought of him at all since those college years, she saw him in his faded green sweatshirt and dilapidated tennis shoes.

He was waiting at the curb and slid into the seat beside her before she could get out to greet him. They leaned toward one another over the center console in an awkward hug.

"You look terrific, Patrick, and *quite* successful, I might add."

He smiled. "I could say the same thing to you, Miss Smooth Hairdo. What happened to your curls?"

"I had to pretend to be in control of things today, so I hid them."

"Speaking engagement?"

"Speaking engagement." She eased the car into traffic and maneuvered it over three lanes to turn left. "I can't believe you called. Do you know how long it's been since we've seen each other?"

"I do. February 1964. Mark and Mary's wedding."

There was something in his voice as he said that, but the light turned green at the same moment, and she had to concentrate on driving.

"Seattle looks really different since I was here last," he said, looking out the window.

"I wondered where you were 'in town' from. Where are you living now?"

"Portland."

"But that's only a three-hour drive. Surely you come up once in a while to visit your folks."

"They moved away too. They're in Yakima now. We just got back to the Northwest a couple of years ago."

"We?" She smiled at him.

"Yes." He paused. "I'm married. Two kids, a boy and a girl. How about you? I noticed you still go by Andrews. Did you keep your maiden name when you got married, like these women's libbers now?"

"Are you kidding? I was Mrs. Paul Gordon, of course. Women didn't even think of keeping their own names back in '63, Patrick, you know that. We were dying to be a Mrs. Some Man's Name. I changed it back after the divorce. I was only married two years."

"Mark told me it didn't work out for you. I'm sorry."

"Don't be," she returned with a laugh. "It was a long time ago, and we are both better off. Believe me! Besides, Protestants are allowed another chance, remember?"

He looked sharply at her, but her eyes were on the road. She was smiling wickedly. They both burst out laughing.

"How could I forget?" he said. "Do you still get your blueprints from God?"

"Sometimes, but I'm not as sure of everything as I was then. You still pray to statues?"

"Every day."

"I'm glad some things are constant."

"I am nothing if not constant," he replied, and Kathleen once again detected a note of something else behind the humor and the words. The conversation was interrupted when she turned into the restaurant's parking area and waited for the attendant.

"This is a new restaurant, so I can't vouch for anything but the view, but I've heard it's good." Kathleen said as Patrick held the door for her. "And something smells wonderful."

"It certainly does."

"We have reservations for Andrews," Kathleen told the hostess.

"Right this way, please," the young woman said.

"Andrews? Boy, some women just talk about being liberated. You really are."

Kathleen couldn't tell if he was teasing or admiring her. She had to admit that in the not too distant past she would have made reservations in the man's name. When had she stopped doing that?

Their table was by the window, and the view of the city skyline across the lake was gorgeous. There was a sailboat race in progress, and the water was ablaze with spinnakers billowing in the early evening sun.

"OK," he said after the waiter had taken their drink orders. "What was the big deal today? What are you doing?"

"I had to convince some city bigwigs to put their hands in their pockets and give large amounts of cash to a center for children's arts that we're trying to get built."

"That's a long way from teaching elementary school, isn't it?"

"I never did teach. I looked into it once, and I would have started at $4800 a year."

"That's horrible! Good thing you didn't have to support a family on that! What did men start at back then?"

"I hope you're just kidding, Patrick," she said, rising to his bait. "The men started at exactly the same salary. It's one of the few professions that pays the same to men as to lowly women."

He laughed then, and she knew he was still egging her on.

"I made more than that working part-time for a professor of mine in the drama department, and after the divorce I just moved into full-time."

"That dervish who got you to start writing journals?"

"Now, how could you remember that, Patrick?"

"I remember a lot of things."

"Yes, she's the one, and she's still a dervish. She had a dream of building a center separate from the university where children could come and participate in the arts, and I caught the fever. We have a small staff now and even smaller salaries until we get this thing off the ground, but I love it."

"She knows which players to send in. I assume you were mightily successful today. You always could wow the crowds."

"Well, I don't know how wowed they were, but the response was pretty exciting. But enough about me. How'd you work your way into that white shirt?"

He laughed again. "You always went right for the jugular, Kathleen. It is a bit surprising, I guess, when you think about how I used to dress. I joined an accounting firm here after college but didn't like what I was doing. So I sent out some résumés and found a job with the government in D.C. If Nixon hadn't been elected, I probably would have stayed there, but I couldn't bear the man. I stuck it out as long as I could and finally left."

"The government or D.C.?"

"Both. An old classmate of mine was starting a new venture in Portland, and he ran into my brother—remember Michael?—who told him what I was doing, and here I am."

"But what do you do? What venture was it?"

"He's a food broker. Ups or downs, people always have to eat. We import spices and cheeses, lots of deli and restaurant items. That's why I'm here in Seattle, in fact. Trade show. We're testing the waters for a new kind of coffee machine for restaurants. If it takes off, it could be a gold mine."

379

"And your wife and kids?"

"Meg is eight and Sean is six. They're incredibly bright and busy and wonderful. My wife—well, I met her in D.C."

"A nice Catholic girl?"

"Full church wedding."

Something wasn't ringing true in his voice. But just then the waiter came to take their orders. When he left, Patrick changed the subject.

"Tell me more about this arts center. Where will it be?"

"We got a huge old warehouse donated to us. It needs lots of work, but it's going to be fabulous."

"Will your office be there too?"

"After a while. We'll need to stay in the Smith Tower for a bit, which I don't mind. I love that old building. We had our pledge dance there once, and we were all so taken by the view from the top. Little did we imagine that what we thought was a giant skyscraper would be dwarfed within just a few years!"

"I can't believe how much the skyline has changed myself, and speaking of changes, tell me what the heck are those things?" he said, pointing out the window.

"It's the latest. They made the old gas works into a park and decided to keep the structures in place rather than tearing them down."

"What next?"

"Now you tell me more about your family, Patrick."

"Not much to tell. My kids are great, and we do the usual—Little League baseball, swim team, and ballet. That's for my daughter, of course, but we don't do much drama. How do you get kids into your program? I don't think they have anything like it in Portland."

"That's my job. I contact the schools and parents and anyone I can think of to spread the word. Lots of folks are so impressed with our programs that they tell their friends. We have a lot of word-of-mouth stuff."

"What about Mary and Mark? Mark and I don't talk often enough," Patrick told her.

"Mary and I still get together. I'm the fairy godmother to Kristin, you know. She's in our program too. She's a little doll. Looks just like her mom. Miss Scandinavia."

"I've seen the Christmas cards. She is a cute one."

The waiter came to ask if they wanted coffee or dessert.

"Actually, what I'd like to do is go see this park. Is that OK, Kath?"

"Sure. Let's go. I haven't been to it yet. That'd be fun."

Patrick paid the bill with a smiling comment as she tried to reach for it, "I invited you, you made the reservations, it's my turn," and they left. They drove the short distance to the park and then walked to the grassy hill next to the old gas works. The grass, long and dry and smelling like straw, rippled like a miniature wheat field in the slight evening breeze. They climbed the short hill and surveyed the view. Lights had begun to go on in the apartments and houseboats that ringed the lake. A few of the brightest stars were just visible.

"As I said, I've never been up here before," Kathleen said. "Just driven by. This is great."

"Let's go down to the water." Patrick took her hand and they went down the rough path together. There were dozens of people wandering about or sitting on blankets.

"Let's sit here," Patrick said. Before she could sit on the bench he was pointing to, Patrick stopped her with a touch on her arm. "But wait, my lady." With an elaborate gesture, he took out an extremely clean and ironed handkerchief and spread it on the dusty bench for her to sit upon.

"Snowy white hanky! Your wife must take good care of you."

Once again he frowned slightly before smiling and sitting next to her.

"Patrick, is everything all right? I don't mean to pry, but I'm a pretty good listener, and I noticed that every time I asked you about your family you changed the subject."

"I didn't call you to tell you my troubles, Kathleen. It's just good to see you again and know that you're doing so well."

"Come on, Patrick. It's me, Kathleen."

There was a long pause, and Kathleen could tell he was struggling with whether to tell her or not. "She's moved to one of those communes in eastern Oregon," he said finally. "Has to 'do her own thing' or whatever they say. It's been really hard on the kids."

He was staring hard at the darkening sky. Kathleen felt her heart break for him. She took his hand. "You must love her very much."

He turned and looked at her. "That's just the problem, Kathleen, I never loved her enough. I couldn't. I've never stopped loving you."

Laughter came from somewhere on the hill behind them, and there was the sound of the tiny waves lapping against the shore, but Kathleen only heard a loud ringing in her ears.

"Patrick, you can't mean that. You must have loved her or you wouldn't have married her."

"I tried to love her. We met at a party shortly after I moved to D.C. She reminded me of you in a way. I think that's why I noticed her. Dark, curly hair. I didn't know anyone in town, so I asked her out. And we just kept doing things together until it seemed like . . . I don't know. She asked me where the relationship was headed, and by then it was nice to be with someone. No surprises. No Chinese food in a carton in front of the TV by myself. You were married to Prince Charming, Kathleen, and living happily ever after, three thousand miles and forever away from me. I thought I could erase you from my memory. I married her a little over a year after we started dating."

"Oh, Patrick."

"I realize now that it was so unfair to her. I love my kids. My daughter is so much like you. Her expression of delight when she makes a discovery is just like what you used to do. Her eyes light up, and she claps her hands together and makes everyone come see. She has to share. My son is a charmer, too, but he's more reserved. Like me." He smiled a lopsided smile.

"Are you getting a divorce then?"

"I suppose it will come to that. She moved out almost a year ago. She started taking pottery classes when both kids were in school. Her instructor was some longhaired hippie who apparently gave her all the attention I never did. She left me a note in one of the bowls she'd made. A black one. How's that for irony?"

"But how could she leave her children? I don't understand that."

"Neither do they. But I won't have them living in that hippie colony. I went there once to try to talk to her. It looked like a diorama of an early man exhibit. No one shaved or bathed. Everyone was in sandals and beads. Everyone had the same vacant expression, talking about peace and love while they seemed to be high on something. It was horrible."

"Oh, dear."

"The worst part, though, the worst part was that I felt responsible. I drove her there because I couldn't love her. I know what it feels like to be in that position."

He didn't look at Kathleen when he said that, but she felt a swift pang of guilt. Looking up at him, however, she realized he hadn't aimed the comment at her. He looked miserable.

"I never thought I could do that to anyone. She was—is—a wonderful person. She's such a good mother. And one day she just flipped."

Kathleen couldn't bear the anguish in his voice. "I'm so sorry, Patrick."

"What am I doing? I've dreamed about seeing you again for years, and now that I finally have, I'm pouring out all my problems. I'm the one who's sorry."

He held her hand tightly and neither of them spoke. They sat looking at the sky as it grew ever darker. Then suddenly a shooting star arced across the sky. Then came another and another. Kathleen could hear people around them making oohing noises like spectators at a fireworks display.

"What is this, Patrick?" she asked, indicating the shooting stars.

"Maybe God's mad at me. Do you think so?"

"If you're the reason, then everyone else is in your debt. I've never seen anything like this."

"Actually it's called the Perseids. A meteor shower that happens every year at this time."

"I'm impressed."

"I heard it on the radio as I drove up to Seattle." He smiled sheepishly.

"There are shooting stars everywhere. Look how many wishes we can make."

She turned to him, smiling, expecting him to acknowledge that their mood had somehow lightened, but he wasn't smiling.

"I made my wish with the first star," he said, folding her into his arms and kissing her deeply. After a moment of shock, Kathleen found herself returning his kiss with a passion that shook her.

Finally she drew back, but Patrick held her close to him. "I've dreamed of this moment a thousand times, Kathleen. I'm sorry if I've come on too fast. I truly didn't plan on this. I'm not asking anything of you. It's just so wonderful to be near you again. I wasn't going to even touch you. I promised myself, but when your eyes lit up like these stars, all the years went away. I'm sorry."

He released her from his embrace but then took her hand, and she felt like the sky, exploding with stars. This casual dinner with an old friend was turning into something for which she was totally unprepared. She studied Patrick's handsome face in the evening light. There was no mistaking his feelings for her. But how did she feel? His kiss had definitely affected her. She was stunned, both by Patrick's kissing her and by her response to it. Looking at him, she could see every woman's dream, a handsome, successful, intelligent, and sensitive man. But he was still married and had two children. She took a deep breath.

"Don't be sorry, Patrick. I'm just so shocked I don't know what to think. Maybe you're in love with a memory. You don't really know me now. We've both changed a lot."

"Some things never change. Every August you can count on these shooting stars, for example. That's a fact." He tried to smile and failed.

"Feelings aren't subject to facts, Patrick. And there's one big fact you seem to be overlooking: you're married."

"I haven't overlooked that for a moment. Well, that's not quite true. For the last year I've just avoided thinking about it. But when I knew I was coming to Seattle again and there was a chance I could see you, all the denial ended. I know I have to deal with my problem." He pulled away to look at her. "And I know it is my problem. Not yours."

"Patrick, I . . ."

He stopped her protest with another kiss, gentler this time—a gentleness that affected her more than the passion. His cheek was smooth against hers. She had no idea what to say. Over his shoulder she saw another star fall. She closed her eyes and tried to make a wish, but she didn't know what to ask for. Being in his arms, inhaling the long-forgotten but familiar scent of him, felt absolutely right and absolutely wrong.

"I need to go home, Patrick. I need to think."

He took her hand again. "I know. So do I. I thought losing you was the most painful thing I would ever have to experience, but I think I'm about to prove myself wrong. I feel like such a rotten person, Kathleen. But I have loved you all this time. I can't stop now. Especially not now."

The next day at work, Jenny asked her how the dinner had been.

"The restaurant was a great choice, Jen. Good suggestion, thanks. It had really good food and great service. And the view was spectacular."

"How about the date?"

"I told you," Kathleen said too quickly, "he's just an old friend. I haven't seen him in years." She busied herself at her desk, not meeting Jenny's eyes. "Thanks again for making the reservations for me."

"No problem." Jenny left, and Kathleen tried to make some sense of what was on her to-do list, but her mind kept wandering to last night. Patrick. After all this time. How did she feel now? He was married. He lived in Portland. He had two kids! What could come of this besides a letter to Dear Abby?

She got up and went to the coffee room and washed yesterday's dregs out of the potbellied mug she'd bought when they moved into this office. It was hand-thrown with a shiny brown glaze. She loved the solid feel of it in her hand. She wished everything felt so substantial. She could tell from the aroma that the coffee was fresh, and she poured herself a cup. Someone had brought in doughnuts, but she wasn't tempted. She couldn't eat.

By 11 she had accomplished nothing at all. She got up to get another cup of coffee and nearly collided with Jenny, who was coming into her office with a florist's box.

"For you. Who's it from?"

"I have no idea. Let me see." Kathleen peeled back the green, waxed tissue to discover a brandy snifter with a gardenia floating in it. The card was addressed to her in Patrick's unmistakable script.

"Well?" Jenny said. "Is it from your Just-a-Friend?"

"It's just a thank-you, I'm sure." Kathleen opened the envelope, hoping Jenny couldn't see her hands trembling.

Gardenias always remind me of you. Now I have the stars as well. Two beautiful things. Could we have dinner tonight?
Patrick

She looked up to see Jenny still standing at her desk, eyebrows raised expectantly. At that moment, Garth poked his head in.

"Flowers! From the Chamber of Commerce?"

"No," Jenny replied with a Cheshire-cat grin. "They're from Just-a-Friend."

"Oh, last night's dinner. How'd that go?" Garth asked, then smiled and added, "Never mind. I can see it went rather well."

"Will you two stop! I just had a lovely dinner with an old friend from college whom I've not seen in ages. It's just a thank-you."

"She says 'just' a lot," Jenny said to Garth.

"She blushes too. I just think this is just serious."

Kathleen knew she could put an end to this whole business by telling them Patrick was married, but for some reason she didn't. Instead she removed the snifter from the box that held it and set it on her desk. The delicious perfume of the flower filled the room.

"Think what you like, you two romantics. I can't be bothered to convince you otherwise. Now shoo! I have work to do, even if you don't."

The intercom buzzed a minute later, and Jenny's voice said, "Line two. He said it was Patrick."

She was not surprised by the call, but her pulse began to race. "Thank you for the gardenia."

"It's not a bribe, but could we have dinner tonight?"

"Everything tells me to say no, Patrick. This is dangerous."

"No, it's not. I promise. No stars. We'll even go someplace very public—with no view. Just to talk."

"Yes, I guess we need to talk. Shall I meet you at the hotel?"

"Lobby at 5:30."

"I'll see you there."

She held the phone in her hand for a few moments longer before replacing it. What was she doing? Her life was pretty wonderful right now, except that she wasn't married and had no children. So what did she need to talk about with Patrick? The very idea of an affair with him was ludicrous. She had read enough to know what a dead end being the "other woman" led to, and she had no desire to cast herself into that role. Besides, she couldn't imagine someone as honorable as Patrick betraying his wife. So what could they possibly talk about? She held the snifter up to her face and breathed in the gardenia's heavy fragrance, redolent of memories.

The rest of the day crawled by as Kathleen tried to keep her mind on anything but the dinner. At 5 o'clock, she tidied up her desk and walked slowly up the hill to the Olympic Hotel. She could have hopped on a free bus, but the longish walk appealed to her. Arriving early wouldn't do. She entered the hotel from the south door instead of the usual turnaround. She stopped just inside the door and took a deep breath. Patrick was standing across the lobby facing the other entrance. As she took another breath, he turned and saw her. A smile spread across his face, and Kathleen knew he had not been sure she would show up. Funny, she had not been so sure herself. Then relief flooded her. How silly she was being. This was Patrick. Things would be fine.

He crossed the lobby and took both her hands, which she held out to him. He made no attempt to kiss or hug her. Kathleen was not sure if she were happy about that or not.

"I thought we could eat right here in the Golden Lion. No windows."

"One of my favorite restaurants, sir. Good choice."

They walked to the restaurant without talking and went through being seated and getting their menus. Kathleen's hands were freezing. The confidence she had felt moments earlier that this would be a simple meal with Patrick had vanished. He looked handsomer than he had the night before. At last night's dinner, he had let her take the lead, albeit expressing amusement with his women's lib remarks. Tonight he was totally in charge. He had made reservations. The Patrick she remembered would have chanced that they could have gotten into such a restaurant as the Golden Lion without any. He asked for the wine list and handled it with aplomb. In her few years with Paul, she had always thought him to be sophisticated. As she watched Patrick now, however, she realized that everything Paul did was done for effect. Patrick did things with an unconscious grace.

Finally, after their cocktails had arrived and their orders were taken, he lifted his glass to her. "I'm sorry if last night was too fast, Kathleen. The last thing I wanted to do was frighten you. Nothing I did was planned. Honestly. So here's to starting over."

She smiled and sipped her drink. Then she set it down and looked at him. "Starting what over, Patrick?"

"Oh, boy. Right to the point she is, folks." He smiled at her, but then his eyes grew serious. "I meant what I said last night, Kathleen. I've never forgotten you. I know that it's been a long time and that things change. I've changed."

"Yes, you have."

"Hmm. Should I say thank you?"

That finally made her laugh. "Yes, actually, you should. You are a far cry from the guy in tennis shoes who'd left his contacts in for two weeks."

He put up his hand as if to ward off that memory.

"I was stupid about a lot of things back then. I let you get away, for one. But I don't want to be stupid now. I know I can't offer you anything, Kathleen. I need to go back to Portland and straighten things out. I thought that just seeing you would be what I needed, and then I could get back to my life and things would go along as they had. But it didn't work that way. When I saw you, everything came flooding back, and I knew that some things hadn't changed."

Kathleen started to say something, but he stopped her.

"No, I don't expect anything from you. All I ask is that you let me call you and see you whenever I can get up here. You may not even be interested . . ." He took another swallow of his drink. "It's just that—it could have been the stars—but I think there was something more last night."

Now it was her turn to concentrate on her drink. "There was something, Patrick. But whatever there was can't possibly matter as long as you aren't free."

"I know that. And I realize I have to deal with my situation better than I have. My kids miss their mom, but who she is now isn't the mom they knew. She's so radically changed,"

"Maybe it's just temporary, Patrick. Have you tried counseling?"

He gave her a wry smile. "Did you?"

She was momentarily taken aback. She remembered the high hopes with which she had gone to each appointment with Paul and the anguish when nothing was resolved. "It didn't work for us either. But we didn't have kids to think about."

"That's the biggest issue. She's so happy with her new life. She thinks that if the kids and I just came to live with her new 'family' as she calls them, we'd all be so much happier. The thing is, she's happy because most of the time she's high on drugs."

He was clutching his drink glass so tightly that the bones in his hand seemed about to burst through his skin.

"She's begged me to try it, convinced that once I see how 'beautiful' everything looks and sounds, I'll never go back to my 'uptight' world, and we can all be happy stringing beads and playing guitars together."

"You sound like you still love her very much, Patrick."

"I love my kids very much, and to see how this is affecting them is killing me. Then hearing about you being so dedicated to helping the children you care so much about and being so . . . so normal." He reached over and took her hand. "I told you last night that I never stopped loving you, Kathleen, but I had pushed all those feelings into a special, safe place. You were married to someone else, and I knew there was no hope for me, so I filed us under 'cherished memories.' I got married and built a family. And the family part worked. In fact, if my marriage had been going along as it had until she left, I never would have called you."

"I believe you."

"The thing that is the hardest is that she always said I loved the kids more than I loved her, and she was right. I can't shake the feeling that this whole thing is my fault. If I had been a better husband. If I could have loved her more. If, if, always if." He took another swallow of his drink. "Well, this is a lot of fun, isn't it? I'm sorry."

"Patrick, I know what you're going through. Not exactly the same circumstances, but breaking up a marriage was hard enough for me with no children. I had such dreams when I married Paul. He was everything I was programmed to marry—good family, good prospects . . ."

"Non-Catholic."

"Of course." She smiled at him then. "Although he wasn't what I thought I would be marrying when I was in Fishers, that's for sure."

"What happened to that, Kathleen? Your religion seemed to be the major wedge between us."

"I don't know what happened to it. Mary and I talked about that once. All I can chalk it up to is that I was so young. We weren't a very churchy family, so it wasn't something I came to college with, but I fell lockstep into Fishers, all right. It was safe and comfortable to believe what they told me, I guess. And, excuse me, but hasn't your church changed radically since then as well?"

"Vatican II. Big changes. No more Latin. Even the sinners can now understand the Mass. We're not exclusive anymore."

"And no hats for women. Don't forget that. What's the world coming to?" She smiled at him, but his face was serious.

"What are we coming to, Kathleen? No, wait," he said as she started to speak. "That was more rhetorical than actual. I know what I have to do. What I need to know—that is, what I would like to know is if there's any reason for me to hope that at the end of everything you might be there."

"You don't think you can save your marriage?"

"Even if I wanted to, she doesn't. I told you I've tried to talk to her, but she's so into her new way of life, the only thing she'd accept is if the kids and I came over to her way of thinking. And you know as well as I do that's impossible."

"What will you do?"

"What I probably should have done months ago. I'll see a lawyer and find out what it will take to get custody of the kids. They're with my folks while I'm here, but they usually go with the mother, you know. That's the scary part. But if the court discovers how she's living, I don't see how they can put young children into that environment."

"I don't either."

"Then to answer your question again, no, I can't save my marriage. It's over, except for the lawyers. And because I have so much to do before I'm free, I know it's not fair of me to ask. But last night I felt something. I think you felt it too."

"Yes, I felt it too. I don't know what it was either," she paused, looking at him, "but it might be worth exploring."

Patrick looked at her for a long moment and then broke into his lopsided smile. He looked 19 again, and she started to laugh. How could she not have seen his earnestness, his quality before? She'd been dazzled by Paul's smooth good looks and by how he made her feel not quite worthy of him. She had felt so lucky to have been loved by him, to have been Mrs. Paul Gordon. What a fool she had been to have traded this wonderful man for the flash in the pan that was Paul!

"I don't know how long it will take, Kathleen," he was saying, serious again. "I can't do anything that will result in their having to live in that commune." He spat out the word.

"There's nothing to say that if we get to know each other again we'll like what we find, you know. What if we don't?"

He raised a fist and quoted in a stage whisper, "'But screw your courage to the sticking place, and we'll not fail.'"

"Lady Macbeth?"

"It's the sentiment, Kathleen, not the speaker."

They laughed, and Kathleen felt a connection she had never felt with Paul. Here was a good man. A man who was a success all on his own. A man who read. A man who felt things. And this time there was no hurry to have a wedding or pass a candle. There was no need to impress anyone with someone's credentials or family fortune.

"Well, there are no guarantees in anything, Patrick."

"Not quite. I can guarantee you that this time I won't go away quietly. We may have a long way to go, but with you in my life, I feel I'm already there." He reached across the table and took her hand, and as his warm fingers closed around hers, she felt a new kind of happiness. And it felt good.

AUTHOR BIO

Photo by Sandy Novak

Cherie Tucker is a Seattle native and a graduate of the University of Washington with a B.A. in English. Through her business, GrammarWorks, she has taught grammar and writing basics to business professionals in the U.S. and Canada since 1987. She also teaches Grammar for Editors in the University of Washington's Professional and Continuing Education editing program. She has won national awards for copywriting, has edited numerous books, and writes a monthly grammar column for the Pacific Northwest Writers Association's online magazine, *Author*. In addition she sings in the Seattle Women's Chorus and serves as an advisor to her college sorority.

ACKNOWLEDGEMENTS

Many thanks to Karen Larsen, wordsmith extraordinaire, for her precise edit; to Perry Jackson and Maxine Barnard for their willingness to read an early manuscript and give such positive feedback; to my writers' group for their encouragement and sharp eyes; to the Woo-Woo ladies (Susie, Beth, Jeanne, Judy) for their support; and to Theresa Truex for always providing clarity and sanity when things seemed muddled.

Cover photo by Anna Wasniewska of Cineart Photography, courtesy of Cathy Mac Rae of Creative Weddings of Calgary, Alberta, Canada

Made in United States
Troutdale, OR
09/11/2025